CLIMATE KILLERS

A BERNADETTE CALLAHAN MYSTERY

LYLE NICHOLSON

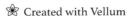

1

THE HEAT HIT Detective Bernadette Callahan as she stepped out of her RCMP Jeep. The sun's rays made her skin itch, the hot air grabbed the back of her throat. A rivulet of sweat began its way down her chest. Her bra would be soaked in minutes. She hated that.

She walked towards the crime scene—an old house frequented by drug dealers. The oppressive heat wasn't stopping the dealers from killing each other. She took a drink of her water bottle. It had been filled with ice a half hour ago but was turning tepid already.

Yellow police tape wafted in the hot breeze. An officer at the door shifted uncomfortably as the wind blew in his direction. He was young and tall with rippled muscles in places where most men didn't know there were places.

He looked up at Bernadette. "Hey, Detective, looks like I won the heat wave pool—it's been fifty-eight days above 35C."

Bernadette smiled. "Yeah, Stewart, you won. Hope that gives you enough for some cold beer." She stood beside him at the doorway. The heat from inside the house was worse than outside. The smell of decomposing bodies hit a gag reflex in the back of her throat.

Constable Stewart saw her discomfort. "There's no need to go in. The CSIs have been here for the past hour, they've taken all the pictures. A pretty clear gang hit. All the victims are known, long lists on their rap sheets... but if you still want to check it out..."

Bernadette paused for a moment, and then donned a pair of gloves. She walked in, took a quick look around and nodded at the CSI team. They looked in pain. It was 37 Celsius outside; it must have been high forties inside.

When the bile in her stomach started to move upward, she knew she'd had enough. She backed out of the room, avoiding the knowing look of Constable Stewart.

"Yeah, you're right. Pretty straightforward," Callahan said. "I'll catch the photos and report at the detachment. She walked straight to her Jeep, started it and hit the A/C on high.

The stench of death started to clear from her nostrils. The bile receded in her stomach as she sucked in cool air. She sipped some water. She looked down at her bra. She cursed, "Damn it, soaked again."

Her phone rang, it was Chief of Detectives Jerry Durham, "I need you back here," he said when she answered. He was always direct. He was a good guy to work with—but direct.

The RCMP Detachment was only minutes away in the small city of Red Deer, Alberta in western Canada. The city was on a flat prairie in sight of the Rocky Mountains with over one hundred thousand people, but there was enough crime there to keep an RCMP detachment and Callahan's serious crimes division busy.

This was Bernadette's second year in the city. She liked it there. The people were straightforward, most working for the oil service companies and the criminals were just as dumb as anywhere else.

Bernadette was in her mid-thirties, a red head with Irish and Native Cree ancestry and definite ideas of right and wrong that made her the perfect candidate for the Royal Canadian Mounted Police, except when she bent the rules, which was too often for her superiors.

Her instincts and work ethic were excellent which kept her one step ahead of reprimand. She put on the radio as the news came on. The announcer went over the latest death tolls from the heat. Eastern

Canada had over 500, western Canada had just under 200 hundred—for the month.

The worst news was the American states. The deaths were hitting the thousands in the mid and southwest USA where temperatures were over one hundred Fahrenheit.

This heat wave had started in mid-August. It was now late October. The Canada Geese should be flying overhead. Instead they were hanging around up north. Maybe they knew something no one else did.

Everyone was talking about this as climate change. Some people were loudly proclaiming the heat wave was the result of all the world's misdeeds and misuse of the planet but Bernadette had a gut feeling there was something more happening. She couldn't put her finger on it. It just felt weird.

She reached the RCMP headquarters and ducked into the women's changing room for a quick shower and change of bra and t-shirt. She carried several changes with her. This was her second one of the day.

She found Chief Durham in his office. He was beginning to look older than his mid-forties. The job, or his three kids had managed to recede his hairline and add a multitude of wrinkles to a once unblemished face.

"Sit down, Callahan." Durham motioned her to the chair in front of him.

"Am I in some kind of shit again, Chief?" Callahan asked.

He shook his head. "No, but if something comes up—you always come to mind." He swiveled his laptop and punched some keys. "We got a Skype conference with Canadian Security and Intelligence Services. You're just in time."

The screen came on. Agent Anton De Luca was in front of them. "Good afternoon Detectives." He greeted them with a beaming smile, looking his usual well-put together self. Bernadette thought De Luca could have been the star of a half dozen Italian soap operas or commercials. He had drop dead handsome looks with a silky voice that sounded like you'd just been placed in a vat of tiramisu.

"What's up, Anton?" Bernadette asked. "You run out of serious international espionage that you have to call up us little city folks? I only got dumb ass drug dealers—but you're welcome to them."

Anton shook his head. "Always with the sense of humor, Bernadette. I hope you keep that as I tell you what mission I have for you."

Bernadette felt her insides take a small loop de loop, like the roller coaster ride that flips upside down and has you screaming for it to come back up. "You got my attention."

"Good, a group of scientists in Canada and America think this latest heat wave cannot be attributed to what we've experienced in normal climate change," Anton said. His demeanor was solemn now.

Bernadette stopped herself from blurting out *I knew it*, instead, she sat forward and said, "Really? Why do they think that?"

"The heat wave has come on too quickly," Anton said. "Several scientists think this is a manmade event."

"I don't get it. How do you heat up a region of the planet like what's happening now?" Bernadette said. She looked up at Durham. "You know, I've been thinking this is crazy odd myself. What are the scientists thinking?"

"They think someone is messing with the ocean currents," Anton said.

"Wouldn't we see something like that?" Durham asked. "I mean... it seems like you'd need something significant to affect a body of water."

"Well, yeah," Anton admitted. He paused for a second as he read from his notes. "Professor Bjarni Sigurdsson, from Iceland, came up with a theory of how we could turn the temperature down or up just from adjusting the amount of heat generated under the ocean floor."

"And, where is the good Icelandic professor now?" Bernadette asked.

"That's the problem. He's gone missing. He was supposed to present a paper in Stockholm on how North America could change the currents and temperature of the Pacific and provide more rain or drier conditions when needed. He never showed up. He vanished without a trace."

"How long ago?" Bernadette asked.

"Back in June of this year," Anton said.

"I take it you want me to go out and look for him?" She cocked her head to one side. "You know, I'm pretty good at finding people, but asking me to head to Sweden on a five-month-old missing persons case is kind of pushing it."

"No. I'm not asking you to go to Sweden. I need you to go to Nicaragua."

Bernadette sat back in her chair. "You found this Sigurdsson guy in Nicaragua?"

Anton shook his head slowly. He looked straight into the screen. "We found Alistair McAllen there. We think he can lead you to Sigurdsson."

"How is McAllen linked to Sigurdsson?" Bernadette asked.

"The Stockholm police found Sigurdsson's cell phone. He had numerous calls to McAllen." Anton said. "There's also some history between the two. They go way back in their University days. The bright boys in intelligence think McAllen's our way to Sigurdsson, and your name came up as the way to get the information."

Bernadette dropped her arms to her side. She looked at her Chief of Detectives then back to the screen at Anton. "Are you serious about this? You really want me to meet up with him again? Why do you think I could convince him to find this missing professor?"

"Because you let him go last time you met. Remember?" Anton said.

Bernadette cleared her throat and sat up straight in her chair. "If you read my report of when we met in Mexico, you'll see I was helping you, Anton. Remember, you were injured and I aided you... then he got away."

Anton smiled into the screen. "Yes, Bernadette, that was a wonderful report. The FBI and the CIA had to swallow hard to digest what they knew was a total fabrication of the facts—now listen,"

Anton put up his hand, "I know you want to throw out a whole lot of rebuttal but we don't have time."

Bernadette closed her eyes, and then opened them again. There was no way she was getting out of this. "Okay, let me have it. When do I leave?"

"You're booked on the 6:55 am flight from Calgary to Houston tomorrow morning. There's a layover in Houston where you'll be met by your partner from the FBI," Anton said.

"Who is?" Bernadette said.

"Agent Carla Winston."

"Oh—my—god, this keeps getting better," Bernadette said.

"You know her?" Chief Durham asked.

"We were in Mexico together, helping in the hunt for McAllen," Bernadette said "She was supposed to be my minder there, you know, look after me so I didn't step out of line... I sort of stepped out of line..."

"Here's your chance to make it up to her," Anton said. "You're on strict orders to find McAllen, see if he has knowledge of where Sigurdsson might be, report that information and head home. This is seventy-two hours tops—you'll be back by the weekend."

"Let me get this straight. Everyone in the intelligence community in North America knows where Alistair McAllen is, and you want me to go see him and not arrest him—is that correct?" Bernadette asked.

"You got it. He's on an island in Lake Nicaragua. Intelligence says he's heavily armed. If we send in the FBI there'd be a shoot-out and an international incident. Nicaragua doesn't like the USA very much; they are getting friendly with China right now. We need you do this quietly. You got that?" Anton said.

"Yup, I got it, Anton." Bernadette smiled at Anton and threw him a salute. She looked at Durham, "I'll turn my file over to my partner and go home to pack a bag."

Durham nodded. "Are you going to be okay with this? I remember you having some history with this Professor McAllen."

Bernadette swallowed hard and looked at Durham. "Yes, he escaped from me once off the coast after he tried to damage world oil, and I kind of had to let him slip away in Mexico..." She dropped her eyes and cleared her throat. "Anyway, you're right, we've had some history—"

"And you're going to be okay with meeting him again?"

"No worries, Chief. I'll handle this with care and be back in time for our weekend barbeque." She got up and headed out the door, a knot growing in her stomach. Was it foreboding of the mission or what she had to say to her fiancé when she got home?

2

THE KNOT in Bernadette's stomach hadn't gone by the time she reached her home. She saw Chris's truck there. She'd hoped he'd be off fishing somewhere, so she could have packed, and headed to the airport in Calgary, and just left a note. That would have been easy. This was going to be hard.

She put the engagement ring back on her finger. She told him she didn't wear it during work as she was afraid she'd lose it in a take-down of a felon, but what she didn't admit to him was that it made her feel like she was caught in a trap.

It reminded her of the traps her grandfather used to set back on the reservation in the far north. They'd find fox, rabbits, and weasels with one leg caught in a steel trap on her grandfather's trap line. The animals would gnaw on their legs to try to get away. She felt the ring burn on her finger sometimes like it was caught in something.

She walked in the door. Her dog, Sprocket, a big lop-eared German Shepard with a semi-obedient personality met her at the door. She bent down and nuzzled her face in his fur.

"You may not want to get too close to him," Chris said from the kitchen. "I think he was rolling in a dead squirrel this afternoon."

Bernadette patted Sprocket and gently pushed him away. "Way to go, big fella, I'm sure you think you'll smell like a star to all the lady dogs out there."

Chris stood at the doorway of the kitchen. "Well, star detective. How'd your day go with the bad guys?" He was dressed in shorts and tight t-shirt, his muscles stretching the shirt fabric to its limits. His hair was wet from his shower. His curls hung down in rings over his brown eyes. Holding a bowl and whisk he announced, "I'm making your favorite dinner tonight, beef wellington and for dessert I whipped up a key lime pie."

"What's the occasion?" Bernadette asked. She felt a foreboding of the storm that was to come with his answer.

"It's been one year since I asked you to marry me—it's also a year since I left the RCMP to be your house husband," Chris said.

Bernadette crossed the room. She embraced him and put her head on his chest. The words *househusband* had been their joke, at first. Chris had left the RCMP on his small island detachment off the coast of British Columbia so they could be together. They wanted to make this work.

He was going to find work in oilfield security but it never happened. There were only security guard positions in their small city. The corporate security jobs were in Calgary, or up in the Oil Sands in the far north. He had offers for Dubai and even a lucrative one from Afghanistan but they were all three- to six-month stints.

Their relationship felt fragile. Both of them had been total loners before, no dependents. Now, they had to be there for each other. It was hard to get used to.

"I have to drive to Calgary tonight, Chris," Bernadette said. She kissed his chest and looked at him. "I have to go to a Latin American country, get some intelligence for CSIS and the FBI and I'll be back by the weekend, I promise."

"Are you going to save the world again?"

Bernadette shook her head. "No, nothing so earth shattering. I just... I need to go down there to meet with someone... get some information on a missing person."

Chris held Bernadette's face in his hands. "I hate to give you the third degree, but can you tell me who you're going to see, or is this the hush, hush shit?"

"Yeah... it's that kind of shit... sorry," Bernadette said. She could have told him it was McAllen she was going to see. She didn't have time for the blow up.

Chris kissed her on the forehead, picked up his bowl and whisk and walked back into the kitchen. "You, know," he said over his shoulder, "maybe this is good, you going away for a few days."

"What do you mean?" Bernadette asked. She stopped in her tracks. She was about to head to the bedroom to start packing.

"Maybe it will give us some time to think. I got an offer for a security detail in Afghanistan. Some American corporation wants their people kept safe over there. The gig pays real well, and I get free medical."

"Does that free medical include the body bag they send you home in?" Bernadette said.

They stood and looked at each other. There was so much more to say, but the words had to be careful. They each knew they didn't have the time for the depth of conversation they needed to have. Chris went back into the kitchen and Bernadette went into the bedroom.

She grabbed her carry-on bag, threw in her usual four to five changes of underwear, t-shirts and jeans with a few pairs of shorts and runners. She stood over the bag, feeling that something was missing. Chris and her were drifting apart.

She went into the kitchen and kissed him hard on the mouth, "Look, big guy, I know things haven't been great with us. But how about you wait until I get back. We'll head out somewhere. Maybe go to Banff, have wild sex in some classy hotel and go hiking along the glaciers."

"Sounds good. How about if I save this dinner for when you get back as well?"

"What's a hungry girl going to eat?"

"How about key lime pie—after we have a shower together."

Bernadette grinned. "You always have great ideas...is that one for the road?"

He pulled her tight, his hands slowly moving down her back, resting on her buttocks. He massaged both cheeks, pulling her into him. She felt how hard he was. "You know, I am feeling a little hot and sweaty, a shower is a great idea."

A few hours later, Bernadette was in her Jeep, for the two-hour drive to the airport in Calgary. She felt better, but unsettled. The sex was always great with Chris. It was sometimes what held them together. She wondered if it was enough.

She stayed in a hotel that night near the airport and boarded the 6:55 am flight to Houston the next morning. Just as she was getting on the flight and about to shut off her phone she read a text from Chris: *Sorry, Bernadette, I decided to take the job in Afghanistan. I leave for Kandahar tomorrow. We'll talk soon. Love you, Chris.*

A flight attendant came by her seat. "Sorry, ma'am, you'll have to turn off your cell phone. We're about to take off."

Bernadette nodded, and shut off the phone. This felt like their relationship was ending. Could she get it back? Would she fight for it?

She slept for much of the morning flight. On her arrival she looked around for Agent Carla Winston in the airport terminal. They'd agreed in a text to meet in front of Hugo's Cocina in terminal D.

Bernadette saw Agent Winston. She looked the same as when she'd seen her last in Mexico. She was African American. A trim little package, all of 5'5" with short black curly hair that showed signs of grey. She was dressed in a light blue casual pantsuit. It still said FBI, but on vacation. Bernadette thought she'd been uptight when she met her previously. It seemed nothing had changed.

Carla Winston turned and saw Bernadette. Her facial expression was one of recognition, then disapproval. The scowl that formed over her eyebrows threw a line of wrinkles all the way up to her forehead. It was obvious to Bernadette that Agent Winston was not happy with her choice of partner.

"Detective Callahan, I trust your flight was alright?" Winston asked in a monotone. She didn't extend a hand for a handshake. She looked Bernadette up and down. Regarding her t-shirt, jeans and black boots as if she'd been subjected to a scan—and failed.

"Ah, yeah, okay flight. But the food was awful. They got anything good here?"

"Best tacos in the airport," Winston said as she walked towards the restaurant.

Bernadette watched Winston walk into the restaurant and muttered, *"My, aren't we the frosty little thing?"*

They took a table away from other diners and let their eyes peek at one another other over the menus. Winston put her menu down and stared hard at Bernadette.

Bernadette cocked her head to one side. "Okay, Winston, let's have it. You want to give me a big piece of your mind about something that's pissing you off. I could see it from across the concourse. So, let it fly so I can enjoy my taco in peace after you get done your speech."

Winston's lips went into a thin line. Her eyes narrowed. Her hands clenched and unclenched. "Okay, I'll tell you what's on my mind. I got a son, a hell of a good one. He's studying to be an Engineer at the University of Virginia. And I have a nice condo in Fredericksburg, Virginia. I'm married to an okay man—no I lie, my marriage is on the rocks...but that's not the point. I got an okay job with the FBI and I intend to retire in twenty years. You get me?"

"Okay, sure. Nice bio by the way. But what exactly are you getting at—?"

"What I'm getting at is the shit you pulled in Merida, Mexico, almost got your partner killed. I know I told you I couldn't fault you for going by your instincts. You did get the antidote that saved the pipelines, but that could have gone the other way. So, here's what I'm saying," Winston leaned forward and her voice was a fierce whisper, "Don't pull any of that crazy shit with me. I intend to go back home to my wonderful son and my useless husband—you hear me?"

Bernadette picked up a nacho chip from the table and dipped it in pico de gallo sauce. "You've made yourself very clear. Now, how about we order lunch? That breakfast sandwich I had in Calgary is long gone."

Winston snapped her menu back open. She ordered the fish tacos and Bernadette ordered the Carnitas de Pato. It was duck with tomato sauce and tortillas. She thought about ordering a beer. She wasn't on the clock, as they were just travelling, but from the cloud she could see over Winston's head, she decided not to push it.

When lunch was over, a quiet affair, with little conversation, they went their separate ways. Boarding time was several hours away. Bernadette decided to find somewhere quiet to see if she could send a text to Chris and Winston said she had some correspondence to catch up on.

When Bernadette came out of the restaurant she noticed a crowd milling around the departure lounges. The departure screens for many flights showed CANCELLED. A small script below said *due to excess heat*.

Bernadette pulled out her cell phone and punched up the local Houston temperature. It read 125 Fahrenheit. She'd read a report those smaller jets like the Bombardier CR7 couldn't fly past 118 F. The flight to Managua was on a Boeing 737-800. Its heat limit was 126F.

Bernadette looked at the time. It was 2:00 pm. Hopefully, a thunderstorm would develop and cool things off before they took off at 5:30 pm. Excess heat made it impossible for the jets to get lift off on the runway. As North America was heating up, more planes were being delayed or cancelled for days on end until the heat waves passed.

She didn't know if she could stand being delayed for hours, or days, with the frosty Agent Winston. She went in search of a newspaper and coffee. Maybe find a quiet place to send a text to Chris. She wanted to write it when she was more composed. Her first response had been to send him a WTF! She needed to rethink that.

Carla Winston watched Bernadette make her way down the concourse before heading in the other direction to make a phone call. She needed to report in. There was nothing about this mission she liked. That she'd been chosen to accompany Bernadette Callahan was strange, the person who was her superior on this mission was stranger still.

Adam Morgan had been in the office of Congressional Affairs, and then was transferred over to the Counter Terrorism group. FBI agents normally didn't drop down into the trenches where Winston was. They rose up the chain.

She'd met Morgan a week ago when this mission was discussed. He'd said he'd receive word from the 'highest level,' how this had to proceed. But what was strange was all their meetings had to be away from the J. Edgar Hoover Building.

Their meeting had to be kept secret. There were leaks in the department he'd said. He gave her a separate burner phone that couldn't be sourced back to the FBI.

Morgan wasn't an easy man to like. He made furtive movements with his eyes. They bounced around when he spoke, never looking at her directly. Slim, with a thin face and pointed chin that did nothing to instill any confidence in the words that came from his small mouth, he dressed well, almost too well for the FBI and always had manicured fingernails. Maybe that's what put Winston off the guy. Who in the FBI would get a manicure? Who had time?

She dialed his number. He picked up right away. "Agent Winston. Have you met with your contact?"

"Yes, I've made contact. I'm in Houston, we board in a few hours for our next destination," Winston said. She couldn't believe how much this man annoyed her.

"Good... listen, there's been a slight change of plans."

"How slight?"

"You are authorized to eliminate Professor McAllen once he's given you the location of Professor Sigurdsson," Morgan said. "Detective Callahan may be eliminated as well."

"Who authorized this?" Winston said, looking around to see if anyone was listening in.

"This comes from the highest levels," Morgan said. "Professor McAllen has been deemed a high value target. Detective Callahan let him escape FBI custody in Mexico. She's believed to be working with McAllen."

Winston couldn't believe what she was hearing. She'd never had this briefing before she left Washington, despite reading the file on Callahan from the Canadian Security and Intelligence Service. Why hadn't they seen anything criminal in her activities? There was no mention of a connection between Callahan and McAllen.

"Okay, I understand what you're asking, but you realize I have no weapons on this trip. The Nicaraguan government would not authorize either of us to have any firearms in our luggage."

"The person you're meeting in Managua will have a weapon for you. He will be discreet in handing it to you."

Winston sighed quietly. "Okay, I got that." She was hoping the lack of weapon would have scrubbed the command to kill Callahan.

"Winston, I can't stress how much this will advance your career if this mission is a success. If you fail... well let's not talk about that..."

"Yes, sir, I understand," Winston said. She ended the call and headed for the ladies' washroom. The elimination of Professor McAllen was understandable. Detective Callahan's kill order was outside her pay grade. What if she didn't do it? Would they fire her for insubordination? She felt sick.

Adam Morgan smiled when he hung up from Winston. Maybe they could get this back on track after all. Sigurdsson should never have escaped. But then, he was dealing with a group of bunglers and half-wits who could barely follow a proper order.

When Sigurdsson was brought back in and the operation was brought back on line, he'd get rid of those who didn't meet his standards. This list was long. Agent Carla Winston would be one of the first to go. That was already planned in Nicaragua.

He dialed a number and heard the long-distance exchanges click in. Matvel Sokolov picked up the phone. "Adam, you have things ready for us."

Morgan winced. He hated to be greeted informally by someone who he considered beneath him, especially this Russian.

He'd found him when he was in the Office of Congressional

Affairs. Matvel was working hard to entice members of Congress and the Senate to give favorable contracts to Russian companies, all owned by the Russian Mafia.

Matvel was good, but Morgan had been better at finding the collusion and bringing in several congressmen who'd swelled their bank accounts. One such congressman was Lawrence Derman. He rolled over so quickly he couldn't get his information out fast enough.

Derman and Sokolov were what Morgan needed. He added a retired and unhappy Admiral Fairborne to his mix and he was set. North America had no idea what they were in for.

"I have everything ready for you, Matvel. Take them all out. You understand. I want no one left to make a report of what happened."

"I have hired the very best," Sokolov said. "There will be no survivors."

3

———

THE FLIGHT to Managua from Houston was three hours. The plane was crowded. Mostly Nicaraguans who'd had enough of the heat and were heading home for some cooler temperatures.

Managua wasn't that much cooler at 28C, with 60 percent humidity, but compared to Houston, this was 20 degrees cooler. Bernadette looked out the window as they landed. A soft blue lake mirrored the mountains and the volcano.

They walked out of the airplane into a small international airport with a mass of humans in the throes of trying to find luggage and family. The presence of heavily- armed security seemed to keep everything in check.

The humid air felt heavy. All around them, they heard Spanish spoken in rapid-fire sentences. Bernadette's Spanish was rudimentary; her second language was French. She turned to Winston. "You understand Spanish?"

Winston rolled her eyes. "I grew up in Virginia, and I slept through my Spanish classes in High School."

They stood there, clutching suitcases, scanning for any signs of the person who was supposed to meet them. A stocky man with a head of black wavy hair and long side burns jostled his way through the crowd and made his way towards them.

"Senora's, encantado de concerte, me nombre es, Elvis Calderon."

Bernadette looked at Winston. "Is this the guy we're supposed to meet?"

Winston pulled out her phone and scrolled through her texts. "Yep, it's really Elvis Calderon." She looked up at Elvis. "Hola, Senor Calderon, you just got the extent of my Spanish—do you speak English?"

"Ah, si, senora, I speak English very perfectly. Please excuse me. Now, may I take you to a hotel close by? You must be very tired from your journey. We will continue to Granada and Lake Nicaragua in the morning."

"Not happening," Bernadette said. "We want to meet our contact in the morning. That means we drive to Granada tonight. Did you not get that in the briefing?" she asked Winston.

"Uh huh, that's what I got. Elvis, you best get on your phone and find us a hotel in Granada, 'cause we're not on vacation. We mean to be finished with our business by tomorrow, and be back on this plane heading home. You *comprendes,* Elvis?" Winston asked.

Elvis's hands fanned out in front of him. "Si...Yes, I understand. I have a good friend at Hotel Dario in Granada. I make a call."

A few minutes later, Elvis returned to say he'd arranged rooms for them before escorting them out of the crowded terminal to his SUV. The next two hours were a blur of traffic. Elvis chatted non-stop about Lake Nicaragua, how beautiful it was and how the Chinese wanted to make a canal similar to the one in Panama.

"The President of Nicaragua, once told the people that he would never dream of making a canal across our beautiful country and defiling our lake—but the money the Chinese offer, I think it is too much for him, and the business people in this country—they are too easily bribed," Elvis explained.

Bernadette and Winston made polite noises from the back seat. The incessant chatter of Elvis stopped them from having to talk to each other. They both thought that wasn't a bad thing.

After passing the intercity mode of transportation—school buses painted in different colours—and threading their way around potholes and near misses with large trucks, they arrived in Granada.

The Hotel Dario was a quaint colonial building, painted in green and white to highlight the columns that tried to make it look more elegant than it was. They were shown into small but nicely appointed rooms with ironclad bed frames and wicker rocking chairs. They agreed to meet downstairs for dinner to discuss the following day.

The dining room was busy at 10 pm. Winston scanned the place. "I forgot the Latinos eat late. You hungry?"

"I could eat road kill right now," Bernadette admitted.

They were seated, ordered some drinks and they squared off again, both eyeing each other as to who was going to lead this discussion.

Bernadette coughed slightly, "Look, how about if I fill in some spaces on what I know of McAllen and his group of merry men. I expect they'll all be there."

"Why don't you fill me in on the *all* part?" Winston said, taking a drink of water and staring at Bernadette.

"Okay. We have four former special forces men from the US military. They served in Vietnam together. McAllen was their platoon leader. Every one of them has a special skill and, although they're many years retired if they exercise those skills it makes them dangerous."

"How dangerous?"

"Percy Stronach was a demolition man, Theo Martin was a weapons expert and Sebastian Germaine was a sniper. McAllen excelled in tactical maneuvers that made him a threat to the Viet Cong on the Ho Chi Min trail."

"You think they're all armed to the teeth on the island?"

"I wouldn't doubt it. Several years ago, McAllen had one of his little science experiments go wrong. He pissed off some big-league Wall Street guys that had paid him big bucks to sabotage North American oil fields so they could make even more money," Bernadette said.

"Yeah, I read a file on that. He had oil fields in Alaska and northern Canada stopped up for a few weeks. I heard there was some kind of fire fight on an island."

"It was a one-sided fire fight. McAllen's boys took the attackers apart. He had deadly crossfire from M-16s and a sniper rifle. He drew them into IEDs and blew them to pieces. Only one attacker made it off the island alive."

Winston took a long swallow of water. "You think that's what we're up against tomorrow?"

"Yes, I think we're going to visit a man with a lot of fire power. The reason he's in Nicaragua is he's paying some nice 'tourist fees,' as in bribes to the local government. Both our governments don't want to go through the legal wrangling to get him out quietly, and no one wants to go in hard due to the body count that would happen if they did."

"So, how do we play this tomorrow?"

"We go in soft as two lambs to the slaughter," Bernadette said. She smiled and raised her beer in a toast to Winston.

They parted ways after dinner. Bernadette went to her room, logged into the hotel's Wi-Fi and looked for anything from Chris. The time difference between them was ten and a half hours.

There was nothing from Chris as he was probably in transit. He'd said he'd left yesterday. The flight would be from Calgary, then probably to Frankfurt and then would it go to Kandahar... or would he fly to Kabul first?

She knew Kandahar was dangerous. Two American soldiers had been killed there in July, and there'd been an attack on the Afghani army base back in May. It was a dangerous place. What the hell was he thinking?

Bernadette put her iPad away and turned out her light. The fan overhead was pushing air in her direction. Tomorrow would bring its own dangers, which she needed to be alert for. Sleep would be a blessing but she knew it wouldn't come.

Carla Winston lay on her bed hoping she'd get a text from

Morgan to countermand the directive to kill McAllen and Callahan. The one for Callahan hadn't been a direct order—or had it?

She'd killed several terrorists in the line of duty. But they'd been armed, they'd fired at her, she'd fired back. She'd won the shoot-out. This was different. This was execution.

She felt good that Elvis had not handed her a weapon on arrival. No weapon, no problem. If Elvis didn't do his job, she couldn't do hers. She was about to turn off her light when there was a knock on the door.

She threw on a t-shirt, pulled on her trousers and walked to the door. Through the peephole she saw Elvis. He was looking left and right. She froze with her hand on the door handle. Could she say she didn't hear the knock?

He knocked again. She closed her eyes, breathed in deeply and opened the door. "What is it, Elvis?"

"Ah, Senora, I'm glad you're still awake. Your FBI people wanted to be sure you had this," Elvis said handing her a heavy plastic bag that could only be a weapon.

Winston took the bag and put it behind her. "Thank you, Elvis," was all she could manage to say.

"One other thing," Elvis said. "I was told to give you these." He handed her a pair of sunglasses. "These will transmit images and the voices of the people you see to me. I'll be recording on shore... you know... for your safety."

Winston looked at the sunglasses. They looked ordinary but she knew they held a transmitter and small camera. Elvis would be sitting on shore and dialing the feed into his phone or laptop and sending it to Morgan. He'd see everything.

"Thank you, Elvis," Winston said once more and closed the door. She broke into a cold sweat. She opened the bag and looked at the gun. It was a Heizer Defense PKO-9. She'd always wanted one for her own use.

This was a nine mm, with a seven-bullet magazine, six inches in length and weighed all of 19 oz. There was a small concealing holster in the bag that she could shove into the back of her trousers or in the waistband.

Winston whispered as she checked the gun sights, *"Someone must really want you dead, McAllen. This thing costs close to a thousand dollars."*

She put the glasses on. They were lightly tinted so she wouldn't look like she was avoiding eye contact when she entered a darkened room. People with dark sunglasses always attract suspicion.

She put the gun beside her bed with the glasses. Tomorrow she'd have to wear a jacket to conceal the gun. The sunglasses she'd put in her inside jacket pocket. She undressed again and got into bed. She knew sleep wouldn't come, she thought of all the possible scenarios for the next day, none of them looked good.

Morning broke with a light rain. It pattered outside the window of the hotel as Elvis came by the rooms of both Bernadette and Winston to wake them. They both looked ragged to him. He told them he'd meet them downstairs and left them alone. He had his own preparations to make.

He'd worked all night to arrange the plans for today. He was under strict orders as to how to proceed, what boat to give them, what time to send them off. Everything must be as instructed. He hated days like this. He needed to remember too many things that he could not write down.

Bernadette had showered and packed her bag when Elvis knocked on her door. She was hoping this day would end with a good result, a lead to find Sigurdsson and a drive back to the airport. That was her hope. Deep in her gut, she knew that wasn't going to happen.

Carla Winston packed and put the gun in its holster and shoved it into the waistband of her pants. She put her jacket on and stood in front of the mirror, turning to the back and to the side. The gun didn't look like it showed but she'd need to be careful. She blew out a breath, grabbed her suitcase and headed downstairs.

Elvis was full of good spirits, greeting them with a bright, *"Buenos Dias."*

Both women muttered a reply, found coffee to go and motioned for him to take them to the SUV. Elvis shrugged. They were not hungry, and he did not want to darken their mood.

The small city of Granada was barely waking up as they pulled away from the hotel at 7:30 am. Traffic was light. A few people wandered the narrow streets with the even narrower sidewalks.

Bernadette knew of some of the history of the place. A colony of Spanish had settled here in 1524. They'd lived in relative peace until they received independence from Spain, then all hell broke loose. A period of dictators and revolution plagued the poor country until somehow they tired of killing one another and brokered peace in 1989.

Winston broke Bernadette's thoughts on history by turning to her. "How do you want to play this with your buddy, McAllen?"

"Ah, he's not my buddy. But that aside, I plan on appealing to his general love of this planet."

"How do you figure that?"

"Simple, if you read his file. He did try to sabotage some oil fields back in 2013, but he also developed an antidote for a virus that was attacking pipelines on land and steel boats in the ocean in 2014."

"So, you think he's a mad scientist, but one with a strange conscience that oscillates between trying to destroy the world and save it, depending on how he feels that day?"

"I guess that's one way of putting it. It's hard to know what makes people tick, especially those that cross the line into criminal behavior," Bernadette said. She looked out the window and then back at Winston. "You know, there's a report I read that McAllen has been financing some major activities in providing fresh water to villages in Africa. There's a rumor that he's also been funding Professor Sigurdsson's research into climate change."

"Um huh, sounds like a real Robin Hood. Now where did this McAllen get all that money to do all these good works?'

Bernadette suppressed a chuckle. "Your own FBI people think he stole it from the Wall Street people that tried to kill him."

"Sounds to me like he's got a big streak of vengeance in him. I hope you're on his good side when we meet."

"Me too." Bernadette stared back out the window.

Elvis said the drive to Marina Cocibolca was only six kilometres and would take only a few minutes. It took longer as they navigated more school buses that were the local transport and donkeys wandering slowly across the road.

The lake was calm at the marina. White Herons stalked the shores for small fish while a lone Osprey hovered overhead looking for fish that would be breakfast.

Bernadette took all of this in. Lake birds were signs of how healthy a lake was. She wished she could read the signs of humans as easily.

Numerous boats lined the dock. Elvis ushered them towards a sleek looking motorboat.

"This I have found for you ladies. See, this is an inboard motor, nice leather interior, it is very fast – you will be across the lake in no time," Elvis told them.

Bernadette scanned the lake. "Is that McAllen's island?"

Elvis followed her gaze, "Si, that is his place. It is maybe one kilometre. You will be in there in minutes with this boat. It's very fast." He motioned back to the boat, waving his hand for them to get in.

"No, we need a row boat," Bernadette said.

"A what?" Winston asked. She was about to get in the boat. She turned to look at Bernadette.

"I said we need a row boat. I told you how much firepower McAllen has. You want to be on the business end of a bunch of lead?"

'But this is loco,' Elvis said. He stared at Bernadette, then at Winston. "A row boat is so much trouble. Only the poor of Nicaragua travel in this."

"Yep, that's right, the poor and the defenseless—ones with no weapons. That's why we're going over in a row boat." Bernadette looked at Elvis. "Now, you want to locate us one or do we have to get it ourselves?"

"No, no—as you wish. I will find you a row boat right away," Elvis said running off down the dock.

Winston stood there shaking her head. "Well, I knew you were crazy, girl, but not this crazy. But if you think this will keep us from getting shot that's fine with me—oh, and I assume you're doing the rowing?"

Elvis ran back, seemingly flustered. "Please, this way. I've found a little row boat that will meet your needs."

Winston sat in the back of the rowboat and put on her sunglasses. Bernadette sat in the centre, unshipped the oars and pushed off. She dipped the paddles deep into the water getting the feel of them.

"You know, this feels good," Bernadette said. "I can use some exercise after that long plane ride."

Winston said nothing. Her body language said it all. This was verification that Callahan was crazy.

Elvis walked back to his SUV, muttering to himself about how his bosses were not going to like this. Sending a text to tell them of the change of plans, he opened the back of the SUV and unlatched a small compartment.

Elvis pulled out a Heckler and Koch MP7 submachine gun and screwed on the suppressor. Looking around, he slipped it under his jacket. He had orders that the two women were not to make it back from the island.

If they wanted to row, that was their problem—he'd be waiting to meet them with a special welcome.

Bernadette was enjoying the rowing. She felt her back muscles flexing and contracting as her arms pulled the oars. Her legs were getting a work out as well. She kept the stern in line with a point on the shore to ensure she was heading for McAllen's island, but what she saw trailing the boat was a bit unnerving. She decided not to tell Winston, yet.

"How close are we to the island?" Bernadette asked.

"About 200 metres," Winston said.

"Good. I need you to row us the rest of the way in."

"You tired?"

"No, McAllen needs to see it's me approaching the island. He doesn't know you and might fire on us." Bernadette put the oars to the side.

Winston sat there staring at Bernadette, not moving.

"Look, Agent Winston, you said you wanted to get home safe. Well, this is making sure you do."

"Okay, I get it. Sounds like a good plan," Winston said as she began to move forward to take Bernadette's place.

"Be careful with your movements," Bernadette said.

"Why, can't you swim?"

"No, I can swim. But there's been a large shark following us since we left the dock," Bernadette said.

"They got sharks in this lake?" Winston looked over her shoulder. She watched the large fin submerge beneath their boat.

"Yeah, bull sharks. Guess they came in from the sea thousands of years ago when this lake was once part of the ocean."

Winston moved slowly forward and sat in the middle seat and Bernadette took her place in the back. She began pulling on the oars while Bernadette made sure she kept her head high so she could be seen from the house on the island.

"I don't think we have to worry about that shark following us," Winston said.

"Why is that?"

"You've got five laser dots from gun sights dancing on your forehead and chest," Winston said.

Bernadette looked at her chest and saw the lasers. "Well. At least we know they're home."

4

"I GOT A SHOT. Want me to take it?"

"Negative."

"They're inside one hundred metres. I have a clear shot. I could take them both out with a single bullet."

"Negative."

Sebastian looked up at McAllen. He had a M40 Sniper rifle with 50 caliber bullets. "You sure about this?"

"You'd make them into pink mist at this range with that rifle," McAllen said.

"And, this is bad, how?"

McAllen shook his head, "We don't kill people who arrive on our island unarmed. That's Detective Bernadette Callahan from the RCMP in the back of the boat."

"What if it's a ruse?" Percy said from a window beside Sebastian. "Maybe they're decoys. Trying to distract us from an attack."

McAllen picked up his binoculars and scanned the horizon. He could see a guy on the shore beside an SUV looking at a cell phone. "Let's see how this plays out. Everyone stay sharp."

Grace Fairchild came up beside McAllen. "How about if Margaret and I are the welcoming committee? You shouldn't be seen outside."

McAllen nodded. "Keep your weapons trained on our visitors. Any sudden movements and they're toast—you copy that?"

A chorus of 'copy that,' came from the other three men in the room. Percy shouldered his M16 with Theo on another sniper rifle.

Grace Fairchild and Margaret Ashley walked towards the rowboat as it approached the dock.

"Good morning, ladies," Margaret said pulling the bow of the boat into the dock and securing the bowline. "Did you row out for coffee?"

Bernadette smiled as she stepped onto the dock. "Sure, I take mine with cream and two sugars."

Winston stepped onto the dock behind Bernadette. "I'm good with whatever."

Margaret motioned for them to follow her into the house. It was a two a story that looked like it had been built in the 1900's and renovated several times. A channel had been dug that allowed boats to drive into the lower level.

They walked into the front room to a welcome committee of four weapons pointed at them. The sound of handguns having their chambers cocked told Bernadette that Margaret and Grace had weapons at their backs.

"Well, well, Detective Bernadette Callahan of the Royal Canadian Mounted Police," McAllen said as he lowered his weapon and came forward from the group. "We've met in some strange places before, but I don't think you've ever come calling on me in a row boat. Mind enlightening us all as to the reason for your visit?"

"How about if we sit down, and maybe you can point those weapons elsewhere? You can see we're not armed. We just came for some information," Bernadette said.

McAllen smiled. "You're right, we're being most inhospitable. Please take a seat. Boys lower your weapons. Margaret and Grace, keep them covered."

Bernadette shrugged. "Well, that's somewhat better." She smiled at Margaret and Grace. "Women usually ask questions before they shoot."

"Not always," Grace mumbled. She raised her gun and pointed at a couch for Bernadette and Winston to sit in.

Bernadette scanned the room. They all looked older now. She felt like she'd walked into a retirement home, but with a group of seniors who'd been cast in a B movie by the Cohen Brothers.

McAllen had a more grizzled look to him. He was tall, with a short grey beard and buzz cut. Gone was his long grey ponytail. Percy and Theo had somehow succeeded to look like old age hippies, sporting long grey hair with Hawaiian shirts, shorts and sandals that made them look like they'd escaped a Grateful Dead Concert.

Grace Fairchild and Margaret Ashley looked like they'd become sisters. They dressed in a similar fashion, native Mayan chic with colorful jewelry.

It was Sebastian Germaine who'd changed the most. Once he had looked like Willy Nelson, with the short beard and long braided hair, but now he sported a goatee and his grey hair was top knotted into a man bun. He wore a stylish t-shirt, designer jeans and slip-on boat shoes in tan leather. He could easily have stepped off a yacht or into the boardroom in Silicon Valley.

"I'll get right to the point," Bernadette said. "An old friend of yours, Professor Bjarni Sigurdsson went missing several months ago in Oslo, Sweden. The Swedish Police recovered his cell phone and discovered it contained multiple texts to you. The FBI and Canadian Security and Intelligence Agency think you might be able to help us find him."

"And, why if I knew where to look for him, would I help you?" McAllen asked.

"Because he was working on a project to cool the Earth. We have Intel that says you were working with him on it." Bernadette leaned forward on the couch, "Look, I know the FBI and CSIS have you pegged as a terrorist, but I saw what you did in Mexico. You came through for the world with an antidote. Now, we need you to help us find someone who can stop the world from heating up before small islands and the coasts are under water."

"You actually think Sigurdsson's invention will help repair the damage we've done to this planet already? The Antarctic ice shelf is ready to collapse. So is much of Greenland's ice. Once they melt, there's no going back. The oceans rise, and *adios* to beachfront property," McAllen said.

"But it's not too late if the world gets turned down by two degrees," Bernadette insisted. "And we have reason to believe that someone is causing the Earth to heat up faster."

"How do you know that?" McAllen asked. He pulled up a chair and sat down a short distance from Bernadette. They stared at each other.

"The scientists say the computer models don't match for the amount of carbon in the atmosphere to what's happening with the temperature. They think it's as if someone is turning it up on purpose," Bernadette said.

McAllen turned and looked at Margaret and Grace. "Barney said that might happen, if his project got into the wrong hands."

"Who's Barney?" Bernadette asked.

"That's Bjarni Sigurdssons' nickname. No one could get his Icelandic moniker," McAllen said.

"So... you'll help us find him?" Bernadette said.

"I didn't say that—"

"We just need to be pointed in the right direction. The scientists need your help, the Earth..."

"Oh god, the world. Why don't you just say the greedy bastards who use up the Earth's resources and pollute the damn place for their own profit because they don't care how they affect the planet." McAllen said.

Bernadette stood up. "I didn't come here on behalf of the greedy bastards. I came for the rest of planet. The one's who can't get a break —they all suffer from when the tides rise and the forests burn. They have nowhere to run—no one to turn to."

McAllen stopped and looked at her, "You know, you're right." He looked at the rest of the group. "The rest of the world will suffer because of the greedy bastards. Okay, the last time I heard from

Barney, he said he was going to be heading to his marine lab off of Key West. You need coordinates for that?"

"I can call it into our people and see," Bernadette said.

Winston tensed up beside Bernadette. This was it. This was the moment she was supposed to do something. How could she? She had a 9mm handgun in a room full of weapons. She was not about to sacrifice her life for the idiot Morgan. Perhaps the transmitter in her glasses was all the FBI needed to find Sigurdsson.

ELVIS SMILED ON SHORE. He could see and hear everything that Winston did. The glasses were transmitting perfectly. He wore an earpiece and heard, *it's a go, execute.*

Two helicopters rose up in the air from an island close by. Elvis cocked his submachine gun and let out a chuckle. He was about to make a lot of money for today's work.

"I HEAR HELICOPTERS," Percy said.

Theo looked out the window. "Affirmative. I hear two."

"What's the problem?" Bernadette asked.

"Sounds like you are," McAllen said.

"What? We don't have any backup. No one in the Nicaraguan government knows we're here. We came with a guy named Elvis—"

"Elvis Calderon?" Sebastian asked.

"Ah... yeah... that's his name. Why?" Bernadette asked.

"He's the worst crook in the country. He works for the CIA, FBI, Russians or Chinese depending on who's paying him," McAllen told her. "Did he give you anything to monitor our meeting with?"

Winston nervously touched her glasses. McAllen grabbed them and looked into the lenses. "Hola, Elvis you little shit. That's you on the shore isn't it?" He dropped the glasses on the floor and ground them with his boot. "Okay, everyone, battle stations. We got company coming."

Sebastian shouldered his sniper rifle. Percy and Theo grabbed M16's, Grace and Margaret stood back from the window with their handguns. McAllen watched the helicopters approach.

"We got a problem," McAllen said.

"What's that?' Sebastian asked.

"I see rocket tubes on the sides of the helicopters."

"Aw shit. That doesn't make for a fair fight now does it?" Sebastian said. He looked up from his gun sights. "What's our plan B?"

"We get them to give us a nice target." McAllen turned to Percy, "You man the 50 cal, Theo, grab the RPG, Margaret and Grace take over the M16s, and we're going for a boat ride."

McAllen turned to Bernadette and Winston. "Ladies, we're about to see if you're telling the truth—that you didn't come with back up."

"How's that?" Winston asked.

"We're about to take a speed boat out with you two in it. If they come after us, they don't know you. If they don't fire on us then these people are your back up."

"What happens if they just fire at the house and ignore us?" Bernadette said.

Sebastian raised an eyebrow. "We'll find out if that big bull shark that was swimming out there likes white or dark meat."

"Doesn't sound like great options, but let's get going," Bernadette suggested.

Bernadette and Winston followed McAllen and Sebastian down a spiral metal staircase to a dark and damp smelling basement. The sound of water lapping on the sides of the boat canal told them where they were before they saw the boats.

McAllen jumped in and started the engine. Sebastian cast off the mooring lines and pushed the two ladies towards the back of the boat. The sleek inboard growled with power when McAllen revved the throttle.

"Now, hold on tight back there, I'm going to come out and make a lot of side to side maneuvers in front of the house. When the helicopters come after us they'll present broadside targets to Theo and Percy."

Bernadette looked at Winston. "Sure, sounds easy."

The speedboat roared out of the channel. A helicopter peeled off its attack on the house and came after it. McAllen threw the boat into sharp S turns. High sprays of water shot out the stern.

Plumes of water erupted on both sides of the boat as a machine gun opened up from the helicopter. McAllen pushed the speedboat to its max. The boat rose up, bouncing hard on the waves.

Bernadette held onto a gunwale. The boat was rocking violently. She feared the boat would hydroplane and flip with so much power.

The boat suddenly slowed as McAllen threw the wheel into a 180 turn and gunned the engines. The helicopter overshot them.

Bernadette saw the helicopter as it passed overhead. Two men were hanging out the doors with machine guns. She could only make out the outline of the pilot in the cockpit.

The helicopter slowed and turned to come back around after them. Bernadette heard a loud whooshing sound from somewhere on the land and the helicopter exploded in a ball of fire.

Sebastian looked at the house where the RPG round had been fired from, "Sonofabitch, that's one hell of a shot."

The other helicopter rose high up into the air moving away from the firing range of the RPG. It came high over the house then dipped its nose. All six of its rockets fired at once. The house exploded.

"You bastard," Sebastian yelled. He picked up his sniper rifle and fired off a round. It missed.

McAllen looked at Sebastian. "You need to kill them Sebastian, not make them angry."

The helicopter turned and came towards them. The side door machine gunners opened up. The water around the speedboat erupted in plumes of water.

Bernadette wondered if McAllen was going to make a run or stand and fight. He didn't rev the engine. He'd made his decision.

Sebastian lifted up his sniper rifle. McAllen stood at his back to steady him. He called in the distance. "1,000 metres, 800, 500, he's dropping down—wait for it—he'll drop down more for a better shot —wait for it—now."

Sebastian fired at less than a hundred metres. Bernadette saw the shot break through the helicopters glass cockpit. The pilot's head exploded, a spray of pink mist covering the glass.

The helicopter roared over them and dived into the water. The rotors thrashed the water as it hit before exploding and sending a water geyser into the air.

Waves rocked the boat. They all turned their eyes to look at the house. It was engulfed in a fireball.

"You think they made it out?" Sebastian asked.

McAllen looked at his cell phone. He had nothing. He drove the boat towards the front of the house. There were no signs of life.

The sounds of police sirens could be heard from on shore. "We have to go," McAllen said. "If we stay here, we'll become guests of the Nicaraguan government. We can never avenge the deaths of our friends that way." He revved the boat and headed for the marina.

5

THE BOAT SPED over the waves. The rowboat ride that Bernadette and Winston had made was covered in minutes by the speedboat. McAllen steered the boat beside the dock. Sebastian leapt off, securing the mooring lines.

"What now?" Bernadette asked, staring at McAllen. In all of the scenarios she'd thought of—this wasn't one of them.

"We're going to find your little friend, Elvis, and he's going to tell us who hired him," McAllen said. "I want to know who's responsible for killing my friends."

"That's no problem," Elvis said, stepping out from behind a shed.

Bernadette looked up to see Elvis on the dock with a machine gun pointed at them.

Elvis waved his gun at Bernadette, "take that rifle and drop it into the water."

Bernadette picked up the sniper rifle. Sebastian's eyes closed as she dropped it over the side.

"Now, you want to know who's trying to kill you?" Elvis said. "I was hired by your American FBI to kill you. Yes, your very own people, Senora Winston." He nodded in her direction, shrugged and sighed. "These are strange times, but you see, whoever pays the most money gets what they asked for."

Winston felt Bernadette's hand in her back. She pulled her gun, and fired three shots into Elvis, the bullets finding their mark in his chest.

He fell forward on the dock. His machine gun clattered at Sebastian's feet.

Winston turned to Bernadette. "You knew I had that?"

"Hell yeah. As soon as you came out of your room with a jacket on. You kept fussing with your back every few minutes. You pretty much broadcasted you had a concealed weapon."

McAllen stood over Elvis's body. "Check him for car keys," he said to Sebastian then looked down at Bernadette. "Do you see his vehicle close by?"

"It's the silver SUV in the parking lot," Bernadette said stepping out of the boat.

A chorus of sirens was coming in their direction, emergency medical services, and police vehicles approaching from Granada. People were lining the docks on the far side of the Marina, staring at the fire across the lake.

Sebastian pulled Elvis's body behind the shed and threw his machine gun in the water. He looked at McAllen. "We'd best make tracks."

McAllen turned to Bernadette and Winston. "Well, are you coming with us?"

Winston looked back from the approaching sirens. "Whoa, what? Why would we come with you? We were just witness to outright murder. The Nicaraguan authorities will want to take our statement—"

"Are you kidding me? Our dead Elvis said your own FBI is trying to kill us. That means all of us," McAllen said.

Bernadette nodded in the direction of the island. "He's right, Winston, if Elvis was lying, the FBI would have made sure you weren't harmed. They don't believe in collateral damage."

"I just don't get it—who in my department would want to kill me?" Winston said.

"Let me break it down for you Agent Winston," McAllen said. "Four of my friends just got killed out there. Whoever sent those guys didn't much care if you or Detective Callahan died in the process. They wanted information. They knew I'd give it to the detective— then you became a liability."

"Aw, shit," Winston, said. "This was a goddamn set up. How could I be this stupid?"

"Welcome to the party," Bernadette said. "I have no idea how the Canadians are involved in this but I mean to find out."

"Hold up for a second," McAllen said raising his hand. "I wouldn't be contacting your people just yet. There's an answer in Florida we need to find. Once we do that, we can go from there."

"What answer?" Bernadette asked.

"Minutes ago, we told the FBI where to find Sigurdsson. They'll be sending a team there to find him. I want us to get there and stop them. Maybe, if we can capture us an FBI agent we'll find out who is behind this," McAllen said.

"This is getting weird," Winston said. "Someone in my own department—"

"On that subject, we need your phone, Winston," Sebastian said.

"My phone?"

"Yes, your phone. The FBI will have a tracking GPS on your phone. The moment we leave here, they'll be on us. Now, give me your phone."

Winston took her phone out of her jacket and handed it to Sebastian. He pulled the sim card out, dropped it on the dock and ground it with his heel.

"I'll get you a new burner phone on the way to the airport."

"We'll pick up alternate passports at a place we know in town," McAllen said. "We can't land in the USA with your ID's. Both your governments will be looking for you."

"You want us to be on the run with you? Are you kidding me?" Winston asked.

"It's not on the run, it's on the hunt." Bernadette turned to

McAllen. "It's getting busy, we'd best get out of here." She nodded in the direction of the ambulances and police arriving at the other end of the marina.

They walked towards the SUV. Winston and Bernadette got in the back while McAllen took the wheel and Sebastian got in the passenger seat with a cell phone in his hand.

They passed the emergency vehicle and made their way into Granada where they picked up new passports in an hour. The old guy who made the passports didn't blink an eye at the FBI and RCMP IDs that he lifted photos from. His bushy eyebrows only rose when McAllen dropped five one hundred American dollars in his weathered hand. He muttered a brief "*muchas gracias*," and they were on their way.

"What's the plan to fly out of here?" Winston asked. "Do we fly to Miami or Fort Lauderdale?"

"Neither," Sebastian said. "We've got a direct flight to Key West International Airport."

"Don't they only take small planes?"

"Yeah." Sebastian turned in his seat. "We got one picking us up."

Winston sat back in her seat and leaned over to Bernadette. "How are these guys getting a personal plane?"

Bernadette whispered, "You remember the story I told you about some Wall-Street guys who tried to put a hit on them?"

"Uh, huh, I remember. Something about them killing all the guys who attacked them on their island."

"Well, a short while later, the Wall-Street guys were executed in their office in New York... and all the money in their accounts was gone."

"How much money?"

"About 300 million."

"Hmm, I guess that buys a lot of private jet time. Also makes our travel companions stone cold killers."

"Guess so," Bernadette said.

Bernadette leaned forward in her seat to get closer to McAllen. "You got some kind of plan when we meet up with these so-called

FBI people in Key West. I don't think a handshake and making introductions will be of much use."

McAllen looked at Bernadette in the rear-view mirror and smiled. "No, we've ordered a friend of ours to have some *toys* ready for us when we land. I'm sure we'll be fine."

"Well, order me an extra-large squirt gun if it's a toy, and anything in a 9 mm with a hollow point if it's not," Bernadette said.

They made it to the airport by noon to find a Learjet sitting on the tarmac waiting for them. Sebastian drove the SUV to the far side of the airport terminal and gave two teenage kids a one hundred-dollar bill to take the SUV back to the Dario Hotel in Granada. He told them the front desk manager would give them one hundred dollars more when they got there. The second part was a lie, but then, Sebastian reasoned, one hundred dollars was easy money for them.

The kids jumped in the vehicle and were gone in a flash. Sebastian smiled as he walked back to the terminal. Whoever was looking for Elvis's vehicle wouldn't find it at the airport. That gave them some time.

The Learjet was small. It had four large leather seats that swiveled to face each other, with a tiny restroom at the back that one with the ability of a Cirque du Soleil acrobat could use comfortably.

Sebastian sat across from Winston, poured himself a glass of Chardonnay and offered one to Winston. She turned away in disgust and poured herself some water.

"Suit yourself," Sebastian said. "You need to relax a bit, Agent Winston. You're very uptight."

"Said by an old man, trying to channel a thirty-year-old." Winston raised an eyebrow.

Sebastian flashed a smile. "Better than trying to channel an eighty-year-old." He sipped his wine and smacked his lips.

Bernadette poured herself a scotch from the self-serve bar and sat across from McAllen. "I wanted to say, I'm sorry for your loss. There was no time until now."

McAllen had his own large glass of scotch. He downed a mouthful, swallowed hard. "You can save your sympathies. I'll mourn my friends in my own time. They all knew if they stayed close to me, that sooner or later this would happen."

"That absolves you of having to feel the pain of their loss?" Bernadette asked.

"You some kind of shrink, detective?"

"No, just trying to figure out what makes you tick… one day you're out to destroy the world. The next day you want to save it."

"Now, just hold on. You're making me sound like half the governments on this planet." McAllen grinned.

Bernadette was about to launch into a more heated discussion when the pilot stood beside them. "Excuse me, Mr. Van Horn," the pilot said, using the fake ID McAllen had presented at boarding. "We have a storm coming into our landing destination."

"How bad is it?" McAllen asked.

"It's going to make for a rough landing, but more importantly, our plane will not be able to stay in the area. We'll need to leave once you've disembarked and fly to a safer location."

"You expect that big of a storm?" McAllen asked.

"Yes, Mr. Van Horn. Key West is about to be glanced by Hurricane Kelly. They've already put an evacuation order on the barrier islands and much of Key West. Are you sure you still want us to land there? We could land in Miami, but you need to know it will be evacuated later today as well."

McAllen smiled at the pilot. "We'll be fine. Just drop us off in Key West, and we'll figure our own way back."

The pilot nodded and walked back to the cockpit.

Bernadette watched him walk away and swirled her drink, "You have no idea how we'll get back, do you?"

McAllen drained his scotch and looked at Bernadette. "Nope, not a clue, we'll make it up as we go. But I do know one thing. Those FBI guys, if that's who they really are, will be in the same kind of weather."

"Great, stuck in a hurricane with a bunch of guys who are trying to kill us. How cozy," Bernadette said and went back to the bar for a refill.

6

AGENT MORGAN COULDN'T BELIEVE the report from Nicaragua. The body of Elvis Calderon had been found on the dock. The last transmission he'd seen from Calderon showed their cover had been blown. The police were sifting through the destroyed house, but it could take weeks before identification of bodies could be made. There was a report from the airport of two women who had the features of Winston and Callahan with two older men boarding a private jet. None of this was good. His entire plan was at risk.

He looked across his desk at Lawrence Derman, a squat older man who seemed to recede further into his chair. Morgan tapped his finger on his desk, something he did when things bothered him. His beautifully manicured nails made a loud sound on the polished mahogany.

"This is what you brought me?" Morgan asked. His eyes narrowed at Derman. "You brought me a bunch of incompetent Russians, Chechens and washed up Arab terrorists who couldn't mount a helicopter attack—armed with rockets I might add—to take out six geriatrics and two women."

"I'm terribly sorry..." Derman muttered, trying to rise up out of the chair. He failed to do so and slouched back down. "Matvel

Sokolov. He said he'd put together a crack team—the very best... I just had no idea they'd fail so badly."

Morgan shook his head and starred hard at Derman, wondering why he'd ever decided to work with him. He'd discovered him several years back when he was Congressman Derman. He was taking bribes from everyone. It didn't matter if it was Russians, Chinese or North Koreans. Derman was the man who made the word corruption into a new standard.

Derman amassed a steady stream of bribes. He had money coming in from everywhere. He could get things done, contracts endorsed, a special meeting with a high-ranking government official that would also take a bribe. What those who bribed Derman loved about him is that he spent the money as fast as he got it. There was never a point where he had enough and walked away. He spent his money on high priced hookers and bad hands of poker. He played high stakes and his losses were big. Morgan couldn't believe the surveillance reports detailing how much Derman blew at the tables.

Morgan studied one of his fingernails. Its cuticle looked ragged. He shook his head and flicked a piece of dust off his desk. "I wonder why I keep you out of jail, Derman."

Derman looked up. His mouth opened and closed, then his eyes locked on Morgan's. "We'd go down together—you must know that, a man of your obvious talents."

Morgan studied the crumpled little man. He wasn't so beaten down after all. Derman was in his early seventies. His features were soft, his hair a wispy grey, and he wore glasses of some god-awful new age design in brilliant red that made him look as if he was about to step into the cockpit of a space ship.

"Hmm, yes, well... we will see..." Morgan let the words trail off. There was no use offending the little turd. He was useful. He'd brought him the craziest scheme Morgan had ever heard of.

If it came through he would become one of the richest men in America. But he was also dealing with some of the most dangerous organizations from three continents. Any one of them, if crossed, would make sure that whatever the American government did to him would be child's play. The Americans would throw him in prison. These people were serious. He let himself relax in his chair and smiled at Derman. "Okay, we need to get this back on track. I'll call Sokolov and make sure he gets the right people in place this time."

"I've already done it," Derman said. "He sent a team to the Key West lab where McAllen said Sigurdsson was. They should be there by now."

"I expect a better performance this time," Morgan said.

"Not to worry," Derman replied. "Sokolov said this team is ruthless. If they find Sidgurdsson there, he'll be brought to us. Anyone else will be taken care of."

Morgan mused a bit. "We need to clean up the mess from Nicaragua. Winston and Callahan are still alive and I think they're travelling with McAllen and Sebastian Germaine. I have a way of tracking Winston, but I need to jump through some administrative hoops to get the tracking activated. Once I have it, I want a team put on it."

Derman lifted one hand in response. "I'll have Sokolov deal with it."

7

Bernadette saw high waves and leaning palm trees as they made their descent into Key West International Airport. The jet landed with a hard thump to keep itself from being thrown around in the wind. They taxied to a private charter hanger to deplane. Bernadette noticed beads of water on the cabin window, not from rain but from the ocean—the wind was picking up. They followed McAllen through the terminal and found a waiting SUV. McAllen and Sebastian opened the back. A duffel bag with guns was inside.

"I guess you didn't make your reservation with Hertz," Bernadette said looking over the weapons.

McAllen handed her a 9 mm handgun and several clips of ammunition. "No, I use my own private members club. I get better air miles." He passed a handgun to Winston and Sebastian loaded a Berretta submachine gun while pocketing some percussion grenades.

Winston smiled at the weapons. "I guess you're expecting the worst scenario, from these FBI guys."

McAllen gave a small smile. "I don't think we tangled with FBI back in Nicaragua. If we had, I think we'd all be dead. I'm pretty sure that was local talent."

"What do you think we'll find at Sigurdsson's laboratory?" Winston asked.

"More of the same. But this time we're ready for them," McAllen said as he checked the sights on his weapon.

"Damn straight," Bernadette said as she put her side arm in her jacket.

"You know," McAllen, said, "this is kinda strange—us being on the same side."

Bernadette winked at McAllen. "Don't get too used to it. Remember, I'm still on the side of the law. And you've got way too many outstanding warrants for me to ignore when this shit is over."

McAllen shook his head and got into the truck. Nothing had changed between them, only the circumstances. She was still an RCMP Detective and he was a wanted criminal.

The jet they arrived on was already taxiing on the runway to take off as they drove out of the airport. By the time they made the highway it was rising up overhead on its way north.

"There goes our ride," Bernadette said. "I heard he's heading for Atlanta to get away from the storm.

They went quiet in the SUV as the wind buffeted the windows and spray from the sea hit the windows. Everywhere people were packing up. A long line of vehicles was heading out of the Keys.

"They know something we don't?" Winston asked.

"Yeah," Bernadette said. "The sea has risen to within its max on the shoreline with global warming. This little piece of land sits only one metre above sea level now. A category 2 hurricane like the one that supposed to glance this place will bring in a four-metre storm surge. They'll be swamped."

"And so will the airport." Winston said. She looked up at McAllen in the driver's seat. "I understand you're a professor of some kind—doesn't that make you some kind of smart guy?"

"You're wondering how I'll be getting us out of here?" McAllen asked.

"Yes, you got it."

"I'll let you know—when I know."

Winston sat back in her seat and looked at Bernadette. "I told myself, do not get in the truck with these guys. Nothing good will come of this."

"Hey, I told you I'd get you back to your son. Relax," Bernadette told her. She looked out the SUV window at the waves pounding over the sea wall. She did not believe her own words.

They pulled a hard left once leaving the highway and came to a dock. A group of men and women were lashing wildly rocking boats to the docks as best they could in hopes that they'd be there when they returned.

McAllen parked beside a 10-metre boat that had a row of dive tanks on it. He jumped out and met with a stocky African American, dressed in shorts and a t-shirt and wearing a Miami Dolphins ball cap. They stood, talked for a minute and McAllen motioned everyone to join him.

"Whoa. What's with the boat?" Winston asked as she joined the others on the dock. "I thought we were going to a laboratory."

"Yes. It's an underwater laboratory," Sebastian said. "I think you missed part of the briefing." He turned to the captain. "This is Captain Darius, and he'll be taking us on our excursion today."

Winston's eyes went wide. "You want us to go out in this weather in this tiny boat? You must be crazier than you are mad."

"Don't worry," Captain Darius said. "Once we get out into the ocean, the waves get smaller. The closer you are into shore, the worse the waves." He looked around at everyone. "Okay, climb aboard. The lab is only five miles out to sea and under 30 feet of water."

McAllen and Darius stopped on the dock for a moment. "Have any other dive boats gone out today?" McAllen asked.

"Yeah, three divers took a boat. They didn't want a captain, said they had their own. They paid a shit load for it. Gave my cousin Ricky enough to buy a new boat for the rental. You expecting trouble out there?" Darius asked.

"Maybe," McAllen said. "Let's just say, I'll be adding a whole bunch onto your fee if we do."

"You're my man." Darius gave McAllen a big grin and they shook hands. "The diving business has been crap this year with all the hurricanes. I'm glad you came my way."

McAllen nodded his head. "Sure, glad to be of help." He watched Darius get on the boat and hoped he'd be better luck for him than he had been for himself.

Winston climbed on board the boat and grabbed a railing to steady her. The boat was rising up and down with every wave that hit the dock. McAllen, Sebastian and Bernadette jumped on and climbed into the wheelhouse with the boat captain.

Sebastian cast off their lines as the boats twin inboard engines roared into life. The boat hit high waves as soon as it left the shelter of the harbor. Waves sprayed over the side and washed the lower deck. Winston fought hard to keep her feet dry on the lower deck before clambering up the steel stairs to the wheelhouse. The boat rocked more up there but at least it was drier. The next forty-five minutes were brutal. Captain Darius couldn't increase the speed much over 10 miles per hour due to the high waves. The boat rose up large waves then plummeted down the troughs and up again like a roller coaster.

Bernadette had been in rough waters on big lakes but this was testing her endurance. She stood on the deck with the others, her legs fighting to stay up as they hit each wave. Her stomach had given up being terrified. She'd thought she'd be sick a few times but didn't relish the thought of leaning over the railing in high seas. She convinced herself she'd be okay.

Finally, they hit calmer waters. The waves lessened, the wind seemed lighter and they picked up speed. A large column of clouds appeared on the horizon. The hurricane was heading their way. How much more forceful it would be would depend on how close it got to Key West.

McAllen turned to Bernadette and Winston. "Do either of you have any diving experience?"

Winston shook her head. She had a look on her face of absolute fear of anything to do with the water.

Bernadette paused, looked at the white caps on the waves, "Yeah,

I've done some resort diving. I'm not PADI certified, but I can do a 30 foot dive."

"Good," McAllen said, "How about if we go below and get suited up. They've got a full selection of wetsuits."

Bernadette followed McAllen to the lower deck. Under the benches were large clear plastic bins with decals listing wetsuits, masks, snorkels and fins. She found a half suit in her size. She didn't like the ones with the full legs.

She went below, stripped naked and pulled the suit on. Although the wetsuit smelled like it had been freshly cleaned, she would rather have had a bathing suit on underneath. She pulled the long zipper up from the back and put her clothes into a dry bag and hung them from the ceiling in the toilet, which is called the 'head,' on a boat.

McAllen stepped out from another small change room. "These things don't feel the same when you got to go 'commando' in them," he observed.

Bernadette blushed. "Ah, yeah you got that right." She instantly felt self-conscious. She shook her head and went back up to the wheelhouse.

Another dive boat appeared in the distance, bobbing at anchor. They closed on it slowly.

"Weapons ready," McAllen said.

Captain Darius looked at the guns his passengers produced. He maneuvered the wheel and throttles. "Some serious shit about to happen," he muttered to himself.

Bernadette felt her pulse quicken. She chambered a round in her 9 mm and took off the safety. The boat came within hailing distance.

A lone man on board looked up in surprise at their arrival. He didn't seem to be expecting visitors. There was hesitation in his movements. He looked down in the water at the bubbles from his divers then back at McAllen and his group.

He made a decision and opened fired with an automatic weapon.

"Everyone down," Sebastian yelled. They hit the deck as gunfire racked the side of the metal-hulled boat.

"Nice welcome," Bernadette said.

"Covering fire," McAllen said as soon as the shooting stopped.

Bernadette and Winston stuck their guns over the gunwale and fired off four quick shots. McAllen and Sebastian stood up with their machine guns.

The man on deck was caught in their crossfire. He fell to the deck without firing another shot.

Darius pulled them alongside. They lashed their boat to it. McAllen jumped on board and examined the dead body.

"A lot of strange tattoos on this guy. He looks a bit Middle Eastern to me," McAllen said looking up at the others. "I don't make him for FBI or CIA."

"I think we're seeing the hired help." Winston stood over the body with her gun.

Bernadette walked to the back of the dive boat. "I see three sets of bubbles from divers."

"Okay, we got to go down there. That's our competition for finding Sigurdsson. Winston and Sebastian, you keep watch up here," McAllen said.

"Ah, Mac," Sebastian said, "You got more than divers down there —looks like there are some special visitors prowling around." He pointed to some fins that broke the surface near the boat.

McAllen looked over the side. "They're black tip sharks." He nodded to Bernadette. "They bother swimmers and spear fisherman. They can be a nuisance when they get curious."

"You mean as in taking an exploratory bite nuisance?" Bernadette asked.

Darius helped her into her dive tank that was harnessed to a large vest called a BCD. The buoyancy control device would help her establish neutral buoyancy once she was in the water.

"When was your last resort dive?" Darius asked as she tightened up her vest.

"About two years ago," Bernadette said.

"Okay, there's no Margaritas afterwards, you need to breathe easy or you'll go through your air too quickly. Just relax." Darius smiled, placing his big hand on her shoulder. It calmed her down.

He slipped weights into her weight belt to help her descend, and handed her a mask that had been dipped in a solution to stop it from fogging. She did some tests of the regulator and walked with her fins to the end of the boat.

McAllen handed her a knife and a spear gun. "Stay close to me and follow my lead. We'll try to drive those divers to the surface where Sebastian and Winston can take care of them."

Bernadette put her regulator in her mouth, nodded and gave him an okay sign by making a circle with her thumb and index finger. The air tasted dry. She had no salvia in her mouth and felt an urge to gag. She stood at the end of the boat for a second. The waves rolled. The boat lifted up high. A deep canyon formed below in the sea. A shark swam by eyeing her. She waited for the boat to drop down again.

Holding onto her mask with one hand, she put one fin forward and stepped off the boat. She plunged into the water. The coolness of the water shocked her. McAllen was beside her. They gave each other the okay sign and started to descend.

The water was murky. They could see only three to four metres in either direction. A shark swam into their vision. McAllen waved his spear gun causing it to flick its strong tail and shoot out into the depths. Bernadette squeezed her nose, blew softly and pressurized as they descended. She checked her depth gauge. They'd dropped three metres. The bubbles from the other divers were below them.

McAllen motioned for them to swim to the right. He didn't want to come on top of them. He wanted to come at them from the side. A light came into view.

Bernadette checked her depth gauge, they'd reached eight metres and the light became a series of portholes in a long orange cylinder. A series of slow bubbles rose from it towards the surface.

They stopped beside some coral and saw three divers outside the cylinder. This was the underwater lab. It was thirty metres long with two hatches. The divers were trying to get into the hatches but seemed to be having problems. Bernadette watched one diver pull something out of large bag. Another diver attached something to a tank. A spark was lit and a bright cutting torch flashed.

McAllen tapped Bernadette on the shoulder. He pointed off to the left. Two shapes were on the seabed. She could make out the forms of two divers in orange wetsuits with logos similar to that of the lab. A trickle of blood streamed from their necks. Their bodies waved with the current. They were dead.

A large shadow appeared overhead. Bernadette looked up to see a big shark circling. Obviously attracted by the blood, it was cautious due to the activity of the other divers. Now, Bernadette realized why the sharks were around.

Bernadette looked back at McAllen. She could see the determination in his eyes. She waited for him to make a move.

McAllen motioned to Bernadette they needed to attack. He kicked hard with his fins and charged at the divers. Bernadette followed. She had her spear gun but couldn't shoot with McAllen in front.

One of the divers looked up, saw McAllen and Bernadette. He pounded on the shoulders of the other two divers to get their attention. The other two turned. One raised up his spear gun shooting at McAllen. It missed him and came at Bernadette. She felt it go over her head where it clanged on her tank's regulator.

McAllen grabbed for the diver's mask. The diver pushed his hand away revealing a knife in his other hand. McAllen grabbed the knife and forced it back into the diver's throat. He pushed it hard until the diver went still. A stream of blood rose from his throat.

Bernadette swam at the other diver and raised her spear gun. The diver knocked it down. He lunged at her with a knife. She grabbed the arm with the knife. She felt him overpowering her. The knife was edging towards her air hose. She pushed back as hard as she could.

McAllen picked up the spear gun. His only shot was the diver's legs. He fired, hitting him in his thigh, it began streaming blood. He turned from Bernadette, kicking for the surface.

The diver with the cutting torch waved the torch at them to ward them off. The torch could cut through metal—it could slice through them in seconds. They were in a stand-off.

Bernadette checked her air—only ten minutes left. The excitement and fight had used up her air much quicker than the one-hour tank. She'd have to start back up in eight minutes.

The door to the lab started to open. The remaining diver turned to look as a spear shot out the door, lodging itself in the diver's throat. The diver clutched at his throat as blood and bubbles shot from the wound.

McAllen motioned for Bernadette to follow him towards the door. She hung back. After seeing the spear in the diver's throat, she didn't like the welcome committee from the lab.

McAllen went to the side of the door and tapped on the hull of the cylinder with his knife. He did a series of taps that seemed to Bernadette like Morse code. A few minutes later, a hand came from a porthole motioning them to come inside.

They swam into a chamber. The door closed beside them and the water started to drop slowly. Bernadette had already gone through her main tank, and then had switched to her spare air. That had only two minutes left.

The air inside Bernadette's regulator was becoming thin. Then non-existent. She had nothing. No oxygen. She held her breath waiting for the water to recede. When it dropped below her face she ripped out her regulator and gasped in air, feeling lucky to be alive.

The water receded out of the chamber. The inner door opened. A young woman in a wetsuit had a spear gun pointed at them.

8

"Becky. It' me—Uncle Mac." McAllen pulled off his mask and his regulator.

Bernadette's shifted her eyes from the spear gun to McAllen.

Becky dropped the spear gun and rushed towards McAllen to help him unclip his diving tank. "Oh my god, Uncle Mac. I had no idea it was you outside. I just hoped you weren't more hostiles." They hugged each other tight.

McAllen smoothed the hair out of her eyes. She was a pretty girl, dark hair with brown eyes. "What happened here?"

"We heard a boat overhead on our sonar. We thought it might be our supply boat," Becky said. "Our radio's been out since yesterday. Carl and Tanya went to meet them. The next thing I knew those divers attacked them..." She buried her head in McAllen's shoulder and sobbed.

"Sorry," McAllen said. "Those guys were looking for your grandfather—this is all my fault. I told the FBI that Barney was here."

Becky looked at McAllen. "He hasn't been back since June. He was helping with the degradation study of the reef, and then all of a sudden he said he had to leave. I haven't heard from him since."

"Did he say where he was going?" McAllen asked.

Becky sniffed, found a tissue and blew her nose. "He said he was going to hook up with grandma."

"Which one?"

"Grandma Sam," Becky said.

"Is she doing the THV study?" McAllen asked.

"Yes, I saw a text from her last week when I was back on land."

McAllen turned to Bernadette. "We best get back to the dive boat. I don't know if these guys have back up. You got more tanks here?"

"I have three left. The supply boat was supposed to refill our tanks. But we don't leave here without taking the bodies of Eric and Tanya to the surface. I'm not leaving them for the sharks," Becky said.

"Understood." McAllen turned to Bernadette, "Unhook your tank and get a refilled one from Becky. You have any more spear guns handy?" he asked Becky.

"This is my only one. I have a couple of long poles. We use them to poke around in the reef to capture small plants," Becky said as she removed Bernadette's tank and replaced it with a full one.

"It will have to do. Those sharks are agitated out there with all the blood in the water. We'll have to stick close together as we rise to the surface," McAllen said.

They put on their tanks and tested the regulators. Becky pulled the inner door shut to the lab and sealed it. She turned the valve to flood the compartment. Bernadette felt a slight wave of panic as the water level rose inside the room. When the water filled the room, they would open the outer door and swim outside.

A large shark swam by the porthole. She tried to calm herself, taking slow breaths. The bodies of the two divers were twenty metres away. They needed to retrieve them and rise with them to the surface. The process was going to be slow. Hopefully the sharks would content themselves with the dead bad guys and leave them alone.

They swam out of the door and took a moment to survey the area. The two divers they'd killed lay on the sea floor near the entry to the lab. A shark had torn into one diver's body; the other was missing an arm. It lay exposed and shredded as small fish pecked at the flesh.

They waved at the swarm of sharks to move them away. They did but hovered in a swarm above them.

McAllen motioned for them to move forward. They came upon the bodies of Becky's dead friends. Their wounds had sealed, making them less of attraction to the sharks. Becky gathered the small girl, into her arms and Bernadette took up the male. He was light, a red head, maybe twenty-five years old. His mask was gone, his mouth open as if he wanted to say hello. Bernadette unhooked his diving tank and turned him around. She hooked both her arms under his armpits and nodded to McAllen and Becky. Becky did the same with the body of Tanya.

Bernadette and Becky held out their poles. McAllen waved the spear gun at the sharks. They looked like a phalanx of warriors bristling with weapons as they rose. The sharks circled. McAllen stayed away from the group to ward off the sharks when they came too close. The reef sharks darted towards them, then shot away. They were smaller, the group of divers looked massive to them. Size wins in the ocean.

They rose slowly. The ascent was going well in a macabre kind of way when a large form appeared out of the shadows. A shark three times as big as any of the reef sharks made its way towards them. It wasn't afraid. It smelled blood. A full-sized Bull Shark. Bernadette recognized the features she'd read about sharks you never want to meet when there's blood around and she was holding onto a dead body trailing blood. Bernadette waved her pole at it. The shark wagged its head side to side. It didn't faze him. His beady eyes were fixed on the body. He'd found a large meal. Bernadette's pole was a mere hindrance.

McAllen came alongside Bernadette, raised his spear gun and the Bull Shark got the message. He turned away—slowly. His large bulk showed scars on the side. He was a fighter and had won most of his battles. Bernadette saw long rows of razor sharp teeth. She felt the wave of water from its body. It scared the hell out of her.

Light appeared. They broke through to the surface. The boat was

LYLE NICHOLSON

twenty metres away. McAllen pulled out his regulator. "Swim for the boat. I'll stay behind to ward off our big friend."

Becky and Bernadette turned on their backs and pulled the two bodies under their chins. The sharks were everywhere around them. Fins darted then turned. The one big fin of the Bull Shark hadn't appeared.

Bernadette feared it would charge up from the depths. She pulled on the corpse of Eric and swam backwards as fast as she could propel herself towards the boat and safety. McAllen stuck his head underwater. He did a jackknife dive and was gone, a swirl of water being all that remained. Bernadette heard a loud hiss and thump from just below her.

McAllen surfaced with a smile. "I put a spear in our big friend's snout as he was heading for Becky. It didn't kill him but he'll have something else to worry about for now."

Bernadette could hear the waves crashing against the boat. She was exhausted by the time she reached the stern. The exertion of carrying the body to the surface with the sharks had worn her to her last raw nerve. She was relieved when three sets of hands reached down and pulled the body of Eric and then her onto the boat. Becky and McAllen came up behind her. They laid the bodies on the deck. Captain Darius found two tarps and covered them. They stared into the sea watching the fins swirl around before they disappeared.

"The sharks are going to go down and clean up the bodies of the two divers that attacked your friends," Bernadette said.

"I hope they don't choke on those bastards," Becky sneered. Her eyes flashed with anger.

Bernadette turned to Sebastian. "One of the divers that attacked the lab was coming to the surface after McAllen put a spear in his leg —you see him?"

Sebastian pointed behind him. A man in a wetsuit was tied to a pole near the bow. A tourniquet was on his leg; his chin was resting on his chest. He didn't look happy.

"He came to the surface. The sharks were all around him. I told him he could either get in our boat all peaceful like, or I'd leave him for shark meat," Sebastian said. "Who says all criminals are stupid?" he snorted.

McAllen, Winston and Bernadette stood around the man.

"Who wants to start our little conversation?" McAllen asked.

Winston looked down at the man in disgust. "Let me give it a go." She nudged the man with her foot. He looked up at her. He had dark hair, eyes and skin. He had a sharp angular nose with a scar that edged the right side of his face. Winston thought this guy could have been cast as the villain in any pirate movie.

"You want to tell us who you're working for?"

"I am saying nothing." He spit at Winston. His voice had a heavy accent. To Bernadette it sounded like Eastern Europe.

"Such a bad attitude," Bernadette said. "He probably doesn't want to tell us his name either."

"You got it, bitch. Give me to the authorities and l get lawyer. Your country is famous for this. I be out on bail and free in no time." The man smiled up at Winston and Bernadette. "Maybe you two like a date when I get out?"

"I don't know about you, but I'm about finished with this suspect? What about you, Winston?" Bernadette asked.

"I've only begun asking him questions," Winston said.

"No, I think we're done." Bernadette looked at McAllen. "How about we help this gentleman up, let him stretch his legs and then see if he wants to go for a swim?"

McAllen smiled. "That's a great idea. I'll bet he needs to move around a bit. I think we'll take this tourniquet off. The salt water will be good for the wound."

"You cannot do this. The other guy told me two of you were law enforcement types. Like FBI and some Canadian police or something. You can't do it—I know my rights," the man said.

McAllen and Bernadette hauled the man up. Bernadette took off his ropes and they walked him towards the stern of the boat.

"Here's the thing," Bernadette told him. "We found out that someone in the FBI is trying to kill us. We're not taking it well. We don't have time to dick around with you and your rights."

"You either tell us what we want to know or we throw you back into the water. Those reef sharks will be nipping on you until a few more Bull sharks come and finish you off. You can think about your rights as you watch our boat disappear into the distance," McAllen said.

They moved him closer to the stern. The waves were getting higher. Shark fins appeared and sliced through the water. The man's eyes grew wide. "No, you would not do this. You're bullshitting me."

Bernadette looked at McAllen. "I hate someone saying I'm full of shit. How about you?"

"Yeah, especially bullshit." McAllen said. They moved towards the stern and leaned him over the water. The only thing between the man and the sharks were their hands.

"Mister, you got ten seconds to start talking. Because this boat is heading for shore with or without you—you decide," Bernadette said.

"Okay, okay, I talk."

They pulled him back and threw him onto deck. He sat there clutching his stomach as if he wanted to throw up.

"Start talking," Bernadette said.

"We were hired by a guy named Sokolov. He said all we had to do was go to this underwater lab and get this Sigurdsson guy out of there. We were supposed to drop him off at a hanger in Miami. That's all I know."

"What hanger?" Winston asked.

"I don't know—some hanger with private jets," the man said.

"Listen," Winston said. "I'll throw your sorry ass over the side if you don't tell us about the hanger."

The man looked up at them. "Sokolov will have me killed when he finds out I gave you this information."

"Sharks or Sokolov. You have shitty choices. But that's what you got. What's it going to be?" Winston asked.

The man sighed and hung his head then looked up. "It's Executive First Charters. The hanger was number 10. We were ordered to capture Sigurdsson, put him on a private plane we had waiting in Key

West then fly him to Miami. We were supposed to get our cash there when we handed him over."

"Do you know where they were taking him?" McAllen asked.

The man stared up at them. "Of course not. I was to get my cash and head home."

"And home is?" Bernadette said.

"Kazakhstan." The man looked down at the deck.

"Are you here legally?" Winston asked.

He shook his head.

"This Sokolov must have smuggled him in," Bernadette said. "That way he wouldn't have raised the alarm of Homeland Security."

They fastened a rope around his wrists and tied him back to a pole on the deck, then went forward to have a conference.

"Who do we give this guy to?" Winston said.

"Yeah, I know what you mean. We drop him off to the Florida State Troopers, they call in the FBI, which means whoever in the FBI wanted to kill us off gets alerted," Bernadette acknowledged.

"And we're all in the United States under fake passports," McAllen added. "Both Sebastian and I are wanted in this country. I'm not looking for attention."

"What do you suggest?" Bernadette asked.

"We take this Kazak guy with us and we put the bodies on ice," McAllen said.

"Whoa," Winston said. "Now you're pushing so many violations of the law that I may want to have the FBI kill me. I'd be locked up for so many years from what you suggest that my life wouldn't be worth living."

"Hey, it's just until we find this Sokolov and who's behind trying to kidnap Sigurdsson and trying to kill us," McAllen told her. "We'd be in Miami inside of a day and have this guy and the bodies back with the authorities inside twenty-four hours."

Winston shook her head. "Yeah famous last words." She looked at Bernadette. "I hate to say it but I don't see any other choice. This investigation leads to Miami." She looked back at McAllen. "Any idea how we're going to get there?"

"Yeah," McAllen said. "Sebastian was on the phone to a Helicopter company out of Miami. They got a Bell 525 on its way to us. They claim they can beat the Hurricane if we make to the airport in the next 45 minutes."

"It's got lots of room," Sebastian chimed in. "We could even take the stiffs if you like."

Winston and Bernadette looked at Sebastian and shook their heads. They looked over at Becky to see if she'd heard the comment. She hadn't.

"I'm going below to change," Bernadette said. "I'm also going to call my contact with CSIS and see what they know of this Sokolov."

She went down the narrow stairway of the boat to a small changing room. She peeled off the wetsuit and found a towel to dry herself. Grabbing her phone she saw she had a text from Chris. It said he'd landed in Kandahar, Afghanistan. The place was dusty, he couldn't find a good beer and he'd call soon.

She smiled and dialed Anton de Luca. He picked up after several rings. "Where the hell are you?" he asked.

"We've gone off mission—a bit." Bernadette admitted.

"Off. Holy Christ, I've been fielding calls all day from Morgan in the FBI. He wants to know what you're up to? What is it about not causing an international incident you didn't get?"

"What do you know about, Morgan?" Bernadette said, ignoring Anton's tirade.

"That he asked for you to be sent on the investigation."

"Did you think it was odd?"

"Ah, yeah I did," Anton, said after a pause.

Bernadette could hear in his voice how he'd felt about sending her to Nicaragua. "You get the command from on high?"

"Yeah, all the way from Ottawa. I couldn't object to it. They agreed with Morgan you were the only one who could get close to McAllen and find Sigurdsson."

Bernadette bit her lip. "You ever hear of a guy name Sokolov?"

"If he's Matlev Sokolov he's ex Russian KGB turned into muscle for the Russian Mafia. One of the worst guys we've ever dealt with. You run into him down there?"

"No, just met an acquaintance. I have a favour to ask, Anton."

"What is it?"

"We've never spoken. You still haven't heard from me. Can you do that?"

Anton sighed. "I should never promise you a favour, Bernadette. How long do you need?"

"No more than forty-eight hours. After that I'll call in and make a full report. Is that okay?"

"I guess so. Is that why you're using a burner phone?"

"Yeah, if you'd send me a picture of Sokolov on this phone, then we have to go off the grid for a bit." She shut off her phone and went onto the deck. She climbed the stairs up to the wheelhouse. The captain was holding on tight as the waves bounced the boat in the high waves.

"How are we doing?" Bernadette asked, looking at McAllen.

"Darius said we'll be in Key West inside of an hour," McAllen said. "But there's one little problem."

"And that is?" Bernadette asked.

"The hurricane has changed course. It's coming inland. That means a higher storm surge. Key West Airport is underwater."

"And we board the helicopter how?" Bernadette asked.

"From the airport roof." Captain Darius looked over his shoulder with a grim smile.

9

Anton DeLuca went from his office to see Mellissa Ackerman. She was good at keeping any confidence he shared with her. She was also one of the few women in the office who didn't come on to him, dropping hints of dinner dates and after work meetings. He enjoyed his conversations with her. He found her funny, and always relaxed.

Tapping politely on her office door he entered. "Mellissa, you were once working on the Russian Mafia and links to US and Canadian Government, yes?"

Mellissa wheeled her chair away from her desk and regarded Anton for a minute. She was in her mid-twenties and a big girl, always had been since she was a kid. She'd grown up with a doting German Grandmother who decided that every adversity Mellissa encountered should be treated with streusel cake, poppy seed cake or pudding pretzels.

She brushed her hand over her wiry hair that seemed unmanageable. "How can I help you, Anton?" Her eyes went soft as she regarded him. He was her reason for late night caramel popcorn binges when her fantasies of him became too much to handle.

"I need some background information on a guy named, Matlev Sokolov," Anton said, taking a seat directly across from her and relaxing. He felt she was more like a buddy than any of the other men in the department. He had no idea how Mellissa felt about him.

"Matlev Sokolov," Mellissa said coughing into her hand and pulling herself together, "He's the meanest of the Russian Mafia. He'd make Tony Soprano look like a boy scout."

"That bad, huh?"

"Yep, one mean mother fu... Excuse me," Melissa said, coughing into her hand again, her face red with embarrassment.

Anton laughed. "Hey, Mellissa, it's okay, just the two of us here. Go ahead; use whatever you want to express yourself. This isn't a briefing. I need to know what one of my team is up against." He reached forward and patted Melissa on the shoulder.

Mellissa felt his hand and her heart went into palpitations. Tonight would require a stop at her grandmother's house for German cake then a full binge of Weeds on Netflix.

"Sorry, you're right, thanks Anton." She sat a little more upright in her chair and began her briefing. "As I said, Sokolov is one bad MF, he came out of the KGB when the USSR was collapsing. He was a mid-grade lieutenant known for his loyalty to Russia and being cruel to opponents. He was well received by the Russian Mafia, or *Bratva*, the brotherhood as they're called."

"What rank is he? And how well is he connected to the hierarchy?"

She turned to her computer and with a few keystrokes brought up a file. "He's listed as an *Obshchak*, that's in the security group of the Russian Mafia. That puts him just below the *Putkhan* or boss." Her eyes squinted as she read a smaller file, "And, he's also A *Vor*—a made man. This is similar to what the American Mafia has. When a recruit shows that he excels in leadership, he becomes a *Vor v Zakone*," She looked at Anton. "That translates to a Thief within the law."

Anton bent down to look at the screen. His face was centimeters from her. She felt his warmth, smelled his skin. He smelled good, a little earthy with a hint of spice. She wanted to groan.

"Has he been in trouble in North America?" Anton asked.

Mellissa cleared her throat. "Yeah, the FBI in Washington caught him in a sting operation. Sokolov was implicated in some collusion to award contracts to companies in the USA that had suspicious links to Russian companies. It seems he had a congressman in his pocket, a guy named Derman."

"Any convictions or jail time for anyone?" Anton asked.

Mellissa blew out her breath. "That is the strangest thing. You'd think there'd be all kinds of serious jail time for this. The congressman got pensioned off. Sokolov was chucked out of the country, and a bunch of billionaires who were in on this threw so many lawyers at the FBI that nothing happened."

Anton stood up and stretched, Mellissa feigned not to notice, "Do you have a list of the billionaires involved?" he asked.

Mellissa pulled up another file. "Yes, we have a Wang Zhoa of China, listed on Forbes as worth 31 billion, Wilhelmina Flowers is a Dutch National living in the USA, worth 28 billion and a Susilo Bambang Yudhoyona of the Philippines...he's worth a paltry 17 billion."

"Wow, some pretty heavy hitters involved in this... Would you do me a favour, Mellissa?"

Mellissa looked up at Anton, her very idea of an Italian hunk, the very man she fantasied making love to her every night and said, "Sure, what is it Anton?"

"Would you run a search of all of these parties and see if anything else comes up. I got a feeling these people are doing illegal things and it may affect someone I have in the field."

"Of course, happy to, Anton," Mellissa said. She gave her imagination a quick slap of reality and turned back to her screen.

10

THE WIND BLEW HARDER. White caps topped the waves. The boat rocked violently. Bernadette gripped the back railing of the wheelhouse; her knuckles were white with the tension. She could hardly make out the shoreline as wind whipped sea spray over the windshield. Darius leaned his large body into the wheel as he was trying to stay with the waves. The dive boat was surfing them as they plowed towards shore.

"I'm going to go around the breakwater," Darius yelled above the wind.

The boat throttled back as a large wave almost swamped their stern. Bernadette looked below to see the Kazak prisoner get submerged then emerge sputtering from the water. She wanted to go down and bring him up to the wheelhouse, but that was too dangerous now.

The two bodies they'd brought up were lashed to the deck. The water washed over them then spilled back. It looked like the sea wanted to take the two of them to their final resting place.

Darius hit the throttle again to stay with the rising wave and not go down in a large trough. If he did the boat's stern would come out of the water, they'd lose power and the waves would have them at their mercy.

Time seemed to register in waves striking the boat, each one sending a shudder up the hull and shaking Bernadette to her core, her legs felt like jelly. She had no idea how the others were doing. They held on to the handrails and stared ahead. Their gaze locked on shore and safety from this maddening sea.

Darius hit the throttle hard. The boat found a big wave and became a surfboard as it careened around the breakwater and found calmer seas.

For a moment they relaxed. They could see the docks ahead. They gave a sigh of relief and leaned against the railing.

Sebastian looked at everyone. "Well, that wasn't so bad. Kind of felt like surfing a really big board." He smiled and looked below deck. "I'm sure even our Kazak friend enjoyed it—ah—what the fuck!" he screamed, pointing to the deck. The Kazak was gone.

McAllen pulled his weapon and charged down the stairs. Sebastian came after him followed by Bernadette and Winston. The ropes they'd tied him with were shredded. They searched below deck. He was gone.

"I guess we were too busy wondering if we were going to live through the waves to watch our prisoner," McAllen said.

"Do we turn around and look for him?" Winston asked.

"We don't know when he got loose. He could be inside the break-water or out to sea." Sebastian pointed out.

"How do we present the bodies without a suspect?" Winston asked.

McAllen laughed. "You think that guy would have ever admitted to killing anyone? He looked at the others, "We've got a helicopter to catch before this hurricane wipes out the Keys. I hope our Kazak guy is a good swimmer or he's fish food."

They went back to the wheelhouse where Darius and Becky had been watching their conference. McAllen gave a thumbs up sign and Darius hit the throttle. The return to the Marina was different. The landmarks weren't there. The shoreline was gone; the sea had washed over it as if it had never existed.

The only thing visible of the dive shop building they'd left from was the divers flag. It blew hard on the roof to mark what was now below. Captain Darius pointed the boat through the parking lot and headed for the number one Interstate Highway. A sign stating Roosevelt Road, Interstate could only be seen when the waves went into a trough.

They pushed on inland, passing a Marriott, Hilton and several beach bars that had been boarded up. Tops of cars and trucks could be seen in some of the parking lots. Bernadette brushed the hair from her face and moved closer to Becky.

The young girl seemed shell shocked. She had been in a quiet underwater laboratory doing experiments when they were attacked. Now, two of her associates were dead and she was racing through a storm with mostly strangers. Bernadette put her arm around Becky. The young woman didn't mind. She moved closer and put her head on Bernadette's shoulder.

They rounded the point of the island on the Interstate, turning onto South Roosevelt Boulevard; a sign barely above water claimed the Key West International Airport was a mile ahead.

They turned again, passing a Benihana's Japanese Bistro and a Timeshare sign. The boat swung hard right on a road between some buildings. A large helicopter was hovering ahead. Sebastian pointed it out to Captain Darius. He nodded his head and increased the throttle on the boat.

They shot passed the car rental lot and come up to the Airport Terminal. The waves were lapping halfway up to its top. Bernadette had remembered seeing a sign on the upper part of the terminal that said WELCOME TO THE CONCH REPUBLIC when she arrived. Only part of the sign was visible.

The boat throttled down and sidled up to the terminal. The roof was above them. There was no way for them to climb up to it.

McAllen pointed to a lower structure on the side of the building.

It looked like a garage. Its roof was connected to the main terminal. Darius finessed the boat towards the structure. The boat came along side and started to rock up and down with the waves.

"Jump onto the building when the wave rises," McAllen yelled over the wind.

Winston looked at the gap that appeared between the boat and the building, and the waves that kept pushing and pulling the boat. "Easy for you to say. You're a tall son of a bitch, and me, I'm so close to the ground my hands could drag."

McAllen pushed Winston towards the side of the rail. When the waves raised the boat, he picked her up and threw her onto the top of the building.

Winston hit the deck of the building, rolled several times and glared at McAllen. "I ain't no god damn free throw in basketball, you maniac."

"She'll thank me later," McAllen said. He turned and looked at Bernadette and Becky. "Anyone else need a hand over?"

Bernadette and Becky looked at McAllen. "Hell no," they said in unison. They jumped over on the next rise of the boat and rolled onto the building. McAllen and Sebastian followed them.

Captain Darius yelled to McAllen, "I'm taking the stiffs to my buddy's ice house in Cudjo Bay. If you're not back in seventy-two hours, they'll get dropped off late one night behind the sheriff's office. You okay with that?"

"That's fine, thanks. And consider your fee quadrupled." McAllen shouted. He knew he had to be okay with what the captain had offered. Leaving him with two dead bodies was not a good scenario.

They climbed to the upper part of the building and towards the helicopter. It was a large sixteen passenger executive copter that the pilot kept hovering just above the roof to keep its weight off the building.

The winds were buffeting it and rocking it side to side. McAllen could see the pilot's face set in a mask of tension. The door opened— the co-pilot waved them in. McAllen and Sebastian guided Winston, Bernadette and Becky to the door and helped them in.

Sebastian was about to step in when the helicopter shuddered to the side. He lost his footing and fell beside the wheel. McAllen grabbed him, threw him into the helicopter and dove in after him. The helicopter lifted off. McAllen lay collapsed on top of Sebastian.

Sebastian turned his head. "Mac, if you want me to thank you for saving my ass out there, you'll have to get off me first."

McAllen rolled off him. "Some things never change."

They took their seats, buckled in and watched the air terminal fall away below them. As they rose, they could see that the Atlantic Ocean had overrun Key West. Tops of building could be seen and some bridges, but everything else was underwater.

McAllen turned to Bernadette. "You see what Global Warming has done? The ocean has risen up so far in the past years that even a category two hurricane swamps this place. In a few more years, this will happen to Miami. Maybe then people will take notice."

Bernadette looked down. The ocean was reclaiming the land. She shook her head at the view. She leaned forward to McAllen. "I kind of feel like a bystander as the Earth takes back what civilization created. It's a strange feeling."

"Well, you'll need to get used to it. There's more of this to come," McAllen said.

Bernadette shook her head. "Sorry, can't fathom it all right now. I need to know what your plan is when we face Sokolov. If the Kazak who escaped is anything like his boss we're not in for a pleasant welcome. What if we call up some of the local Miami Police Force? I could call in an officer assistance request to my people in Canada. What do you think?"

McAllen shook his head. "Too risky. Any request for assistance between your government and the USA will get bounced through at least two or three channels and I'm sure the FBI will pick it up. I think it puts us in danger."

"So, the four us face off whatever Sokolov has for muscle when we arrive?" Bernadette asked.

"I'm hoping he didn't bring more of his henchmen with him. He'll be expecting to pick up Sigurdsson, a seventy-one-year-old with the fighting skills of a scientist—which means none," McAllen said.

Bernadette didn't reply. They'd managed to bring their weapons with them in a dry bag that Darius had given them. She only hoped that when Sokolov saw them he didn't start shooting.

11

WILHELMINA FLOWERS SAT at the head of the boardroom table in a small conference room in the Four Seasons Hotel on the Hawaiian island of Lana'i. She'd booked the time, the hotel and provided the agenda. She arrived one day before, reserved a penthouse with a prime ocean front view at a reasonable cost, to her, of 5,425 USD per night and made sure she had time for some yoga and a spa treatment. She wanted to look refreshed and relaxed for the other members at the meeting. She felt anything but.

Wilhelmina had always been anxious and high strung. She'd grown up in The Hague, the third largest city in Holland. Her father had been a prominent lawyer in the United Nations International court of justice. She'd had to grow up in the shadow of this man who brought civility and justice where there was greed and lawlessness. She hated her father for that. After all, what was wrong with greed?

Greed produced a lavish lifestyle, power, and a life of indulgence in the finer things in life. Wilhelmina wanted all that and more. Her family name was Uittenbroek, which she hated as well, almost as much as her father's good deeds and unfathomable good humour.

She'd planned and executed her own path to riches. It led to the

London School of Economics, the top University of its kind in Europe. With a finance degree, a top bank in Berlin in mergers and acquisitions employed her the day she graduated. By the time she was twenty-seven, she'd formed her own company of corporate raiders to buy corporations, sell off their assets and move on to the next one after the carcass of the company and employees had been laid to rest.

She met a man named Flowers, an Englishman with an infuriating laugh and a habit of providing off colour jokes at parties. They married on a whim after a big acquisition that produced her first billion. She divorced him three months later, kept the name Flowers, and her billion. There was no looking back after that. Climbing the Forbes list of the world's billionaires was her passion. The day she got on the list she was ecstatic. It was like rarified air, what someone would experience climbing Mount Everest. She had arrived. There were by some counts, only 2,325 billionaires on the planet, and of those only 286 were women. Wilhelmina Flowers, the gangly little Dutch girl with the blonde hair, blue eyes and hatred for sports had become one of the elite. By the age of thirty, she'd surpassed Oprah Winfrey and Donald Trump with their minuscule three billion. Then, she shot passed the billionaires with retail stores, beer manufacturing and real estate holdings. Wilhelmina, or Willa, to her closest friends, and there were not many, was on her way to the ten billion mark, by the time she hit thirty-five.

Willa no longer cared what the riches brought her. Monet's and Rembrandts' hung in her New York Penthouse, a Gulfstream G550 worth fifty-three million dollars was at her command to fly her in total comfort to any destination in the world, and she still had eyes on becoming richer than Alice Walton, the daughter of the Wal-Mart founder. She was only a few billions away.

To become the richest in the world and to top Bill Gates and his eighty-six billion, she'd need something special. What was about to happen in this room tonight would give it to her. So she hoped.

Susilo Yudhoyona and Wang Zhao entered the room and sat across from her. They noticed she'd taken the seat at the head of the table. Neither said anything. The expression on their faces mirrored their feelings. A woman had assumed control. Yudhoyona was tall, totally bald with black rim glasses so large that they dominated his face. He wore the customary Filipino Barong shirt in white with white embroidery. He was known for his adherence to customs and traditions, which seemed odd for man in his late twenties.

Zhao was short, wore a blue golf shirt, plain white pants and an 85,000-dollar Rolex in white gold. The massive watch overmatched his pudgy wrist. Willa thought he looked like a little kid with his dad's watch.

The men sat down, busied themselves with their cell phones and ignored Willa. She was used to this. Almost every meeting she'd had with men started in the same way. She'd have their attention soon.

But in fact, she would not be in control of this meeting. The chair beside her was reserved for Ivanovich Volkov, the Russian that had brought them together a year ago to collude on bribes to get American contracts. The one that had almost brought them to ruin, was now the one who was about to bring them the biggest deal and the most riches they'd ever seen.

Volkov entered the room in his usual late fashion. His presence commanded attention. He was built like a prizefighter with a dark brush cut, wide set eyes and a broad face. When he entered a room, his eyes prowled. He did it like he was entering the lair of another animal. He looked for weakness in others.

He stared down Zhao and Yudhoyono, both men flinching and dropping their eyes. Volkov was elated. He locked eyes with Willa. She looked back at him. He put all his concentration into his stare. He'd made Russian Generals shake with this look. A mafia strongman once wet his pants with this stare. Willa stared back at him and smiled. Volkov dropped into the vacant chair, and set his gaze on the two men. He was put off that Willa had taken the head of the table, it should have been his, he was after all the major player, and he was the one leading the pack. His name in Russian meant wolf—what was this woman thinking?

"Has everyone been brought up to date?" Volkov asked.

"No," Willa said. "I thought you'd do that for us, Illy."

The name Illy hit like a punch in Volkov's gut. He was not used to being referred to in such patronizing tones. This lady would need some taming. He would do it tonight, after he'd dealt with this meeting.

"Okay, let's get started," Volkov commanded. "The one billion dollars that you each put into this project has been put to good use." He looked around the room to see if the others had assimilated his words. Deep in his soul, he thought these billionaires were trash. These were pawns that would be used and disposed of.

"How exactly? Have you been spending our money?" Zhoa asked.

Volkov stared back at him, his eyelids closed slightly as if he was finding a target on that soft Asian body, "We have put together three underwater drilling sites in the Pacific Ocean in strategic locations to provide the maximum increase in temperature to the ocean currents that affect the climates of North America."

"Really? I thought you'd flushed our one billion down the toilet, because so far the temperature of the planet has gone up only a few degrees. Everyone, even the stupidest school boy, or politician, knows you need to increase the climate's temperature by four degrees to have any real effect," Yudhoyana said. He'd now lost his fear of Volkov. His money was involved, he feared losing money more than this Russian.

Volkov poured himself a glass of water; his large fingers gripped the glass tightly, but the thick crystal glass withstood his death grip. "These things take time. What we're doing is unparalleled in history. For a group such as ours to change the climate of the Earth in such a short space of time, takes exact measures."

"I understand you've been so exact that you've lost the chief scientist who was leading the project? Isn't it true that Professor Sigurdsson is no longer on the project?" Zhoa asked. He was emboldened by Yudhoyana's attack on Volkov. This project needed to be brought under control. It was his one billion dollars at stake, not this ridiculous Russian who looked like a washed-up boxer.

Volkov's massive hand slammed down on the mahogany table. The crystal glasses bounced. "Enough!"

He rose out of his chair. A large vein pulsated in his neck. "This project will make you richer than your wildest dreams. My people will see that everything is brought under control." He realized he was panting, out of breath. He sat down again and smoothed his jacket.

"I realize there have been some difficulties. This Professor Sigurdsson, will be returning to the project shortly. You will have your four-degree rise. In a very short time the Earth will be in throws of panic. Crops will fail, governments will fall, and you, my friends will profit from your knowledge of when we cool the Earth again. Any more questions?" Volkov asked.

"Yes, I have one," Willa said. "Just who are all the people you work for. You've never told us that."

"That, my pretty lady, is not something that you need to know," Volkov said. He winked at her moving his left foot in her direction. Their feet met under the table. Her shoe was off; it caressed the top of his pant leg. *Good,* he thought, she is hooked. He would take care of her tonight.

Willa smiled. "Okay, Illy, we'll take your word for it, for now." She turned to the other two at the table. "Gentlemen. I suggest we give Illy and his people one week to show us results, then if not—"

"Then what?" Zhao interrupted.

Willa winked at Zhao. "We are not without our resources. I'm sure Illy and his people would not want to incur our displeasure."

Zhao smiled at Willa. He had no idea what she meant. He'd made his money from real estate and commodities. There was nothing in his experience of dealing with Russians' or anything as illegal as what they were doing. He was hoping this tall Ms. Flowers had a plan. He hated the idea of seeing one billion dollars disappear without a decent return.

Wilhelmina Flowers adjourned the meeting. They wandered off to their own rooms. There would be no meeting for dinner in one of the many fine dining rooms in the hotel. They would each have dinner on their own, in their own suites with a butler bringing them a sumptuous meal as they contemplated whether they'd just been involved in the biggest losses of their careers.

They couldn't write off this loss. They'd funneled the money into this project from various sources to be untraceable. If this failed, at best they'd be in jail, at worst, and this was the very worst, the world would find a way to make them pay for this crime with their lives.

12

VOLKOV PACED in his hotel room. He'd placed a call to Pacific operations but needed to wait until they rose to periscope depth to return it. A few moments later his cell phone rang. It was Andrew Drummond, the captain of their submarine and manager of the drilling operation.

"What progress have you made with the drilling?" Volkov asked.

"Oh, aye, we've made progress, but not the kind you'd like to hear about," Drummond said. He was a Scotsman from Glasgow with a thick accent that sounded to Volkov more pirate than Scottish.

"What do you mean? You've been drilling for two weeks. The other locations report another thousand metres drilled. What's the problem?"

Drummond was silent for a moment. "As I've told you countless times, Volkov, we're drilling blind. Oh sure, my boys can run pipe to the centre of the Earth if that's what you wish, but I've no idea whether I'm about to tap into the mother of all volcanos or a wee thing that will fart no bigger than a sparrow. You get my drift, man?"

Volkov's large fingers gripped the phone. He breathed deeply for a second. He wanted to fly to where Drummond was and rip his vocal chords out. "Yes, I think I get your drift."

"Aye," Drummond continued, "Sigurdsson had the calculations. Without him, this is an expensive operation that's burning money."

Volkov winced at Drummond's words. This operation had cost three billion so far. They were close. They'd bought three submersible drilling platforms, and a crew of twenty men manned three used submarines, that had to be continually resupplied by a surface ship.

Sigurdsson had stowed away on a resupply ship, slipping away before someone noticed he was missing. He'd left a note saying he was going to drown himself. No one thought to check the supply ship before it docked. Volkov was positive there was collusion in getting Sigurdsson off the submarine. Had he bribed someone?

Volkov raised his voice slightly. "Drummond, I need you to keep drilling, do you hear me? And, I want you to keep venting the hot volcanic gases that are coming out into the ocean current. Is that clear?"

"Aye, clear as mud. Now, when do my men get some time off? They keep getting notices of all the money in their accounts, but they can't get at it until they get off this bloody rusted out tin can you have us floating in," Drummond said.

"I've told you, they will all get paid handsomely for their work when it's done. Then they can access their accounts. As a matter of fact," Volkov said with a smile, "I'm going to authorize an extra fifty percent raise to everyman on the boats. And, Drummond, I'm putting you in for a one hundred percent raise."

"That's most kind of you, I'll pass the message along to the lads... now, when can I let them know they'll be getting on land to spend all the cash?"

"Very soon. I expect inside of a week," Volkov said. He ended his call and poured himself a large Vodka. He had no intention of paying the men. They were sending each of them a weekly notice of how much money was in their accounts for their work, but told them they couldn't touch it until the work was completed.

Every week ten thousand dollars was placed into their accounts. It was a bogus transfer that did not exist. Volkov would have a cleanup team make one final trip to the submarines when the drilling was done. The submarines would be sunk to the bottom of the ocean and the drilling equipment destroyed. The men on board would be blamed for the world's catastrophes.

Volkov made sure each man on the boat had emails and links to numerous terrorist groups. He loved how his mind worked.

His next call was to Sokolov, who answered on the second ring. "Where are you?" Volkov asked.

"I'm in Miami, waiting for my package," Sokolov said.

"How soon?"

"Not sure, I lost contact with my courier. There is a hurricane here. The delivery is late."

Volkov massaged his forehead, he hated these delays. " I just thought of something. When you get the package. See if you can get some extra insurance for it, before you bring it home... you understand me?"

"Perfectly," Sokolov said. "I'll contact our FBI agent, he should be good for something besides whining. I'll find out where Sigurdsson's nearest relative is, and if they are dear to him. It seems everyone's heart melts a bit when I'm about to cut off a loved one's fingers."

Volkov thought Sokolov was brutal even by his own standards. "Good, get it done, and tell me when you have our package."

He put his phone down and gulped the rest of his Vodka. The doorbell of his suite rang. He hadn't ordered anything from room service. As a precaution he pulled out his switchblade knife, holding it behind his back as he peered through the peephole.

He smiled as he saw Willa standing outside in a bathrobe. Tonight he would teach her how to be more submissive. He opened the door wide and grinned. "Ah, nice of you to visit."

Willa breezed into the room with a flourish as he closed the door. She shed her bathrobe.

Volkov let out a gasp. She stood before him in a leather corset with metal studs. She pulled out a riding whip and smacked it hard on her hand.

"Well, Illy, now who's been a bad little boy, lately?"

"I have," Illy said weakly. "Where did you learn... who told you I like these things?"

Willa smiled, her eyes shining with a wicked glint, "I spent some time with your favorite girl in Berlin, Jana. She taught me so many wonderful things I almost went over to the other side." She brought the whip up, tracing it down his lips then down his body, resting it on his thigh.

"But... I don't know if I want to do this... with you..." Volkov said. He didn't move the riding whip. Willa ran it over his crotch. He let out a small moan.

"Why don't we see how it goes, Illy? I was told by Jana that I was her best student."

Willa slapped his thigh with the whip. She kissed him hard on the lips, biting his lower lip and caressing his crotch, she pushed him towards the bedroom. He went willingly.

Volkov had no idea how she had found out about his perversions. Everything would have to wait until she had assumed control over him and brought him to climax. If she had learned from his lovely Jana in Berlin, then tonight would be magnificent. Tomorrow, he would dominate the world again, but tonight, the skinny rich bitch would give him everything he desired.

13

SOKOLOV DRAGGED HEAVILY on his cigarette and dropped it to the ground. He didn't have the prizefighter look of Volkov. He was short and slim, slightly balding with soft blue eyes and thin lips. To most he wouldn't look like a threat. He had been schooled in Combat Sambo, the Russian form of mixed martial arts. He'd been good at it. So good, that few wanted him as a sparring partner. He watched the wind blow his cigarette away and pulled his jacket collar up. He'd been here with his men, waiting, all day for his captive to be delivered.

He hated waiting. But it had been in his training from his early days in the KGB to his career in the Russian Mafia. You waited for things to develop; sometimes it took months or years. In this case, the waiting was changing by the minute. The hurricane was approaching. The city was being evacuated. It had been upgraded to a category 3 and news reports said it might hit a 4 with possible wind speeds of 200 kph. This wasn't good. Neither was the situation Sokolov was in.

The staff of the executive hanger wanted to send Sokolov on his way so they could evacuate. The jet that he'd hired wanted to leave. They had orders from their owners that their plane was in danger if they stayed longer. Bribes no longer worked with these people. The airplane crew was tied up with the hanger crew. His men stood guard over them. They'd been told they'd be untied and set free once they reached their destination.

This was not going well. He'd have to kill all the personnel in the hanger before they left and kill the pilot, co-pilot and flight attendant of the plane if they did not agree to a large bribe once they landed. Hell, he'd most definitely have to kill them anyway. He took bribes, hated giving them.

He looked over the tarmac. Not a plane was in sight. He heard a helicopter approaching. The sound grew louder. Suddenly it appeared over the top of the hanger. It was descending.

Sokolov looked for his men. They were inside the hanger. Had his team in Key West commandeered this helicopter? He took a few steps towards it then held back. Something didn't feel right. He reached inside his jacket and pulled out his gun.

14

"Is that Sokolov on the ground?" McAllen asked as the helicopter descended.

Bernadette looked at the picture she on her cell phone from Anton, and at the man on the ground. "Yep, that's our guy."

"Weapons out, everyone," McAllen yelled. He looked at Becky. "You stay in here."

Sebastian pulled out the dry bag and passed around weapons to Winston, McAllen and Bernadette. The pilots in the cockpit were too busy landing the helicopter to notice what their passengers were doing.

"Uncle Mac, I'm not leaving you." Becky said. Tears welled in her eyes.

Bernadette could see she was panicked. She grabbed her hand. "It's for your own safety. We'll have the helicopter take you a safe distance out, then call them back when it's all clear."

"What if you get hurt?"

"Hey, it's four against one," Bernadette said. She squeezed Becky's hand and gave her a wink.

The helicopter dropped to the ground. McAllen forced the door open and jumped out drawing his weapon. He yelled for Sokolov to put his hands up.

Sokolov drew his weapon. He dropped into a crouched position and fired at McAllen. His men appeared out of the hanger. They opened fire with machine guns. Bullets hit the helicopter's engine, it began to smoke. Bernadette pushed Becky out of the helicopter in front of her and lay covering her on the ground. The pilots jumped out of their cockpit.

Sebastian crawled over to Bernadette. "We need to get away from this chopper before this thing blows up."

A stream of bullets sprayed the tarmac in front of them.

Bernadette looked at Sebastian. "Which way do we go?"

"Count to five after I throw this," Sebastian said. He pulled a percussion grenade out of his jacket, armed it and gave it an overhand throw. It arced high and landed in front of the hanger entrance. The grenade exploded. It was all noise. But enough noise to disorientate their attackers. Bernadette pushed Becky towards the side of the hanger. It put them out of the direct firing line.

Bernadette chambered a round in her gun. She needed to get Becky to some kind of cover then help deal with the attackers. She looked up to see a man come around the corner with a machine gun. He raised it to fire. His chest exploded. He slid to the ground, his gun falling beside him. Bernadette looked over her shoulder. Winston had dropped the man with her high caliber handgun.

"That girl can shoot," Bernadette said to Becky who lay beside her.

The entire hanger was erupting in small arms fire. Machine gun fire was coming from inside the front door. McAllen, Sebastian and Winston were returning fire from the tarmac.

Bernadette saw a side entrance. She picked up the machine gun of the dead man on the ground and looked at Becky. "Can you shoot a hand gun?"

Becky took the gun from Bernadette; "The bullets come out the pointy end, right?"

"Shoot only the bad guys. You got that?"

"Sure, these are the same bastards that killed my friends. I'm accurate with a spear gun. I'll be happy to put a hole in one of them."

"Good, aim for the centre of the body. Just like you would a fish," Bernadette said. She motioned to McAllen with hand signals that she was going in the door.

She checked the machine gun, it was loaded—she slipped through the door. Four men were taking turns returning fire inside the hanger. Sokolov was on the far side.

Bernadette raised her weapon and fired at the three men in front. One went down, the other two whirled and fell back. Sokolov stared at her in surprise then jumped behind a counter.

A percussion grenade bounced in the front door and exploded with a bang and echo that reverberated through the hanger. Smoke filled the air. A second later, McAllen, Sebastian and Winston appeared. They shot the two men.

The smoke cleared. Bernadette walked forward slowly, her weapon scanning the area around her as she came up to McAllen, "Did you see where Sokolov went?"

Sebastian went behind the counter then down a hall searching for him. He shook his head when he returned. "He commandeered a UPS van and left the driver dead outside."

Bernadette looked around the hanger. "Let's see if these guys left anyone else alive in this building."

The offices and waiting room were empty. Winston found a woman and four men tied up in the bathroom. They were very happy to be set free.

"I've found two pilots and a lady flight attendant. They were supposed to fly Sokolov out of here," Winston said.

"Did they have a flight plan?" McAllen asked.

"San Francisco." Winston replied.

McAllen walked up to the pilots. The older one, a man with salt and pepper hair, bushy eyebrows and face with crevasses that looked like it had seen too much sun identified himself as the captain. "You hear anything about where these guys were headed after they landed in San Fran?" he asked.

The captain shook his head. "They were pretty tight lipped. The head guy, he said his name was Smith." He raised his eyes at the irony. "He said we were to wait for someone to arrive and then fly out of here."

"Why'd they tie you up?" Winston asked.

"We told this Smith guy, that we needed to fly the plane out of here due to the approaching hurricane. We didn't want to wait any longer."

"And, I assume Smith didn't like that?"

"Ah, yeah," the captain said massaging his wrist where he had been tied. "When I told him his flight was cancelled and we were leaving, he pulled guns on us and pushed us into the men's room. When we got there, we found the hanger staff there as well. They'd tried to close the hanger down and leave. He didn't like that either."

"What size of plane do you have?" McAllen asked.

"A Challenger 300," the pilot said. "But, look, thanks for setting us free, we're happy to give you guys a lift somewhere, but it's got to be out of the path of the hurricane."

"How's Bermuda?" McAllen asked. "And consider your plane chartered, I'll have money deposited to your company."

Bernadette was standing beside McAllen. "Why Bermuda?"

"Simple, his wife Samantha is there. She might know where he went," McAllen replied.

"It's not an underwater lab again is it?" Winston asked.

"Nope, it's above water."

"Above water? What the hell does that mean?"

McAllen walked off in search of Becky, waving his hand as he left. "You'll be fine."

Winston looked at Bernadette. "I hate it when he says that. It means the shit is going to hit the fan again, doesn't it?

"I'd say so," Bernadette admitted. She looked over the situation of three dead men, one dead UPS driver outside and two helicopter pilots that were in need of an explanation, as well as the Executive First Flight Center staff. If they were going to get out of here, without a visit from the Miami Police she needed to do something. It was time to make some tea.

"You want to help me make some tea?" Bernadette asked Winston.

"Tea, who the hell drinks tea after a gun fight?"

"I find it great to calm the nerves," Bernadette said. She found the executive lounge, pulled out some teacups, poured in hot water and dunked in a tea bag from her pocket.

"Now, I want you to be very careful with this tea. Give it to the helicopter pilots and the hanger staff only, okay," Bernadette said.

"Why, what's in it?" Winston asked.

"It's an old native remedy from my grandmother back home. She used it to calm everyone down. It's also going to put them to sleep for about four hours. We'll be long gone by the time they wake up. I'll call my people in Canada and have them file some kind of a report of us fighting some terrorists."

"Really, you think someone's going to believe that?"

"They'll have to. I'll file the report, and I'm sure our dead guys have a rap sheet that extends all the way back to Russia or some place that looks equally as bad."

Winston shrugged and walked away with a serving tray full of tea. She distributed it to the helicopter pilots and the hanger staff who gratefully sipped it and were asleep in minutes.

Winston came back and dropped the serving tray on the counter beside Bernadette. "That's quite tasty."

"What's tasty?"

"I spilled some of the tea in the saucer. I sampled it," Winston said. "A real nice sweet yet pungent taste."

Bernadette took Winston's arm. "You'll need to sit down."

"Why... I don't... feel..." Winston said as her knees buckled.

Bernadette carried Winston over to a couch and laid her down.

"Winston opened her eyes slowly. "That's really potent stuff. Why do you carry it... was it for me?"

"How'd you guess?" Bernadette said. "I'd planned to drug you in case you wanted to interfere with my plans to capture McAllen."

"... Oh... I see... I'd planned to kill you... and him... interesting..."
Winston said as she nodded off to sleep and started to snore.

Bernadette shook her head. She turned to see McAllen standing
beside her.

"Interesting conversation I just overheard," he said

"Hmm, yeah, well about that—"

"No, I get it," McAllen said. "You can't get over the fact you're an
officer of the law, and still need to exercise an outstanding warrant on
me—isn't that it?"

"Yeah, that's pretty much it," Bernadette said, massaging the back
of her neck, "You know, I'm just like that scorpion in the old tale
about the river crossing with the frog."

"Which one is that?"

"Well, the story goes that a scorpion wanted to cross a river, and
he asked a frog to take him across. The frog said, no way, you'd sting
me. The scorpion convinced the frog he won't and he climbed on his
back and half way across the river, the scorpion stung the frog. The
frog yelled to the scorpion, now we're both going to drown, and of
course the scorpion says, sorry, couldn't help myself... I'm a scorpion."

"So, do I call you Detective or Scorpion?" McAllen asked with a
chuckle.

"Detective will do. I think I'll be putting my stinger away for the
duration of our journey."

"Speaking of that. What do we do with our FBI lady? We could
leave her here," McAllen said looking over at Winston on the couch.

"I think we should keep her with us," Bernadette said. "If
someone in the FBI is trying to kill us, then she's also on the menu.
Perhaps with her we can draw them out once we have some more
answers as to who is behind this crazy scheme to heat up the Earth.
At least now we've confirmed that Sokolov is connected to someone
in the FBI who wants us dead."

McAllen shrugged. "Well, in the spirit of keeping your friends
close and your enemies closer—what the hell. There's lots of room
on the plane." He turned to the airplane captain. "What's the ETA to
Bermuda?"

"Two hours and fifty minutes after wheels up," the captain said.

"Let's get going," McAllen said.

He helped Bernadette pick up Winston and they carried her to the hanger with the private jet. They also had to carry the drugged body of the flight attendant on board as Winston had given her tea by mistake. The pilots did a system check, and were rolling down the runway a short while later.

Bernadette pulled out her cell phone as they lifted off the runway and headed for Bermuda. She went through all of her text messages. There'd been nothing further from Chris. Somewhere, in some time in this day or the next, they needed to have a conversation. It was the conversation they should have had a month ago, actually six months ago, before everything had fallen apart.

She gazed out the window and saw the big fluffy clouds that were forming in the south. This was the hurricane that was bearing down on Miami. They were being pushed by the elements and threatened by humans. It was hard to know which was worse at this point. There was an answer out there. She looked down at the deep green of the Atlantic. She realized there were some questions she needed to ask McAllen. There was a lot he wasn't telling her.

15

SIGURDSSON LOOKED over his shoulder twice before he entered the street. He felt he was being followed. He called himself a *halfviti* in his native Icelandic language, it meant idiot. He walked down the street of Anchorage, Alaska.

He looked all his seventy-one years, and with maybe a few more added on. A full head of grey hair was draped down over his neck and needed a cut several weeks ago. His eyebrows were bushy and sat over eyes that were once a bright blue and now faded grey. His tall frame was slightly hunched over, not from arthritis but from fatigue. He shuffled when he walked. His feet hurt.

He'd been here for two days now. The journey had been perilous. First, he'd stowed away on the supply boat. His fellow Icelanders and some Norwegians on the submarine had come to his aid and smuggled him off.

They knew there was something wrong with the drilling job. Sigurdsson wished he'd known when Volkov approached him all those months ago. The Russian knew how to apply enough praise and money to get him to come on board.

What had Volkov said? Something about Sigurdsson's talent being wasted, how the private sector would take his ideas and show the world how amazing he was. Sigurdsson scoffed at that thought now. They'd shown him what an amazing idiot he was. It sounded better in the language of Iceland. *Halfvitii,* the word resounded longer on the tongue.

His problem now was whom could he tell? Who would believe a washed-up professor from Iceland roaming the streets with hardly enough money in his pockets to get another few nights in a flop-house. Soon he'd be living on the streets.

To get here, he'd hitched rides out of San Francisco on trawlers, shrimp boats, anything going north. Now, he was at the end. The technology necessary for Volkov to succeed with his plan was in his head. He'd been careful to never make notes.

Now, the only way to make sure he erased any possibility of the Earth heating up, he needed to erase himself, one step off the pier would do it. He'd dreamed up the plan last night. He'd pick up some big rocks by the river, put them in his pockets and jump off the pier. The fisherman would find him sometime the next day, but then maybe they wouldn't. The crabs would. He shuddered at the thought.

He tried to put these imagines out of his head. He needed a drink. Not just one, many. He needed to get very drunk. He had that need deep inside of him and knew where to go. Maybe this would be his last night, then the rocks, and then the pier. A plan was formulating in his head. It was the best plan he'd had in some time. He shuffled down the street, looking once more over his shoulder. *"Halfviti,"* he muttered to himself.

16

BERNADETTE FOUND some food in the plane's galley. An elegant linguine with shrimp in an unpronounceable sauce, that went well with a chilled Chablis and some warm rolls. She threaded her way by the sleeping Winston and flight attendant and served up portions of the meals to McAllen, Sebastian and Becky.

"Don't get used to me serving you," Bernadette said. "I'm terrible at anything but tear back foil and heat—this is as good as it gets."

Becky looked up and smiled. "My stomach hasn't seen food since this morning, and this is wonderful. And, hey, I'm happy to scavenge in the galley for seconds."

Bernadette thought Becky looked like she was coming around, to almost normal for a human under stress. They'd pulled her out of an underwater lab, she'd seen her friends killed, been almost attacked by sharks and seen several men killed in Miami. The girl was resilient. They'd found some shorts and t-shirt for her to wear, and she looked like a regular young lady travelling in a very swanky private jet.

Bernadette sat down with McAllen out of hearing of Sebastian and Becky; "You want to fill me in on how you're related to Becky?"

McAllen wiped some sauce off his lips with his napkin. "I'm sort of an uncle, through my long friendship with Sigurdsson. We spent a lot of time together in our early years in university. We even had jobs together working on fishing boats out of Seattle to pay our tuition."

"And, you kept in touch with him all these years?"

"Yeah, I've been around the Sigurdsson family on and off for years. I kept in touch with Barney when I went to Vietnam, he of course didn't have to serve, as he was an Icelandic national. We reconnected when I went to Canada."

"When did you two hatch your plan to save the world?" Bernadette asked. She took a sip of her wine. "Sorry, I don't want to sound so trite... When did you decide to do something about climate change and turning down the temperature?"

McAllen winked at Bernadette. "No, you were right the first time. Barney and I did want to save the world. He had come up with a way to cool off the oceans currents. It would have dropped the Earth's oceans by three to four degrees.'

"Wouldn't that be too much?" Bernadette asked. "I mean, don't we need some heat in the ocean? Wouldn't that have created another ice age going that cold?"

"Not a chance of that happening," McAllen said. "That hurricane we just escaped from is one of several barreling down on the East Coast of the USA. They've been building like a chain. They gain their force from the ocean's heat. Hurricane season has now moved to May and ends in late December."

"And Sigurdsson could stop that?"

"Partially. He was also going to find a way to lower the water temperature to take some of the carbon monoxide out of the ocean. That underwater lab we saw in Key West, that was to see how fast the reefs are dying. Ocean temperature and carbon monoxide are bleaching the reefs, the coral is dying and the fish are losing their habitat. None of that is good for the oceans—unhealthy ocean, unhealthy planet."

"How far did your plan progress?"

"We were just getting started, but we needed a lot of money, more than I had, or that I could even steal," McAllen said with a grin, knowing it would get a rise out of Bernadette.

"Was Sigurdsson trying to get government funding when he was in Stockholm?" Bernadette asked. She chose to ignore McAllen's remark about stealing money.

"Yes, that was it. There were governments there with big bucks. Most of them had coastlines that were starting to go underwater from the rising sea, and many of them like Canada and the USA were losing massive hectares of land due to forest fires. He had their attention," McAllen said.

"So, what went wrong?"

"Barney texted me that someone else was coming to the table. He was all excited. These people claimed they could get things done right away. They had the money. All he needed to do was to show them the plan, and they'd be cooling the Earth in no time," McAllen explained.

"Then you lost contact with him?"

"That's right. All of a sudden he disappeared." McAllen shrugged, tipped back his glass and drained his wine.

Winston woke up from the couch. She sat up, shook her head and looked at Bernadette. "How long was I out?"

"About two hours. I should have warned you about even tasting the tea. It's very potent."

"Where are we heading?"

"Bermuda."

"Really? I thought that was just a joke. Where are we headed for there... no don't tell me... you're probably going to say the Bermuda Triangle or something crazy like that," Winston said.

McAllen poured himself another glass of wine. "Ah, pretty close. The Bermuda Triangle, which the US Government claims does not exist, by the way, is a triangle from Miami to Bermuda and back to Puerto Rico." He sipped his wine and smiled. "We'll be going somewhere into that triangle to find Becky's grandmother, Samantha Sigurdsson."

"And, why exactly are we trying to find her?" Winston asked as she opened a bottle of water.

"Because, Becky said Sigurdsson was going there some months ago," McAllen said.

"You think he's there?"

"Oh, hell, no, I think he's been gone for some time. But Sam always knew what Barney was up to. She could almost read his mind. I need to find out where he might be heading. And, I also want to find out from Sam how The Ocean Conveyer is doing?" McAllen said.

"The Ocean what?" Winston asked.

"The Ocean Conveyor. Oceanographers see it as a series of currents and heat transfers that moves warm and cool water from one place to another on the planet. Without it, Norway would be a sheet of ice, and Alaska would be even colder in the winter than it is now," McAllen said.

"Sounds like some pretty scientific stuff," Winston said.

"Nope, not that hard to understand really. If you watch the currents rise and fall in a stream you see how things move from one place to another. That's the same for the ocean. It's just that it moves hot and cold water from the depths up to the surface and transports it around the world." McAllen looked at his watch. "We should be landing soon, we've got to do something about getting Becky off this plane."

"What do you mean?" Bernadette asked.

"I don't think she had a passport stuffed in her wet suit when we got her out of that lab in Key West. She'll need one to clear customs in Bermuda."

Bernadette looked at Becky, then at the sleeping flight attendant. "I have an idea."

17

VOLKOV WOKE UP IN BED. He was naked. The sun was shining outside the window. He thought it must be morning but what time? He tried to raise his arm to see his watch but his arm was tied. So was his other one.

Raising his head he saw that both his feet were tied and a bright red ribbon was affixed to his penis. He screamed in anger. "That bitch!"

He yanked his right arm hard and the bindings came loose. The one on the left came away just as easily. He was about to remove his leg binding when the housekeeper came in. She screamed and ran out of the room with a mumbled stream of apologies following behind her.

Volkov laughed. This is exactly what his lovely Jana in Berlin used to do to him. Willa had probably left the *Please Make Up The Room* sign on the door to ensure he was awakened.

His mind glanced over the memory of last night. Willa had been exceptional. She'd brought him to new delights that even Jana had never dreamed of—or dared. At one point she'd strangled him, taking him to the brink, then bringing him back. He couldn't remember how many times he'd had an orgasm.

He sighed deeply as he thought of it. This would make it much harder to kill her when all this was over, but then some of the best things in life must pass. He pulled open his drawer, took out his phone and dialed Sokolov.

The phone rang many times until Sokolov finally answered. There was the sound of wind in the background.

"Where are you?" Volkov asked.

"I'm in a UPS van driving down the highway," Sokolov answered.

"What! Where's Sigurdsson? Why are you not in the airplane heading for San Francisco?" Volkov screamed into the phone.

"McAllen showed up in a helicopter, shot my men and stole my plane," Sokolov said. "He must have overcome my men in Key West and found out our plans. He must die."

Volkov drew in a breath and closed his eyes tightly trying to assimilate this piece of information. "Do you know where McAllen took your plane?"

"Yes, I called the idiot FBI agent and he had a way of tracking someone on the plane. It's headed for Bermuda."

"Really, you lost your plane and your men and you're calling the FBI agent an idiot. Do you have a plan now, or have you decided to deliver the packages in the UPS van?" Volkov said putting a hand to his head and massaging his temples.

"Yes, I have found a plane at another airfield outside of Miami and another team of men. I'll be leaving inside of thirty minutes."

"Good. Do not screw up this time. You know what I do to people who fail me?"

"...Yes, I do. I will not fail," Sokolov said, his voice trying to sound strong.

Volkov ended the call. He picked up the hotel phone, ordered breakfast then dialed a number on his cell phone.

A voice answered, "Admiral Fairborne."

"It's me, Volkov. Are you in a secure area?"

"Yes."

"Is the present climate change causing the amount of disruption we expected in the US government?"

"Absolutely. Congress and the Senate are blaming each other, and the President can't get them to agree on a course of action. Of course, half of them think this is all some kind of fake news brought on by either the Republicans or the Democrats or some right or left faction. I'd say the USA government has ground to a standstill, it's become redundant."

"Excellent. What is the military doing?"

"They are waiting for the President to make some kind of a decision. Right now, the Atlantic fleet is on high alert, but that's only to provide aid to the Eastern Seaboard that's about to be hit by one hurricane after another. The army is fighting forest fires, and the air force... well most of it can't fly because the temperature is too hot for their jet engines."

"Perfect, Admiral," Volkov said. "You will be remarkably rewarded in the new America that is created once we turn the temperature down. It is people like you who see the future, and know how to correct it. I will call you again with further instructions."

Admiral Fairborne put down the phone and breathed a sigh of relief. He had done everything they'd asked of them. He'd provided the information they needed and he would be rewarded in the new America. He smoothed his hair and straightened his uniform. He still looked good for a sixty-two-year-old naval man. He was formerly the head of the US Atlantic Second Fleet that had been dismantled in 2011. In his mind, an Admiral without a fleet was not an Admiral.

He looked up at a painting in the hallway of his Annapolis home, there, prominently displayed was a portrait of his ancestor, Sir Stafford Fairborne of the British navy. Sir Stafford had cleared the British coast of pirates and taken part in the glorious revolution of 1688 that instigated the overthrow of King James II of England by a union of English Parliamentarians with the Dutch, the Prince of Orange. The successful invasion of England with the Dutch Fleet and army led to William III of England with his wife Mary II, James's daughter to produce the bill of rights of 1689.

Admiral Fairborne ran a soft cloth over the four stars on his shoulders. Once this was over, he'd be Admiral of the American Fleet.

He had officers ready to assume command at several bases. Once the government fell, his men knew what to do.

The Russians would be invading, but to establish a new order, which would set America back on its true path again. And he, Admiral Fairborne, would go down in history, just like his ancestor. He smiled up as the picture of Sir Stafford Fairborne and walked out the door. He had much to do to get ready for his big day.

Volkov walked out of the shower and devoured the breakfast of eggs, bacon and biscuits he'd ordered. This was almost all going to plan. Yes, they needed Sigurdsson for the final details, but they'd find him.

Then, they'd turn up the oceans a few more degrees and America would suffer like never before. There would be crop failures and a heat wave that would kill hundreds of thousands and the seas would invade the low-lying cities on the American coast.

The great climate holocaust would call for drastic measures. Already the American government was almost powerless. The Russians had offered to help but at present they were being rebuffed. But for how long would the Americans hold out?

Volkov smiled at the American psyche. Sure they were tough in battle, strong warriors, but when their media showed their civilians dying in the streets they'd lose their resolve and call in the Russians to help. He knew Russians would suffer with the heat of Climate Change as well. But to him, Russians were born to suffer. They would handle the heat, the forest fires, and the rising waves. Once they saw that this was to defeat America, they would understand and accept what they'd been through.

He dressed in linen pants and fine Hawaiian silk shirt, admiring his features in the mirror. He knew in time the Americans would cave over this tsunami of climate change he'd created with his Russian colleagues. Some were government, but most like him, were Russian Mafia. They would make a new order all right, an order that would produce more power and money than any of the world had seen.

Volkov walked out of room on the lookout for Willa. He needed to thank her for last night. In the new world order, maybe he would make her his slave, if he didn't kill her. Then again, who knew what would happen? They might have need of some of these billionaires in America, perhaps to show them how to really get the most out of what America had to offer. He whistled a tune as he walked down the corridor of the opulent hotel. Everything smelled of fresh cut flowers. He breathed deeply and smiled.

Willa Flowers was on her plane, toasting her domination of Volkov with a rare early glass of champagne. The island of Lanai disappeared as her jet climbed into a bank of clouds and she turned her attention to her computer. In front of her were the list of companies she wished to take over once the climate catastrophe had reached its climax.

There were major food companies that were already losing share value, they'd be a steal in a week, plus forest products, at the rate of forest fires, their production was shut in. She had placed a large order to buy the controlling shares in three of them. Inside of a week she'd have two more. And then, there were the airlines. So many of them couldn't fly with the extreme heat that many would soon have to file for bankruptcy.

Her own plane was heading to Panama City, a safer bet during this heat wave crisis in the USA. She'd wait for the temperature to return to normal before she'd set foot on American soil again. By then, she'd be one of highest ranked billionaires in the world. She smiled, sipped her champagne and settled down in her large leather chair.

18

GETTING Becky off the plane without a passport was a problem that Bernadette solved by finding a spare flight attendants uniform and getting Becky into it. That was the first hurdle, and then it was to have her use the flight attendant's passport.

"Oh my god, this girl is Polish and she's blonde," Becky said, walking behind Bernadette towards the passport control desk in the charter terminal.

Bernadette turned to Becky, "Look, you're a flight attendant. You don't have to say anything. Smile a bunch and flash your eyes at the customs agent. He'll turn to putty."

"Ah... the customs agent is female," Becky said, motioning to Bernadette with her eyes.

"Uh, oh, yeah, okay, well then... say nothing, make like you don't understand English so well," Bernadette said.

Becky rolled her eyes and followed everyone to passport control. The customs lady was even easier than they thought. She glanced at their passports and waved them through.

Winston, Sebastian and McAllen followed and they met outside the small terminal where taxis and limos were pulling up looking for passengers.

"We don't all need to meet with Becky's grandmother," McAllen said. "I think Sebastian and Winston need to go in search of a few clothing items, then Sebastian can find us another plane out of here."

Sebastian shrugged. "Where are we going after this?"

"No idea. I'll know more once I meet with Sam. I don't think we'll be more than a few hours."

"A few hours?" Winston asked. "I thought you said this lady was somewhere out in the ocean."

McAllen winked. "I lied, Becky told me in the helicopter that Sam's research ship is docked in Hamilton Harbour, a short cab ride from here."

"And you lied—why?" Winston asked.

"I liked the look on your face when I told you we were headed out to sea again," McAllen said.

Winston walked away muttering invectives regarding McAllen's possible lineage.

Bernadette touched Winston on the shoulder as she turned away. "Look, get us some underwear and I could use a few t-shirts, and maybe a light shell jacket in size medium, and a few toiletries like a tooth brush would be nice."

"Oh, yeah, I'm now the den mother for a bunch of people on the run from the law, oh wait, I am the law. You know if someone had remembered to get our suitcases out of the truck that went under-water in Key West we wouldn't have this problem," Winston said.

"You're right, they would have washed overboard on the dive boat," Sebastian said.

McAllen hailed a white taxi van and jumped in the back with Becky and Bernadette. They pulled away from the airport, the cab bumping along in the left-hand lane, and the driver asking them all kinds of questions about their 'vacation on the island.'

McAllen quieted the driver with a response of "they were on the island for some serious business matters."

The driver turned up his radio and let them talk.

"You want to tell me why we couldn't have contacted this Sam by phone from somewhere in Miami?" Bernadette asked.

McAllen turned to look at Bernadette; he lowered his voice as Becky was in the back of the van. "Look, Becky has no parents. Her mother died when she was young and her father passed away last year in a diving accident. Sam is Becky's only close relative who will look after her."

"Okay, I guess I'm fine with that. I'm a big believer in family, but that still doesn't answer my question as to why we couldn't have found the information from this Sam person over the phone, and you could have told her we were coming."

"Oh... well... there is one small thing," McAllen said looking out the window.

"And what small thing is that?"

"Samantha Sigurdsson hates my guts."

"Oh, that kind of small thing." Bernadette looked out the other window and tried to relax. It was times like these that she needed to breathe and absorb the scenery. It calmed her mind for whatever craziness McAllen might bring later.

The taxi van moved slowly along the narrow road. Houses shuffled by in bright colours of green, blue and pink, with the occasional white one with green shutters thrown in. White washed brick walls melded into white picket fences then a wall of green. Some pine trees, almost unrecognizable from her native Canada appeared, then the ubiquitous palm trees, in every size and shape dotted the road.

The background to all of this was a blue green sea that dazzled in the bright sunlight. It lapped upon the rocky beaches and the white sands. Dropping its waves on the shores, it sighed ever so slightly before retreating again.

She was caught in a trance at the beauty of the island. Part of her wanted to dream she was on vacation. The van would stop in front of nice hotel and she'd get out and meet Chris out front. They'd go up to their room and make love for the afternoon then come down for a swim. She was feeling hot when the van stopped.

She broke out of her trance to see them parked in front of a sixty-metre long research vessel with a deep blue hull and orange wheelhouse. A bright red crane was on the stern with a large winch. The name on the side read, Nemo II.

McAllen got out of the taxi, paid the driver and motioned for Bernadette to follow Becky and him up the gangplank. Bernadette wondered what kind of reception they'd get.

A tall woman with bright red hair stepped out of the wheelhouse. She was dressed in t-shirt and jeans with deck shoes. The way she moved along the deck and shot down the ships stairs you'd have assumed she was part monkey, she moved with such agile grace. She planted herself in front of them.

"Grandma Sam," Becky said.

"Oh my god, Becks it's you. I didn't recognize you in the uniform." Sam picked Becky up in a bear hug and smothered her with kisses.

McAllen stepped forward. "Hello, Sam."

Sam dropped Becky and threw a punch so hard into McAllen's jaw that it spun him backwards. Bernadette was able to catch him before he tumbled down the gangplank.

SEBASTIAN AND WINSTON made their way by cab to the shopping area of St. Georges, one of the main cities of Bermuda. The cab ride didn't take long; it was longer standing in line to exchange money into Bermuda Dollars.

The people of Bermuda liked their own currency or plastic but Sebastian had no plastic. Credit cards were too easy to trace. They used a central booking service for their private plane service that charged an offshore account. The rest was in cash. He always carried a large amount of cash.

They first shopped at a local store, bought some underwear, t-shirts and jeans for themselves and McAllen and Bernadette, then, Sebastian saw a store that caught his eye.

"Follow me, Winston," Sebastian said leading her down Water Street.

Winston followed behind as fast as she could. She was amazed at how fast this little guy could move. How old was he, seventy? He was damn quick for his age. Winston thought.

They arrived at The English Sport Shop. The place smelled expensive. Winston felt out of place. Her hair was a mess, her trousers and shirt had needed changing for over two days and she was sure she smelled bad. Sebastian walked up to the line of fine linen pants and polo shirts. He smiled at the store clerk that thought some shipwrecked old man had walked into his store.

"Ahem, may I help you?" the clerk asked with an icy tone that showed his apparent disdain for this vagabond image in his store.

Sebastian looked at the man; he was dressed in proper Bermuda shorts in bright green and a polo shirt in a pale blue. "Not if you're fixing to have me wear clothes like yours," Sebastian said pulling three pair of linen pants off the pile. "Here, put these in the fitting room for me. I'll want four polo shirts and a linen jacket, no bright clashing colours. I don't intend to stop traffic on my way out of here."

Winston smiled at Sebastian's manner. The clerk, his name was Donald, went red in the face and began putting aside clothes for Sebastian.

Sebastian looked at Winston. "And find the lady something in some nice slacks and tops as well." He winked at her.

Winston and Sebastian left the shop forty-five minutes later looking like they'd just stepped off a cruise ship.

"You always do things like this, Sebastian?" Winston asked.

"Like what?"

"Well, do whatever comes to your mind." Winston was walking beside him as they made their way to a seaside bistro for lunch.

Sebastian waited until they were seated in the bistro, and ordered some wine before he answered. "You know, I used to be a real pain in the ass. Like a stickler for details and regulations."

"Like me?" Winston asked.

"Oh yeah, like you, but even more so," Sebastian said as he sipped the wine the waiter had poured. "I found ways to tie myself in knots with wanting to please everyone, to make them all happy and it didn't do a damn thing for my own personal peace."

Winston sipped on her wine. She'd now gone over to the other side. No longer caring about regulations or drinking on the job. Especially working for people that were trying to kill her.

"So, I should be more like you and cut myself some slack," Winston said.

"No, you should be yourself and set yourself free," Sebastian replied. He leaned across the table. "You know, you're a very attractive woman, there's no reason why you got to put all this scary vibe out there that pushes men away."

"Me, I don't do that... do I?"

"Oh, yeah.

"Really?"

Sebastian tilted his head, "Look, I don't know if you know my past—"

"The one where you were a stone cold killer?"

"No, not that one. I was a sound engineer for some of America's greatest rock and roll legends after the army." Sebastian buttered a roll and took a huge bite out of it.

Winston sipped her wine and regarded this strange little old man over her wine glass. "I didn't know that. Whom did you work for?"

"The greats, Janis Joplin, The Eagles, and then of course my special guy...Marvin Gaye."

"Oh—my—god, you did sound mixing for Marvin Gaye." Winston clasped her hand over her mouth. She'd said it so loud other patrons looked at her.

Sebastian swallowed his bread. He swirled his wine and sipped it, smacking his lips as if he'd tasted the best Chardonnay on the planet. "Yes, the last song I helped him with was Sexual Healing."

"Now, don't be lying to me, Sebastian," Winston said.

Sebastian raised he hand. "No, as god is my witness, I did the sound for his song, Sexual Healing in 1982."

"But you're a white man."

"Ah, yeah, but I got me an ear for soul. Marvin knew that about me. He knew what I'd done for The Eagles, well before they broke up, and of course Janis Joplin was incredible, until her overdose."

"I'll be damned. I'm in the presence of the man who has been in the presence of Marvin Gaye. That must have been incredible," Winston said.

"Well, yes and no."

"Why's that?"

"I had to help Marvin with his lyrics, and with his own healing... you know—"

"Now, stop it, now you're lying to me. Nobody had to teach Marvin anything."

"Well, I did. I helped him get to his true sexual side. You see I've had that way about me. I'm not only a Shaman in the truest form but also a sexual healer," Sebastian said lowering his voice.

Winston said nothing. She sipped her wine and stared into his eyes. Sebastian thought this afternoon was going remarkably well.

~

WHEN HIS LEAR JET landed at Bermuda Airport Sokolov couldn't believe that the jet McAllen had stolen from him was still at the Charter Terminal. He ordered his pilot to park as far away from it as possible.

He had picked up two Cuban exiles to accompany him, but he wasn't happy with either of them. They were low life criminals who could use a gun. That was it. They had passports that claimed they were American and no active warrants on their present identities.

What he was going to use these two idiots for was going to be a problem. He'd given them both submachine guns with orders to never shoot at anyone unless he ordered them to. He hoped they got that. They hadn't looked too stoned when he picked them up, but they looked a little high now.

The one who called himself Rozales, had pupils like pinholes, and the one called Fuentes now had a smirk on his face. He'd never seen them pop any pills on the plane, but they'd gone to the bathroom five times in flight.

The problem was Bermuda. This place was uptight. In Miami he could get away with some gunfire and leaving a few dead bodies on the street. Here, they absolutely frowned on it.

The island was tiny. There was no escape once they'd hit McAllen and his people. He'd have to tread carefully here. If he could find McAllen and his people in some seclude place, he'd kill them all, dump their bodies and get back on his plane and head back to San Francisco.

His cell phone rang. It was Adam Morgan. "I hope you have something for me," Sokolov said.

"You wanted next of kin for Sigurdsson I have them. I'm sending a text of pictures of his granddaughter and one of his three wives," Morgan said.

"Three, what the hell? Is this guy an Arab Sheik?"

"No, two of them he divorced, and from what I see, if you took either one hostage he'd tell you to shoot them."

"Sounds like a few of my ex-wives. Where is the third?"

"Samantha Sigurdsson runs a research ship out of Hamilton Harbour in Bermuda."

"Bermuda?"

"Why, are you close?"

"I'm right fucking here." Sokolov grinned into the phone.

"Good, maybe you can also find his granddaughter, Becky, she was doing a reef study off Key West. The place your people attacked. Did you see her with McAllen?"

Sokolov nodded. "Yes, I saw a young lady with them in the helicopter in Miami."

"Then, this is easy. Find them, get them to tell you where Sigurdsson is and he'll come to us. And kill McAllen and his accomplices" Morgan told him.

"Yes, easy," Sokolov said ending his call. He did not like taking orders or advice from this sniveling FBI agent. He'd faced many American agents in battle. They were good, this Morgan was a pansy—he imagined breaking his neck when the new order was established. But he'd do it slowly; first he'd do something horrible to those manicured nails of his.

His Cubans were outside, smoking cigarettes and whistling at any woman who walked by. He called them over and gave them directions to watch from behind a maintenance shed.

"Here is a picture of this McAllen and the FBI Agent and this Canadian woman. You will text me the moment you see one of them arrive. You understand me?

They nodded and smiled and with their machine guns tucked under their jackets then sauntered off towards the shed. Sokolov hoped they stayed awake. How he wished he'd had the Kazak he'd sent off to Key West with him.

Winston and Sebastian finished their lunch at the bistro. The wine was good, the conversation stimulating and Winston hadn't felt this good in years. She was a little high on the wine. Had Sebastian ordered a second bottle?

They fell into a cab together. Sebastian sat close to her now. She felt his heat. He smelled good. Like a man, one with all hormones and hair and, damn, he made her feel sexy. They hummed the tune of Sexual Healing, he rested his hand on her leg and by the time they got back to the charter terminal she was ready to jump this little old guy. He'd somehow morphed in her vision into a man who would transport her to someplace she hadn't been to in some time. Orgasm Ville.

Her relations with her husband were strained. There'd been no sex in...so long she couldn't remember. Here in the bright sun of Bermuda, wearing fine linens and silk, she was someone 'else. And that person needed to get laid.

Sebastian subtly guided her to the Charter terminal, told reception they needed a room to freshen up in before their next flight and in a heartbeat they were in a private room with shower, bed and soft music.

"Now," Sebastian said as he kissed her slowly while removing her clothes, "I want you to know, that the doctor is here and the sexual healing session is about to begin."

Winston groaned softly as Sebastian moved down her body. She began to tremble as he disrobed her and walked her to the shower. The next hour was lost in her own private heaven... she was in Orgasm Ville many times.

THE CUBANS FUENTES and Rozales had seen Sebastian and Winston enter the terminal. They'd spotted them the moment they got out of the taxi van. For the next half hour they discussed whether this was the *una mujer negra,* the black lady, they were looking for. The man didn't match the picture of McAllen.

She'd been arm in arm with a *viejo hombre blanco,* old white guy. Fuentes laughed and told Rozales the Viejo hombre probably had a *pene pequeno,* a little penis which had them laughing until they had tears in their eyes.

It was when Sokolov called them to ask if they'd seen a black woman of small height perhaps with an older white man that they began to fear for their lives. The Russian was not to be messed with. They responded that yes, they'd entered the building just a few minutes ago and they were just about to report it.

Sokolov walked into the Charter Terminal. There was no one there so he walked out to the tarmac. The Challenger jet was being refueled and the maintenance crew was working on the plane. A team of cleaners was entering.

He walked back into the terminal and approached the front desk. "Excuse me, madam," he asked the lady with a smile, "I'm looking for my friends, a black lady, about this tall with an older gentleman. Have you seen them?"

"Ah, yes, they've taken one of the private rooms, to rest," the lady said. Only one eyebrow went up in a slight sign that this was mildly interesting.

He smiled. If Winston and McAllen were in the room together, he could kill them easily. But to do so he'd have to kill this lady as well. He did his calculations as he reached inside his jacket for his gun.

The doors to the terminal opened and three policemen entered escorting a dignitary of some sort. Sokolov shoved his gun back inside its holster and slunk away to a chair to wait. He hated waiting.

19

MCALLEN WOKE with a damp cloth on his forehead. Bernadette was standing over him. "That woman has one hell of a right cross." She said.

He massaged his jaw and sat up. He was on a cot in a room below deck. "How did you get me here?"

"Becky and I carried you down. I had to convince Sam, that she couldn't stomp on you when you were down. I also told her we were looking for her husband."

"Where is she now?"

"Outside this room, standing guard. I think she wants us out of here now that we've dropped her granddaughter off. You know, McAllen, I didn't realize you had this kind of effect on people. But now, I kind of see how you can rub people the wrong way."

McAllen shook his head to clear the two Bernadette's dancing in his eyes, "Well, some people don't always get my drift."

"Oh, she drifted you alright." Bernadette chuckled.

"Not what I meant."

"I know, but it's still funny as hell. How about if I see if she's ready to make nice?" She poked her head outside the door.

Samantha Sigurdsson was in a muted conversation with Becky. She looked up at Bernadette. "Is he conscious?"

"Yes," Bernadette said. "And, it would be nice if he could stay that way for a while. Maybe we can go to your mess hall and get a cup of coffee?"

Sam shrugged. "Sure, follow me."

Bernadette took McAllen by the arm and they followed Sam to a mess hall beside the kitchen. Becky found coffee mugs and placed them in front of Bernadette and McAllen.

Becky whispered, "It takes my grandmother a little while to warm up to Uncle Mac, but she usually comes around."

Bernadette smiled at Becky. "Yeah, I've faced a few Grizzly Bears in Northern Canada with the same attitude."

Sam leaned forward on the table and stared across at McAllen. "Well, what crazy ass story have you got for me this time?"

McAllen sipped his coffee, to buy some time and let his jaw relax. "Well, I was going to tell you—"

"Stop right there." Sam raised her hand. Bernadette thought she was about to jump over the table at McAllen.

"I don't want no more of your bullshit lies—you hear me?"

"No, Sam, I've only come here with the truth."

"Really? Is that so? Well isn't that something." She looked at Bernadette and Becky. "Seems, like you're about to experience a first ever from this man. The truth."

"Look, we may have gotten off to a bad start," McAllen said.

"Bad start. You call filling my Barney with all kinds of crazy ideas about cooling the planet's ocean a bad start?"

"I know I may have given him an idea or two, but listen Sam, some of those crazy ideas were his, I just gave him a little direction," McAllen said.

"Oh, really?" Sam asked, her eyes going wide. "Fertilizing the ocean to produce plankton blooms that would supposedly absorb carbon dioxide from the atmosphere was his idea?"

"Well... okay that was my idea," McAllen admitted.

"How about inserting large vertical pipes in the ocean to bring up cool water from the deep to the surface—Barney's idea?"

"Ah, no... that was my idea as well." McAllen lowered his eyes from Sam's gaze.

Sam looked from Bernadette to Becky. "You see. Mac here has been leading Barney on all kinds of silly experiments that have got him nowhere."

She sipped her coffee and looked back at McAllen. "I'll tell you what's happened in the year that these two wannabe geo-engineers have been playing with their experiments, the Earth's oceans have been getting warmer at an alarming rate."

"How bad is it?" Becky asked.

"We've seen a rise by two degrees in all of our heat transfer and current studies. I have data from the Pacific to the Atlantic and it's all the same. A constant rise," Sam said.

Becky nodded. "You know, Grandma, we thought we were getting a strange anomaly in our reef study off Key West, but the reef is dying at an alarming rate. The fish can't handle it. Their numbers were dropping."

"Did you notice any cruise ships in the harbor when you arrived?" Sam asked.

"No, should there be?"

"This is their season. The oceans have heated up so fast that they are producing hurricanes one after another. Becky told me you brought her up from her lab in a category 2, well, there's a category 5 coming behind it, and another one forming after that. On top of that —the oceans are rising so fast they'll swamp all the lower islands in the Caribbean."

"It's all caused by the warming ocean?" Bernadette asked.

"Yeah, that's the cause. I know there's a bunch of climate deniers running around saying this is just a blip, but this started in August, and hasn't let up," Sam said.

"Before I left Canada," Bernadette said, "I was told a group of scientists thought this latest temperature increase wasn't normal. They were sure it was a man-made incident. They sent my partner and me out to use McAllen to locate your husband. You think there's any truth to this?"

Sam put her hand on her forehead and sighed. "Well, our data is showing a definite spike. We've been monitoring a gradual increase and sending in our data to the world's governments. Not that it's done any good. I guess someone in Florida is going to have to see their house flood from the sea before they get excited."

"Doesn't the present model show 2030 for that to happen anyway?" Becky asked.

"Yes, that's the forecast. But something else is happening. The increased sea temperature is causing the ice sheets to melt in the Arctic and Antarctic far too fast. The increased fresh water shuts down the ability of the oceans to move the water from one place to another—"

"That means a total shutdown of the ocean conveyer," Becky said.

"I assume it's really bad," Bernadette said.

"Yeah, most of the European coast goes into an ice age, and so does Alaska. The rest of the world suffers from strange droughts as moisture is no longer carried properly by the currents," Sam told her.

"How do you think someone could be affecting this?" Bernadette asked.

"As much I as hate to say it, I think your scientists are right. Someone is messing with the ocean's temperature. And, I think I know what they might be up to," Sam said.

"How about if you enlighten us," McAllen said. He was smiling now. The focus was no longer on his crazy antics.

"Barney was working on a strange phenomenon, it had to do with rivers of fresh water under the ocean," Sam said.

"I remember that," McAllen said. "There was a study of one off of Australia. And everyone knows about the ones in Yucatan called Cenotes. Did Barney tell you what he found?"

"Yes and no," Sam said. "When he was at the PEARL lab in Canada, he came upon some references to it. He was excited; said it confirmed some rumours he'd heard about it back in Iceland."

"What's PEARL?" Bernadette asked.

"The Polar Environment Atmospheric Research Laboratory," McAllen said. "It was just finished being built in 2017 on Ellesmere Island, then the Canadian Government pulled the funding."

"Sounds like the forward thinking of a government," Bernadette said turning to Sam. "Do you think that your husband might have returned to the lab, maybe to retrieve his notes?"

"Maybe to hide out?" Becky asked.

"Pretty barren place to do so. But that's a possibility," Sam said. "Barney kept most of his information in his head, but then, if he found clues to a giant underwater river, it might be there."

"What's our next move?" Bernadette asked. "We need to either find Professor Sigurdsson or whatever he was working on. If he was looking at an underwater river that could cool the ocean, maybe that's where we should look."

"I agree," McAllen said. "There are so many things that don't add up. The minute we go looking for Sigurdsson we have someone else on our tail. Matter of fact, they're trying to get there ahead of us to get to him."

"Do you think someone wants to capture Sigurdsson to force him to work for them?" Bernadette said.

McAllen tilted his head sideways as if a thought had just hit him. "What if he'd been working for them and he escaped?"

"I doubt it," Sam said. "How could he be helping someone increase the temperature of the earth's oceans?"

"I don't know. What if he was telling them to drill for volcanic vents in hopes he'd find the rivers. Maybe he left when he couldn't find his rivers," McAllen suggested.

"Great speculation," Sam said. "Do you think he'd be foolish enough to gamble on a tactic like that?"

"You never saw him play Blackjack," McAllen said. "That man would go bust more times on a seventeen, when everyone knows the odds are in the dealers favour."

"The world isn't a card game, McAllen," Sam said.

McAllen rolled his eyes. "I think you're wrong. It's a high stakes card game, and too many people are playing as if they have the winning hand. In the end, mother nature always has the trump card."

"Okay, great, McAllen. You can sit here and spout cliché's all day, or get the hell off my ship and go do something about it," Sam told him.

"Good, I'm going with them," Becky said.

McAllen put his hand on her shoulder. "No, Becky, you need to hang here with your grandmother. Besides. I can't keep passing you off with that Polish flight attendant's passport. I need to get that back to the plane."

"But... I..." Becky protested, a tear forming in her eye. Bernadette could see she loved McAllen and wanted to be with him.

McAllen closed his eyes. "Not going to happen, Becky. Now, get yourself out of the flight attendant's uniform. I'm sure your grandma has something for you."

Becky walked off in a huff towards a cabin that Sam directed her to find some clothes. She came back dressed in shorts and a t-shirt with the uniform in a bag.

Sam stood on the gangplank and gave McAllen a hug,

"Does this mean all is forgiven?" McAllen asked.

"Hell no. It means if I have my arms around you I can't sock you again with my fists," Sam said. She stood back from McAllen. "Look, I know you love Barney. You two go way back. But you've got some really strange ideas. It kind of makes me crazy."

Bernadette smiled. "You're right, Sam, you and the rest of the world. I'll make sure he stays out of trouble, or gets into the right kind."

They hailed a cab and headed back to the airport.

"That wasn't so bad," McAllen said.

"Really, did you expect a worse reception than a punch in the face?" Bernadette asked.

"Yeah, one time she took a shot at me." McAllen smiled ruefully.

20

SOKOLOV SAT in a chair in the waiting room of the charter terminal. He wore his sunglasses and peered over the top of a newspaper at the policemen. He was calculating. He wondered if McAllen walked out of the lounge with Winston now, if they'd recognize him? Did they have weapons on them—would they draw them or try to run? What about the police officers?

Then, it got worse. Another officer walked in. This one was a female police officer and, by her uniform, he assumed she outranked the others. She shook hands with the dignitary and looked around the room. She was maybe in her late twenties, dark hair pulled back over amber-coloured skin. He couldn't see her eyes, imagined them as hazel. The look fit. Sokolov liked to have a description of everyone. The young policewoman's eyes took in everything in the room until, eventually, her gaze rested on the small Russian. He was used to being watched, being tailed. This young lady should be no problem to him.

He was, after all, off limits to the FBI because of Adam Morgan's meddling in the central bureaus data banks, but Bermuda was a problem. They weren't under any American jurisdiction. Bermuda was a British Protectorate. As such, they had the local police and a direct link to MI6, the British Foreign Intelligence service, which also worked closely with Interpol.

There was a worldwide alert out for him. Interpol wanted him bad. MI6 would love to have a few words with him before they handed them over. MI6, however, wasn't as kind as most British believed. Their methods of interrogation were quite sophisticated and rough.

The policewoman took off her sunglasses and took out her cell phone. She was pointing it in Sokolov's direction. Before she could adjust the image to bring him into focus, he took out his cigarettes and began a sideways slide out the door.

He turned his face towards the wall and kept his head down, working furiously to pull a cigarette out of a pack that was somehow not producing his nicotine delivery system. He swung the door open and breathed a sigh of relief until he saw the two police cars with uniformed officers. Sokolov stuck the cigarette between his lips and put his lighter up to his face.

In seconds he had made his legs move him to the other side of the terminal building. He looked around for Fuentes and Rozales who were nowhere to be seen. Walking down the short road towards the main terminal, he saw them hanging around the taxi stand. They were smarter than he thought. If they'd stayed where they were, the police would have questioned them. Any search of their person would have produced their weapons.

He was walking towards them when he saw a taxi van approach. Instinct told him to stand behind a palm tree. In that moment he saw McAllen and Bernadette Callahan returning. A feeling of rage came over Sokolov. There was no way he could touch them. They'd outmaneuvered him, and they didn't even know it. He cursed his luck as he walked towards his Cuban henchman. Then he stopped.

He realized that the young lady he'd identified as Becky Sigurdsson wasn't with them. They must have dropped her off on the island. He grabbed his phone and dialed Morgan.

Morgan answered on the second ring.

"You said Sigurdsson's wife was on a research ship somewhere off

Bermuda. I want the name of the ship and I want you to put your global tracking system on it now," Sokolov said.

"I don't know if I can get that to you right away. I'm in the middle of something." Morgan said, bristling at the Russian's tone.

"My friend. You could be in the middle of the river with a weight tied to your ass if I don't get this information in the next hour," Sokolov insisted.

Morgan almost hung up the phone. He wasn't used to being talked to that way, but he knew whom he was dealing with. Russian Mafia killed those who disobeyed or displeased them.

"I'll have the information to you shortly." Morgan put the phone down and brushed the sweat from his brow. This was getting worse, not better. There would be a breaking point; he hoped he wasn't at the center of it.

McAllen and Bernadette saw the police cars as they approached the terminal. The taxi van stopped in front and the driver opened the door. There was nothing else they could do but pay the taxi driver and walk inside. Any other move would have drawn attention. Had their covers been blown? Had someone identified Alistair McAllen, and Sebastian Germaine as they'd left the airport?

If they had, then they would be walking into police custody. Bernadette wondered how she'd explain this to the Bermuda Police. She was travelling on a false passport to do police business... would that even work, she wondered? They took a deep breath and walked into the terminal. Three policemen and a policewoman were standing in a corner with a man in a beige suite. Sebastian and Winston were nowhere to be seen.

A door opened and a giggle was heard, followed by a laugh. The two of them came out of the lounge as if they were teenage kids on a first date.

Winston saw Bernadette and McAllen. Her eyes dropped down and she let go of Sebastian's hand. She put her hand up to her neck, as if this would hide her recent actions.

"I see you two have been taking in some valuable rest time," McAllen said with only a hint of sarcasm.

"Hey, great showers, Mac," Sebastian said pointing behind him to the lounge. "Here, we got you some new clothes. I suggest you hit the showers before you put them on."

"Thanks," Bernadette said, eyeing Winston. "I'll see if they have another room available."

"Oh, heck no, we're done with the room. Your turn," Sebastian said.

McAllen grabbed the clothes and headed into the room. "No one needs to tell me twice. I can smell myself from two hundred metres. How about if you get us another plane, Sebastian? This time we're heading for Montreal and a little place called Ellesmere Island. I'll work the details out with the pilot once you've found the transport."

"I'm pretty sure the plane we fly in on, is still here," Sebastian said. "I heard the pilot say he couldn't fly back to his base in Phoenix due to the heat, and the storms are keeping him from the Eastern USA."

"Great, then he'll love where we're going," McAllen said.

Winston looked at Bernadette. "Where is this Ellesmere Island? Is it in a lake near Montreal? I've always wanted to go there."

"Well, you can plan that some other time. We'll stop to refuel there, but Ellesmere Island is in the Arctic Ocean," Bernadette told her.

"How far north is that?" Winston asked.

"About 1,000 kilometres from the North Pole," Bernadette said. "Pretty much the top of the Earth."

Winston looked down at her new linen slacks and blouse. "I guess I should have bought some different clothes."

Bernadette waited until McAllen was finished with his shower, and out of the lounge before she went in. She found ample towels and fresh toiletries. The shower felt amazing. She couldn't remember the last time she'd had one. They'd been washed over by the Atlantic Ocean and dripped dried in the helicopter, so being clean with fresh underwear was the next best thing to heaven she'd felt. She found

McAllen when she came out. The police had left the building. He was in a muted conversation with Sebastian.

She waited patiently for them to finish. McAllen looked at her; he could see there was something on her mind. "What's up?" he asked.

"I think we're going at this wrong," Bernadette said. "Here we are chasing after Sigurdsson, but we need to find out who is behind this ocean temperature rise."

"And, you're going to do this how?" McAllen asked.

"I'm going to contact my people in Canadian Security and Intelligence. I'm going to feed them what we've found and see what I can find," Bernadette said.

"You don't think that will get back to the FBI guys who are trying to kill us?" Sebastian said. He'd come up behind Bernadette.

"The guy I'm going to contact is a bit outside the loop. He'll be discreet," Bernadette assured him.

"I hope so. If this gets out as to where we're heading, we'll have one hell of a welcoming committee waiting for us," McAllen said.

"I hear you." Bernadette went to a quiet corner and dialed Anton de Luca on her cell.

～

SOKOLOV and his Cuban thugs pulled up in front of the Nemo II in Hamilton Harbor. They'd rented a van and picked up two large duffel bags and some chloroform and cotton wool in town.

The three walked up the gangplank and were met by Samantha Sigurdsson. "May I help you?" she asked.

Sokolov stuck a gun in her ribs, "You will say nothing, move quietly towards the lower deck. If you shout, I will kill you and everyone on this ship. You understand me?"

～

BERNADETTE REACHED ANTON. "Where are you now?" he asked.

"Bermuda."

"Nice, I've always wanted to go there. I take it you're not hitting the beach."

"Nope," Bernadette said. She filled him on the conversation she had with Samantha Sigurdsson.

"And you're heading for Ellesmere Island?"

"Yes."

"Okay... strange travel plans, but I understand. Now, what is it you want me to do?" Anton said.

Bernadette smiled. He was always to the point. "This Sokolov guy was in the Miami Charter Terminal waiting for Sigurdsson to be delivered to him. He could only have got his orders from someone in the FBI. Who transmitted McAllen's information about Sigurdsson being in Key West?"

"You're right. I hate to admit it, but the dots connect," Anton admitted.

"I think you start following the rabbit down the hole. If you go back to Adam Morgan, who gave you the order from the FBI to have me come with Agent Winston to find McAllen, we could progress up the chain."

"Okay, I'm on it," Anton said.

"But you'll have to keep your investigation quiet. If Adam Morgan gets wind of it he could shut it down and destroy any evidence."

"Trust me, Bernadette, this investigation won't leave here. I'll have a crack team work on it and I'll get back to you with what we've found out."

Bernadette turned off her phone and found McAllen and Sebastian with Winston in the terminal. She motioned for McAllen to join her.

"I've got someone in Canada working on this. He'll report whatever he finds," Bernadette told him.

"Good, now we'd better make tracks. We have a lot of airspace to make up to get to the top of the world," McAllen said.

"Is the pilot going to take us all the way there?"

McAllen chuckled. "You know, he actually said he'd like to, but the landing strip in Ellesmere Island is small, and gravel. He'll take us as far north as he can. We'll make alternative arrangements for the final leg."

Bernadette smiled at the phrase, 'alternative arrangements.' She'd flown in the far north of Canada before. Some of the planes could look less than airworthy but the pilots were always capable.

21

THE CRACK TEAM that Anton De Luca promised Bernadette Callahan was really only Mellissa Ackerman. Her attention to detail and imagination in research far surpassed the other analysts', which made her a 'team,' and a force all by herself.

She was a loner, spending lunch breaks on a walk or reading a book, not hanging in the break room sharing stories with other analysts. To Anton, that meant a project or conversation with her, went no further. He loved that about her.

He walked to her cubicle and found her peering at the computer. "Hey, Mellissa, I hope you're not too busy, but I really need you on a project."

Mellissa whirled around in her chair. "Of course not, whatever you need, Anton." She was hoping he'd drop into her office again. She'd been up nights working on the connections of the billionaires, Congressman Derman and Sokolov.

That very day she'd planned to present it to him. She'd worn her blue dress with the lower cut neckline. It revealed just a little of her ample bosoms that, in her dreams, she wanted Anton to caress. Four times that morning she'd wanted to go to his office with her research and each time she'd lost her nerve. She couldn't believe he was in front of her. Her heart raced and her palms went sweaty.

"Did you find anything about those billionaires and the Russian guy?" Anton asked.

"Oh, yes..." Mellissa began slowly. She didn't want to seem too rushed. Not wanting to appear like a flustered schoolgirl.

"I've found a few things since we last spoke." She pulled out a large file beside her desk and turned it towards Anton. He pulled up a chair and sat beside her.

"What have you got?"

Every pore of Mellissa was vibrating with Anton beside her. She pulled the first piece of information and cleared her throat. "Ah, I ran a cross check of our three billionaires first. I put them into the Interpol database, their Ballistic Information Network and I got a strange hit."

"How strange?"

"All three of them were on the same island of Lanai in Hawaii a few days ago. I did some further checking and found they'd checked into the Four Seasons hotel there."

"Were they all attending a conference?"

"Nope, I checked that too. The Fuglemans had a wedding, but they weren't on the guest list." Mellissa allowed herself a small smile. She was sweating so much with Anton beside her she thought there'd be a puddle forming around her chair.

"Well, I guess it's not that strange the three of them were together. They were involved in some crooked dealings in the USA, maybe they were trying to come up with some new ones,' Anton suggested.

"Yes, but Illy Volkov was also there," Melissa said.

"Volkov. Are you sure?"

"Absolutely. I had a friend of mine in Homeland Security do me a favour and run a facial recognition scan of all persons who entered the Lanai airport. They all arrived by private jets but Homeland Security has made all private charters put in cameras to feed into their scanners."

"Isn't Volkov the boss of Sokolov?"

"You bet. He's the head boss of Sokolov and the key Russian Mafia figure that heads the controlling group of most of Russia's government. They say that nothing in Russia happens without a bribe being paid. There's even a saying that you don't take a shit without paying the Mafia for the toilet paper." Melissa cringed, "Oops, sorry, I didn't mean to be so crass..."

Anton shook his head and smiled. "It's okay, Melissa, it's just us here. I don't mind you embellishing on the information."

Mellissa's face went a deep red. She couldn't believe her silly slip of the tongue in front of Anton. Was she trying to impress him? She wanted to die inside.

"This is excellent work. Now there's something else I'd like you to do for me," Anton said.

"Anything—I mean... how can I help?" Mellissa wanted to slap herself at this moment for blurting out her feelings.

"One of our people in the field thinks that someone might be doing some underwater drilling on the Ocean's floor. If they were doing this, they'd have to purchase some pretty substantial equipment. Can you see if you can find any correlation to this with our billionaires and Volkov?"

"Sure thing. I have someone in the US FBI Forensic Accounting Department I can talk to—"

"This has got to be super discreet," Anton cut in. "No one, not even the FBI can know what we're looking for or why."

"That's not a problem. The person I'll be contacting will be through a backchannel. There will be no record of our conversation and any information passed on will be your eyes only," Mellissa assured him.

"That's excellent," Anton said. "I knew I could count on you." He got up, patted her on the shoulder then left the office.

Mellissa was a puddle of emotions as she watched him walk down the hall. She finally took her eyes off his firm butt, sighed and got back to work.

She couldn't wait to call her secret contacts—what she told Anton was her back channel. They were all young women with fantasies just like hers. She'd met Tina Engelbach from Homeland Security and Lisa Burkhart from the FBI Forensic Accounting Department over a year ago at a Cyber Security Conference in Orlando.

They instantly connected. Three big girls with oversized hand-bags and bad hair that gravitated to the same table at lunch amongst the sea of skinny people in their cool Banana Republic outfits and comments about the lack of 'carb free food,' on the buffet. Mellissa, Lisa and Tina shared their passion for law enforcement, then, they all admitted to their fantasies of the male agents they worked for. Their meeting evolved into a pizza party in their room, away from the prying eyes of the skinnies. They watched their favorite hero, Melissa McCarthy in the movie Spy. She'd played an analyst with Jude Law as her love interest.

From then on, the three connected by Facebook, and used FB Messenger to communicate. They did everything, 'off campus,' which meant using burner phones to communicate. Any data sent would be to a private server. None of their transmissions showed up in FBI or CSIS files. They felt they could chase bad guys this way, and they hoped they'd impress the hell out of the hunky Agents they worked for. It worked that way in their imaginations. And their imaginations worked overtime.

22

SOKOLOV WATCHED the faces of Samantha and Becky Sigurdsson. He could see the fear in their eyes. It was always the same with his captives. Their eyes would dart back and forth. They would breathe heavily; their chests heaving to take what they thought would be their last breaths. "I promise I won't hurt you," he said.

"And the gun is for—what, a party game?' Sam asked.

"You make jokes, I like that in a woman."

Sam set her mouth in a hard line. She wondered if this Russian would leave without killing them. The odds didn't look good.

"What have you done with my crew?"

"We locked them in the engine room. They will be safe there."

"Safe from you? I doubt it," Becky said. "Do you plan to kill them?"

Sokolov lowered his gun and smiled. "We are only here for information. No one needs to die. You tell us where your Mr. McAllen and his friends are headed and we let you go."

"How about if you get the hell off my ship and I tell you nothing?" Sam said.

"Not an option," Sokolov said. "Here is what is going to happen." He pulled out a switchblade knife. "I am going to cut pieces out of your beautiful granddaughter until you tell me." He snapped the blade open. It shone in the light. He took its edge and sliced his hand. Blood dripped to the cabin floor.

"Ellesmere Island. They're going to a research station to find evidence of a river that runs under the oceans. Maybe it will stop what you bastards are doing to heat the ocean. And you won't find Barney there. He's long gone," Sam said. She hoped the last part was true. She wasn't sure.

"Excellent. Now, that wasn't hard, was it?"

"Okay, you've got what you want. Leave us alone," Becky said.

"Oh no. You will be coming with us." Sokolov said. "We have a little flight planned off the island."

"You'll never get us out of Bermuda without half the police force seeing you taking us away," Sam said. "This is a small island. People will see us leaving. You'll never get away with it."

Sokolov grinned. "My dear lady, I have been involved in smuggling my whole life. Getting two people off this island is easy."

He signaled to the Cubans who came at Sam and Becky from behind. They both struggled with the chloroform-soaked rags over their mouths but the fumes overcame them. They slumped to the ground.

Fuentes opened up two large nylon bags and fit each of them into one. He zipped the bags and with Rozales at one end, they hauled them down the gangplank and into the waiting van.

Darkness was falling. The lights had not been turned on in the harbor yet. Sokolov loved this time. The time between darkness and daylight, perfect to move someone with no one to notice. Once the two women were loaded into the van, he ordered Fuentes and Rozales to shoot the crew. He'd saved them until now, just in case he needed to torture them to get Sam to speak. You never knew how close a family was. One time he had had to kill two sons to get the mother to give up her husband. It was only when he threatened her daughter that she weakened. Turned out the mother didn't like the sons but loved her daughter. He'd been doing her a favour by killing them.

They had no problems transporting the drugged women to the airport and getting them on the plane. The pilot only nodded at the unusual cargo. Sokolov called Morgan once they were airborne.

"I have Sigurdsson's wife and his granddaughter," Sokolov said when Morgan answered."

"Good." Morgan wanted to say it was about time Sokolov did something right but the man scared him. "Take them to our facility in San Francisco. What about my FBI agent Winston, and McAllen? Were you able to deal with them?"

"No. The opportunity did not present itself," Sokolov said. He'd decided if Morgan pressed him on this he would personally land in Washington, drive to his location and shoot him on the spot. He found him that infuriating.

"I see. Did Sigurdsson's wife know where her husband might be?"

"Yes, your FBI agent and McAllen and friends are heading to a place called Ellesmere Island. She tried to convince me her husband isn't there but I think she's lying. Why else would someone go to the ends of the Earth?"

Morgan punched up the name of the island on his computer. He couldn't believe what he was seeing. "My god, it's at the end of the Earth."

"There's a research lab there. I suspect Sigurdsson is there and has all the information you need to keep the drilling operation working. Do you have someone you can send?"

Morgan ran his mind over several of his assets and none of them were a fit for this. It would be impossible to send a team of FBI agents to such a remote location without arousing suspicions of the Canadian Government that would fall back on him.

"I don't have a team that I could put together that fast. Do you have someone available?"

Sokolov wondered why they had even bothered to involve this man. "I have the perfect people for this—Russians. They are close by."

Sokolov ended his call and dialed Volkov.

When Volkov answered he told him what he wanted.

"You're serious?" Volkov asked.

"I'm very serious. It's time we got them involved. They will be showing themselves inside of a week to ten days. Why not use them now?"

Volkov took a deep breath. "I don't know if one of them is available at that latitude."

"Are you kidding me? The Russian fleet is all over the Arctic. They've been under the ice all winter. The channels are completely open now. There will be no interference from the Canadians. Their small navy is a joke."

Volkov nodded his head as he listened. He was right. The Russians owned the Arctic Ocean. The Canadians, Americans and those in Denmark and Greenland laid claim to huge territories, but the Russian Submarine fleet prowled the waters below the ice in the winter and above in the summer.

"I will make a call and let you know," Volkov said.

He ended his call and sat back in the large leather chair on his private jet. He'd been brooding over the departure of Willa Flowers before this phone call and this gave him something to focus on.

His next phone call was to Russia. Every Mafia head had at least three top Russian officials on their payroll. A Russian official could be bought for one million Rubles. That was less than 18,000 USD. But they wanted this every month now. What annoyed Volkov was that the officials were getting involved in offering *krysha*, the Russian word for roof that meant protection. This had been the sole domain of the Mafia. He hated competition.

Volkov chose only those who listened to his instructions, took bribes and didn't flash their money around. A new anti-corruption department had been established some years ago. Only those who were stupid or went outside the good graces of the Russian Mafia ever got caught in corruption scandals.

Volkov had chosen Anatoly Polzin, who checked all the boxes he was looking for in a high-ranking official. He was in the ministry of defense. He was middle aged, not too much of a social climber and kept to himself. His needs were simple—ten million Rubles per year and his daughter was sent to a top university in the USA with her full tuition and all of her expenses paid. Money flowed to Polzin through his wife who was set up as a public relations consultant and did nothing but go for lunch with her friends in Moscow. It was nice life for both of them and Volkov ruled them.

Polzin answered his phone after several rings. "How may I help you?" he said once Volkov identified himself.

"Is this line secure?"

"Yes, as secure as it can be in the Ministry of Russian Defense."

"I want you to send a submarine to Ellesmere Island in Canada."

"Okay, and what is it to do there?"

"There is a research lab there, The Polar Environmental Atmospheric Research Lab. Have the crew take all their data in regards to rivers under the ocean, and to capture any scientist that fits the description of a picture I'm going to send you," Volkov instructed.

"Ah, you do realize that the Canadians will not like this, and they have an intelligence base several hundred kilometres away," Polzin said.

"When your men come ashore have them do so without insignias or markings. It worked in the Crimea, it will work there, and you can deny that the sub ever landed," Volkov said shaking his head. He couldn't believe this high-ranking bureaucrat hadn't thought of this.

"And, what will we tell the Russian Prime Minister and President when they come looking for a head to chop off?"

"Let me worry about that. I'll take care of you. Haven't I always been your *krysha?*"

Polzin sighed audibly over the phone. "Yes, Volkov, you have always been my roof and given me protection. However, this could have international implications."

"How is your daughter doing at university?"

"She is doing well. Top marks in her law faculty."

"And your wife? Enjoying her lovely lunches with her friends?"

"Yes, yes... of course... but—"

"There is no but. You will send a submarine to this island immediately. They will land, and do as I ask."

"And if they meet opposition?"

"Kill everyone. You can claim it was terrorists. Goodbye." Volkov said.

Volkov hung up his phone and sat back in his leather chair. In a few weeks time, Russian ships would be landing on the shores of America to give them aid. The massive Antonov Cargo planes capable of carrying 150 tons of food would be landing in the American mid-west. The optics would be wonderful. Russia would be saving America from the largest drought in its history. Russian soldiers would serve arm in arm with Americans to quell riots and bring peace.

Volkov smiled as a shapely air attendant brought him Vodka. No one would know the Russian Mafia had orchestrated all of this and the Mafia would rule America inside of six months. He would offer a *krysha* to all who needed it. And everyone would need a roof for protection. He'd make sure of that.

23

BERNADETTE LOOKED at her phone to see their route north as the plane reached altitude over Bermuda. Their charter jet would take just over two hours to get them to Montreal. Sebastian had ordered cold weather clothing for the four of them in Montreal when they arrived. Bernadette was impressed that he thought of everything.

Then, they had a three-and-a-half hour flight straight north to a little place called Iqaluit in the territory of Nunavut. There they had to say goodbye to their luxury jet and take a little six or eight seat propeller plane, called an Otter, to the final destination of Ellesmere Island. If you needed to fly to a desolate and cold destination, the Otter was your plane.

Winston sat across from Bernadette. "You seem wrapped up in your phone. Anything interesting?"

"I'm looking at our travels. It's going to take us about eight hours and three different airports to get us close to the top of the world and most of the time we'll be going straight north," Bernadette said.

"You ever travel that far north?" Sebastian asked.

"Nope, I've been a tree line girl all my life," Bernadette said.

"What's that supposed to mean?" Winston asked. She looked out the window and back at Bernadette.

"We'll be going into what we Canadians call the Barren Lands. There are no trees there. You may see a few low-lying shrubs and rocks, but there won't be a tree anywhere."

"How do people live there?" Winston asked.

"Well, the Inuit as they're called, which means 'The People' have been happy to live there for thousands of years. Until, civilization and warming atmosphere destroyed their ice. They relied on it to hunt for seals. Now, much of the ice is gone from there. As the ice disappears, so too does their way of life."

"A life of hunting seals in freezing conditions... isn't that a life they'd want to get rid of," Winston said. "I mean, look, I'm all for tradition and such, but my god, the temperature up there hits minus 50C. Who'd want to live up there?"

Bernadette pursed her lips and put down her phone. "I can't explain the love that some people have for their land. I'm only half native, and sometimes I feel like I just want to live inside the forests and on the lakes. It something that resides in you and it's hard to explain."

"Well, I'm African American, and you won't get me longing for the jungles of Africa," Winston said. "Hell, I don't even like the parks of Washington DC."

"Those are the most dangerous," Sebastian said.

"Amen to that," Winston replied.

Bernadette picked up her phone and scrolled through messages. "I think we got a problem."

"What is it?" Winston asked.

"I got a text here from Anton at CSIS that the Bermuda Police discovered the crew of The Nemo II were murdered on their boat."

"Oh my god. Do you think it was Becky and Sam? I can't believe we left her there," Winston said.

"Look, we don't know for sure. The report said they found several victims shot in the engine room." Bernadette said.

Winston looked towards the back of the airplane. "Do we tell McAllen?"

"No, we wait until we know more. I'm going to ask Anton for more Intel."

"That also means someone knows where we're heading."

"Yep, from one shit storm to another. Happy days," Bernadette said.

24

Mellissa Ackerman left the Canadian Security and Intelligence Services building to call her contacts. She picked her usual spot, a Tim Horton's Donut shop three blocks away. The trendy agents never came here. They frequented Starbucks a block from the building. This donut shop was full of working people from warehouses across the street and truck drivers and contractors in denim jeans and boots covered in dirt.

Mellissa loved the place. The crullers were covered in sweet frosting and the maple creams oozed with enough sugar to give her a headache. She loved it, called it her 'buzz.' She bought a cruller and a maple cream and large double cream double sugar coffee and found a table beside a group of young electricians who were talking loudly about last night's hockey game. You couldn't get better cover for a covert operation.

She dialed Lisa at Homeland Security and when she came on, she muttered, "Three way, *sub rosa*."

"I'm on it," Lisa said.

Mellissa put her phone down and picked up her cruller. She bit into it and savored the sickly sweet icing sugar wending its way around her tonsils. She sipped her coffee and waited. Their '*sub rosa*,' code was an ancient code of secrecy meaning 'under the roses,' in Latin, where all things private were once spoken. Lisa would be hurrying out of her office with her burner phone and Tina would be doing the same. After Mellissa had consumed her cruller, her phone rang.

"I got a big juicy one, girls," Mellissa said.

"Did it come from your dreamboat, the Italian hunk?" Lisa asked.

"You got it."

"What did he smell like this time?" Lisa asked.

"Old spice aftershave and pasta with a hint of Parmesan Reggiano cheese," Mellissa said.

"Oh my god, I could rub a guy like that all over me," Lisa said, her breath audible over the phone.

"Easy, Lisa," Tina said. "You'll be making your panties wet again."

"A girl can fantasize," Lisa insisted. "Now, what have you got?"

"Okay." Mellissa looked to see if the group of electrical contractors was still deep in their hockey game discussions. "Listen up ladies. We have to go total black on this. No one can know what you're investigating. I have it on authority from my dreamboat that his people in the field will be compromised. You copy that?"

"We copy that," the girls said in unison.

"Okay then, I'm going to be sending you profiles of three billionaires, all of them have been in trouble with the US government for playing with government contracts," Melissa said.

"Any of them get caught, do time, or get their hands slapped?" Tina asked.

"Nope, nothing. They lawyered up and walked away."

"That figures," Lisa said. "With lots of money you get to do lots of crime and get away with it. They have anyone else involved?"

"Yes, there was someone named, Sokolov, you'll find he's a Russian Mafia, but we're more interested in his boss, a guy named Illy Volkov."

"What exactly are we looking for?" Tina asked.

"Any companies that the three little piggy's set up—sorry that's my pet name for the three billionaires—and any connection to a guy named Volkov. I found a record of him meeting with the three piggy's recently," Melissa said.

"Anything specific?" Tina asked. "Like what do we think they're into?"

"You have to promise me you won't breathe a word of this," Melissa said.

"It's in the vault. Now, spill," Tina said.

"Okay." Mellissa dropped her voice low, even though it mattered little to the men discussing last night's hockey game. "We think all these people are trying to do something to the Earth's oceans. As in, they are trying to raise the temperature."

"Shut the front door." Lisa screamed into her phone. "Seriously? You've landed the big score, the big investigation."

"Oh, yeah." Mellissa took a triumphant sip of her coffee. "We are in the biggest of the big investigation. It doesn't get any better than this."

"Okay, this time, maybe I wet myself a little," Tina, said. "This is ridiculous—but wait, we can't take credit for it if we link all these people to climate change. How shitty is that?"

"I know, ultra shitty, but that's what we do for our dreamboats. That's why we stay up at night watching Netflix and eating Rocky Road ice cream."

"Because we're losers?"

"No, Tina, it's because we see the cause to be so much deeper than ourselves," Mellissa told her.

"I'll give you a deeper cause. You, getting laid by your dreamboat, and you wouldn't give a damn if the water was rising around your ankles," Tina said.

Mellissa heard Tina loud and clear, sighed silently and said nothing. She was totally right in her assessment.

"Okay, I think we've got the plan here Mellissa," Tina said. "We'll get right on this and report everything we get. I'm sure between myself at Homeland, and Lisa at FBI Forensics, we can come up with something. These people always think they can hide their money trails but we always find them."

"Thanks, girls," Mellissa said. "I'll talk to you both soon." She ended her call, finished her donut and walked out of the coffee shop. She smiled, not one of the young men arguing over the latest hockey game had heard a thing.

CAPTAIN RUSANOV DID NOT like the message he'd received from Moscow. The sender was Anatoly Polzin who was the most sniveling money-grabbing bastard in the ministry of defense. Rusanov and every other sailor knew what the Russian Navy had been before the Soviet Union fell to those bastards in the Mafia. They were once a great super power, feared and respected by the Americans and the British. Now, they were always playing catch-up.

They had too few ships in too few places. Rusanov's submarine prowled around the Arctic Ocean. Yes, he could defeat any ships of the Canadians, Greenlanders or Danes, but he avoided the Americans at all cost. His Borei class Submarine was formidable, however, it was one of only three. There should have been many more on the way. The corruption in Russia meant every ship was over budget and built at a snail's pace as tradesmen made sure they got their share of bribes before they did anything.

Rusanov looked at his message again and called his second in command. "Yuri, look at this bullshit they want us to carry out."

Yuri scratched his day-old whiskers and adjusted his cap. "Is it the usual bullshit or something new?"

"This is new, alright. They want us to go ashore at Ellesmere Island, steal any documents related to some river under the ocean and kidnap some Icelandic Professor named Sigurdsson."

"Really, how about a partridge in a pear tree? Did they ask for that as well?"

"I don't understand. What the hell does a partridge and a pear tree have to do—"

"Never mind, it's a silly English Christmas song. And how exactly are we to hide the fact that a Russian Submarine has landed on Canadian soil and done this?" Yuri asked.

"We're supposed to kill everyone and blame it on an Arab Terrorists."

"Ah... there you go... perfect Russian logic," Yuri said. "Now, when are we supposed to do this silly and terrible thing?"

"Right away. We need to sail there immediately. We can be there in ten hours," Rusanov said.

"And if we disobey? What can they do?"

"This comes from Polzin, you know he's connected to the Mafia. He'd have all our families killed then have us killed when we come back to Russia."

Yuri lowered his head. "You make one hell of a compelling argument for us turning into Arab Terrorists."

25

BERNADETTE SAT in the lobby of the luxury charter terminal in Montreal in a large leather chair staring out the window, sipping on a latte from the lounge. It was past midnight. The terminal would close soon. They needed to leave, find a hotel for the night and resume their travels in the morning. But there was a problem. The airplane they'd flown in on was not going to take them any further. The charter company did not want their luxury jet flying into the far north of Canada. The pilot had cold feet as well, which Bernadette thought was a good expression for where they were going. He'd never been that far north, and the thought of a severe winter storm leaving him stranded there was not appealing. The pilot, co-pilot and the flight attendant had left for a nearby Hilton Hotel two hours ago.

McAllen had taken a taxi to pick up their arctic gear for their trip north. He seemed to take their situation in his stride. He'd said he'd find them a hotel on his return and Sebastian would find them another plane.

Sebastian was in the corner on a phone in a high back executive chair in front of a mahogany desk trying to find another flight. A large black sculpture of a Walrus was behind him. Bernadette could see the back of Sebastian's head in the Walrus's belly in the darkness of the window in front of her. He was balding just above his man-bun.

She wondered if they'd ever get to Ellesmere Island. But, did it matter anymore? From what she was seeing on the news, the oceans were pouring into New York, and London.

Winston sat down beside her. "My god, you look sad. What the hell is on your mind?"

"Sorry, I've been looking at the newscasts on my phone. It looks like people are running for high ground all over the world. There were more deaths from the heat in the American Midwest. I'm wondering if all of this is too late."

"You mean, we should all go home, put our heads in the sand and wait to see who survives?"

"Yeah, that's it. I've got this little cabin in Northern Canada. Maybe I could patch things up with my guy, and take him and my dog up there. We could hunt and fish and wait for the world to get its shit together."

"Then what?"

Bernadette put her coffee cup down and stretched out her legs. "Yeah, then what...? That's the problem."

"Look, you know you're a do-gooder like me. It's in our blood. We are lumped into all the great breed of first responders. Whether it's the World Trade Centre attack or someone harassing an elderly couple. We jump in. Just can't help ourselves."

"You mean that's why we're destined to go to the top of the world to try to find some crazy scientist for a way to cool the Earth?"

"Yeah." Winston winked at Bernadette. "It's in your DNA, girl. You can't stop once you're on the hunt. You have to follow through and you know it."

"Aw, shit, and here I thought I had something called free will," Bernadette said.

"Never going to happen." Winston said. "I think I'm going to find me one of those fancy coffees." She got up, stretched and headed for the executive terminal kitchen.

Bernadette checked her phone. There was a message from Chris.

He was leaving Kandahar in a convoy. She tried to call him but there was no answer. His phone went to voice mail.

She thought of a message she could leave. Something that would encapsulate the loneliness she felt without him. The turmoil she was in trying to make it work with him. She almost dialed again and stopped herself.

Her phone rang, it was Anton, and with a sigh of relief she answered the phone. "What's up, Anton? You have anything new for us?"

"Yeah, Bernadette, two things, neither are great, but here they are,"

"Let me have it. I never expect good things these days."

"Okay, first, I found the report from Bermuda. There are two dead males and two dead females found in the engine room."

"Any IDs yet?"

"No, whoever killed them, started a fire. The bodies were unrecognizable. They'll be doing dental records for ID and that takes time," Anton said.

"Great, I'll have to tell McAllen that his friends might be dead, but we're not sure. Always a comforting message," Bernadette said. She rubbed her left temple. The thought of passing this message along was giving her a headache.

"Sorry, that's all I got for now. But there's something you need to know that's much worse."

Bernadette chuckled. "Great, I always love to know what's worse than the situation we're presently in."

"The FBI has declared Carla Winston a rogue agent. This Adam Morgan has been lighting up the phone channels here in Canada trying to have you listed as a rogue as well. You know what that means."

"Yep, other than bad for our pension plan, it means we are to be approached with extreme caution and apprehended," Bernadette said.

"I wish it was that simple. Morgan wants a shoot on sight order put out."

"What! No one in the FBI or the RCMP would agree to it," Bernadette said.

"Morgan claims he has emails from Winston saying she wants to destroy US targets, and she names you in the emails as her accomplice."

"Wow, Morgan can really make up some good shit. That's kind of a classic, to have us branded as dangerous terrorists. I have to hand it to him, getting the FBI and RCMP as his hit squad is creative."

"There's an alert in Canada that anyone who makes contact with you must report it immediately," Anton said. He looked around him as he said it. He was in a shopping mall using a burner phone.

"I think we must be onto something if Morgan wants us dead, don't you think?" Bernadette asked.

"Yes, I'd say so. Look I have to go. I've been getting some major heat from my boss asking me to give you up."

"Thanks, Anton. I know this is hard to keep getting us information. Anything on the connections of Sokolov?"

"No, nothing yet, I've put some of my best people on it. I'll call you when I get it."

"Great. Look, as we head into the far north, cell coverage can go from sketchy to non-existent. I'll contact you when I can."

"Great, be careful, Bernadette."

"Sure, with all the FBI and the RCMP trying to take us out that should be a breeze."

Bernadette put her phone down and let out a breath, realizing how hard this mission was getting. As she got up to look for Winston she saw two men come in the front door.

They walked in and made hand motions to each other. One wearing a blue suit nodded and headed towards the executive lounge, the other wearing a leather jacket wheeled and headed towards the reservation desk. The way they clutched their jackets, Bernadette could tell they had weapons.

26

BERNADETTE WATCHED the men walk by. They hadn't seen her. She scanned the terminal. Sebastian was still in the corner at the desk on the phone locked in conversations to get another plane. McAllen hadn't returned yet. Would the men open fire the minute they saw Winston, or would they try to take her into custody? Were they FBI or RCMP undercover? Her mind raced. She slowed her breathing to think.

The first man walked to the charter desk. The person behind the desk had walked into the back office. The other man was approaching the executive lounge. Winston had just headed there to get a coffee.

Bernadette jumped out of her chair and headed towards the lounge. She didn't run. Running would make too much noise with her boots. She made it to the lounge at the same time the man in the leather jacket did.

He stood there surveying the room. Winston turned and walked towards him with her coffee. He opened his jacket. He didn't say a word as he drew his weapon. Bernadette hit him from behind with a blow to his ear that knocked him unconscious. He crumpled to the ground, his weapon falling on the rug.

Winston dropped her coffee. "What the fu—"

"Quiet," Bernadette hissed. "There's another one outside."

Winston ran forward, picked up the gun and stood beside Bernadette. "Where is he?"

"In front of the charter desk. You see him?"

"Yes, I see him. What now?"

"We go and take him out." Bernadette said.

"It's over a hundred metres to that desk. The moment we start walking towards him he'll see us and open fire. This guy pulled his weapon the moment he saw me—he didn't ask me to surrender. You want a shoot-out in this building?" Winston asked.

"Okay, we get him to come to us." Bernadette said.

"Good plan. How're we going to do that?"

Bernadette stepped out of the door and yelled to the man at the desk, "Hey, shithead, over here."

The man turned in Bernadette's direction, pulled his gun and ran towards the lounge.

"Nice work. Now what?" Winston asked.

Bernadette ducked back in the lounge and picked up a chair. "He's going to put his head down to look at his partner when he enters. Then, I hit him with the chair, you cover him with the gun."

Winston nodded her head and checked the weapon. It was equipped with a silencer. She hoped she didn't have to fire it.

The man pulled the door open and saw his partner on the floor. He swept his weapon to the right. Bernadette was there with the chair. He fired.

The silenced weapon made a sound of air with the click of the chamber. The bullet ricocheted off a chair leg as Bernadette launched it at him. It hit him in the chest. He dropped his gun and reached down for it.

Winston tackled him, dropping her weight on his body and pushing his head into the floor. Bernadette landed an elbow on his head. The cracking sound of his head told her he was lights out.

Winston fell back off the man breathing heavily. "Well, that went as planned."

Sebastian walked into the room, stared at Bernadette and Winston on the floor with the two unconscious men. "Wow, did I miss a party?"

Bernadette looked up at Sebastian. "You know, your timing is amazing."

"What happened?" Sebastian asked.

"I just heard there were some FBI and RCMP out looking for us. It looks like they found us," Bernadette said. She rolled over and checked the pockets of the man in the leather jacket.

"Any ID?" Winston asked.

"No, he's clean. Check your guy," Bernadette said.

Winston went through his pockets. "Same here. Not a thing."

"These aren't regular card-carrying law enforcement types." Sebastian pulled up the sleeve of the man in the leather jacket. "Yep, a lot of tattoos." He pointed at one. "You see this, that's the Russian Orthodox Cross."

"We just took out two Russian Mafia hit men," Winston said.

"Yeah, sent by Morgan of the FBI. But how did they find us?" Bernadette asked.

"That's the million-dollar question. One of you ladies has got to be wearing a tracking device. And, my money is on you," Sebastian said nodding his head in Winston's direction.

"Me? Why the hell you think it's me?" Winston asked jumping to her feet.

"Because it's a common practice of the FBI for field agents. They put a GPS tracker under their skin so they can track them if they are taken hostage," Sebastian told her.

"Well, I've never been important enough to be implanted with one of those," Winston said.

Bernadette looked at Sebastian and Winston. "Look, we can figure that out once we decide what to do with these two."

Sebastian picked up the handgun with the silencer. "That's easy, I pop a shot into each of their skulls and we leave them here. The cleaners are in the building. They can deal with it."

"Sorry, that's murder," Bernadette said.

"You think these guys were kidding around. They intended to kill you," Sebastian pointed out.

"Shooting an unconscious man is against everything in the law enforcement code. And about sixteen different religions," Bernadette said.

"Okay, how about if I wake one of them up, give them a gun, and you can have an old-fashioned shoot-out?" Sebastian asked. His eyebrows knitted in concentration as he waited for Bernadette's answer.

"No, you know I don't mean that either. We don't shoot criminals we've apprehended," Bernadette said.

"You want to leave them here, so when they wake up they get to have another crack at finding us?" Sebastian asked.

"That's not an option," Bernadette said. "But we do know one thing. Morgan in the FBI sent this hit team."

"How do you figure?" Winston asked.

"I got a call from my guy in CSIS, who said Morgan had put out a search and destroy on us. He told me we'd been labeled terrorists. If we were found dead, it wouldn't matter by whom, it would be condoned by the FBI."

"Very nice, and he sent Russian Mafia to make sure they didn't capture us to tell our story. The dead are silent," Bernadette said.

"Yes, and the living fill in the details," Sebastian added.

Bernadette looked at the two Russian goons; both were starting to moan a bit, the beginnings of rousing to consciousness. She turned to Sebastian. "Give me that silencer." With a puzzled look he handed it over. She grabbed a facecloth from the washroom and wrapped it around the butt of the gun, lifted one of the goons by his hair and whacked him hard at the base of his skull. It was a dull thud; the guy slumped to the floor. She did the same with the other goon. "That should do the trick, they'll be out for a long time."

Winston looked stunned. "What's that all about?"

"An old Chicago mob trick, the 'black jack'. No flesh wounds and no broken skull, but a hefty shock to the brain stem puts you out for several hours, sometimes up to two days."

The door to the lounge opened and McAllen stepped into the room with a large duffel bag. "Wow, what the hell did I miss?"

27

Bernadette looked at McAllen. "You missed a Russian Mafia hit team. We figure they were sent by Adam Morgan, we now know who in the FBI is after us."

"But we still don't know why," McAllen said.

"Hmm, the more we search for Sigurdsson, the more we run into Russians. I think we can see a theme shaping up here," Winston said.

"Are they alive?" McAllen asked.

"Yep, we knocked them out," Bernadette said.

"Check their pockets for car keys," McAllen said.

Bernadette and Winston checked each of the men. "Bingo," Winston said, "this guy rents from Avis."

"Let's haul these guys out of here. We'll take them to their vehicle and figure it out from there," McAllen said.

Bernadette and Winston took one man and McAllen and Sebastian grabbed the other one; they dragged them towards the door.

The door opened. Two cleaners stared at them with their vacuums and mops in hand and a stare of disbelief on their faces.

"*Excusez-moi*," Bernadette said in French, "*Mais amis ont trop bu.*"

The cleaners smiled, rolled their eyes in sympathy and stood aside. "What did you tell the cleaners?" Sebastian asked.

"I told them our friends drank too much," Bernadette said.

"That's not a stretch for Russians," McAllen commented.

They dragged the men outside and into the parking lot where only a few cars remained. McAllen hit the button on the key lock and a van flashed its lights at the far end of the lot.

"Great! These guys had to park far away. What kind of hit men are they? They never read about the getaway part after the hit?" Bernadette asked.

McAllen opened the back doors of the van—they pushed the two men in. Sebastian climbed in after them and began looking around the van. He tore open two backpacks and rummaged through them.

"Whoa, we got a whole bunch of cool spyware in here," Sebastian said. "There's night vision goggles, a GPS finder and oh my..." He looked back at the other three, "We got a whole medicine chest of Lorazepam, Ambien and Restoril. These are the classic sleep drugs. Take a few of these and it's nighty night."

"Anything else?" McAllen asked.

"Some scalpels and pliers to pull your teeth or finger nails out one by one. These guys came prepared, crude stuff but it works," Sebastian said.

"Let's get in the van and out of sight of anyone in the building and decide what we're going to do with these two," Bernadette said.

"So, the killing thing is off the table?" Sebastian asked.

"Yes," Winston and Bernadette said in unison.

"Okay, just asking," Sebastian waved his hand in resignation.

"I think I got an idea," McAllen said. "First, you told me you think Winston is carrying a tracker."

"Yep, that's my take on how they found us," Sebastian said.

McAllen took the GPS from Sebastian and approached Winston. He held up his hand. "Don't be offended, I'll be checking Bernadette as well."

He ran the tracker over Bernadette and got nothing. Turning to Winston the device made loud beeping noises as soon as it was near her. It was loudest over her chest.

"Okay, it is me with the tracker," Winston said, "but I've no idea when they put it in me. I never authorized it."

"Were you put under for any dental work?" Bernadette asked.

"No."

"How about any surgery?"

"Nope, not a thing. I've been totally conscious except when sleeping," Winston said.

"Have you ever woken up one morning, feeling a little groggy and felt you had something bite you in the night, like a small bug bite maybe?" Sebastian asked.

Winston started to scratch under her breast. "Yeah, I felt something like that about two weeks ago. I thought maybe a spider or some kind of mosquito bit me overnight."

"There you go. Someone got into your bedroom at night, put you under with a mild dose of chloroform and injected you under the skin with the tracker," Sebastian said.

"In my own house. Holy shit. I can't believe it."

Sebastian took out the scalpel. "Only one way to find out."

"I don't think so. You are not going to be feeling my breasts for a microchip," Winston said.

"I'm a bit hurt," Sebastian said. "You were somewhat more amiable in the shower yesterday."

"I'll check," Bernadette said quickly.

They went into the front of the van, turned on the overhead lights and Winston lifted her shirt and pulled up her bra. Bernadette felt under her left breast and found a small bump. She squeezed it, then ran the scalpel on the side of the bump. A small piece of glass popped out. She wiped Winston's small wound with an antiseptic wipe and gave her a band aide.

"Okay, we've got it. What are we going to do with it?" Sebastian asked.

"We got any water?" McAllen asked.

Sebastian found two water bottles in the van and handed them to McAllen. He took the water, the tracker from Bernadette and a handful of the sleeping pills and opened the mouth of the man with the leather jacket.

The man choked a little as the pills and tracker went down. His eyes eased open a bit, but it was not certain if he realized what had happened to him; at least his swallowing reflexes worked. He tried to turn his head away.

Sebastian leaned over him with the muzzle of the silencer, pushing it into his mouth. "You will swallow hard my friend, or I will make an extra-large hole in your mouth to make it easier for you. You understand me?"

The Russian nodded and swallowed hard. McAllen forced more water down his mouth. Sebastian black jacked the Russian on the head with the butt of the gun to send him into unconsciousness again. They did the same with the second man.

"Okay, great, we've got two Russian's in la la land, who are going to sleep for at least two days. Now what?" Bernadette asked.

"We need to find a truck stop," McAllen said.

Sebastian took the driver's seat, while Bernadette did a Google search of truck stops nearby. There were several close but none that suited McAllen. He wanted one that serviced big rigs, long distance haulers. The one they found was twenty kilometres away. They drove in silence, the light snow brushing the windshield and the street lamps making pools of light on the darkened asphalt.

A few highway cruisers of the Quebec Police floated by, one even kept pace with their van for a while. The officer looked briefly at Sebastian behind the wheel until he moved on, perhaps to a coffee somewhere warm or to something that looked more suspicious. They crossed a long bridge and came into a large truck stop with a crowd of big rig trucks all softly purring with their diesel engines running, while their drivers were inside eating or taking showers.

McAllen cruised the ranks of trucks until he found what he was looking for. He parked behind it and told Sebastian to get out the Russians' tool bag. The truck they found had a long trailer with an advertisement for a hardware store on it. The license plates were from British Columbia, a mere 3,500 kilometres away. They picked the lock and heaved the men in the back. Sebastian closed the lock again. It looked like it had never been touched.

"I'd say our two Russians are off on a journey," McAllen said as he got back into the van.

"You think that will buy us enough time to find Sigurdsson?" Winston said.

Bernadette turned in the passenger seat. "Yes, but it's time we go on the attack."

"What do you mean?" Winston asked.

"Time we take it to Morgan," Bernadette said. "McAllen, I think you and I should continue north and Winston and Sebastian take a trip to Washington, see some sites, and get that bastard Morgan. Maybe he'll tell you who he's working for."

"I like that," Sebastian said. "I always wanted to meet my Congressman, you know talk about the declining salmon population off Seattle."

"Hey, I'm glad to be going home. Maybe I can check with some of my people and get an update," Winston said.

McAllen turned to her. "Not a chance. You need to stay off the grid. When you and Sebastian get there, you make no contact with anyone. You got that?"

"What the hell. I have people I can trust in the FBI, not all of them are shitheads like Morgan," Winston said.

"Okay, sorry. There's a lot on the line, especially your lives if Morgan finds out your closing in on him." McAllen looked at Sebastian. "Use her contacts, but make sure she follows your lead."

"What the hell is that supposed to mean?" Winston asked.

"I improvise a little more than most people," Sebastian said.

McAllen shook his head. "Sure improvise, but don't be killing Morgan when you do it."

They went silent for a time until they picked out a motel near the airport. They checked in then Sebastian drove the van to a hotel next door and left it there.

Bernadette looked at her watch, it was 4 am, and her flight was at 10 am. A luxury of three hours of sleep, if she could make it happen

—chances are she couldn't. She rolled everything over in her brain. What was Morgan's angle on this? How deeply was he involved with the Russians? None of it made sense. But then most crimes never made sense. They were about money, about greed and about some score someone wanted to settle to feed their egos.

Bernadette had often thought she should have used her brain to pursue a career in science. She'd excelled in high school in math and science. She could have developed something for the brain that would have made it turn towards good instead of stupidity. She closed her eyes tight and let that thought leave her head. Tomorrow's journey came into her head. McAllen hadn't been able to find a private plane. They'd be taking commercial airline.

A First Air flight would fly them straight north to the little town of Iqaluit, and then they would be on small charter flight on a twin engine De Havilland Otter. The little workhorse planes were configured from nine to nineteen seats. Bernadette knew tomorrow's plane would be short on seats and long on cargo space. Airplanes were the only means of transport in the high Arctic. Roads ended on the outskirts of the little towns.

Her main concern was how they were going to get through the airport. Would there be RCMP out looking for them there? Would a facial recognition scanner be activated somewhere that would give off their location?

She turned over and tried to sleep. Thoughts of the two Russians in the back of that truck tugged at her. She'd have to fix that in the morning. Finally, to the sounds of Winston's snores, she drifted off to sleep.

28

Morning came with the shrill sound of Bernadette's phone alarm at 7 am. She needed to be showered and down in the lobby in thirty minutes. Rubbing the sleep from her eyes she headed for the shower. Winston was still sound asleep.

Bernadette looked at the GPS tracker as she was toweling off. It was active. The truck with the Russians must have left soon after they'd dumped them in the back.

All night, visions of the Russians waking up, untying themselves and jumping the unsuspecting truck driver when he opened the cargo door had crept into her dreams. She couldn't let anything happen to the driver. Her mind raced with the possibilities of who to reach out to. Anton was already under watch at CSIS, she dared not get him involved. She needed some local help.

She stared at the GPS tracker. The truck had made its way past Ottawa and was now on Highway 17 heading for Thunder Bay that would connect back to the TransCanada Highway. She almost pounded her head for the answer—then it came to her. She'd gone to RCMP cadet school with Andrea McKinnon. Her Facebook page said she was living in North Bay and attached to the Thunder Bay RCMP Detachment.

Bernadette accessed the Hotel's Wi-Fi on her phone and pulled up the detachment's phone number. She asked for Andrea, telling reception it was urgent and personal.

Andrea answered the phone.

"Andrea, it's me, Bernadette Callahan."

"Holy crap, Bernie, I just read an arrest warrant for you on the BOLO this morning. What the hell are you up to, girl?" Andrea asked.

"Really complicated. First, the warrant is bogus, you know that, right?"

"Okay, good to hear it coming from you. Do you want to come in? I can make sure you're taken in safely."

"Hell, no." Bernadette realized she'd raised her voice causing Winston to stir under the covers. "This warrant is to throw us off the track. Look, I can't give you all the details, but I'm on the hunt for someone who can turn the world's temperature down."

"Whoa, Bernie, you always did get the big stuff. Here I am in Thunder Bay looking after traffic accidents and domestic disputes. Obviously, you're reaching out to me for help. What's up?"

Bernadette let out a sigh of relief at Andrea's tone. "Okay, there's a transport truck coming your way. It's a Pro-Hardware Truck with BC license plates Delta Echo Foxtrot One, Seven, Niner, you got that?"

"Yep, I got it. What am I supposed to do with it?"

"There are two individuals in the back. They're kind of drugged and tied up—you need to take them out of the truck, let the driver go as he knows nothing about them being there and hold the two individuals," Bernadette said.

"Did you happen to put these individuals in the truck?"

"That's affirmative."

"And, what am I supposed to do with these two? Am I to charge them with anything?"

"Attempted murder, but I can't be there to testify—not yet anyway."

"And when would you be able to testify?"

"Might be a few days, maybe a week."

"You know I can't hold them—with that whole Canadian Legal System and all…"

"Can you put them somewhere?"

"Ah, where would you want me to put them? The moment I take them into custody I have to write a report. They have to go through processing. My god Bernie, you passed your exams as an RCMP officer. You know that."

"Here's the deal. It's life or death, my death if those two are let free. I need some time. And I need those two held. You get me?"

Andrea paused for a moment. She could hear the tension rising in Bernadette's voice. "Yeah, I get you…"

"They need to be out of the system, can you do that?"

Andrea nodded her head as she listened to Bernadette. "Yeah, I got a place for them. This is so illegal, and against everything I stand for. You sure you're going to save the world, Bernie?"

"Yep, stop the forest fires, lower the oceans and drop the temperature by four degrees—How's that?" Bernadette asked.

"Okay, works for me. I have to get my partner, Constable Roy Danchuck involved to make it work, but I don't' think it's a problem. He's so off the grid himself, he'll love this."

"Thanks, Andrea, oh and one more thing."

"Really?"

"Ah, yeah the guy wearing the leather jacket, we made him swallow a GPS tracker. You need him to throw it up. Leave it by the side of the road or drop it off somewhere. It's how those bastards found us in the first place." Bernadette said.

Andrea shook her head. "Yes, Bernie, you were always a treasure, even in cadet school. Can I text you on this number when we've made the collar and put your goons on ice?"

"That'd be great. Thanks so much for this, Andrea. You don't know how much this means to me." Bernadette put down her phone and headed for the lobby.

Andrea put her phone back in her pocket. Constable Danchuck was coming out of the coffee shop. "Roy, we're about to do something to help save the planet, but it's totally illegal and will put our jobs in jeopardy."

"Do I have to write a long report later?" Danchuck said.

"I'll write the report," Andrea promised.

"Okay, I'm in. I was hoping to get out of traffic duty today."

Andrea turned to Danchuck as they got into their police cruiser. "Do you know how to make someone throw up?"

"Eat my mother in laws cooking. A sure bet every time." Danchuck said with a grin.

29

BERNADETTE MET McAllen in the lobby. He had two small blue duffle bags by his side. He handed one to Bernadette.

"Here's your Arctic kit." McAllen said. "I hope it's your size."

Bernadette pulled a short down jacket out of the duffle. There was a larger full length one stuffed inside that had been bought for Winston. She wouldn't need it where she was going. There was a pair of boots with felt lining and a pair of down gloves and scarf. At the bottom was an Aviator hat, in shearling wool with flaps. She smiled when she saw it, pulling it out and putting it on her head.

"Oh my, I'll be styling in the Arctic in this."

"Yes, you will," McAllen said handing her a pair of dark sunglasses. "We'll need these to get us through the airport cameras. I'm just a bit worried about some facial recognition scanner sending our image to FBI Headquarters in Langley."

"I'm more worried that Morgan sees it before Langley does." Bernadette said pulling on the jacket and adjusting the hat on her head. "But with this hat and these glasses, I hardly recognize me."

The airport shuttle arrived outside. They climbed inside and sat in silence as the shuttle hit the freeway on the way to the airport. The van's heater blasted overhead and made Bernadette sweat in her new wool hat.

Outside the weather was a mix of rain, snow and sleet—the eastern Canadian message that winter would soon be arriving. Here, the weather was oscillating from sweltering hot one day, then an Arctic cold front dropping in the next.

The people of Montreal took all of this in their stride, so far. Bernadette once spent a summer here. She'd felt like she was going to die in the heat and humidity that summer. The French had shrugged it off, went to the outlying lakes, then partied into the night on the weekends with a meal of poutine, French fries smothered in gravy and melted cheese curds to ward off a hangover the next day. Bernadette had tried that—it didn't help.

The van bumped and groaned over the uneven roadway. The ones that the politicians were supposed to fix with Montreal's tax money, but somehow had ended up in graft payments to numerous contractors and heads of Quebec Mafia. The Russian Mafia could learn a thing or two about doing business in Montreal. Here, the money exchanged hands and few people died. It was far more civilized.

Finally, the shuttle van dropped them in front of the First Air departure gate. They took out their duffels, and McAllen tipped the driver a twenty-dollar bill. The driver, an East Indian with an Orange Turban and long beard clasped his hands together and said, *"Merci Beaucoup,"* in French mixed with a Hindi accent.

"You're a generous man," Bernadette said.

"It's the smallest I had," McAllen said. "But, if we're not successful in cooling the planet, that twenty bucks won't help him much."

They punched through the double doors and into the line with the rest of the passengers. Bernadette sized up the people in line. Northerners. You could tell them from their dress, their looks, and their quiet demeanor.

The dress of the High Arctic is never fancy, no fashion show. It's jeans mostly, sweaters and sweatshirts. Maybe they wore one from a favorite southern hockey team, or the cherished University of the

North, TUK U, the University of Tuktoyaktuk. That's a running joke with the northerners. There is no such university; they just like wearing TUK U.

The look of northerners is one of determination. The barren lands as some people call them are not for everyone. You either fall in love with it, or you're running screaming from it the moment you can. The quiet way of the northerners was mostly from the Indigenous people. They were Inuit; once named Eskimo, which was a derogatory term given to them by the Indians in the south. Eskimo, means "eater of raw flesh". The name Inuit means, "the people".

Bernadette had seen a rig worker in the north once call an Inuit an Eskimo. That young Inuit man had landed a punch so squarely on that man's face that he was lights out before he hit the floor. They shuffled forward in line. There was quiet conversation amongst the line, most of it unrecognizable to Bernadette.

McAllen stood beside her. "You understand this Northern Native tongue?"

"Nope, not a word of it." She adjusted her hat. "I don't really speak much of my native Cree either, I understand some, but this is Inuktitut."

"So, I take the Cree and Inuit didn't get along if they never figured out each other's language," McAllen said.

"Ah, good point." Bernadette lowered her voice and moved closer to McAllen, "My people, the Cree and the Inuit fought for over one hundred years. I remember learning in school that they made peace in 1770." She turned to McAllen, I was told that the Inuit name for the Cree was 'Adla,' which means enemy."

"Wow, that's harsh," McAllen said.

"Yeah, you'd think with the high Arctic being so sparsely populated we could have gotten along."

"What'd you fight over?"

"Probably fish and seals."

"Wow, imagine if you'd fought over oil and minerals. That fight would have lasted a lot longer than one hundred years," McAllen said with a slight grin.

They checked in and went through security. The security guards were looking for illegal drugs and didn't scan their identities.

Once they got into the waiting room, Bernadette opened her duffel bag. "You know, we don't need these extra parkas we bought for Winston and Sebastian."

"Well, I didn't want to leave it in the hotel room, might have seemed suspicious," McAllen replied.

"Here, give me the one you had for Sebastian." Bernadette said.

She took the two parkas and the extra gear and went to an elderly Inuit couple. After a muted conversation and many smiles, she left the gear with them.

"That was smooth," McAllen said. "What did you say to them?"

"I told them I was half Cree, and I'd heard a story that the Inuit had given a Cree hunting party a seal skin rope to make peace. I wanted to make a gift to them from my people of western Canada."

"Very nice," McAllen said. "I hope they enjoy those one-thousand-dollar goose down parkas."

"Up in the north, it's not the price of things, it's the meaning of a gift and the giver. And, you never know what will come in return," Bernadette pointed out.

30

Constable McKinnon and Danchuck spotted the transport truck just outside of Deep River. They put their siren on and pulled it over. Both constables approached the driver and asked him to get out of his cab. They told him they needed to check his cargo.

The truck driver got down from his big rig. He was a young guy, big chested with large biceps. He looked like he's most of his free time in the gym. He wore a skintight muscle shirt that had McKinnon trying to find her focus.

He adjusted his baseball cap as he walked with them to the back of the truck. "What's up officers?" His sauntering walk showed attitude, and defiance.

"We had a report that you may have two people stowed away in the back of your truck. We just have to check, sorry for the inconvenience, sir," McKinnon said in her calmest voice possible.

In all traffic stops, she always stayed calm and even. Drivers could escalate things in a hurry. This one looked like a candidate for that.

"Not, f 'ing possible. This truck has a padlock on it, and I got the only key. I checked the back doors before I left Montreal and it hadn't been tampered with. You got the wrong truck," the driver said.

"Well, sorry to inform you, but we have information that two men were seen getting into this truck at your last stop in Montreal. We need you to open the back," McKinnon told him.

"I got to call my company before I open the back," the driver said.

McKinnon raised her hand. "Well, you can do that. Then we'll have to file a report that you aided some fugitives if I find someone there. Do you want that?"

"Whoa, what the hell! I ain't done nothing. I didn't let anyone in the back of my truck."

"Didn't say you did. Someone is using you to transport these people. Now, you can open the back, or this constable and I take you into custody and have your rig towed into our compound. You decide."

The driver seemed to deflate. His big biceps seemed to grow smaller with his shrinking options. He went back to his cab, pulled out his keys, jumped on the back to open the back doors.

McKinnon and Danchuck drew their side arms, just in case the two men were fully awake.

"This is bullshit, you ain't gonna find nobody—holy shit—"

McKinnon and Danchuck smiled as they viewed the sleeping bodies of two men on the floor of the truck.

"Look. I didn't let these guys in here. You gotta believe me. If the company finds out, I lose my job." The driver became flustered.

McKinnon holstered her weapon. "Not a problem. We'll take these two into custody, you get on your way—this never happened, okay?"

"Sure, sure thing officer, look you RCMP, you're the best...I'm so impressed by your dedication and all—"

"Thanks for your comments, now please, on your way."

"You got it, I'm out of here."

They'd placed the two men on the side of the highway in the culvert. Danchuck pulled out a bottle of Ipecac syrup and mixed it with some water.

"It says here to put in a larger dose for immediate results."

"Well, more is always better, don't you think?" McKinnon asked.

"Sure thing," Danchuck said as he placed the bottle near the lips of the man in the leather jacket.

The effect was immediate, the man gagged and then with the help of Danchuck he bent over retching on the side of the road.

Danchuck peered on the ground at the contents of the man's stomach. "What are we looking for? I see this guy likes sausages... eweh, that's gross."

"Callahan said it was a tracking bug. Might be shiny—I think I see it. I need my gloves," McKinnon said.

Danchuck followed her to the police cruiser, then stopped and turned to watch the two men. "We might need those tweezers I got in the trunk, the ones I use to sort through evidence."

"You mean the ones you use to check suspects for drugs?" McKinnon asked.

"You think I'm going to stick my hand in some suspect's pockets and get poked with a needle full of Fentanyl? Hell no, I'll use those tweezers every time," Danchuck said.

Cawing sounds made them look up. A flock of crows landed near the culvert.

"Ah shit, you think they got the tracker?" McKinnon asked knowing what the answer was.

"Oh yeah, they probably saw that shiny tracker glisten in the sun," Danchuck said.

They ran back to the culvert as the crows took off in a flurry of black. "Yep, they got the sausage and the tracker. Did we need that for evidence?" Danchuck asked.

McKinnon shrugged. "I don't think so. Callahan said to drop it off somewhere. I guess it's now on a path to somewhere."

"Straight as the crow flies," Danchuck said dryly.

"Okay, let's get these two in the back of the squad car."

"Where are we taking them?"

"My friends cabin up in the woods. I figure we keep these two drugged up with some of these pills I found in their pockets."

"What if something happens to your friend, detective Bernadette Callahan?"

"You know it's her we're looking out for?"

"You said her name twice."

"Oh, I guess I did. Well, if something happens to her, then we're screwed." McKinnon said as she sent a text to Bernadette.

31

FBI AGENT ADAM MORGAN watched his monitor with curiosity. The tracker they'd placed on Agent Winston had done strange things in the past few hours. Now it was bizarre. The hit men Sokolov had sent to the private charter terminal hadn't reported in, but the tracker showed that Agent Winston must have been put into their van. The tracker was moving through a desolate part of Canada. Where were they taking her? The tracker stopped for a moment, then it seemed like it had become airborne and travelled off the road over the forest. How could this be possible, he asked himself?

Morgan wanted to call Sokolov to get some answers. He picked up his phone then put it down again. Every time he'd talked to the Russian he felt like he was the one in the wrong. He sweated when they talked. His fist tightened around the phone, his throat constricting. What had he gotten himself into? Was it worth the money and the position of power he'd have once the Russians controlled the government?

Morgan turned off his computer and left the office. He'd done enough for the day. He put a few files in his briefcase to make it look like he was taking work home and smiled at several agents as he left the building and headed for his car.

He decided he'd go to his health club for a swim, then a sauna and a massage. Tension was growing in his neck, begging to have the masseur, Vincent take it out with his large hands. Afterwards he'd order food from his favorite Italian restaurant that he'd pair with one of the fine wines in his well-stocked wine fridge. He put his BMW 5 Series sedan in drive and headed for the club. When everything had settled, and he was the director, he'd be driving a much more expensive car, maybe a Maserati or an Aston Martin. He smiled at the thought and pulled into traffic. He didn't see the white van pull out from the curb to follow him.

Sebastian rode in the back seat of the van, with Winston sitting beside Agent Luis Valdes, the only FBI Agent she could trust.

"Don't lose him," Winston said.

"I've got a tracker on his car," Valdes said. "I attached it this morning in the parking garage after you called me."

"Good thinking," Winston said.

"Whoa, an atta boy from you. Those cool clothes you're wearing must have changed your disposition," Valdes said.

Winston rolled her eyes. Sebastian had told her the only way they'd get through the recognition scanners at Dulles airport in Washington was if they drastically changed their appearance. Sebastian had picked out some clothes in Montreal that made him look like a rock-and-roll promoter.

He was dressed in tight jeans, a black t-shirt leather vest with silver studs. His hat was a black leather baseball cap worn backwards. He'd added the right amount of chains around his neck to finish off the look.

He'd convinced Winston she needed to look like Mary J. Blige. She'd worn a blonde wig, large hoop earrings, oversize glasses and a black push up bustier, with shiny black tights and a white denim jacket.

Valdes had picked them up at the airport and almost lost it the moment he saw her. It was only by Winston threatening to shoot him if she got her hands on a gun that he calmed down.

They followed the BMW down Pennsylvania Avenue. The car

took a left past the White House on 15th street and another left on H Street. It was when Morgan took a right on 16th street that Valdes knew where they were heading.

"He's going to The University Club."

"I didn't know he was a member. Isn't the Club invitation only and costs a small fortune to be a member?" Winston asked.

"Uh huh, you got that right. You wonder how he's driving a fifty-thousand-dollar BMW and going to an exclusive club." Valdes looked sideways at Winston and suppressed a grin. He still couldn't get over not seeing her in FBI blue jacket and slacks.

"I think this confirms his connection to the Russian Mafia. Now, all we need to do is pick him up, have no one see us do it and convince him to talk," Sebastian said.

"That's going to be difficult. I know it's getting dark, but finding somewhere to grab him between his club and his home will be tough. It's too well-lit and populated," Valdes said.

"You know where he lives?" Sebastian asked.

"I sure do,' Valdes said. "He has a Brownstone over in Arlington, just across the bridge from here."

"You have any B&E tools in this van?" Sebastian said.

Valdes smiled. "Hey, you're with the FBI, we don't call it break and enter, it's more enter and reconnaissance."

"Whatever you call it, let's get over there. We have work to do." Sebastian said.

MORGAN FELT wonderful after his swim, sauna and relaxing massage. The club was a great place to unwind. He'd let his mind wander over the things he was going to do in the new order of America—it felt good.

He had a list of people in the FBI he wanted thrown in jail. He knew that in many cases the Russians would ensure they weren't in jail long. Many would die soon after they got there or on the way. That didn't matter to him. He thought of adding his ex-wife to the list. Would men have to pay alimony from a divorce in the new order? He wasn't sure, but if alimony was kept in force, he'd ask Sokolov to take care of her, and her mother. Actually he'd like to watch that when they brought them in. He smiled at the thought.

He pulled his BMW into the driveway of his brownstone and hit the garage door opener. He parked the car and shut it off. He left his briefcase in the car. He wouldn't be doing any work tonight. The work was being done for him. The security system made a comforting beep as it went from red to green.

He walked into his hallway. A gun was thrust into his back. Four hands grabbed him, took his gun and threw him to the floor.

He yelled, "Look, if you want money, my wallet is in my inside suit pocket. Please take it and go. Just leave me alone."

A hand grabbed his hair and pulled his face to the side. Agent Winston smiled down at him.

"You looking for me, Morgan? Here I am."

32

BERNADETTE SMELLED SMOKE. She awoke in her airplane seat and looked around. No one in the cabin seemed to be in a panic. They read books and watched their electronic devices.

McAllen stirred in the seat beside her. "You get some sleep?"

"Yeah, but I smell smoke. Has the captain said anything?"

"He sure did. Half of Northern Canada's forest is on fire. The crews can't do anything with it. The smoke you smell is from those fires. He said there's some half million acres burning right now."

Bernadette took a water bottle out of the seat pocket and took a long drink. "I guess the only good thing about where we're going is there are no forests."

"I've never been there," McAllen said. He pulled an airplane magazine out the seat pocket and turned to the information piece on Nunavut. "Says here this territory is two million square kilometres. And look here, you could drop both Texas and England in there and lose them both. How about that?"

"Yeah, and the place has about 35,000 people. There are more seals than people up there," Bernadette told him.

"You know, if we don't stop whoever is trying to mess with the planet, I think a lot of people are going to have to develop a taste for seal meat."

"You think the Earth's population is going to move towards the north and south poles?" Bernadette asked.

McAllen paused for a second. "It seems to me, that if we've heated the planet to a temperature that's no longer livable, then the only recourse is the movement of populations."

"It's happened many times before," McAllen continued. "One of the strangest was the settlement of Greenland and Iceland by the Vikings. The historians and climatologists claim they settled there because of a four hundred year warming period that was widespread in Europe. It must have extended to the North Pole as well."

"Wasn't there a little ice age that made the Vikings leave?" Bernadette asked.

"That's the accepted story. Around 1360 to 1460 AD the weather changed. There's archeological evidence of the Vikings eating their seed grain and even teeth marks on human bones which means extreme starvation as the weather turned colder and they couldn't tend their animals."

Bernadette said with the hint of a smile, "And all that time the Inuit were out hunting seals on the ever-forming ice and living large."

"That's pretty much the size of it. The Vikings that were strong enough, got into boats and fought the sea ice to get back to Denmark, and the Inuit thrived in the cold temperature."

"So, perhaps we're about to see a reverse. People from the south fleeing north to get away from the fires, drought and starvation," Bernadette said.

"You're right, this could be one of the greatest reversals of global population in Earth's history."

They sat in silence for a while, taking in the conversation they'd just had. A short time later the pilot announced they'd be landing.

The airport was a small two-story building in bright yellow with one gate for arrivals of large jets. The smaller planes picked up passengers and cargo from the tarmac. Bernadette and McAllen followed the passengers into the terminal. The signs were in English and Inuktitut. The latter looked like a combination of Hebrew and Arabic with no known letters that Bernadette could make out in English.

A young man with a broad face and smile approached them as they entered the terminal. "Are you Van Horne?" he asked McAllen. "I'm Danny, your pilot to Ellesmere. You want a tour of the town first, or are you good to go?"

"No, we're ready to go now," McAllen said. "How'd you know it was us?"

"You both look pretty white. And Van Horne wasn't any native name I'd ever heard," Danny said.

They picked up their bags and followed Danny outside the terminal and back onto the airport tarmac. They walked 700 metres to a hanger with several small planes in front.

"This is our plane," Danny said, pointing to a twin-engine Otter with large tires. "This thing can handle the short runway in Grise Fiord."

McAllen coughed slightly. "Ah Danny, we've had slight change of plans, can you drop us off at Eureka? We want to visit the PEARL station there. That okay with you?"

Danny shrugged and smiled. "Sure thing. They aren't far by air. A hell of a long hike overland with no roads, so no problem, I can drop you there."

"You don't need to file another flight plan do you?" McAllen asked.

"Hell no, we drop in on Eureka all the time, I tell them I'm coming when I'm on my way there," Danny said.

When Danny walked away, Bernadette turned to McAllen. "Why did you do that? Book our flight to Grise Fiord and change it with the pilot?"

"I thought if he filed a flight report to Eureka which is a research and weather base, the information would go to your Canadian Security and Intelligence people. I'm just trying to keep our tracks covered," McAllen explained.

They climbed aboard the aircraft, which was surprisingly

spacious inside. It had nine seats for passengers and the rest was loaded with cargo for Ellesmere Island.

As Danny fired up the engines and put on the seat belt sign, Bernadette realized they were the only passengers. The little plane roared with its big engine. It taxied onto the runway and with a powerful surge of its engines became airborne in what seemed a matter of seconds. It seemed to literally jump into the air.

Danny smiled from the cockpit. "Hell of a takeoff, eh? These babies can take off and land on almost any runway. These are the workhorses of the High Arctic. There's next to no roads up here in summer and the winter roads are by snowmobile and ATV's, so we're in use all year round."

The little town of Iqaluit grew smaller as they rose into the air. The snow-covered mountains were bathed in the setting Arctic sun. Bernadette checked the sunset time of where they were going. There was none. They would be travelling into Arctic night. There would be no sun again on Ellesmere Island until January 23rd. Almost four months of total darkness.

"Hey, I forgot to ask," Danny said from the cockpit. "You meeting someone in Eureka?"

"Well no, this is kind of a surprise visit. We're both with Environment Canada. We're a surprise drop in to see how the research station is being kept up," McAllen said as he leaned forward to answer Danny.

"Not a problem. I'll call ahead about an hour out. There are only a few people there now. When the Government pulled the funding on PEARL, I was picking up people for the homeward journey. Man, there was a bunch of pissed off scientists." Danny got on the radio and gave his position to Iqaluit tower.

"Is the station still manned?" McAllen asked.

"Yeah, they got like two or three guys there keeping the lights on and all that expensive equipment from freezing. The rest of the people work at the weather station that's fifteen klicks away, I'll give them a heads about your arrival and they'll take you by truck or ATV to the research station."

"That's great," Bernadette said.

"Don't worry, they got lots of places you can sleep tonight. The place is mostly empty," Danny said.

McAllen and Bernadette sat back in their seats and watched the rugged landscape of the Arctic flow beneath them. There were mountains covered in snow, and an expanse of sea. None of the sea was full of ice. Both of them knew it should be at this time of year.

The ice should be forming; seals, polar bears and walrus would be making their homes on it. But it wasn't happening. Global warming was hitting here and changing the way the people interacted with the land.

Bernadette fell asleep in her seat and woke an hour later to hear Danny on the radio. He was repeatedly calling Eureka. There was no answer.

"They might be out doing some outside stuff. I'll call later. But don't worry, when they hear my plane come in, there's always at least three or four of them show up at the landing strip," Danny said.

Bernadette looked at her watch. It was 3 pm. They were supposed to land in an hour. She got out of her seat to stretch her legs. There was a perfect view of the horizon through the cockpit window. They were flying into total darkness.

33

ADAM MORGAN OPENED HIS EYES. He was tied to a chair in the basement, his feet, hands and body bound with a rope. He hated the basement. He hadn't been down there since his wife left him. All of her things were there. He realized the rope he was tied with, was hers. The rope was supposed to secure a kayak to her car. She'd left it there telling him, *"I hope you hang yourself with it."* He struggled against the rope as he heard footsteps descending the stairs. The little guy in the rock n' roll outfit appeared in front of him holding a large bundle in a kitchen towel.

"My companions are upstairs hard at work on your computer. You have a lot of password-protected files. You want to save us some trouble and give those to me?" Sebastian asked.

"Go screw yourself," Morgan said. He wanted to spit at Sebastian but that was extremely bad form.

"I was hoping you'd say that."

Sebastian moved another chair closer to Morgan and placed the bundle on it. "Now, before I start, do you have any allergies? Like gluten, peanuts or lactose?"

"No, why do you ask?"

"I'm just screwing with you." Sebastian chuckled as he opened the kitchen towel. He laid out an assortment of kitchen knives and a large kitchen shear with care.

Morgan's eyes grew wide. "What do you think you're going to do with those?"

"Oh, these knives? They are nice, aren't they? You have excellent taste. I love your Japanese Santuko Knife. Excellent craftsmen, the Japanese." Sebastian admired the blade as it gleamed in the light. He ran his thumb across the blade to test its sharpness.

"Tsk, tsk, Mr. Morgan, this hasn't had a proper honing in a while. I mean, it will cut but it's going to leave a ragged edge," Sebastian said with reproachful eyes.

"You can't do anything to me that the Russians won't do worse. Don't you know that?" Morgan said.

"Now, that's a good start. Admitting that you've been working with the Russians. You want to tell us your boss's name?"

"No, he'd kill my entire family."

"We know a few things about you. You're divorced and you never see your mother. You're not making much of a case, Morgan."

"They'd kill me. Is that what you want to know?"

"Okay, fair enough." Sebastian took the kitchen shears and tested them on a Bic Pen. The pen was cut clean in two. He laid the pen on the towel and let it bleed out its blue ink.

"My agents won't let you do anything to me. This is just a ruse to get me to talk. Besides, if you try anything I'll scream my head off and have the neighbours calling the cops," Morgan said. He looked at Sebastian, trying to see if this had any effect.

Sebastian walked over to a workbench in the corner and found a roll of duct tape. He pulled off a long piece, cut it cleanly with the Japanese knife and stood over Morgan.

"Let me tell you something, Morgan. Your people upstairs don't give a shit about you. If I torture you to death, they're fine with it. We need the information to get into your computer. I will gag you with this duct tape and start taking off your fingers. Then I might take off some toes. Sure you'll pass out, but I've got the chemical know-how to bring you back to consciousness."

"What kind of monster are you? You couldn't possibly do such a thing to another human being."

"You wouldn't think that would you? I was trained by the United States Government to interrogate Vietnamese prisoners. I was told American lives were on the line—to use whatever means possible to get information. I'm about to do the same to you. Because the stakes are the same."

Sebastian walked slowly forward with the duct tape. Morgan shrank away. Before Sebastian could place the tape over his mouth he screamed, "Okay damn it. I'll talk."

"Wonderful. Let me get a pen and I'll write the passwords down."

"You don't need that. They're all the same."

"Okay, what is it?"

"The password is mywifesabitch, all lower case." Morgan sighed.

"You really do harbor some major resentment. But, I get it, I had three wives and some of them could be a bit testy." Sebastian turned and headed for the stairs.

"None of this will do you any good," Morgan said.

"And why is that? We'll have all of your contacts in your network and we can prove what you've been up to."

"You may have my contacts, but there is nowhere in there detailing what they're up to. Sure I have an idea they're screwing with the Earth's core temperature, but I don't know the whereabouts of the project," Morgan said cocking his head to one side.

"Really? Well, how about if we check your files and get back to you when we need some clarification?"

"Suit yourself, but you won't find anything more than a bunch of emails and files concerning my dealings with some disreputable Congressman and some shady business people. Most of my files are from ongoing FBI investigations."

"And, where will we find the files on you and Sokolov and your Russian friends?" Sebastian asked.

"They were hired help. My operatives in the FBI were busy at the time. I needed to contract out," Morgan said with the slightest of smiles.

"Don't you mean you needed contract killers and the FBI wasn't up for it?"

Morgan shrugged in his ropes. He looked away.

Sebastian went upstairs to the den that Morgan used as an office. Valdes and Winston were there, searching his paper documents. He gave Winston the password Morgan had given him.

Winston raised an eyebrow. "Hmm, I'm sure a lot of women could use this password as well. No wonder hackers have such an easy time."

Valdes got busy with opening the computer and reviewing files. "I see mostly FBI stuff here. He's careful about putting things in here that could incriminate him if he's caught."

"Can you access some of his hidden files?" Sebastian asked.

"Yeah," Valdes said. He went to the file menu and typed a command, *chflags nohidden/path/to file-or-folder*. A set of files appeared.

"What's this *Climate Killers* document all about?" Winston asked.

Valdes started to read it out loud. "The plan to take over the United States Government by manifesting a Climate Catastrophe. It has names of everyone in the USA that is involved." He read down the page. "This is a step by step diagram of how the Russians would increase the temperature in the Ocean and cause major drought and killing heat to the US heartland. They drop in a little tidbit about a forecast for forest fires that would be devastating."

"Isn't that nice of them to give a full narrative on what they plan to do to us?" Winston said. "Does that document say if they plan to attack us?"

"No, nothing like that. But on this third page it talks about how they would infiltrate the USA in relief planes," Valdes said.

"Clever bastards," Sebastian said. "The old Trojan Horse scenario. They send in help with their transports loaded with Russian soldiers. We should have thought of that in some of our wars. Might have saved us some casualties."

Winston looked up from the computer. "How do we get this out to the US government? Whom do we send this to?"

"If you send this to the government, they'd call it fiction. They're so busy right now battling forest fires and trying to shore up the coastline that is flooding cities, they'd laugh us out of the room. Then they'd throw us all in jail for taking Morgan captive," Valdes said.

"But he's the one that was trying to kill us." Winston put her hand on her neck and massaged a knot of tension that was building itself towards a headache.

"He could say there was a leak in the FBI, and the Russians were trying to get to Sigurdsson before we did," Sebastian said. He placed his hands on Winston's shoulders and gave her a deep massage. She almost groaned with pleasure.

"I think we need to work on our guy in the basement. Morgan knows a hell of lot more than he's letting on. This is going to be my pleasure for the evening," Sebastian said.

He left the room and headed for the basement. On the way down the stairs he heard the garage door open. A car engine started. Tires squealed. He ran down the basement steps. Morgan was gone.

Morgan hit the accelerator. The BMW's tires burned rubber, making a loud screeching sound as he made his escape.

He chuckled once he made it onto the freeway. They'd never catch him now. The moment Sebastian had gone upstairs, Morgan bounced in his chair until he got to the knives that had been left there to torture him. With the Japanese chef's knife, he'd sawed through the ropes on his hands. He'd thought of grabbing a handgun he had in the hallway upstairs and killing them but it was too much of a gamble. If they'd seen him first he'd been a dead man. He was never a good marksman.

He placed a call to Sokolov using his car's voice activated phone.

"You're calling me from your car and not a burner phone. What's the problem?" Sokolov asked when he answered.

A chill went down Morgan's spine. He had to report what had happened. He needed his help.

"I ran into a problem. Those people you were supposed to kill turned up at my house a few hours ago."

"And?"

"They made me give them my computer passwords. I'm blown—don't you get it? They know about what we're up to. I need to get out of America, fast," Morgan said.

He braked hard to avoid rear-ending a slow moving pickup truck in the right lane. He maneuvered around the truck and hit his accelerator, cursing as he drove.

"I don't understand. How can you be alive if they tried to get information out of you? All of my men would have died before they gave away secrets," Sokolov said.

Morgan sputtered, "I escaped, damn it."

Sokolov went silent for a moment.

Morgan waited. He was in the Russian's hands now. His escape was up to him.

Sokolov's voice was slow and deliberate. "Go to the Elite Charters Hanger at Dulles Airport. I'll have a plane take you out of there in an hour. You will meet a person named Katia. Follow her to your plane. She'll take good care of you," Sokolov said.

Morgan blew out a breath of relief. "Thanks. I'll meet you for a drink in Moscow when this is over."

"Yes, we will do that. Safe journey."

Winston and Valdes looked at Sebastian as he told them the news of Morgan's escape. "I guess we're totally screwed," Valdes said.

"You think he's going to run back to the FBI and put a lockdown on the capital to capture us?" Winston said.

"I don't think so," Sebastian said. "I figure he thinks he's been blown. He'll probably run to a safe house or try to escape the country."

"But you told us he said we had nothing on him?" Winston said.

Valdes looked at the computer. "No, there's even more hidden files here. He's put in notes on who'd be in charge of the FBI once the takeover happens and it's none other than Adam Morgan. There's even a guy named Derman who'd be taking over as Secretary of Commerce and an Admiral that would take over the combined Russian and US seventh fleet. Looks more than fiction to me."

"How do we get this out there?" Winston said.

"I'm going to download this to a USB flash drive and make copies. Then I plan to send these little gems to the Washington Post, the New York Times and every major newspaper in the USA," Valdes said.

"It's going to be called fake news by the White House. You know they have a standard response for that kind of thing. They've been saying that this weather catastrophe is a blip in the weather pattern," Sebastian said.

"Well, hopefully the reporters will start to verify and call enough of the people on this list that it will shake them up," Winston suggested.

Valdes made his copies and they left Morgan's home. As they walked out the door there were several children playing in the street. Not an FBI agent to be seen. They breathed a collective sigh of relief and drove away.

MORGAN'S DRIVE to the airport was slow. The traffic was heavy. He kept checking his rearview mirror to see if he was being followed. He pulled into the parking lot. The tension melted away.

He was going to miss his good life in America. But he reasoned it would be for a short time. America would be brought to the brink of disaster and Russia would come to save it. They would just stay, permanently. He smiled as he saw the vision of him returning as the director of the FBI.

He left his lovely BMW with a backward glance of regret and made his way into the building. A young blonde woman in a blue business suit stood up as he entered.

"Mr. Morgan, I am Katia. Please follow me. I've been told to take special care of you."

Morgan relaxed. The lady was pretty, nice features and an athletic sense about her. Sokolov only hired the best.

They walked to a private lounge. Katia opened the door and smiled for him to enter. He walked into the room. There was a plastic sheet on the floor.

Morgan turned. Katia had a gun with a silencer. She shot Morgan twice in the head. Sokolov only hired the best.

34

THE PLANE'S engines changed their pitch as it began its descent. Bernadette could only see darkness. Clouds were covering the moon. Danny was busy at the controls and calling to the Eureka weather station to inform them of his arrival. He got no response.

Bernadette and McAllen grabbed their duffel bags and took out their down jackets. They'd been advised that they needed to wear their outerwear in case of a crash landing. The last thing you wanted to have is severe exposure if the plane landed too short of the runway.

"I'm going to do a quick fly over to make sure there's no equipment on the runway," Danny told them.

He banked the plane and dropped towards the ground. A sliver of moonlight appeared through a broken cloud revealing snow-covered mountains surrounding a fjord with ink black water. They dropped lower. The water looked dangerously close.

Lights of buildings on shore appeared ahead. Bernadette looked at them and saw something else in her side vision. She turned her head to see a black shape in the water. A small blue light shone down on what looked like a platform. It only appeared for a moment then it was gone as the plane flew inland. Danny made a pass of the airfield. It was narrow with reflectors on both sides, some on top of weighted down oil drums to keep them from being blown away in the Arctic winds.

There were several low buildings and a dome-like structure that Bernadette took to be the weather station. Oil drums and a collection of vehicles surrounded the buildings. She could see large orange snow removal equipment and a few trucks in the pools of light from the buildings. There was still no sign of people.

The plane gained altitude and did a go around. Danny hadn't seen any problems with the runway so he told them to "buckle up, we're going in."

The plane came in low again over the ocean and landed on the short runway. Its big wheels bounced softly on the snow and came to a stop short of the buildings. Danny turned the plane around to have it ready for takeoff and turned off the engine. He came out of the cockpit, opened the door and released the stairs. Lights of two vehicles came towards them as he jumped out of the plane.

"I told you'd they'd arrive to pick you up," Danny said with a smile. "That's Arctic hospitality for you."

Bernadette and McAllen climbed down the stairs shielding their eyes from the headlights. One truck stopped directly in front of the plane, turning sideways as if to block it. The other one pulled up beside them. Five men dressed in white military parkas glared at them behind machine guns pointed in their direction.

"Holy shit!" Danny exclaimed. "Who the hell are you guys?"

"Hands up. Hands up," one of the men yelled. He waved his machine gun in the air and pointed it skywards.

They put up their hands.

McAllen whispered, "We got Russians."

"No talk," the Russian yelled.

Three Russians jumped down from the truck. They were joined by four more from the other truck. With shouts and gestures the three of them were forced towards one of the trucks then hoisted into the back. The Russian pounded on the truck cab and yelled a command; the truck started up and headed away from the plane and the buildings. They went from the bright lights of the buildings towards the mountains.

They were huddled together with their backs to the cab. The Russians kneeled and sat on the truck bed with their machine guns trained on them. Bernadette could make out their faces in the moonlight. They were young, clean-shaven and uncomfortable with the guns they were pointing at them. To Bernadette, these didn't look like soldiers; there was something about them but, currently, she couldn't register it.

The moonlight began to fade as they headed inland. It was like closing down the aperture on a camera lens. In slow gradients it faded until they were in darkness. The truck sped up.

SOKOLOV CALLED Volkov and told him about his conversation with Morgan and why he eliminated him.

"Okay, this is not good, but then not so bad," Volkov said.

"But I think this FBI Agent Winston will give whatever information Morgan had in his files to the media.

"Yes, you are right. How close is Derman to getting Congress to ask for Russian assistance?"

"He's close, but many are worried how it will look to the American people. They've always given aid to Russia. They would have to receive it on a mass scale. I think they are worried about their next election."

Volkov laughed. "These Americans know nothing about how to fix an election. If they did, they could run the country the way they wanted and screw the people. Like we do.

"Yes, I know, but if Congress doesn't vote for aid, we cannot bring our planes in. This plan will fall apart."

"Leave it to me. I have something that will make them come screaming for Russia," Volkov said. "We have infiltrated all of their crazy militia groups. There are Nazi's and white supremacist, and these ultra-right groups that are all armed to the teeth. They have weapons that we Mafia would like to have."

"What can you make them do?"

"We've already done it. Our infiltrators have been telling them for months that the time to take over the American Government is coming. I will give the word, and our people will tell all these groups the time is now."

"You think this will work?"

"Of course. We will also flood their Facebook and social media with messages that the people need to rise up and take control. In one week, Congress will be begging for our aid."

Sokolov marveled at how devious Volkov was. Even he couldn't have thought of such a plan.

"Okay, boss, I'll be here in San Francisco waiting to hear from you."

"Good, and how is Sigurdsson's family? Are they keeping well?"

Sokolov turned and looked into the window of the room where they were being held. "Yes, the wife and the granddaughter are well."

"Good keep them alive. Sigurdsson will contact them, then he will come to us, and do whatever we ask."

Sokolov put down his phone. He wandered out to look over San Francisco Bay. The ocean was rising fast. He might need to move them to higher ground.

THE TRUCK CAME TO A STOP. Bernadette, McAllen and Danny were pulled to their feet and shoved towards the back of the truck. One by one they were dropped to the ground and pulled along by the soldiers.

One of the soldiers pushed McAllen, he whirled and muttered, "*Skhodite, ya ustal.*"

The other guards laughed and clapped McAllen on the back and smiled at him.

Bernadette got beside McAllen. "What did you say to them?"

"I told them, go easy I'm old."

"You speak Russian?"

"No, I'd learned that from a Russian hooker in Barcelona," McAllen said.

The soldiers propelled them forward into a large Orange building. The place was the PEARL lab. The walls were covered in maps with an array of computer equipment scattered throughout the room.

The place looked like it had been ransacked. Papers were everywhere, file drawers open and desks overturned. In the middle of the room lay the body of a man face down in a pool of blood.

It looked like a usual crime scene to Bernadette, but in this case she knew the killers. Two men and a woman were crouched against a wall with their hands on their heads. She could see the fear in their eyes.

A soldier pushed them towards the other captives with his hand on the butt of his machine gun. He yelled, "Sit down."

"Great English skills," McAllen said. "They must have learned taking captives 101."

"No talk," another guard yelled.

They slid down the wall beside the others. Bernadette was shoulder to shoulder with a man who looked in his early thirties. A knitted cap was pulled down over his head with wisps of long blond hair poking out. His face wore a mask of terror.

He leaned over to Bernadette and whispered, "We thought you might be our rescue squad."

Bernadette looked at him and raised her eyebrows in a gesture of resignation. She glanced around the room. Two small satchels caught her eye. They looked out of place for a research facility.

She whispered quietly to the man beside her, "Are those explosives in the bags?"

"Afraid so. Looks like C-4, the soldiers put them in here and played with the timers. I don't know if they've been activated."

The soldier with the machine gun came back and stared down at them. He was furious.

Bernadette looked up at him and smiled. "No talk," she said.

The soldier walked back to huddle with his compatriots in the middle of the room. A door from the outside opened and they stood to attention.

A small man with a grey beard walked in. Bernadette could see from the salutes of the soldiers he was their commander. His steely blue eyes took in the captives. He walked towards them, taking wide berth to avoid the body and blood on the floor.

"I am here to find some information on the research of a Doctor Sigurdsson. We know he was working here, but unfortunately he is not here now. You will direct us to this research and we will leave you in peace," the man said.

"Is that what you call this? You're here to find some research? Is that why you killed our colleague?" the man with blond hair said.

The bearded man looked down at the dead man, "Unfortunate. I understand he was trying to communicate with your military. We could not allow that."

"Well, for your information, buddy, my dead friend did get hold of the military. He told the base at Alert that a bunch of Russians arrived in a submarine and attacked our station. The Canadian Forces are on their way to take you out." The blonde man said.

"That is amusing. Thank you for this funny scenario. The base you called at Alert is 400 kilometres away. They have only seventy personnel, half are civilian weathermen the other half are trained as military observers, and there is no fighter aircraft."

He knelt down in front of the captives. "You see, you are in the High Arctic, you are in front of the commander of one of the greatest submarines in the Russian fleet." He smiled and winked at them. "Let me tell you the situation. The Canadians have a few submarine hunters. They are called Auroras. They are stationed over 7000 kilometres south of here on your east coast in Newfoundland. If they took off the minute we arrived they are now maybe 700 kilometres closer.

He stood up and paced the room. "You Canadians have a small air force of CF-18 fighters but they cannot even reach here with their short flight range. You are all alone. I am the only friend you have and I want your cooperation or your lives. Isn't that simple?"

"If we give you what you want, you'll let us go and return to your sub?" McAllen asked.

"Of course. I am reasonable."

"Give us a minute to confer with my friends," McAllen said.

The Russian captain walked away from the captives.

McAllen turned to the others. "Okay, we're searching for the same thing. Professor Sigurdsson's wife told us he had found evidence of a secret river under the ocean. He said he could cool the planet with it. But these guys know it also has a river of magma beneath that could heat the Earth. You guys get my meaning?"

"I'm Doctor Curtis Weppler," the man with the blond hair said. He pointed to the woman and man beside him. "This is Doctors Jane Russey and David Maslam."

"Great," Bernadette said. "What do you know about Sigurdsson's research?"

Doctor Weppler was taken aback by Bernadette's sharp reply. He straightened his hat and looked at the other doctors. "We know quite a lot about it. We helped him find it. Well, let's say so much as we came up with a premise that it might in fact exist."

"Really, Curtis," Doctor Russey said. "How can you even try to take credit for Sigurdsson's research? You told Sigurdsson his idea was daft and that if there was such a river there with a magma flow beneath, every geological survey ever done in the ocean would have known about it."

Weppler's eyes went wide in disbelief, "I never said such a thing—"

"Okay," Bernadette cut in. "Let's just say you two agree to disagree. Now, do either of you know where he may have hidden this file?"

"But, if we give the file to them, they'll kill us anyway," Maslam said.

"You're absolutely right." Bernadette said. "But we need to make like we're looking for it so we can stall them until help arrives."

"The Russian said it was hours away," Weppler pointed out. "You heard how long it's going to be before help arrives."

"The Russian may know his distances but he doesn't know squat about Canada's Northern defenses. Six months ago, they moved the Aurora sub hunter and six F-18s with supporting air tankers for refueling to Rankin Inlet, the former North American Defense system base," Bernadette said.

"Rankin Inlet, that's only 1,500 kilometres from here," Russey said.

"That's right. The Aurora has a max speed of 750 kms an hour and the F-18's can do 1,800 kms an hour. I figure with the big shots in Ottawa having to have a shit fit on taking on a Russian sub, then getting the balls to actually do it, that they scrambled the planes over an hour ago," Bernadette said.

McAllen moved closer. "What we need to do is get ourselves into position to do something the moment these guys hear aircraft overhead."

"But... we're not fighters... we're scientists. I don't even have my pepper spray on me," Maslam said.

"Don't worry about that. You get us standing and walking around and making like we're searching for this file and we'll take care of the rest," Bernadette said.

McAllen looked at the Russian captain. "You got yourself a deal. You let my scientist friends and me have access to the computers and we'll get you the information you seek."

"That is better," the Russian captain said. "Now, one wrong step and my men will be happy to kill you."

"Of course, with that in mind let's get to work," McAllen replied.

McAllen and Bernadette moved into the main computer room with the other scientist and Danny. McAllen shooed the soldiers away, telling the leader they needed to be able to confer in private. The Russians wandered off to the far corner and lit up cigarettes.

Dr. Maslam looked at the soldiers in disgust. "Don't they see the *no smoking* signs?"

"The only smoking you should be worried about is if one of those guys shoots off one of his machine guns. Then you'll have some smoke you don't want," Bernadette said.

McAllen got everyone around the computers and made like he

was pulling up files. He looked at Weppler. "When did these guys arrive?"

"About two hours ago. The guys in the weather station saw the sub surface in the moonlight and their zodiacs come to shore. They went out to meet them. They shot two of them but the other guy escaped and got up here in a truck. He screamed that the Russians had landed in a submarine and got on the radio the Canadian Forces in Alert, the nearest base to us.

"Did he make radio contact with Alert?" Bernadette asked.

"Yeah, the guy in Alert said help was coming. Told us to sit tight," Weppler said.

"Then the Russians shot him?" Bernadette asked.

"Yeah," Weppler said, "they burst into the lab twenty minutes later and saw our guy on the phone. He screamed at them that our military was on its way—waved the phone at them like it would stop them. They shot him right in front of us."

The Russian captain came over. "You have some results yet?"

"No, we're in conference," McAllen said. "Please let us work on this."

"I have a way to help you," the Russian said.

"What's that?" McAllen asked.

"I will shoot one of you every twenty minutes that you delay."

"Thanks, nice pep talk, now, let us get back to our work," McAllen said.

The captain walked back to his men. They got busy crowding around the computers.

"Do you think he'd do that?" Russey asked. Her face was screwed up with the question and the tension.

"He's already shot someone for trying to call our military. I'm certain he's going to shoot one of us if we delay," McAllen told her. "Now, which one of you knows where Sigurdsson left his data?"

Weppler leaned forward into the group. "You don't get it. Sigurdsson never left any notes. He came to us with this story of the underground rivers, saying he knew how to find them."

"You mean there's nothing here?" Bernadette said.

"Not a damn thing. Sigurdsson was here from May to June this year; he came up with his idea then headed off to Stockholm to give a paper on it. We thought he'd be laughed out of the conference," Weppler explained.

"But that didn't stop you from telling us you knew all about this river did it, Weppler?" Bernadette asked.

"Don't mind him, he hasn't had an idea of his own for years, and is always trying to piggy back on other people's research," Russey said.

"If I may interject," Maslam said, "and, if you'll discount the statements of my two colleagues, as the two of them are going through a trial separation and using me and this Arctic lab as their sounding board."

"Really, Maslam, if we're so tiring, perhaps you'll offer yourself up as the first one to be shot in the next twenty minutes," Russey said.

The three scientists eyed each other with a hatred that had developed over a long summer of Arctic isolation.

"This is getting us nowhere," Bernadette said. "We either come up with something to stall them further or have something that looks like information."

"I know what you can do," Danny said.

They turned and looked at Danny. He stood there his hands thrust firmly in his pockets, his smile wide. His eyes gleamed with an answer they hoped would save them all from imminent death.

35

"WHAT IS IT? Bernadette asked.

"The River of Thule. You'll find it on Sigurdsson's file. We used to work on it remotely. Me in Iqaluit and him when he was at this lab or on his travels," Danny said.

"The River of Thule, okay, I'm typing that into the lab's data base." Weppler said. He watched as the file came up. "Oh, my god, this is a freaking video game. Are you trying to get us all killed at once?"

"No, you don't understand. I worked on it with Sigurdsson from our ancient Inuit legends. The Thule was our ancestors. They replaced the Dorset people, and then we took over from them. All of our history is in the spoken words, so Sigurdsson and I figured we'd make a game out of it. He put the river in there as he said he'd found it in legend and knew of its existence in the real world."

"You want me to show this video game to our Russian submarine commander and hope he doesn't put a bullet in my head the moment he sees it?" Weppler asked.

Danny shrugged. "You got anything else?"

"How does it work?" Russey asked.

Danny came forward to the computer and punched in a code to initiate the game.

"You see here, there's an Inuit warrior with spears and arrows. You have him capture seals. Each seal gives him 50 points. Once you get to 500 the arrows and spears turn to gold, then you're in the big time."

"What happens then?" Russey asked. Her face was flushed as she moved closer to the screen.

"Well, that's when all the good stuff happens – you get to meet up with the golden walrus and the shining polar bear. They become your companions to capture the narwhale who will lead you to the sea goddess and the hidden river." Danny was starting the game as he spoke, his hands moving quickly as his Inuit warrior speared seals.

"This is disgusting," Weppler said.

"Really?" Russey asked, turning to Weppler. "You think this is any more violent than World of Warcraft or King's Quest?"

"Ha, I wouldn't know about that. But you probably would," Weppler said, his eyes narrowing in accusation at Russey.

"Yeah, it's what put me to sleep at night and satisfied me, because it certainly was never our sex."

"Okay, okay, we need to take this down a notch." Bernadette looked at Danny. "Does this video game show exactly where this river goes, or was this just a mythical animation put together to amuse both Sigurdsson and you during the long dark winter?"

"No, it's real alright. If you play the game all the way to the end, the river extends underground all the way from here in the Arctic down to Antarctica. I've done the game several times and each time it ends there but it goes under North America and through the Pacific."

McAllen stared over Bernadette's shoulder at the screen. "I think our good scientist placed the map into the video game where he thought no one would ever find it."

"Your time is up," the submarine captain shouted.

They all jumped at the sound of the captain's voice. It shook them out of their concentration on the video game and back into the reality of their situation.

"Can you give us a few more minutes?" Weppler asked in a pleading tone.

"No, you can tell me which one of you wants to die first or I will choose one of you myself."

"I think he's serious about killing one of us," Maslam said.

"No shit, Maslam," Russey said. "You're the best at deductive reasoning. That's why you ran this team. Why don't you offer yourself up as our first candidate?"

"I'll do no such thing. As I am the team leader, it's me who makes the decisions, and, as you Dr. Russey, are the most junior in our group, I suggest that it's you who is shot first."

"Really? That's what you think? And that wouldn't be because you're a misogynist son of a bitch, Maslam?" Russey asked. She crossed her arms and stared him down in an accusing look.

"Holy mother of god. How about if I shoot both of you—just to keep you quiet?" the captain suggested.

"You don't need to shoot anyone," McAllen said. "We've found what you want. You'll need to come and look at this screen."

The captain turned to his men and shouted a command as he approached. "I told my men to shoot all of you if you try to take my gun from me and take me captive." He placed his gun in his holster and walked among them with a swagger.

Bernadette and McAllen exchanged looks. That very thing had been on their mind.

The captain looked down at the screen. "What is this? This is some kind of a cartoon diagram?"

"No, it's the way that the scientist Sigurdsson hid the river inside a game," Bernadette said.

The captain's head turned from side to side. "You expect me to believe this? You think I am stupid? I'll have you all shot."

"See, I told you," Weppler said, wringing his hands.

A droning noise could be heard. Low and growling at first until it grew in strength. It became a vibration. A glass of water on the table started to shake. The captain looked up at the ceiling. His eyes went wide.

"That noise got your attention?" Bernadette asked. She moved closer to the captain. "That's the sound of the Canadian Air force

Aurora sub hunter. The one you said was too far away to get here in time."

A loud whoosh of jets coming in low shook the lab.

"And that would be a couple of those F-18 Fighters you claimed were so ineffective that they couldn't be a threat to you."

The captain screamed at his men in Russian. The men raised their weapons.

One of the men ran towards them. He tore the computer's hard drive from under the desk and ran towards the door. The captain followed him out with the rest of the men.

"It looks like our captors are leaving." Bernadette said.

"Yeah, but not with that hard drive." McAllen ran to the satchels of explosives against the wall. He picked up one and motioned for Bernadette to grab the other one.

"How's your throwing arm?"

"Fast pitch baseball champion," Bernadette said.

McAllen thrust a satchel into her hands. "Follow me."

They ran with the satchels out the door. The Russians were getting into the trucks. McAllen set a two second timer on the explosives and they heaved them at the trucks then took cover inside the building.

The sailors didn't see them in the darkness. One sailor heard a thud and asked a question of the man next to him. A loud roar shredded the sailors and ripped the truck in half.

McAllen and Bernadette peered outside. The flames of the burning gasoline from the trucks tanks lit up the darkness. The smell of bodies and rubber tires wafted towards them, cutting the pure Arctic air like a knife.

The three scientists came up behind them. Maslam screamed. "I can't believe you killed all those men."

McAllen turned on him. "Really, you want to know why I killed those men? They wanted to kill you minutes ago, and if they'd returned to their submarine the captain could have launched missiles to destroy everyone in this facility."

Maslam went quiet as another fuel tank exploded, producing a fireball. They threw up their hands to shield themselves from the blast.

Explosions came from harbor where the submarine was. Several rockets roared into the sky.

"Those are from the submarine," McAllen said. "The Russians are firing rockets at the Canadian Airforce."

"What happens if the Russians win?" Russey asked.

"You mean, if they knock the Canadian fighters and the sub hunter out of the sky?"

"Yes, exactly," Russey said as she watched the fighters and sub hunter do evasive maneuvers and fire off countermeasures. The sky was being lit up with a deadly display of fireworks.

"I'd expect the other Russians would come ashore looking for their captain and his men," McAllen said.

Bernadette turned to Danny. "Can you help us disappear if that happens?"

"Sure," Danny said. "But the nearest settlement is over those mountains and hundreds of kilometres away. We can hide out in the dark for a while, but it's going to be a cold wait."

They watched as one fighter was hit by a missile and exploded. They all went silent knowing the pilot had probably been killed. The other fighter descended in a spiral, shooting two missiles in quick succession before gaining altitude. The submarine hunter dropped torpedoes. The splash sounded like a whale hitting the water. A minute later a loud explosion rocked the valley and the sky lit up.

"I don't think we have to go anywhere," Bernadette said. "I think our Canadians just got themselves a submarine."

The harbor became illuminated as explosives erupted from the submarine. The conning tower was visible for a second, and then it submerged as more explosions convulsed the hull of the submarine.

"Time for us to go," McAllen said.

"Yeah, I agree," Bernadette replied.

"But, what about the hard drive?" Russey asked. "Wasn't that what you came for?"

"We wanted to keep it out of the hands of the Russians,"

Bernadette said. She turned to Danny, "You said that was a game you'd made with Sigurdsson. You must have copies somewhere?"

Danny winked. "Are you kidding? We made it into an app. Kids and adults all over the Arctic play the game. You can download it onto your phone as soon as we get back into cell range."

"There you have it, McAllen," Bernadette said. "We need to get out of here. The military will be sending in a team to check this place out, we'd be detained for questioning when they do."

"Who exactly are you two people?" Russey asked. She moved closer to Bernadette. "I've never seen you at any of our Climate Change Symposiums. What were you doing here at our research station?"

"That's way too many questions. We don't have time for the long or the short versions," Bernadette told her. She turned to Danny. "Can you fly us out of here now?"

"I sure can," Danny said. He turned to the other scientists. "Look, it's better for everyone if you don't tell the military that I flew in here with these two."

"How do we explain how the Russians were killed?" Weppler asked. "They'll think we did it."

McAllen put his hand on Weppler's shoulder. "Tell them the sailors had some explosives in their truck and they went off prematurely."

Russey laughed. "Hey, Weppler, you're an expert in premature events. I'm sure you can sell that one."

Bernadette looked at the three scientists. "We need you to keep our visit a secret, for now. Hopefully we'll find Sigurdsson and make some sense of what's happening in the world right now. Can you help us out?"

"Sure," Maslam said. "Scientists are good at keeping secrets as most of the time we aren't believed anyway."

Bernadette and McAllen followed Danny to a truck that was parked beside the lab. They rode in silence the fifteen kilometres back to their plane. When they got there, the plane was where they'd left it.

There were only flickers of flame coming from the sea below to show where the submarine had been. A small fire burned on one of the mountains where the jet had crashed. As the plane roared into the Arctic night, Bernadette wondered if they'd be able to find an answer to the world's heat, before the world turned to weapons for its answers.

36

Sɪɢᴜʀᴅssᴏɴ ᴡᴀs desperate to hear his wife Samantha's voice. He wanted to tell his wife everything. How the Russians had made him believe they were using his inventions for good, how he'd failed the planet by working with them, and now, how he was going to save the planet by killing himself and taking his knowledge with him. All this went through Sigurdsson's mind as he threw back another shot of Jagermeister with a beer chaser. He was sitting in Humpy's Great Alaskan Ale House on Sixth Avenue in downtown Anchorage Alaska.

He'd been here for the past four hours staring at a payphone in the corner. It looked forlorn and unused. With each shot of Jagermeister that tasted somewhere between cough medicine and an elixir that would produce a powerful force of reasoning in the mind, that was only one more drink away and never arrived, he came to the conclusion he had to call Samantha.

What good would it do to kill himself without giving the reasoning, he thought? He was, a scientist after all. All his actions were documented and as this was to be his last and definitive action, he would need a record, a recording, someone like his wife to explain to the world, that although he had erred in his judgment, he'd made things right again.

He rose up from his chair at the bar and fixed his sight on the pay phone. He calculated it at twenty metres away. He then computed the number of steps it would take to reach the phone with his level of overall drunkenness. The Jagermeister was now having the effect of producing a severe list to his left side or in nautical terms his port side. He muttered *hard to starboard* and righted himself.

He made it to the phone and grappled with the handset as if it was a life ring thrown from a ship. He fumbled around in his pockets and found a handful of quarters, which he began to plug away into the top of the phone.

For a moment he stopped. What number would he dial? He knew of one number in Bermuda where Samantha came ashore off her research ship and the other one was her cell phone that was only in use when on land. He hesitated for a second as the thoughts and the numbers collided and then reappeared in his brain. Then, it dawned on him, he'd dial Samantha's cell phone. It was the only one he knew right to the end.

The phone rang. Sigurdsson closed his eyes as he imagined Samantha picking up the phone. Five more rings. His eyes opened and he looked to the ceiling of the phone booth. Someone had written a profanity on the ceiling. *Fuck you if you're looking up here* it said.

He was about to put the phone down when a voice came on, "Hello."

"Samantha. Is that you?"

"Oh my god, Barney. You shouldn't have called me."

"No, I needed to talk to you one last time," Sigurdsson pleaded into the phone. "Please don't hang up."

"She won't be hanging up," a male voice said.

"Who's this?" Sigurdsson demanded.

"You don't get to ask questions. You get to answer them," Sokolov said. "I have your wife and your granddaughter here. They are safe, for now. How healthy they stay will be up to you, Professor Sigurdsson."

"Don't you touch them," Sigurdsson screamed into the phone.

The patrons of Humpy's Great Alaskan Ale House looked up in alarm at the screaming drunk.

"Don't worry, nothing will happen to them if you agree to come back and finish the job you started. All of your mates are lonely without you on your submarine. You finish your job and we'll send your wife and your granddaughter off to a nice little vacation spot where you can join them."

"But, I know you're lying. You've lied about everything. You fooled me into thinking you were good—you're evil. I don't want to work for you."

Sokolov fired a gun in the air. "Did you hear that?"

"What did you do? Where's my Sam, where's my granddaughter?"

Sam got on the phone. "It's me, Barney. I'm okay, so is Becky. He's trying to scare you. Don't listen to him."

Sokalov tore the phone from Samantha. "Now, your wife is the one that's lying. I'll keep them both alive as long as you help us. We already have your coordinates from tracing your phone call. Stay where you are and we'll come get you. Agreed?"

Sigurdsson's hand covered his face. "I agree. I'll be here. Just don't hurt them."

37

MELLISSA AKERMAN SMOOTHED her hair and straightened her dress. With the file tucked under her arm she made her way to Anton De Luca's office. Her heart was beating fast—way too fast. She took a deep breath to slow it down.

Olivia Chapman was in Anton's office. Mellissa found it hard not to hate her. She was tall and beautiful in a Vogue Magazine way with perfect teeth, blue eyes and flawless skin. *Who the hell looks like that?*

Mellissa cleared her throat at the door. Olivia looked up. A frown graced her perfect eyebrows in annoyance. How dare Mellissa intrude on her conversation with Anton? She was a level two analyst, one grade above Mellissa. Office decorum dictated that Mellissa should wait until Olivia had left Anton's office. Mellissa was in no mood for office politics or decorum. The file under her arm was pure gold. This was the key to get Anton's attention; this was *screw you* Olivia Chapman material. She cleared her throat again, louder this time and stood her ground.

Anton looked up at Mellissa. "Yes, what is it?"

"The file you asked for, on that *special assignment* you gave me," Mellissa said. She drew out the words special and assignment with raised eyebrows and a nod to the folder under her arm.

"Would you give us few minutes?" Anton asked Olivia.

She looked defeated. She threw a quick smile and wink with a "sure, no problem," but the look she gave Mellissa was one of pure disgust as she made her exit.

Mellissa's heart beat even faster on entering Anton's office. "I found everything you were looking for... and more," she said, drawing out the 'more,' and trying not to sound like a breathless debutant from Gone With the Wind.

"That's great," Anton said. He motioned for her to open the file beside him on the front of the desk.

Mellissa opened the file and pulled out sheets of paper. "I had my two amazing contacts with the FBI Forensics and Homeland Security find all of this for me—plus a bit of digging by myself and I think I've found what we're looking for."

"And none of this will lead back to you or this department?" Anton asked.

"It's been confined. My girls... uh... my contacts assured me that everything they obtained was through back channels."

"You're amazing, Mellissa."

"Why, thank you." She lowered her eyes, hoping the heat she felt in her face hadn't produced an embarrassing blush on her face.

"Show me what you've found."

Mellissa pulled out the first sheet of paper, "What I did was correlate all the data of the times that the billionaire bad guys—sorry, that's the name we gave them—met up with the head of the Mafia."

"Volkov?"

"Yes, I found out they'd been together in several different locations throughout the world through facial recognition technology used by Homeland Security. Once, I had these dates we then ran all of their company transactions through the FBI's TFO section."

"What's the TFO section?"

"That's the Terrorist Financing Operation Section. It was set up after 9/11 to help agents trace transactions and track patterns to help identify anyone who might be related to a crime."

Mellissa pulled out a second piece of paper; it had the name

Regent Marine Projects in a logo on the top. "This is what we came up with."

Anton looked at the paper. It had a list of equipment and transaction dates going back two years. "This looks like submarines and drilling equipment."

"That's exactly it. There were three submarines and three submersible drills capable of deep water drilling purchased for a value of 2.5 billion dollars as well as a warehouse rented in San Francisco," Mellissa said.

"My god, this all fits. Callahan was told that there might be something to do with submerged drills and submarines. This is amazing work, Mellissa."

Mellissa's face went red. Her hands were sweating. She ran them over the back of her dress to avoid sweat marks on the papers in front of her.

"Do we know where these submarines have been put to work?" Anton asked.

"No, sir. Regent Marine Projects lists itself as a private company. It hasn't taken out any drilling permits for work in the ocean."

"Which is why they bought submarines and these type of ocean floor drilling platforms." Anton looked at the list of equipment then pulled up the identifiers on his computer screen. "You see these drills? They could be operated by the submarines which means they could do all of this below the surface and not be seen."

"No need for a drill permit if you can't see what's being drilled." Mellissa said. "They could be operating anywhere in the ocean."

Anton nodded. "That's a lot of ocean to look for three submarines. I have no idea how'd we'd find them."

Mellissa leaned forward and whispered, "Way ahead of you. These submarines are old Whisky Class from the Russian Navy. They're diesel and their engines give off a distinct hum. I've had my American contacts reach out to several companies that are doing seismic surveys in the ocean and I've been able to do the same with two Canadian companies as well."

Mellissa had to stop for a second. Her voice was becoming louder in her excitement. "I'll be notified anytime a Whisky Class submarine is heard from in the Pacific and report back to you."

"What about the Atlantic?"

"The climate model we're seeing is the direct result of the exaggerated El Nino and La Nina weather patterns. This can only happen in the Pacific Ocean."

"You really have done your homework, Mellissa." Anton put his hand on her shoulder. "If I'm ever allowed to report this, and we don't all get fired for this, I'll make sure I recommend you for a promotion."

Mellissa's face grew hot. She was sure she could set off the fire alarm with the heat she felt for Anton. "That's really wonderful, sir."

"Call me Anton."

"Anton... sir... I mean Anton. Sorry..." Melissa's hands could hardly hold onto the files anymore. She shuffled them together, and then realized that Anton would want them. Her hands fumbled as they touched his—the files dropped to the floor.

Anton smiled. "It's okay, Mellissa, I'll pick them up. You've done an amazing job on this." He looked out the office door at the waiting Olivia and moved closer to Melissa. "Would it be too forward of me to take you to dinner?"

"Dinner? Ah, no, I mean yes, I mean dinner would be nice... thank you," Mellissa said as she stumbled out the door.

Olivia watched her leave the office with a mix of disgust and wonder. Somehow, this oversize girl with the wiry hair and poor taste in clothes had just been asked to dinner by the best looking and available man in the entire agency. She would need an entire night of watching Netflix and a large amount of Ben and Jerry's ice cream to get over this.

38

DANNY LANDED the airplane back at the Iqaluit airport a little past 10 pm. Bernadette looked out at the twinkling lights of the small city of 8,000 people and had a surreal feeling wash over her. She'd just been to the farthest point north in the Arctic, fought with a submarine crew and watched young men get incinerated in a bomb blast and here she was back in the closest thing to civilization the far north had.

Danny switched off the engine and turned to Bernadette and McAllen. "I'm avoiding the main terminal. I received a radio message the RCMP is looking for two people in the area. They claim they might be some kind of terrorists or something like that... I told them I haven't seen anyone."

"You think the main terminal isn't a good place to go right now?" McAllen asked.

"The RCMP is there. They say that two people of interest boarded the flight from Montreal to Iqaluit and haven't been seen since. They want me to bring them my passenger manifest. I told them I would be stopping by my office to pick it up. You need to disappear."

"You know who we are?" Bernadette asked.

"Sure, you're the Cree lady that gave two parkas to my grandmother and grandfather in the airport in Montreal."

"Those people were your relatives?" Bernadette asked.

"We're all related up here, and no good deed goes unnoticed in the Arctic." Danny said. "My cousin Omar is outside in a truck. He's going to take you to another relative of mine where you'll spend the night."

"How are we going to get out of here tomorrow," McAllen asked.

Danny smiled. "Don't worry, people of the Arctic have been smuggling things right under the noses of the RCMP for years. Tomorrow you'll be flying out of here as cargo. You'll be listed as seal meat and muskox horns."

McAllen and Bernadette got out of the plane and squeezed into the front of the truck with Omar. He was a big guy, too tall for an Inuit. Bernadette figured from his features and long black hair he had to be of Cree like her.

"Hi, I'm Omar," he said extending his hand across Bernadette to shake McAllen's hand, and then shaking Bernadette's hand. "I'm taking you to our uncle's place tonight. He's got one last Walrus pot roast from last spring's hunt. We'll be in for a good feed tonight."

Bernadette put her head back on the seat. She tried to close her eyes. Tiredness washed over her. She had a feeling they were losing control, losing purpose. Dead bodies were piling up and answers were few.

They drove down the gravel roads of the town. A few streetlights shone revealing small dogs roaming the streets. The truck was of mild interest. The little house they arrived at was set back from the town. A few snowmobiles surrounded it. Some looked like they worked, some looked like they once had and were now parts for others.

It was evident that the lack of snow was causing a problem to the people of the north. There should be snow, and snow roads, and ice building up on the sea for the Polar Bears to climb on to hunt for seals. None of that was happening, winter was late. The late season hung like a question mark on the north. Without snow and cold, the people of the north did not function properly. Ice and snow were essential to their way of life.

Bernadette and McAllen followed Omar into the small house. The place was warm with a wonderful smell of cooking. Garlic, onion, and spices wafted into the air and made them all instantly ravenous.

Omar's uncle, a squat little man with twinkling brown eyes and an easy smile motioned them to come into the house. "Welcome, Danny told me you've had a hell of a journey. Here, this will make you feel better." He thrust two mugs of a frothy substance into their hands.

Omar smiled at them. "It's Moose Milk, Uncle Peter makes it the best. He puts in lots of condensed milk, coffee, nutmeg and of course some good rum." He introduced everyone to Uncle Peter and handed out the Moose Milk.

Bernadette took her first sip of the drink. The mixture of rum and sweetness first assaulted her tonsils with sugars then warmed her all the way down as the large portion of rum hit her stomach. A wave of tiredness swept over her. She found a chair in the kitchen and almost fell into it.

Uncle Peter put a plate in front of her with a large portion of Walrus pot-roast and a big piece of bannock bread. She loved bannock. It was something her grandmother always made for her. The stuff was made from sugar, salt, baking powder, flour and water, patted into a pancake mold and fried in about a ton of butter and oil. Bernadette dipped her bread into the juice of the walrus pot roast. Her mouth was assailed with a pleasant taste of butter and walrus fat. A little piece of heaven she thought, right here in a kitchen in the high Arctic.

"Hmm, Uncle Peter, you are the best," Bernadette admitted.

Uncle Peter winked at her and refilled her mug of Moose Milk. "I'm always glad when people like to eat."

McAllen put his face deep into the pot roast, breathed deeply and took a large forkful. He smiled up at Uncle Peter and gave him a nod and two thumbs up. McAllen and Bernadette let Peter and Omar talk while they ate. They were both too exhausted to respond. Peter spoke of how bad the Arctic had become with the late winter.

"Nobody understands how we need the snow. You know, the people in the south, they think it's going to be all right having warm weather up here. But it's not. It's no good. The warm weather is bad for the fish; they don't come towards the shore or the rivers. The same with the animals, I had to go a long way to get this walrus, the seals are going higher to colder weather. But if we lose the Arctic cold... then what's going to happen?"

McAllen swallowed his last bite of walrus. "The Earth will lose its natural cooling properties. Both of the poles, the Arctic and the Antarctic are essential for the planet to have a stable temperature. We could be thrust back into an age where the Earth is tropical and the ocean covered much of the land. All of this, "McAllen waved his fork around, "was once a tropical forest."

"See, there you go, I'm right," Uncle Peter said. He brought over more walrus pot roast and bread for McAllen.

Bernadette put up a hand to signal she couldn't take any more. The meal was great, but that much grease combined with the fried bread would set her stomach on a collision course with the toilet that she didn't want to see happen.

She looked up at Peter and Omar. "I'm not sure if Danny told you, but we're up here to try to find a way of stopping the earth from getting too warm. We're trying to find an ancient underground river. Danny said he was working with a professor on some kind of a game that might show the whereabouts of this river."

"You mean the River of Thule game?" Omar asked.

"You know of it?"

"Every kid in Iqaluit knows it. My son, Michael, is the best player of the game. He's hit level ten at least twice," Omar said.

"What's level ten?"

"It's shows where the river goes," Omar said.

Bernadette pulled out her cellphone. Danny had told her how to download the app on the plane flight back to Iqaluit. She hit the start button and an Inuit warrior appeared.

"How long does it take to find your way to the source of the rivers, or where they go?" Bernadette asked.

"Are you kidding? Michael spent most of the summer on that. You need to talk with him," Omar told her.

"When can I see him?" Bernadette asked.

Omar smiled. "Probably right now. He's supposed to be sleeping in the back room, but knowing him he's in the middle of one of his games. Let me check."

Omar walked to the back of the house. There were two bedrooms and a bathroom. He peeked into the bedroom on the right. "Ah ha, I knew you weren't sleeping. I need you to come out here and bring your game with you. Our guests need your help."

Michael came out of his room. He was all of ten years old, tall for his age like his father with thick black hair and intense dark eyes. He was dressed in pajama bottoms and a t-shirt. He'd been dressed for bed, but he looked like he'd been far from sleep. An iPad mini was in his hand.

"I was telling our guests how you got to level ten on the River of Thule game. You want to show them how you did it, Michael?"

Michael grinned and shrugged a 'sure' gesture and went to Bernadette's side. "You need to get seal points first. They're the easiest. Then you work your way towards getting a golden walrus to help you." Michael looked at Bernadette with serious eyes. "You have to be careful, if you don't use your walrus right, you'll never get to the narwhale—that's where all the good stuff happens."

"What good stuff?"

"The narwhale leads you to the source of the hidden rivers. Then you're at level ten," Michael explained.

Bernadette stared hard at the game for a moment then looked at McAllen. "This is like a real map of the world."

McAllen looked at it. "You're right. This isn't a pretend map or animation. It starts off in Ellesmere Island then heads south with every time the Inuit Warrior gains points."

"Can you get the game to level ten?" Bernadette asked Michael.

"Sure, I might take a few minutes," Michael said with another shrug of his shoulders.

Omar winked at Bernadette. "Kids these days. They can spend hours on these games and it's hard to get them to go fishing or hunting like we did when we were their age."

Peter slapped his nephew on the back. "Are you kidding? When you were his age, you wanted to stay in front of the television. I had to drag you out the door to the trap lines in the winter."

Bernadette chuckled—nothing had changed. She's seen the same problem when she was young, the only difference was, she was the one heading out the door, her brothers watched television.

Michael went back to his room for a few minutes. He told them he needed to concentrate. When he came back, he wore a shy smile.

"Here it is," he said handing the iPad to Bernadette.

McAllen stared over Bernadette's shoulder. "Well, that doesn't help much."

Bernadette looked at the screen. Two narwhales with their long ivory horns waving were pointing to an island. But the island was off the west coast of the USA.

"I have no idea of an island like this. It looks like it's about one thousand kilometres off the coast of California, about the same latitude as San Francisco," Bernadette said.

McAllen stared at the screen. "This must be some kind of message that Sigurdsson left, and maybe there's another puzzle to solve to get from there, to somewhere else, the final goal."

Michael shook his head. "No, there isn't. The game ends there, at this magical island. It says right here I've reached the source of the River of Thule."

Bernadette rubbed her eyes. "Look, I'm starting to see the narwhales wave at me. I think I need to curl up somewhere."

"I've got some cots for the both of you in the back. You'll be sharing Michael's room. You can get some shut eye at any time," Peter said.

Bernadette washed her face in the bathroom and hit the cot like a log falling in the forest. She was asleep in seconds, dreaming that night of narwhales. A large pod swam before her. They played and clicked their long ivory tusks against each other. The narwhales were pale in colour, white with spots of black. They looked like a big porpoise with a long tusk coming out of their nose.

The Unicorns of the Sea, that's the name that floated up to Bernadette. She watched them play in front of her, moving in a slow rhythmic dance. They wanted her to follow them. They motioned to her with their long tusks to keep coming, to keep swimming with them. They swam deep.

But she became afraid. They were moving towards dark water. She couldn't see anything in front of them. She stopped for a moment. A chill came over her. Then a light appeared from up above. It was a strange light, seemingly filtered through a lens.

She woke up in a sweat. McAllen was in the cot next to her snoring. She glanced at her watch. It was just past 6 am. It was pitch black outside the window. She knew sunrise wouldn't be until around 8 am at this latitude, and sunset would come around 4 pm. She had to think of their next move.

She smelled the welcome aroma of coffee coming from the kitchen and the unmistakable smell of more bannock bread being deep-fried in oil. She did a mental check of her stomach. It had somehow processed the walrus and bannock bread from last night. She could probably handle some more fried bread this morning, but any more than that and her intestines would not be happy and would let her know about it.

Throwing on her shirt she made her way to the bathroom and to the kitchen. Peter greeted her with a coffee. She loaded the big mug with milk and two sugars and after some small talk with Peter she excused herself to make some phone calls.

She needed to get back in touch with Anton. She glanced at her watch. It was 6:45 am. A quick mental calculation told her it was way too early. But the situation demanded she call him before everyone else got up. Peter was busy in the kitchen. She parked herself in the small living room.

She dialed his number and hoped her wouldn't be too upset with her. The phone rang three times and sleepy voice answered, "Hello."

"Sorry, Anton, but I had to get hold of you. I have no idea what this day holds for us," Bernadette said. She gave him a quick overview of their trip to Ellesmere Island, the fight with the Russians and her present situation. She left out the details of the River of Thule game, as she wasn't sure how to explain that, yet.

"I'd heard about the situation in the Arctic. The Russians are claiming they were coming ashore looking for assistance and the Canadians attacked them."

"Of course, a likely story. How's it playing out?"

"The entire Russian Arctic Brigade has been put on red alert and a fleet of their submarines is heading up there to assert their territory. I think you started World War III in the Arctic Ocean."

"Are you serious?"

Anton chuckled. "Sorry, Bernadette. Look, a whole bunch of diplomats are working things out. The Americans are on our side, thank god. They've already responded that the Russians should have given clear indication if they needed aid. They're all just posturing at this point. We have at least a week or two before the nuclear missiles start flying."

"Always with the snappy sense of humor, Anton. Do you have anything else for me besides your Armageddon speech."

"Sorry, yes I do," Anton said. He filled her in on the information that Mellissa had given him about the billionaires and their submarine drilling operations and warehouse in San Francisco.

"You know, I'm getting a feeling that some of this is starting to fit together," Bernadette said.

"Enlighten me, Bernadette," Anton said rubbing the sleep from his eyes. "It's 4 am here, you've put the world on nuclear alert and I could use some good news."

"You said Regent Marine had a warehouse in San Francisco?"

"Yes, I did. What does it mean to you?"

Bernadette sipped her coffee. She had a note pad beside her with the words San Francisco on it. "You need to give me that address. I think I know where we're going next."

"I'd be happy to. At least in San Francisco you won't be running into the Russian Fleet and we'll only have one small war to deal with," Anton said.

"Again, you should have been a comedian, Anton. Good Italian-Canadian humour is hard to come by," Bernadette said. She wrote the name and address of the warehouse in San Francisco down and circled it.

"You have no idea where Sigurdsson is? Anton asked.

Bernadette shook her head. "I'm sorry, we're no further ahead than when we left on this mission."

"And how's your partner, Detective Winston doing in the far north?" Anton asked.

Bernadette almost choked on her coffee. "She's fine. Not happy with the cold up here but she's fine." She realized that she hadn't given Anton any details that she was travelling with McAllen and Sebastian Germaine. At this point, this was information she wouldn't pass on; it would be hard to explain.

"Good. I haven't heard anything from her boss, Adam Morgan. I phoned him yesterday and no one in his department seemed to know where he was. I know he's a strange guy, but going absent during a major case like this is odd."

Bernadette felt a tingle in her spine. That could only be the work of Winston and Sebastian in Washington. Her next phone call would be to Winston for an update.

"Well, you know those FBI types. They can be strange," Bernadette offered as a weak reply.

"Just keep me updated on your movements," Anton said. "I'll see what information and assistance I can give you."

Bernadette was about to say something when she thought she heard a female voice. "Do you have someone with you?" She couldn't believe she blurted that out. "Oh god, sorry about that. If you do that's none of my business—sorry."

Anton sighed. "It's okay, Bernadette. How about if we say good-night or good morning and we both get back to saving the world."

"Sure, sure thing," Bernadette said.

Mellissa Ackerman rolled onto Anton. "Do you think we could take a little time from saving the world for one more gigantic orgasm like the last five?" she asked, kissing his chest.

"I'm sure we can make time for that," Anton said. He kissed her deeply as she grabbed him and pulled him inside her. The world would just have to wait.

Bernadette got another coffee from Uncle Peter and greeted McAllen as he came out of the bedroom. He looked a little worse for wear, but awake.

"We need to talk. There have been a lot of developments," Bernadette said.

"How about if we meet in our outer office," McAllen replied.

39

THEY PUT on their parkas and went outside. The cold morning air grabbed at their lungs and produced steam from their coffees. A thermometer on the outside door read minus five Celsius. A light snow was falling; the flakes came out of the darkness and dropped on their hair.

Bernadette brushed some snow off her brow and sipped her coffee, giving McAllen a briefing of what she'd learned from Anton. She waited for him to digest the information.

"They've got a warehouse in San Francisco and you think that fits with what you saw on the River of Thule game. Is that how your intuition is working this?" McAllen asked.

"Yeah, that's where I'm going with this, plus dreams of narwhales and unicorns dancing in my head overnight."

McAllen turned his face up to the snow and let some rest on his face, and then turned to Bernadette. "You know, that sounds just bat shit crazy enough to work. We've got nothing else at this point. You mentioned Adam Morgan has gone missing, how about we call our compatriots in Washington and see what they've been up to?"

Bernadette dialed the number she had for Winston's cell phone. The phone rang several times before Sebastian answered in a sleepy voice. "Damn it, this better be important cause I was having a great dream."

"Sebastian... we're looking for Winston. Is she somewhere close?" Bernadette asked.

"Yeah, she's here, let me wake her up," Sebastian said.

They could hear a muted conversation and Winston came on the phone. "Hey, Bernadette, McAllen, how are you two doing? We've heard all kinds of action from your area. Did you kick the ass out of some Russian Submarine?"

"Well, not exactly," Bernadette said. "That was the Canadian Air Force, we just happened to arrive at the right moment."

Winston laughed. "We thought it had your fingerprints on it. The world is on high alert for a nuclear war. CNN has stopped covering the rising tides and forest fires."

"Is that why you two decided to sleep together tonight?" McAllen asked. He looked at Bernadette who couldn't believe his direct question.

"I needed to continue this fine lady's treatment of sexual healing," Sebastian said.

McAllen turned to Bernadette and muttered, "That's his line with all the women. I'm amazed it works."

"Besides," Sebastian continued, "we found all this great information on Morgan's computer. It looks like the Russian Mafia was behind this scheme to raise the world's temperature. They wanted to take over the United States."

"You have evidence of this?" McAllen asked.

"Sure, we got it off his hard drive. We turned it into the Washington Post and sent copies to the New York Times and several other leading world newspapers, but your antics in the Arctic have buried the story for now. Who's going to care about this story when everyone's running for cover from a world war of nuclear missiles?" Sebastian asked.

"He's right," Bernadette said. "Even if we could get someone to print this story about Russian involvement in this, it won't see a front page until this crisis blows over."

"What do we do now?" Winston asked. She'd moved closer to Sebastian. He was resting his head on her breast and stroking her tummy. She smiled down at him.

"If you two love birds can break yourself out of bed, how about we meet in San Francisco," McAllen suggested.

"Sure, I love the clam chowder and sourdough bread in San Fran, but what else is there?" Sebastian asked.

"We found a warehouse we want to check out, and we've got a possible location of where the Earth's ocean temperature is being messed with. A good chance it's some 1,000 kms off the coast of San Fran. We found a kind of map in a game Sigurdsson developed called River of Thule," McAllen explained.

"I remember that game. I played it with Theo and Grace down in Nicaragua. Both of them were kick ass at it, they killed me when we played it," Sebastian said.

"Well, thanks for that," McAllen said.

Bernadette looked into McAllen's eyes. He looked back up into the sky and breathed in deeply. It was obvious the pain of losing them was still there and raw.

"If we're heading off shore we'll need a boat," Sebastian said. "I think I know where I can get us one."

"Now, don't get no Tuna boat or something industrial," McAllen cautioned. "We need some speed. There's no use in getting on board something that chugs at ten knots and takes us over three days to get there."

"You know me, Mac, I always come through. I'll get us a nice ride for the waves," Sebastian said as he winked up at Winston and patted her tummy.

"How soon can we meet up?" Winston asked.

"We have to find out when we're leaving here," Bernadette said. "I understand we're being smuggled out of here, but not sure when. As soon as we have an idea of the final flight to San Francisco, we'll send you a text."

"Sounds good," Winston and Sebastian said in unison.

Bernadette heard a distinct giggle from the two of them before they clicked off their phone. She wondered if the entire world was having sex because of the situation they'd caused in the Arctic?

A lump came into her throat. She missed Chris at this moment. She wondered where he was and what he was doing. She looked at McAllen. "Could you give me a moment. There's someone I need to talk to."

"Sure, I need more coffee anyway. Can I bring you some?"

"No, I'm fine."

Bernadette punched in the numbers she had for Chris and listened to a distant ring that was somewhere in Afghanistan.

"Hello, Chris here."

"Hey, fella, it's me, Bernadette—"

"Wow, where are you calling from? I've just heard on the international news that the RCMP and FBI are looking for you. I had some uptight FBI guy call me and ask me if I'd heard from you."

"Did you tell him anything?" Bernadette asked weakly. She felt it hard to compose herself. She was realizing how much she missed him.

"Of course not, Bernie, you know I'd never give up my best girl. Didn't I always say we were outlaws in our last life, I was Butch Cassidy and you were—"

"Calamity Jane," Bernadette interrupted with a smile. "I miss you so much, you know that don't you?"

"I miss you too."

"Did you want to prove a point, to see how crazy I'd be knowing you're in danger?" Bernadette asked.

"Okay, I guess I may have been pushing the limits on this one," Chris said. "This mission is pretty nuts. The guy we're protecting has us going into some dangerous areas. We got these Hezbollah guys coming at us daily with all kinds of shit. It keeps me on my toes, but sometimes I wonder if it's worth it for the cash their paying me."

"Wouldn't you rather be my houseboy? I'd pay in amazing sex," Bernadette said. Her face went hot as she mouthed those words.

"You know, Bernadette, right now I'd about throw this whole

thing over just to be next to you watching bad gangster movies and falling asleep together on the sofa."

Bernadette squeezed her phone. A tear made its way down her face and started to freeze. "What do you say, when all this is over, maybe we meet somewhere in Europe?"

"You mean if I live through the next rocket attack and you don't get captured and put in jail?"

"Exactly. We'll meet in Paris. A friend of mine told me about this cool little street called Rue Mouffetard in the Latin Quarter. It has wonderful restaurants and markets."

"Great." Chris laughed. "As long as it has a decent hotel with a nice bed where you and I can work up an appetite, I'm in."

His phone started to cut out. "I need to go, we're about to leave on our next trip outside the wire and my connection is fading. Listen, girl, you know I love you. I'm a rare idiot some times, but I love you madly. You know that and—"

The phone clicked off. Bernadette stood there as the sun rose up in the high Arctic sky staring at the phone, her lifeline to Chris. He was gone. She sighed and put away her phone. She felt a shiver; she needed to go back into the house.

As she walked into the house a wall of warmth and the smell of cooking breakfast greeted her. Uncle Peter looked up from the stove where he was frying something that smelled like more walrus with eggs. "Danny called, he's arranged a flight for you out of here after sunset."

"When's that?" McAllen asked.

"It's at 4:00. Be ready to leave at 3:30." Peter said.

40

Admiral Fairborne watched the news and clenched his jaw. His fists were balled and he found it hard to restrain himself from pounding on his armchair in the officer's club. CNN was showing the American submarines that were entering the Arctic Ocean to defend Canadian Sovereignty.

A news clip showed the fighter jets taking off from Eielson Airforce base near Fairbanks Alaska. Four Ohio Class Nuclear submarines were listed as entering the Bering Sea and steaming for the Arctic. Even the English and Danes were committing ships and planes to back up Canadian Sovereignty in the Arctic.

Fairborne knew this was the Americans using the pretense of defending Canada to reassert its own rights in the region. With the melting ice in the Arctic Ocean, it was virtually ice free in the summer. Ships were now making regular passage through and saving hundreds of thousands of dollars in fuel instead of going through the Panama Canal.

But what was at stake was all of the offshore oil and minerals found on the ocean floor. Fairborne had seen the secret documents of what America stood to profit from drilling and mining in the Arctic. It's what his Russian handlers had told him would be the riches that he, the great Admiral Fairborne would be part of once they'd taken over the American government.

This latest, unseen incident was derailing that. A Russian submarine was destroyed off Ellesmere Island in the Canadian Arctic. The Canadian's claimed the submarine fired upon them as they came to the aid of their civilians. A commentator was claiming how close the world was to nuclear war over this incident and started to list the firepower of the submarines headed for the Arctic.

With a smugness that couldn't be missed, the commentator explained how the Ohio Class submarine, with its 192 warheads that could enter back into the atmosphere at Mach 24, separate into eight multiple warheads with up to a 475 Kiloton warhead could wipe 24 Russian cities off the map. He then said, "That would be a bad day for Russia, back to you."

Fairborne almost choked on his coffee. The utter morons, what were they thinking? This was removing the attention from America's plight of forest fires, drought and rising seas to see who would stand down first.

This was not going well. Fairborne walked out of the officers' club. Two men in uniform stood on the steps of the club. "Admiral Fairborne?"

"How may I help you, Lieutenant?" Fairborne asked. He noticed that neither the lieutenant nor the young corporal at his side had saluted him as he neared them. He drew in a breath and calmed himself before he gave his reprimand.

"I'm Lieutenant Moskowitz. You need to come with us, Admiral, you're being taken in for questioning for charges of treason against the United States of America."

"Treason?" Fairborne sputtered. That's absurd."

"No, sir. There's been a complete report from the Washington Post on your activities. The Judge Advocate General's office wants a meeting with you. This is not a request, sir. It's an order."

"The Washington Post. You can't be serious. Any news from them is fake news," Fairborne said.

Lieutenant Moskowitz spun Fairborne around and put handcuffs on him. "My wife is a reporter for the Washington Post, sir."

41

Omar took Bernadette and McAllen back to the airport just as the sun was setting at 4 pm. There was a threat of more snow, but it wasn't coming down. In late October there should have been piles on the ground already. The truck tires crunched on gravel as it headed for the airport.

They parked away from the terminal and entered a small Quonset hut that was Danny's headquarters for his airplane. The hut was crowded with wooden pallets and boxes that had either been shipped in or were to be shipped out.

Bernadette couldn't see any specific order to the warehouse; Danny seemed to be the organizer. He wandered from one crate to another, with his helper, a tall man with greasy coveralls and a Montreal Canadiens Hockey hat that had seen better days, as had the team.

McAllen found himself a space on a packing crate and surfed the net on his phone. He was looking for islands just off the coast of California. Other than the Channel Islands off Los Angeles, only Alcatraz came up. After a while he gave up, turned off his phone and stared into space.

The door opened into the warehouse. Bernadette whirled. She

expected to see the RCMP with guns drawn to do a takedown. Her stomach had been feeling anxious all morning from more fried walrus.

A little Inuit lady walked in. Bernadette recognized her as the one she'd met in Montreal and she'd given the parkas to. She approached with twinkling eyes. She was speaking in her native Inuktuk so Bernadette called Danny over to translate.

"My grandmother says she heard you are going to search for the headwaters of the River of Thule," Danny said.

"How did she find that out?" Bernadette asked as she jumped off her packing crate and dusted off her jeans.

"Ah... well... I maybe told her," Danny said as he found something interesting to look at on the warehouse floor.

"Is there anyone who doesn't know what we're up to in Iqaluit?"

"Not if they're native. We've pretty much in the loop on this one. The River of Thule could reduce the temperature of the Arctic, bring the ice back and keep the Kallunak out of here," Danny said. "Sorry, Kallunak means white people. But what she means is if the ice returns in the winter and into the summer we won't have the ships and Kallunak hunting for oil. We can get back to our traditional ways of hunting and fishing. My grandmother thinks it's a better way of life for the Inuit."

"I couldn't agree more," Bernadette said. "From what I've seen of civilization, it's based on buying things online and watching Netflix. Not much competition with the Inuit."

The grandmother approached and took Bernadette's hand. In it she placed a rock that felt odd, like it had many facets in it, but she could only feel them and not see them.

"What is this?"

"This is a rock my grandmother found many years ago. She said she fell asleep on the beach and had a dream of Sedna, the goddess of the sea. Sedna gave her a rock, told her it was from the headwaters of the River of Thule. One day a woman would appear who would take it back to its origin."

Bernadette felt the rock in her hand. It had a heaviness that far outweighed its size. "Is it from a meteor?"

"No, it's from Sedna," Danny said.

Bernadette smiled at Danny's grandmother. "I will do my best for you and your people. I will search for the River of Thule and place this back there."

They exchanged goodbyes with the grandmother. She watched them walk towards the plane. Her head was nodding and a low chant came from her lips, as if she was throwing a good luck song in her native tongue to speed them on their way.

"You believe any of what you just said back there to the old woman?" McAllen asked.

"Damned if I know, but it seemed the right thing to say. But I don't know, the more we get into this journey, the stranger it gets. Maybe this River of Thule is real. Maybe this rock is real. And as far as Sedna being the goddess of the sea, who knows? I'm Catholic, we have so many patron saints and visions bouncing around, that I can't judge anyone else's."

They found places amongst the packing crates on Danny's plane. He wasn't joking about Muskox horns and seal meat, the plane had the smell of meat and a musty odour from the horns. Within minutes of them putting on their seat belts Danny turned the plane onto the runway and they were airborne.

Bernadette sat back in her seat and closed her eyes. She hadn't slept that well last night and she hoped to nap on the flight to Yellowknife in the Northwest Territories. The journey would take just under four hours. There was nothing to see below in the darkness and she needed her mind to go blank for a while. It had been on overdrive the past few days and it needed a time out.

The engine's big single propeller lulled her into a long nap. When she woke her head was lolled to one side and a stream of drool was coming out of her mouth.

McAllen was on his cell phone next to her confirming their next flight. He'd been able to hire a NetJets Gulfstream G5 that was to fly from Edmonton, a city just under a thousand kilometres south of them to pick them up in Yellowknife.

They were to fly straight to San Francisco, another long haul of over 2,400 kilometres. As the plane started its descent into the Yellowknife airport Bernadette got a queasy feeling in her stomach. Was it all the landings and takeoffs, or another possibility of meeting with airport officials and being recognized? She wiped her face and tried to pat her hair into shape.

The lights of the small city of 20,000 came into view. Apartment buildings and government buildings shone their lights into the northern night as the plane flew towards the airport.

The little plane bumped along the airstrip and Danny powered the engines towards the industrial hangers. The Gulf Stream had already landed. It was a short distance from where they parked their plane. Bernadette felt a sense of relief. They could board the jet without going through airport security.

She grabbed her duffel bag and followed McAllen out of the plane. A welcome wind of cold air washed over her that was refreshing after the stifling airplane trip.

She stopped for a second and stretched. Out of the corner of her eye she saw two uniformed RCMP officers making their way towards her.

42

THE TWO OFFICERS were all business. One was a tall dark male, Bernadette thought he was Cree, like her, and the other was a short female who had the unmistakable features of an Inuit.

They walked passed Bernadette and approached Danny. The female officer, her name badge stated Corporal Aglukkaq, seemed to know him.

"Hey, Danny, we got word of someone doing some smuggling up here in the North. That wouldn't be you would it?" Aglukkaq asked with a smile.

"Hey, Daniele, you know I'm so legit it hurts my business," Danny said with a grin.

Bernadette watched the exchange carefully. Her training as an RCMP officer told her all the body language of an officer and a suspect. There was none of that here. The officers' hands were not on their guns, but thrust deep into their pockets to keep warm. Not a ready position for a take down.

"So, what are you bringing in?" Aglukkaq asked.

"Oh, just seal meat and some Muskox horns from the Inuit Cooperative store," Danny said. He was still smiling at the female officer, his hands down by his side.

"And these two are your passengers?" The male Constable asked. His name badge said Ladamer. He didn't seem as impressed with Danny as his female counterpart.

"Ah, just two people that needed a lift from Iqaluit. They're catching a ride on the Global G-5 over there," Danny said pointing over his shoulder to the big private jet with the crew standing by to receive Bernadette and McAllen."

"Nice ride. Must be some pretty important folks you're flying around these days, Danny. You mind if we get their names?" Aglukkaq asked.

"Ah sure, um... you want to give the officers your names?" Danny said to Bernadette and McAllen.

"You don't have them on a passenger manifest?"

"Not handy. It's in the plane," Danny said. His hands went from his sides as he crossed his arms.

Bernadette shivered inside. To an RCMP officer, this was a sign someone was lying or uncomfortable with the facts. If this young female corporal were any good she'd see it in a heartbeat.

"Why don't you get it for me, Danny," Aglukkag said turning to McAllen and Bernadette. "Could I see your identification please?"

"Is there a problem, Corporal," McAllen said. "We're running behind for an important meeting in the USA."

"Well, since you have your own plane, I doubt if they'll leave without you. Now, I need to see your IDs."

McAllen and Bernadette pulled out their fake passports and handed them over. Constable Ladamer shone his flashlight at the document and then up at their faces.

Constable Ladamer stared hard at Bernadette's passport. "You remind me of someone," he said shining his flashlight in her face.

"Really? Who's that?" Bernadette asked.

"A girl I knew back at Twin Pines Reservation in Northern Alberta. Her name was Bernadette Callahan. She left when I was young. I think she got into some trouble there," Ladamar said.

"Twin Pines, nope, never heard of it. You say it's in Northern Alberta?"

"Yeah, you say you've never been there?"

"No, Constable, if you look on my passport I was born in the USA. This is my first time in Northern Canada," Bernadette said.

"And what exactly are you doing this far north?"

"We work for a private art collector out of San Francisco. We were looking at Inuit soapstone sculptures in the Arctic," McAllen said.

"Who's your collector?"

"Sorry, he's real shy, as I said, he's a private collector," McAllen said. He let his words sit there for the constable to mull over.

Danny came out of the plane with a clipboard. "Here we are, Daniele, sorry I should have had it on me when I got out of the plane, my bad."

Danny walked up to the four of them and handed the papers to Corporal Aglukkaq. He felt the tension in the air. Constable Ladamer's jaw was clenched.

"You didn't just write their names on your manifest in the plane did you, Danny?" the corporal asked, staring at the papers.

Danny had a pained look on his face, as if the officer had asked him an offensive question. "No, that would be wrong."

"Okay, we're fine here," Aglukkaq said. She smiled at them. "Have a nice flight."

"But, this lady looks an awful lot like the one on the APB," Ladamer pointed out.

Aglukkaq shook her head and smiled at Bernadette. "Sorry, but my partner thinks he's going to make the big collar of some rogue RCMP Detective all the way up here in Yellowknife." She gave him a gentle push. "Come on, Ladamer, it's your turn to buy coffee and donuts and I'm getting cold out here."

Danny, Bernadette and McAllen watched the RCMP officers walk away.

"That was close," McAllen said. "Did you actually know that constable?"

"Hell, yeah," Bernadette said. "I used to hang out with his older sister. He was a total pain in the ass five-year-old brat. I beat the hell out of his cousins, the Cardinals, before I left the Reservation."

"Do you think they were looking for you?"

"Well, if they were, that's the worst interrogation I've ever seen," Bernadette said. "I can't believe how quickly the corporal shut it down. You know anything about her, Danny?"

"Yep, her grandmother is tight with my grandmother. They're both into the ancient ways and believe that the River of Thule exists. My guess is she came to check out the lady who's about to return the stone to the headwaters," Danny said.

"Really, you think that's why she came to check us out?" McAllen asked.

"I'd bet you a whole load of dried walrus," Danny said.

McAllen and Bernadette said goodbye to Danny. Bernadette gave him a hug and they boarded the private jet. The pilot and co-pilot were female and so was the cabin attendant.

Bernadette kicked off her boots and slunk down into a white soft leather chair. The cabin attendant introduced herself as Meghan and brought them both a large glass of single malt scotch and some glasses of iced water.

Once they'd attained cruising altitude, Meghan informed them that she'd be preparing Filet Mignon with roast potatoes and vegetables for dinner followed by a cheese course and then a crème brulee for dessert. She placed the wine list beside them and left them to relax.

The jet taxied down the runway, then took off with a smooth acceleration. Bernadette looked down at the little city and watched the lights fade into the night.

She sipped her scotch and placed her hand in her jacket to feel the rock. There was something odd. When she received the rock it was round. It was now narrower with a point. Bernadette took the rock out and stared at it. She looked over at McAllen to see if he'd noticed anything but he seemed lost in thought. Maybe she'd tell him later.

The captain came on the intercom to tell them their destination of San Francisco was 2,400 kilometres away. Their air speed would average 880 kilometres per hour and the flying time would be two hours and 45 minutes. The captain told them to please enjoy the cuisine and beverages provided by the amazing Meghan.

Then the captain came back on and explained that they were intending to land at the Hayward Private airstrip in San Francisco, however, they were still monitoring the rising seas in the inner harbor.

"At present," the captain continued, "San Francisco International airport is under water and no longer operational. We've been informed that Hayward has several dykes in place to stop the rising sea, however, if these become too tenuous we'll be diverting to an inland airport."

"I'll keep you advised as we get closer to San Francisco, and our flight and ground crew will make every effort to ensure that you reach your final destination."

McAllen and Bernadette exchanged looks. "Where are Sebastian and Winston supposed to meet us?" Bernadette asked.

"I told him the Hayward airport, but then if things change we'll have to deal with it," McAllen said.

"Do we have a plan when we arrive?"

"Yeah, we'll make a visit to the Regent Marine location."

"I'm with you on that. What do you think we'll find?"

"No idea, but I asked Sebastian to bring along a few things, just in case."

43

As they stepped off the plane they smelled smoke. It grabbed at their throats and stung their eyes. The captain was at the bottom of the airplane stairs and informed them there were numerous forest fires in the area and smoke coming in from the massive fires burning in the Los Angeles area.

The captain said, "I hope you'll be okay here. We won't be able to wait for you and we've been informed not to land at this airport again. The dykes could break at any time. Our company can arrange to pick you up in Sacramento or San Jose on your next journey. Please stay safe."

Bernadette spotted Winston and Sebastian coming out of the building to greet them. "Well, this is a nice surprise," Bernadette said.

"Hey, for us too. When we heard of all the action up in the Arctic, we thought you two were casualties," Winston said. She came up to Bernadette and gave her a hug. "Glad to see you're with the living."

"Always glad to be above ground," McAllen said as he engulfed Sebastian in a bear hug.

"Hey, don't mess my new threads," Sebastian said pushing himself out of McAllen's hug and straightening his jacket.

"No, he was never one for bromance," McAllen said. "Only likes hugs from the ladies."

Sebastian gave McAllen a sour look. They followed him out of the terminal to the Lincoln Navigator he'd rented. He opened the back of the SUV and showed his new purchases.

McAllen looked around to see if anyone was watching before he picked up one of the submachine guns.

"You couldn't get us some Israeli Uzi's or German MP5's?" McAllen asked looking at the American MAC-10 submachine gun.

Sebastian shrugged and shook his head. "Look, this was short notice. There so many people buying guns right now to protect themselves from what they think is the next Armageddon, that all I could get was what people don't want."

McAllen picked up the Smith and Wesson 9mm handguns and smiled. "These you had no problem getting?"

"Are you kidding? A handgun in America is a staple. I'm surprised the drug stores don't have them in the aisle with the pain killers."

They armed themselves with the weapons. Winston, Sebastian and McAllen chose the submachine guns and a handgun each while Bernadette chose only a handgun with some extra clips.

Bernadette checked the sites of the handgun and looked at Winston with the submachine gun. "You know, Winston, those things just spray bullets. I like to aim at what I'm going to shoot at."

"Whatever knocks the bad guy down the fastest is where I'm at," Winston said. "I'll ask them if my aim was okay when they're on the ground."

"Now, that we're all armed and dangerous, how far are we from the warehouse of Regent Marine?" Bernadette asked looking around at everyone.

"The place is about twenty minutes from here just off the Nimitz Freeway. Winston and I scoped it out when it was light. The place has a doorway at the front with large freight doors at the back. There's a little plaque on the front door giving their name, but we didn't see any signs of people in the building."

"I guess we go check it out." McAllen looked at Sebastian. "You have anything else you want to add?"

"Nope, I got nothing," Sebastian told him.

Bernadette looked at the two of them. There was something in their exchange that was stranger than usual. She got into the back of the SUV with Winston and checked her gun again.

It was just past midnight when they got onto Nimitz Freeway. The surrounding area looked unusually quiet. From the reports Bernadette had seen on her phone, people were evacuating. They were heading to higher ground. The rising sea was flooding the bay.

Evacuation centers had been opened in Sacramento, however, with the forest fires and smoke, there was a stream of people heading north towards Oregon. Much of the population of America was on the move. Looking for either relief from the rising ocean or the smoke and fires caused by the lack of rain and the extreme heat.

They motored passed a Costco, auto body shops and warehouses until Sebastian took an exit that led them down a street with a row of darkened warehouses.

They stopped half a block away from a low grey cement building. The building had covered windows and a door with a small sign that read Regent Marine. There was a van parked out front. No light shone from inside. One floodlight shone over the doorway.

"You see any signs of an alarm?" Bernadette asked.

"There's an alarm company sign on the door, but I looked at the outside of the building, and the phone lines aren't hooked up. So, if they have an alarm it's not going anywhere."

"Unless it's working on a wireless system."

"Ah, yeah, forgot about that. I've been out of the burglary business for some time," Sebastian said.

"So, what do we do? Should we just go in?" Winston said.

"My money's on a bust down the front door, Winston and Mac, you cover me with your submachine guns and I'll drop low and fire a spray of bullets to take down anyone inside," Sebastian said.

"And if that's the people who are cleaning the building, you're okay with filling them full of bullets?" Bernadette asked.

"Ah... no... not to kill the cleaning people... if that's who's in there..." Sebastian said as he trailed off into thought.

"How about if we go, jimmy open the front door, and take a look around to see what's going on. If we meet any resistance—other than the people cleaning the place we'll deal with it. Okay?" Bernadette asked.

"Fine. Let's go." Sebastian pulled back the lever on his submachine gun to chamber a round.

They left the SUV, staying on the side of the streets and away from the streetlights until they got to the side of the warehouse. Sebastian went to the front door and crouched down to start with his entry tools.

Winston came up beside him and tried the door handle. "Sebastian, sweetie, it's open."

Sebastian pushed the door open slowly. He crouched low and made his way inside. He was in a long hallway. Sebastian motioned for them to cover him as he moved towards the light that was coming from an office at the end of the hall.

Winston and Bernadette took up positions inside the door while McAllen followed Sebastian. There wasn't a sound coming from the lighted room.

They moved slowly, crouching low, their weapons at the ready. McAllen got to the window and looked inside. He saw Samantha and Becky inside.

He moved to the door to open it.

The lights of the warehouse came on. A voice yelled, "Drop your weapons or she dies."

McAllen looked behind him. Sokolov was standing beside Winston with a gun to her head.

44

"DON'T DROP YOUR WEAPONS!" Winston yelled. "He'll kill us all anyways. Shoot him."

Bernadette stood two metres away. She looked at the options for a shot. Her gun was raised. She could see only a fraction of Sokolov's head. *Should she chance it?*

She felt a gun barrel at her head. "Drop your weapon," a thickly accented voice said. Bernadette dropped her weapon on the floor and looked at Winston.

McAllen and Sebastian were at the end of the hallway. They had their submachine guns pointed at them. What would they do? If Winston and Bernadette both hit the floor would McAllen and Sebastian open fire? How could she get the message to Winston?

"This is a nice standoff, no?" Sokolov asked. He was smiling with his gun at Winston's head.

"The odds aren't in your favor," McAllen answered. "You shoot those two women—I'll finish you off and free the other two hostages. It doesn't seem worth your while. You die for very little."

"I do not intend to die. You will not let me shoot this lady. You Americans are very soft on your people. You always try to negotiate your way out of conflict. We Russians embrace conflict—it makes us stronger. We could teach you all many things, when we've taken over your country you will see—"

A hissing noise sounded. Sokolov's head exploded. Bernadette heard another hissing sound behind her. She turned to see the man holding her fall to the floor, a pool of blood spreading from his head.

Percy Stronach strode into view behind Winston holding a gun with a smoking silencer. "Was anyone else getting tired of that Russian's speech—cause damn—I sure was."

Behind Percy was Grace Fairchild. Bernadette looked behind her to see Margaret Ashley and Theo Martin with their weapons walking towards her. Margaret was congratulating Theo on his shot.

"It helps when they stand still like that," Theo replied.

"But, I thought you were all dead back on Lake Nicaragua," Bernadette said.

McAllen strode up the hallway and hugged Margaret then looked at Bernadette. "We had our plan B. When attacked we separate, it's also good to let the enemy think that some of you are dead. They then work on the objective—from the grave."

"How did you escape the rocket attack from the helicopter?" Winston asked as she cleaned Solokov's blood off her face.

"We'd built a safe room in the basement," Percy said. "When we saw that helicopter rise up to a firing position we ran downstairs and buttoned up a steel door. Sure the house burned down on top of us, but we had a tunnel we'd built to the other side of the island with another boat there. We watched you as you drove away to make sure you were safe."

"They've been working on this case from the moment we arrived in Key West. How do you think I've been able to get chartered planes and firearms so quickly in each location?" McAllen said.

"I'm impressed," Bernadette said. "Now, what's in that room at the end of the hall?"

"The best surprise yet." McAllen could hardly suppress a grin. Bernadette followed him to the room to see Samantha and Becky. She felt tears well up in her eyes as they hugged.

Samantha looked at them. "I can't tell you how glad I am to see you. The reason we've been kept alive is that they found Barney up in Alaska two days ago. They picked him up and took him back out to the site where they're drilling again."

"Do you know where they're drilling in the ocean?" Bernadette said.

Samantha shook her head. "They were always secretive about that. I know it's off this coast somewhere as they used this warehouse for resupply of the submarines. But I have no idea where."

"Did you get us a boat?" McAllen asked Sebastian.

Sebastian looked at Percy. "Yeah, Percy picked us up a little something down in Los Angeles. I think you'll like it."

Percy looked up and winked at McAllen. "You said you wanted something with some speed. I got us a super-fast yacht that will top out at 30 knots."

"I hope you didn't break our bank account to get it," McAllen said.

"Oh no worries. We stole it," Percy told him, giving him a nudge and a wink.

McAllen clapped Percy on the shoulder as they moved out of the building into the night. The sky was now a red glow from the fires in the hills. They needed to get out of there as fast as possible.

Sebastian, McAllen, Bernadette and Winston followed the other four in their rented van to a road that turned into water. They got out and slogged their way up an embankment until they reached a pier.

"Most of the piers that aren't floating are under water," Theo said as they walked along what was left of the pier that looked like it was about to float away.

At the end of the pier was a long silver yacht. To Bernadette it looked about seventy or eighty metres long. As she approached, she saw a strange looking boat on the stern.

"Is that a mini submarine on the back?" Bernadette asked.

45

"YES, IT IS," Percy grinned, "We had a bit more trouble stealing this one. But when Mac reported the bad guys could be using submarines, we figured we'd best get one of our own."

Bernadette walked to the stern and examined the small, compact submarine with the bubble in the front. "How safe is this thing?"

"Supposed to be the ultimate in a mini, it's got a six hour mission time and a depth of 1,000 metres," Percy said. He stood beside Bernadette and caressed the clamshell dome of the observation deck with one hand.

"I hope you're the one going down in this thing," Bernadette said as she walked back towards the others. "At a thousand metres deep I want more than that bubble between me and the ocean."

Bernadette found the others in the wheelhouse. Theo was showing McAllen and Samantha the bridge and detailing how state of the art this yacht was that they'd stolen.

"Ah, I just have a question?" Bernadette asked, stepping in between Theo and McAllen.

Theo looked at Bernadette; he was annoyed at having his description of this beautiful yacht interrupted. "What is it?"

"Don't all of these high priced yachts have GPS tracking devices installed so that when they are stolen they can be traced?"

"Sure they do," Theo said. "Percy found the tracker on the bridge and disabled it. My god, they placed it right behind the helm, what a bunch of goofs."

"Maybe, they were some smart goofs," Bernadette said. "Can't they track this yacht with its satellite signature?"

"You're right," Percy said. "I have been in the boat building business all my life. These big yachts communicate with shore by satellite. They all have a distinct signature, just like an airplane. We need to turn it off."

"Does that mean we're navigating blind?" Bernadette asked.

"No, it just means we can't communicate with anyone other than by ship to ship radio or if we're close to shore if we don't want to be recognized. You can use your burner cell phone when in range of shore and that's about our communication with the world." Percy turned to everyone. "And use the computers only for web searches or downloads. If you try to face time with someone from this ship, I'm sure it will get picked up."

"Who cares about satellites?" Sebastian said. "There is a million-dollar sound studio on this thing. I can make some great audio and video tapes."

Margaret laughed. "That's great, we can do a video of our pleas for clemency when we get caught. By the way, what's a boat like this worth?"

"About 80 million US. That's not including that little mini sub and the outrageous sound studio. I think we're floating on over 100 million."

"When you want to be in the theft over 5,000 dollar category. I guess this is it," Bernadette said.

Winston came up beside her. "We've gone from international terrorist to international thieves. I hope our rap sheet doesn't extend too long or I'll never see my son's grandchildren. Of course, that's even if we live through this and I get to see my son."

"I think it's time to be getting under way," McAllen suggested.

Bernadette nodded and followed McAllen, Theo and Percy to help them cast off the ropes. The big yacht's engines growled as they moved away from the pier and into the harbor.

Becky and Margaret went forward to call out any floating debris that could pose a danger to the hull. They motored slowly past oil drums, lumber and a few shipping containers that had floated off the docks as the seas had risen. Several times, the yacht had to either go around or reverse to miss objects in the water.

Bernadette had seen a sign that said San Leonardo before they got on the ship. They motored slowly by the shadow of Oakland Airport. The runway was underwater, all planes that could fly had left and only a few lights showed through the smoke from the fires.

As they passed by Oakland there was an eerie silence. Sebastian stood beside Bernadette. He looked at the city and shook his head. "There was a rumour of a tsunami in the Pacific Ocean. The people were leaving here in droves when we flew in yesterday. Probably only the looters left in town."

To confirm Sebastian's words, they heard the sound of gunfire and sirens. They turned away and watched Treasure Island and Alcatraz glide passed them. Alcatraz Island was in darkness. The ocean had breached all of its docks. Boats that had been there to ferry tourist across to view the once famous prison had all been moved to safer places.

Fisherman's Wharf came into view on their left side. Few lights were on. Grace said she'd heard they'd had a massive power outage from the forest fires in the hills.

The Golden Gate Bridge loomed over them as they passed under it at one in the morning. Bernadette felt the ocean breeze. It was cold, but it pushed away the smoke from the fires. It felt good. She pulled a blanket around her shoulders, taking one last look at the darkened city as they sailed away.

"That's the Point Bonita Light House on the starboard side," McAllen said, pointing at a sweeping light off to their right. "The last point of land."

Bernadette came beside McAllen on the bridge. "Any idea where in this big ocean we're heading for?"

McAllen shrugged his shoulders. "I figure we go straight west. That River of Thule game mentioned it'd be out in that direction. What's your rock doing?"

"My rock?"

"Yeah, that little piece of rock you were given in the Arctic. That old woman told you it came from the River of Thule."

Bernadette reached into her jacket pocket. The rock was now warm to the touch. When she pulled it out, it had a slight glow to it.

"Put it up here on the helm," McAllen said.

Bernadette placed it on the helm with its point towards San Francisco. The rock turned itself around to point out to sea.

"Did you see that?" Bernadette said.

McAllen's mouth hung open. "I sure as hell did,"

Grace Fairchild came onto the bridge. "Where did you say you got this stone from?"

"An Inuit woman gave it to me in the high Arctic. She said it was from the goddess of the sea and asked us to return it to the headwaters of the River of Thule." Bernadette said.

"Well, I think we just found our guide," Grace said.

"Looks like we follow its heading," McAllen said. "I'm increasing our speed to 30 knots. It's going to take us about forty hours to get where I think this place is, so everyone, get whatever rest you need and take turns keeping a lookout for small floating debris. And, if you see any patrol boats from the US Coast Guard or Navy, we may have to outrun them."

Bernadette looked up at the stars that were coming out into a moonlight sky. In front of them was only sea, and somewhere a drill that was producing heat from the Earth's ocean that was damaging the planet.

She hoped they arrive in time to shut it down. That shutting down part was the question that rolled around in her mind. How does a yacht, even a multi-million-dollar one, stop a submarine?

46

BERNADETTE SAT in the ship's galley with the rest of the crew that wasn't on watch or piloting the yacht. Grace had bustled amongst the kitchen stores and produced a passable mac and cheese with several amazing bottles of wine.

Theo decanted a 1960 Bordeaux wine that probably cost several thousand dollars. He felt it would complement the pasta and 'bring out the aroma of the cheese.'

Bernadette dug into the mac and cheese and tasted the wine. It tasted earthy, complex and damn good going down. She smiled at Theo and complimented him on his choice.

Becky and Sam were sitting around the table. They didn't look too bad from their ordeal of captivity. Neither of them had been abused at the hands of Sokolov, and both were happy that the nasty Russian was dead.

"Do you think we'll find my grandfather alive?" Becky asked as she pushed her plate aside.

"I have no idea," Bernadette said. She always thought honesty was the better answer than the positive thinking bullshit faction. It covered all bases.

Sam turned to Becky and stroked her hair. "Your granddad is a survivor, he's escaped from them once, and he can do it again. We'll do everything we can to help him."

Bernadette put her wine glass down with a thud. "That's it. We need more help."

"What're you thinking?" Sam asked.

"I just realized how crazy we are. We have this super yacht with a mini sub and some pissy assed weapons to take on a submarine. We need some serious back up," Bernadette said.

She went below to the cabin that she now shared with Grace and Margaret and found her cell phone. The phone had power and it still showed some bars of service. They hadn't come that far off the coast yet.

She glanced at her watch. It was 2:00 am, which meant 3:00 am mountain time where Anton was but it couldn't be helped. She dialed the number.

The number rang several times until a sleepy Anton answered, "If this is who I think it is, I hope you saved the world, cause damn I'm tired."

"You have the sexiest morning voice, you know that, Anton?"

"It's 3:00 am, how sexy can I be?"

"I'll be brief. You need to call in some backup for us. We're on our way to where Sigurdsson is."

"You know where he his?"

"Not exactly."

"What's not exactly mean?"

"We're pretty sure we know where he is," Bernadette said and went on to explain how they found the warehouse in San Francisco, saved Samantha and Becky and killed Sokolov and his henchman.

"So, you have the coordinates of this submarine and the drill site?"

"Well... no, not yet"

"What do you have?"

Bernadette explained the stone she'd received from the Inuit woman in the Arctic and the yacht they'd stolen to get to their destination.

Anton paused for a long moment. "So, let me get this straight. You want me to call in the American Navy and Air Force to back you up in a stolen yacht where you're heading out to sea on the direction of an ancient stone? Did I get that right?"

"Exactly."

"You woke me up for this?"

Bernadette winced. Anton did not sound happy. She waited silently on her end of the phone, hoping that the phone would stay in service while he made up his mind.

"Okay, Bernadette. What can I say? That is one hell of a story. But so far, you are closer than anyone else to possibly solving this. I'll call my liaison in the Canadian Forces and they'll contact the American forces in San Francisco. I can't promise you anything, but I'll see—"

The phone went dead. Bernadette stared at the phone's screen. It was showing no service. She only hoped that Anton would come through. She went back on deck. McAllen was there with Percy and Margaret.

The stars were coming out in a massive blanket of light overhead with a full moon. The super yacht glided over a calm sea leaving ribbons of silver wake.

Bernadette looked at the rock on the helm. It was starting to glow with a faint reddish tinge.

VOLKOV STOOD on the bridge of the supply ship, hoping this would be the last trip he'd have to make on this terribly slow and ponderous vessel. He preferred to travel by yacht, or to have flown by helicopter or seaplane. None of these options were open to him.

The operation was now hemorrhaging money. He had to watch their expenses or start to dip into his own capital and he was not willing to do that. He suffered the slow trip on the supply ship in silence, but boiled on the inside as to the time it was taking.

He'd been told they were making headway with the main submarine. The volume of steam and temperature they needed was imminent. This would be the last trip. He'd make sure they killed the submarine crew and placed depth charges on the drill. Several months from now, Volkov would hire a company to come out and seal up the vents, 'the ones he'd somehow found,' making himself and his people heroes.

The men he had on board were his clean-up crew. They weren't deck hands; they were killers and would ensure no one made it from the submarine alive to tell the tale of what his people had done.

What bothered Volkov was Sokolov's failure to report in. He'd called several times with no answer. San Francisco, he knew, was experiencing severe fires and floods. Perhaps the cell phone towers had been damaged by the fires?

He cursed his decision to not give him a satellite phone, as they were too expensive. He tried Sokolov again, got no answer and stuffed his phone back in his jacket. He would take great pleasure in killing Sigurdsson himself when this project was over. It would give him some sense of closure.

The final closure he was missing was with that tall rich bitch, Willa. When he was finished with Sigurdsson, he'd be tracking her down. He had special plans for her. He smiled and walked back to his cabin.

47

SIGURDSSON SAT on the deck of the submarine and looked up at the stars. There was a smell of sea air mixed with cigarette smoke. He hated the latter, but there was nothing he could do about it.

Every night, the submarine surfaced to take in fresh air and for the diesel to recharge its batteries. It gave the crew time to relax on deck, smell the air, and have a cigarette. A few cast a line to try their luck at fishing.

Sigurdsson had been back on board for two days now. The crew had greeted him with mixed emotion. Some thought him a traitor for deserting them and others, with a knowing eye, thought how sad it was he'd been caught and brought back.

The past few days had seen much activity. Sigurdsson had directed the seafloor drill once again. The Geotechnical drill could work at depths of 3,000 metres.

A surface ship had dropped off the drill several months ago, and once it had descended to the ocean floor, the submarine took over the command of the robotic arms to drill to depths of up to 500 metres by remote.

They drilled down, inserted a probe to get a temperature of the core, then Sigurdsson would assess if this was a spot to insert a blasting rod. Once the charge was inserted the seafloor drill was moved by its own propulsion system to a safe spot and the charge was detonated.

The blast hole was assessed again to see if they'd ruptured a hole big enough to let out the steam from the volcanic magma that was flowing below the seabed. Sigurdsson was working on intuition and a series of guesses that his imagination had formed over the years. He knew that somewhere near this volcanic magma was also a great underwater river. They somehow flowed in concert, water and fire. He had no idea how they'd been formed.

He'd heard of this phenomenon not in scientific circles but in legends, first in his home country of Iceland, and then in Canada's high Arctic. The River of Thule flowed beneath a river of fire the ancient rumors had said.

Sigurdsson pulled a blanket over his shoulders and sat upright against the submarine's conning tower. He looked up at the bright stars. Was he chasing an ancient rumor? Was he a fool for believing it?"

He shuddered as the thought surfaced. If he'd done all this, put his wife and granddaughter in peril and hundreds of thousands of people's lives at risk because of a rumor? If that were true he did not know how he'd live with himself.

What he knew was every day he stayed alive and was useful to Volkov and the people on this ship he kept his wife and grand-daughter alive. But how much longer could he do this, while putting others in danger? He also knew he would no longer be useful and neither would his family, once he'd increased the ocean's temperature.

There was something he could do. It would be at great risk, he could find The River of Thule and unleash it. A light came into his eyes at the thought. Tomorrow, Volkov was supposed to arrive on the supply ship.

What if he drilled down, unleashed the river and the eruption killed everyone in the area? Sure, he'd be killed, but so would everyone else and the project would be gone.

"*Would Sokolov kill my Sam and Becky,*" Sigurdsson whispered to himself. The probability was high. Both Sam and Beck would understand and agree with his actions. They'd see he'd done the right thing. He sighed deeply, wrapped his blanket around him and, staring once more up at the stars, committed his soul to the universe, because tomorrow he might no longer be of this world.

48

ANTON's first call was to the Canadian Armed Forces in Ottawa. There was one person who he could call to give Bernadette and her crew some back up. Major William P. Baumgartner, nicknamed Boomer by his close friends, had a way of getting things done.

They'd worked together on joint Canadian Security and Intelligence and Armed Forces missions before. Although this one was weird, it wouldn't be too weird for 'Boomer.'

Major Baumgartner, 'Boomer' answered on this first ring. He was in his mid fifties, a navy lifer with a salt and pepper beard who would rather be at sea than sitting at a desk in Ottawa surrounded by politicians and bureaucrats who only saw the military as pawns to be moved around at their own discretion.

"Hey, Boomer, Anton here. I got a hot one for you. You ready to have your world turned?"

"Last time that happened it was an Asian girl in Singapore, but why don't you enlighten me, Anton?"

"I got a super-yacht full of my people heading for a destination in the Pacific that needs the help of the US Navy."

"You'll have to be a bit more specific, Anton. You've given me the first scene of Gilligan's Island. I need something more."

Anton proceeded to give him the inside story on how he'd sent Detective Bernadette Callahan to work with Alistair McAllen and their mission.

Boomer let out a breath. "Jesus H. Christ, Anton. Is this the same Detective Callahan who was assumed to be off of Ellesmere Island and involved in our latest dust up with Soviets?"

"Yes, sir, that's her."

"Okay, just wanted to make that clear. So now she's with a band of other wanted criminals heading to an undisclosed location to head off a supposed climate disaster and she needs the help of the navy. Do I have that right?"

"I couldn't have stated it better myself," Anton said, smiling to himself at how fast Boomer worked on things.

"Okay, you got one little problem," Boomer said.

"What's that?"

"A Russian Submarine and three light destroyers are on the way to that same area."

"Do you know why?"

"No idea. American Fleet operations in the Pacific have been watching this since yesterday. Everyone thought the Russians would be putting everything they had into the Arctic because of the sinking of their submarine. For them to throw a submarine and three surface ships in the Pacific is odd."

"I wonder if they are heading for the same place as Bernadette Callahan?"

"Could be. Maybe they're trying to stop what's going on with this project of ocean temperature rising or trying to keep it going. Right now, we're working with diplomatic channels. That news article that was published about Russia's attempted takeover of America through disaster relief has sent heads rolling on an international scale. The Russian Politburo claims they knew nothing about it."

"I'm sure they'd claim that."

"We've had their admiralty on the phone to us. They say this is the work of a group of Mafia inside their government. They are working on expelling them. Seems this is all coming to a head quickly."

"So, they can get some assistance?"

"I have some good contacts in the American Pacific fleet. They'll be sending shadow patrols to be watching the Russians. It's something both sides do when the other side gets anywhere near the other's coast. I'll let them know about Callahan and her little pleasure cruise and they'll provide whatever assistance they can."

"That would be appreciated, Boomer."

"Just one more thing."

"What's that?"

"If the Russians and the Americans decide to start shooting at each other, tell Bernadette Callahan and her friends to keep their heads down."

Anton put his phone down. Bernadette was out of phone range, and he had no way of getting a message to her. He hoped the Americans arrived in time to provide back up.

49

BERNADETTE AWOKE on the second morning of their voyage with visions of narwhales waving their long ivory tusks at her, motioning for her to come towards them. The island they pointed to was pure white in the sun but it shone back with an eerie dull light.

She rubbed the sleep from her eyes, found coffee in the galley kitchen and went up to the wheelhouse where she found McAllen standing at the wheel. Becky and Samantha were standing beside him in a muted conversation.

Bernadette looked out the front window of the ship towards the bow. The sea was restless this morning. Small whitecaps whipped up by a steady breeze made a blue carpet that folded into a grey haze on the horizon. They seemed to be travelling into a vast nothingness. Bernadette had never been this far out in the ocean before. She felt a chill and hugged her arms around herself.

Becky appeared at her side. "Hey, Bernadette, did you sleep okay?"

Bernadette turned back to Becky. The young lady looked good for someone who'd been in captivity for the past several days with people who were bent on killing her. "Yeah, I slept fine, but I've been plagued by dreams of narwhales waving their tusks at me."

"Sounds like they're trying to tell you something."

Bernadette sipped on her coffee and stared back out into the vast ocean. "You believe in dreams, Becky?"

"Always have," Becky said following Bernadette's' gaze towards the horizon. "When you've spent as much time as I have both under and on the water, you get to sense things, like the ocean is trying to tell us something. Trying to get a message across."

"Like it's saying, quit polluting me, and warming me up?" Bernadette asked.

"Yeah, kind of like that. I hope you don't mind me prying into your dreams, but what are these narwhales doing? Are they pointing to anything, or trying to get you to follow them?"

"They've been waving at me and pointing to an island, which is funny, because there're no islands this close to America. We'd have to get to Hawaii before we find another land mass."

"Did you see any of the island?" Becky asked.

"Yeah, it had this dull white sheen to it. There was a bit of sun on it, but hardly any light reflected back." Bernadette said.

Becky's scratched her forehead, "There's only one island like that in this area."

"Really, are you serious? There's a white island a thousand kilometres off the coast of the USA?"

"Yeah, it's called garbage island or sometimes even plastic island," Becky said. "It's become a floating vortex of all the accumulated plastic that's been dumped into the ocean over the past fifty years." She motioned for Bernadette to follow her into the wheelhouse where she found a laptop. She pulled up a Google search.

"You see this? Google states there are three large garbage patches. One off the coast of Japan, it's called the Western Garbage Patch, then there's the Subtropical Convergence Zone in the north, and we're heading right towards the Eastern Garbage Patch in the North Pacific Subtropical High," Becky said.

Bernadette traced her fingers over the screen. "It says here that the floating garbage is the size of Texas, some seven hundred thousand square kilometres. You'd think you'd see it from space?"

"You'd think so, but a lot of it is in tiny particles of plastic and it's submerged just below the surface," Becky explained.

"Could they be hiding a submarine under that?"

"Well, if they were, the large amounts of plastic and floating garbage would distort any attempts to find them by using sonar," Becky said. She turned to Samantha who had moved closer to them. "What do you think, Grandma Sam?"

"I totally agree. From what I understand of the great garbage patch islands, there's so much stuff floating around underneath from toilet seat covers to plastic water bottles, that sonar would bounce all over the place," Samantha said.

Bernadette walked over to the stone that she'd received from the Inuit woman. It was glowing now. She could feel the warmth of it from standing nearby. "Where is this pointed to?" she asked.

McAllen looked at the chart that was appearing on his screen above the wheel. "I'd say we're heading dead center of the big bulk of plastic junk you three have been talking about. Hopefully, we'll find our submarine in the midst of all that garbage."

Bernadette looked at the screen. It showed only dark blue sea, with no island. "Any idea how we're going to take on a submarine when we get there?"

McAllen raised one eyebrow then motioned for Bernadette to come closer. "Go below and talk to Sebastian and Percy. Both are weapons experts. They can come up with something."

"Did they bring some weapons with them?" Bernadette asked.

McAllen shook his head. "No, not that I know of, apart from some small machine guns and a few handguns. But both of them have been known to improvise. That's what we need now. We need brains over brawn. This little cruiser would be kindling if the submarine has a deck gun, and we're a sitting duck if it has usable torpedoes. We need the boys below to figure out something they don't expect."

Bernadette had no idea what McAllen was talking about. She had a sinking feeling their mission to find a submarine and stop it was doomed from the start. She went below to find Sebastian and Percy. A chord of guitar music floated up the passageway as she headed down the plush stairs.

She first followed her ears towards the music, then her nose. The distinct smell of marijuana reached her nose as she approached, making it wrinkle. The weed was legal in Canada and some states in the USA, but it still unnerved her to smell it, as she'd had years of prosecuting people using it. As the music grew louder, she opened the door of the sound studio and a cloud of marijuana smoke billowed out. Percy and Sebastian sat in two chairs with guitars and joints.

Sebastian looked up and expelled a plume of smoke. "Hey, Bernadette, we're just having a morning consult. You want to join us?"

"No," Bernadette said, crossing her arms, and trying not to look too judgmental. "McAllen sent me down here, said you might improvise something that we could take on a submarine with."

Sebastian passed his joint to Percy. "I thought you'd never ask. Yes, we have a plan." He expelled a large plume of smoke and smiled.

50

LIEUTENANT COMMANDER AKASAWA scanned the daily reports from Pacific Fleet. He couldn't believe what he was seeing. A small convoy of Russians, consisting of one submarine and three light destroyers were heading for the California coast.

Why had they left the task force that had been steaming towards the Arctic? Akasawa was in the command room of San Diego US Pacific Fleet Operations. His job was to decipher Russian Fleet movements sending recommendations to fleet commanders as to which threats they should consider hostile and which ones they should shadow. He sighed, picked up his cold cup of coffee and sipped on it. The bitterness of the cold liquid almost made him gag.

Petty Officer Milken appeared at Akasawa's side with a memo. "I just got this, sir. It's for your eyes only." Milken saluted and walked away.

Akasawa looked at the paper. It was from his friend, Baumgartner in Naval Operations in Canada. They'd served together in the Gulf of Aden, stopping Somali pirates from boarding merchant ships and taking the sailors hostage.

He had to read it several times before he understood what Baumgartner was asking, but he still couldn't believe it. He grabbed his phone and dialed his number.

"Hey Aka. What's up?" Baumgartner asked.

"God damn it, Boomer. I need you to be serious. We're not chasing pirates anymore and hanging out in Arab bars. What the hell is the meaning of this memo?"

"It's simple, Aka. We need you to provide some cover for a private yacht that is in search of a rogue submarine doing some hazardous drilling on the ocean floor that we believe is being funded by the Russian Mafia," Baumgartner answered.

"But this is a stolen yacht."

"Borrowed."

"Really. Did the owner get notification?"

"A matter of poor communications."

"Hmm, is this some Canadian bullshit?"

"We call it *merde* in French, and possibly yes. Can you help?"

"Who's on the yacht?"

"An FBI Agent, an RCMP Detective working on behalf of CSIS and several Americans and Canadians who have various warrants out for them for some charges that we won't go into at this time."

Akasawa closed his eyes and let his head sink to his chest. "Do we apprehend the people on board the yacht once we've established their safety?"

"Once they've established their objective and stopped this Russian sub from drilling, I think they'd return the yacht to the Coast Guard for its return to its rightful owner. As for laying charges, why don't we see if they've done any good before we proceed?"

"This sounds as bad as when we were catching pirates off the Somali Coast," Akasawa said.

"It has that air about it, yes."

"You mean, smell?"

Baumgartner sighed. "Okay, you were the one who was good at semantics. Can I count on you? Can you send some ships or air support?"

Akasawa looked at a screen that showed what ships and planes he had available. "This is going to be tough. Most of our fleet is being sent to back up the situation that's happening in the Arctic. We sent a complete task force of destroyers and cruisers up to the Bering Sea to blockade anymore Russian ships trying to enter the Arctic."

"How about aircraft?"

"Sure, I have a P-3 Orion Sub hunter I can send out, but you need some surface support." Akasawa scrolled down his screen. "I have two LCS that are in the area. I can send them."

"The Littoral Combat ships? The ones that have been plagued with technical bugs and keep having to be towed back to port?"

"Look, other than that, you got the Coast Guard. They're busy trying stopping looters from entering the port cities," Akasawa said.

"It's that bad?"

"You remember when we first did tours in the Gulf of Aden, and there were pirates everywhere trying to board ships?"

"Oh yeah, I will never forget those days."

"This is worse. Every jackass with any size boat can float into a compromised city and start to loot it. I've got problems from Chula Beach right into Coronado."

"Sorry, I know this is a pain in the ass I've handed you, but our Security and Intelligence thinks the people on the yacht might be able to make a difference. You know, like do some cooling of the ocean, and drop the atmospheric temperature."

"Holy shit. If you could promise that, I'd divert my carrier task force and every fighter aircraft I've got to cover them."

"Can't promise it, it's a hunch my security guy has."

"Is he any good?"

"Remember that bug that was infecting pipelines and shut down the Mediterranean Sea a year back?"

"Your guy did that?"

"No, it was Detective Bernadette Callahan who figured where the antidote was—she's on the yacht."

"Okay, you got your backup. I'll divert whatever I can to help them out. But I can't guarantee how well my little boats will do against three Russian Udaloy I Class Destroyers and a submarine. If things get hot for them, I'll tell them to pull back and let the Airforce handle it."

"I'm sure you'll do your best, that's all I ask," Baumgartner said as he ended the call.

Akasawa called his Petty Officer over to give him instructions. He hoped his best would be good enough. None of this was looking good.

51

BERNADETTE THOUGHT the island of garbage was a mirage when she first saw it. It rose like a thin grey line on the horizon. The ocean was dead calm.

Not a breeze stirred. McAllen slowed their speed to a crawl as they came within view of the mass of plastic refuse the sea had captured into a swirling vortex of currents and made into the fake island that could neither provide life nor give any sustenance to any creature that came upon it.

"I didn't realize it was so big and so visible," Bernadette said as she stared out at the island of floating garbage.

Samantha came up behind her and put her hand on her shoulder. "Up until this year you wouldn't have seen this at all. Most of the garbage was below the surface and lot of it was smaller. However, with the rising oceans, millions of tons of debris have floated off the shores and ended up here."

"How do we find Sigurdsson and his submarine beneath this island of garbage?" Percy asked walking up to the wheelhouse.

Bernadette walked over to the helm and gazed down at the stone from the Inuit woman. "What if we used this stone?"

"How about hanging off the bow with a string tied to it and see if starts to pulse downward, like a person with a divining rod looking for water in the desert?" Percy suggested.

"That's a great idea," Bernadette said. "Get me some strong cord that I can use."

Percy grinned. "You know that I was just making a silly suggestion. I had no idea you'd think it would work."

"Why wouldn't it? If the stone came from the headwaters of the River of Thule, then it should point the way to it." Bernadette's eyes were wide with excitement.

Samantha and Becky ran to the lower cabins and came back with some strong cord and a nylon mesh bag. They put the rock into the bag and secured it with a strong bowline knot. Bernadette went to the bow. She lay on her stomach and extended the rock out as far as she could reach. Samantha and Becky held the extra cord to ensure the rock didn't get loose.

"Tell McAllen to head slowly into the garbage patch. I'll relay to Becky when I feel the stone pulse downwards."

Percy yelled back to Bernadette, "No worries about McAllen going slow. You see how much garbage is out there? We could poke a hole in this boat with all that floating crap."

McAllen threaded the yacht past shipping containers, plastic crates, fishing nets and an entire set of a plastic bouncy castle that was still inflated and bobbed about as if some children would suddenly appear, to spend countless hours playing in it while the parents drank cocktails and ate roasted hotdogs.

Bernadette's arms were starting to ache when she felt a strong tug of the stone. She yelled to Becky, "Stop the boat."

McAllen put the engine in reverse then to a full stop. The yacht bumped into plastic bottles and a large sign for fish tacos.

"You think the submarine is under there?" Percy asked staring over the side into the debris and the water below.

"If it's drilling near the underwater river, it has to be there," Bernadette said.

"Now what? How do we take over a submarine?" Becky asked.

"With the superior forces of sound and magic," Sebastian said with a silly grin on his face.

Sebastian no longer looked stoned. As far as Bernadette could see, his pupils were now a regular size, and his speech wasn't slurred. He just seemed giddy from the plan he'd formulated.

"Okay, Captain Nemo," Bernadette said. "What've you got planned?"

Sebastian licked his lips and rubbed his hands together. "You're going to love this. We downloaded a whole fleet of warship sounds from the ship's computer and made it into a tape. I've got submarines and destroyers with their props churning, and pings from the hulls that will make anyone below think they've got a whole shit load of trouble bearing down on them."

"And why wouldn't they just cut their power line to the drill rig and run?" Samantha asked.

"From the information I found on this type of drill, it's got to be done manually. They attach the power lines on the surface then descend. They're a sitting duck down there. I lower an underwater sound amplifier and make like they are about to be run over by the American Navy, then we transmit a radio message that we're about to drop depth charges on them if they don't surface."

"Great, and when they surface and see a yacht, what then?" Becky said. "How many men have they got down there? Aren't they all armed?"

"Sure, but we have weapons—and my magic," Sebastian said with his silly grin going wider.

"Magic? What magic?" Becky asked.

"This lovely yacht has a hologram program. I've been testing it out overnight. I can make this little luxury boat look like a US Naval Destroyer with the flick of a switch. I've never seen anything so amazing."

Bernadette put her hand on Sebastian's shoulder. "Okay, are you sure it wasn't some really good weed you were smoking last night?"

McAllen stepped forward from behind the helm. "I can attest to the hologram. This yacht uses a hologram program to disguise it as different sizes of naval warships to scare off any would-be pirates. As long as we have power to the engines the hologram stays secure. I was with Sebastian overnight while he tested it—before he got stoned."

Sebastian wasted no time in getting his plan in progress. He had a long cord with an underwater speaker attached. He lowered it over the side and went below to start the sound program.

Margaret and Grace opened up the arms locker of the yacht handing out automatic weapons. Becky and Samantha wanted a quick lesson on their use but Bernadette put a stop to that.

"Just point the guns. You'll get respect. But don't pull the trigger," Bernadette said. She didn't need anyone opening fire by mistake. She made sure the safety was on both weapons.

McAllen punched in the hologram for a US Naval Destroyer. He decided to go with a replica of the USS Higgins. Once the speaker was in the water McAllen started to broadcast on his radio.

"Attention unidentified submarine. You've been deemed a threat to our vessels. Our destroyer, the USS Higgins and our submarine USS Jefferson City have targeted you. You will surface or be destroyed. Do you read me?"

There was no answer on the radio. They could only hear the sound of plastic rustling on the waves around the boat. McAllen repeated his message. There was still silence. Then they felt something. The yacht was moving—its bow began to lift into the air. McAllen ran to the helm to start the engines.

"The bloody thing is coming up from below us," McAllen yelled. "Everyone, hold on!"

52

THERE WAS the sickening sound of metal on metal as the massive submarine rose up from the sea with the yacht caught on its fore deck. The crew of the yacht was thrown back against the plush white leather sofas on the top deck. The drinks carts with silver platters lurched wildly towards the stern spilling ridiculously expensive bourbon in its wake.

Sebastian and Percy held fast to bar stools and watched in horror as a bottle of fifty-year-old brandy did a header on the deck and exploded into pieces.

"Such a waste," Sebastian muttered in the direction of the carnage of liquor.

The yacht was sliding backwards as the submarine rose. It finally rested; nose high with three quarters of its bulk out of water and nestled against the conning tower of the submarine. Men appeared out of the conning tower of the submarine. They couldn't believe their eyes. To them, they saw the hologram of a US Naval Destroyer resting on their submarine.

"What the hell do we do now?" Samantha asked looking at McAllen. She was holding onto the helm with him. The rest of the yacht crew had fallen into the massive leather sofas. They lay there not sure of what to do next.

"Maybe we get them on the loud hailer and ask them to surrender," Becky yelled. She was sprawled out on the sofa, with her feet up and a machine gun in her arms.

McAllen reached for the microphone. He punched the on button and pulled it towards him. "Attention submarine. Come out with your hands up. We have you surrounded."

"You mean covered, don't you?" Samantha said rolling her eyes.

"That would be too obvious," McAllen said, holding the microphone away from this mouth.

The crew of the submarine came out of the conning tower and deck hatches with guns. They looked at what they thought was a destroyer on top of them, dropped their weapons and fell to their knees with their hands up.

Bernadette pulled herself off the sofa, and with much effort made her way to the railing. "Look, it's working. They're surrendering. Get your weapons out and let's take over that submarine, everyone."

A chorus of cheers broke out from the yacht. Sebastian and Percy helped Theo, Margaret and Grace to the railing. They shouldered their weapons and trained them on the captured crew below. There was a feeling of elation from what they had just pulled off.

Then, the engines shut down.

"What happened?" Theo asked. His face went from jubilation to shock. "Did we just lose the engines?"

"Water must have seeped into the engine room," McAllen said.

Percy looked at Sebastian, "Does that mean we lost the hologram—?"

"Yep, and we're screwed," Sebastian said.

The men below saw a sleek yacht replace the naval destroyer and picked up their weapons. Shots rang out. Bullets bounced off of metal bulkheads. The crew of the yacht returned fire.

"Can we open fire now?" Becky asked Bernadette.

Bernadette looked at Becky. They were outnumbered four to one by the men on the submarine. She crawled over to her. "Go ahead, pointy end to the front, just like a spear gun."

Becky let off two quick bursts of fire that cleared the conning tower. "Like that?"

"Damn, you're a natural. Keep their heads down, I'll see if we've got any percussion grenades."

She moved down the railing to McAllen. "We got anything besides machine guns? Nothing is going to penetrate that submarine hull."

McAllen yelled to Sebastian over the gunfire. "Sebastian. You got anything else? We need magic or a bloody bomb."

Sebastian jumped back from the railing just as a bullet hit a bulk-head above him. Paint chips splattered over him. "Why didn't you say you wanted a bomb in the first place?"

He lurched along the deck; holding onto whatever he could until he reached the stairs leading down below.

"You think he'll come up with something?" Bernadette asked McAllen.

"I hope so, either that or he's gone to smoke a joint and get some inspiration."

The crew of the yacht had stopped firing. They were getting nowhere. The crew of the submarine had realized the same. Small weapons fire was having no effect on metal hulls.

"We're like the old iron warships that met in the American Civil War," Percy said sitting next to McAllen. When they met the first time none of their armaments could penetrate each other's armor. The battle ended up a stalemate and they both slunk off back to their lines."

"The problem is, we can't slink off anywhere until we can get rid of this submarine. You think he'll submerge?" Bernadette asked.

"He could. Then back up and ram us," McAllen said. "But they can't do it with the drilling rig attached to the sub. If we can keep them from getting forward on the deck, they'll have to stay where they are."

"This really is a stalemate," Bernadette said.

"Only until we run out of ammunition," McAllen replied.

Sebastian appeared with several canisters. "I've got it."

Bernadette pulled her head back from the railing as a barrage of gunfire ricocheted on the rails making her flinch. "Got what?"

"I've got bombs," Sebastian said with a noticeable look of glee.

"What, C-4 explosives? That could harm this boat if you throw that over the side," Bernadette said.

"Hell no. This ain't no C-4. The guys who owned this yacht were rock in roll musicians. This shit is a psychedelic love bomb. It's filled with Magic Mushroom dust. These guys used to lobe this into their rock concerts so everyone would get stoned," Sebastian said.

"But you have no idea how long it would take to have an effect," Bernadette said.

"What's the difference? We could be hung up here on this submarine for hours or days. I figure the dust in this will act pretty fast, otherwise the musicians would never have used it," Sebastian said.

McAllen nodded his approval, took a canister, primed it and threw it over the side. It exploded in a cloud of fluorescent colours on the deck of the submarine.

The men on the submarine stopped firing their weapons.

Bernadette looked over the railing. The men put down their weapons. They were looking at their hands. Some were wondering around the deck and looking at the plastic garbage on the side of the sub. A few giggled, some sat cross-legged and stared into space.

"That's awesome," Becky said. "Can I throw one?"

"Sure, knock yourself out," Sebastian said. "Just make sure to click the primer and give it a good toss."

Becky took the canister, clicked the operating primer to one side and took her arm back to make a throw. The canister slipped out of her hand and fell on the deck.

"Aw shit," Becky said.

"Wow, that's far out," Sebastian said.

Bernadette tried not to breathe. She held her breath and crawled backwards, away from the canister. Was it too late? Had she ingested any of the magic mushroom dust? How soon would she know?

She'd studied hallucinogenic drugs in the RCMP. Magic Mushrooms had hallucinogenic side effects. There was a feeling of oneness with the universe. She remembered reading that surfaces may tend to ripple. How would she know that? What would it look like?

She looked at the canister. The colours were coming out in waves and patterns. The rest of the crew was staring at the cloud of fluorescents in awe.

Bernadette felt nothing. Maybe the dust hadn't affected her? She looked down at the wooden deck were her hand was, it had disappeared into the wood.

Her conscious mind saw a small cloud descend in front of her. The cloud was blue and green with a hint of gold. Where had she ever seen something like that before she wondered?

She remembered she had a bed cover like that back in her room when she lived with her parents. A warm feeling came over her. She heard herself moan with pleasure.

A figure appeared in front of her. She wasn't sure who it was at first, then she realized it was her Grandmother Moses. She bent down and took Bernadette's hands and raised them to her face and began to speak.

Grandmother Moses was saying something very grave. It sounded like a message. Bernadette tried hard to hear, but there was a humming sound in her ears.

She leaned closer to Grandmother Moses. "What are you trying to say?"

"You're being boarded by Russians. Your life is in danger."

53

BERNADETTE FELT THE SHIP MOVE. Did the submarine submerge? Had the stoned submariners remembered to close their hatches before they dived?

A feeling of loss came over her. She had no idea why. Then the ship's floor became level. She no longer had to lean to one side to keep from sliding backwards. That was a nice feeling. A level feeling —she thought she might like to explore that.

She heard shouting. Large men were climbing over the railings of the yacht. They didn't look like nice men—muscles, tattoos, unshaven faces and guns.

The men removed all the weapons from the yacht crew. One very large man came and stood over Bernadette. He had a strange face. He looked like a wolf.

"I am Volkov," the man said. "You must be Detective Bernadette Callahan, and I assume that is Alistair McAllen and FBI Agent Winston lying over there on the floor."

Bernadette blinked her eyes twice in reply. She thought that was satisfactory at this point.

Volkov surveyed the yacht and looked over the side at the submarine. "You have been a colossal pain in the ass. You have come close to destroying our plans and our billions of dollars in expense."

Bernadette blinked three times. She wanted to show how much she appreciated his words. She tried to move her mouth; words did not seem to want to form. She mumbled a subtle, "Hmmm."

Volkov stood directly over Bernadette. "You think you have stopped us by exposing our plans to the newspapers? You have failed. The Russian Mafia is much stronger than you think."

Bernadette's mouth made a benign, "Oh," in response.

Volkov took this as a sign that Bernadette was being argumentative. "Ha, the Russian Mafia bows to no government, and we will prevail. We do not need the Russian Military. We have infiltrated all of your fringe groups in the United States. Once we've finished here, and raised the temperature of the sea, we will watch America fall into chaos, and our operatives will lead all the factions. This will be the greatest takeover of another country ever orchestrated by us."

Bernadette shook her head to clear her eyes and try to focus. She was starting to come out of the hallucinations.

"You don't have to worry about your fate, my dear," Volkov continued. "I'll make sure that all of you die after we've finished here with the drilling. But I will make sure that your death will be especially painful and I will exact whatever pleasure I see fit off your body before I see the light fade from your soul."

Bernadette now understood why the vision of her grandmother had appeared to tell her about a dangerous man. He was also vicious. Volkov shouted instructions in Russian to his crew. Bernadette and the crew of the yacht were pulled up from the deck and pushed to the railings. Sebastian resisted. He was clubbed to the floor with the butt of a rifle.

Bernadette felt a large hand over her face. "I will be sending you all to my ship." Volkov said. "This very nice yacht will be a lovely prize for me, lucky for me; the submarine did not put a hole in it. I do not want the bother of having to clean up your blood from these beautiful decks."

His breath was on her face. He smelled of stale meat and alcohol.

Her heart was racing; her arms began to shake of their own accord. If these were to be her last moments on Earth she wished it could have been in the arms of her lover, Chris. Her mind reached out to him. Wherever he might be in the world, she made a desperate plea that she would one day be with him again.

Another pair of hands grabbed Bernadette. A face appeared close to her. It was a thin face with scars. It looked familiar.

"Don't you remember me?" the face asked.

"Hmm, no," Bernadette mumbled in an attempted reply. Her tongue was just starting to make itself useful in her mouth.

"I am the Kazak you wanted to throw to the sharks in Key West—now you remember me?"

Bernadette stared at him hard. "You must be a good swimmer."

The Kazak laughed. "Yes, I am very good. I escaped your boat in hurricane waves. You should have killed me. I make sure I kill all your friends in front of you. You will watch as I feed them to the sharks."

Bernadette shook her head. "You're not a nice man."

The Kazak roared with laughter. He translated Bernadette's words to the Russians who broke into a chorus of laughter.

The laughter brought Bernadette to her senses. The fog left her brain. Sharpness came. She could see all the Russians, what weapons they had and where they stood. A large red ship was 500 metres off their starboard side.

Her crew had been moved to the railing. She needed a plan. It appeared in flash of silver. A silver canister rolled onto the deck. McAllen had kicked it towards her. She knew what to do. She dropped to her knees and grabbed the canister. With one twist she released the cap. A stream of fluorescent colour shot out of the canister. Bernadette pointed the canister at the Russians. They raised their guns—not one fired.

"Everyone. Over the side—now," Bernadette yelled.

The yacht crew leapt over the side with no hesitation. The fear of the Russians was far greater than the five-metre drop to whatever lay in the water.

Bernadette followed them over. She expected to land on hard plastic or fall through the debris into the cold Pacific Ocean. But she bounced.

She bounced high the first time and almost collided with Margaret Ashley. On her second bounce she landed on Grace Fairchild. She gave out a loud whoosh of air and several invectives.

Bernadette rolled over to her side and looked up. They'd fallen onto the bouncy castle. One of the inflatable playthings used to amuse children at birthday parties. It was at least ten by ten metres with tall-inflated pillars that resembled palm trees. Colours of blue, yellow and green rotated in an inflatable maze.

A slide was in the centre. Sebastian and Percy were hanging onto the top. Both of them were having difficulty understanding whether this bouncy castle was real or part of the magic mushroom hallucination.

McAllen came towards Bernadette, bouncing as he did so. He looked somewhat comical, bouncing over an inflatable frog to get to her. Bernadette lay on her side. Trying to stand on this thing was impossible. It floated on the waves. Small flags fluttered overhead proclaiming this the fairest bouncing castle of all.

"We need to get onto the other ship," McAllen said, pointing to the supply ship that Volkov had arrived on.

Theo picked up a toilet seat cover from the water "Maybe we could paddle this floating plaything over there if I could find a few more of these. It's only a few hundred meters but it'd take time."

"Look around for anything we can use as paddles, we need to get moving before the Russians come out of their hallucinations. They probably have weapons on their ship," McAllen said.

"I don't think we have to worry about any of that, Uncle Mac," Becky said.

"Why's that?"

"There are more Russians coming." Becky pointed towards the stern of the yacht. A large destroyer with a Russian flag had dropped anchor. Three zodiacs full of sailors with weapons came towards them.

54

THEY WERE TAKEN aboard the Russian destroyer and handcuffed. Bernadette wondered if their luck would ever change. They stood in line on the deck. An officer approached them yelling instructions to the sailors. The handcuffs were taken off.

"I apologize for my men putting you in handcuffs. I am Captain Anatoly Yelchin of the Russian Navy. We have come here to destroy this drilling operation. The article that was published in your American Newspapers alerted our government to the disaster that the Russian Mafia has been trying to make on the American people. We are here to put a stop to it. I assume you are one of the ones that helped uncover this?"

"Yes, with a lot of help from the people I'm with," Bernadette said

Captain Yelchin took Bernadette to one side, away from his men. "I understand you are in possession of the stone of Thule. Is this correct?"

Bernadette stared into the face of the captain. He looked too young to be the captain of the Russian Destroyer that bobbed alongside the yacht. He looked all of twenty-something with bright blue eyes and a light beard that struggled to frame his face.

"How do you know of this?" she asked.

"My wife's family are Russian Inuit, they are called Yuits from the Chukotka Territory. Your journey has been all over the Arctic Peoples Facebook group. I have strict instructions from my wife and my mother-in-law that I'm supposed to aid you any way I can." He looked back at his men. "My men know nothing about this. I will tell them I'm aiding in the destruction of the drill," Yelchin said.

Bernadette tried not to smile. The little Inuit woman from Iqaluit had expanded her reach farther than she could have imagined. "The stone is on the yacht, but we have no idea what to do with it."

"Sigurdsson will know," McAllen said. He had moved closer to Bernadette and the captain and overheard the conversation.

They climbed into the zodiacs and motored to the submarine. The crew of the submarine was coming out of their hallucinations to find Russian sailors with guns trained on them. They put their hands up, again.

McAllen, Bernadette, Sam and Becky went on the submarine with the captain and the sailors but there was no sign of Sigurdsson on deck. They went below into the confined space of the submarine. The boat smelled foul. Stale air with rancid human odors assailed them. They searched each small room until they came to a room marked, 'private-keep-out', in large letters.

McAllen swung the door open to see Sigurdsson sitting at a desk looking at a laptop with swirling colours.

"Barney. Are you okay? Samantha asked. She rushed over with Becky and they wrapped him in a hug.

"I knew you'd come," Barney said in muffled voice from the huddle that engulfed him.

"We're glad you're safe," Becky said.

Sigurdsson looked at McAllen. "Sorry, Mac, I've failed everyone. I thought I'd be able to drill down below the magma and unleash the river, but every drill bit I've used becomes useless once it hits the underground lava flow. I've only increased the temperature of the ocean."

"What if you had a different drill bit? Maybe tipped with something stronger?" Captain Yelchin said.

Sigurdsson shook his head. "I've tried everything they've sent me. Titanium, diamond, nothing works."

"I was given a rock from the high Arctic by an Inuit woman," Bernadette said. She said it was from the headwaters of the River of Thule. Damned if I know what she was talking about, but my gut feeling tells me we give it a try."

"The drill became detached from the submarine when your boat backed off. It's a thousand metres on the bottom of the ocean and I have no way of reattaching it," Sigurdsson said.

"We'll use the mini-submarine on the back of the yacht. It has a robotic arm. We could attach the stone to the drill bit with it," McAllen suggested.

"Excellent. I will have my sailors take it down, and have it attached," Captain Yelchin said.

"I think I have to be on board the submarine," Bernadette said.

"Why is that? You need to go 1,000 metres deep in a small glass bubble?" McAllen asked.

Bernadette closed her eyes. "No, the thought scares the hell out of me, but the old woman in the Arctic said the stone was in my care to get it to the headwaters of Thule. I feel responsible for it."

"Fine, you will go down in the small submarine. Anyone else?" Yelchin asked looking around the group.

"I need to go as well," Sigurdsson said. "This whole fiasco is my fault. I need to see the drill bit is affixed properly."

Samantha hugged him harder. "You know if you unleash the water under the magma there will be one hell of an underwater explosion?"

Sigurdsson shrugged. "Yeah, I know, but we have to stay down there to monitor the drill, to make sure it's working."

"Let's get going," Captain Yelchin said. "I have reports on my radio that American ships are approaching and some submarine hunting aircraft. We need to be finished with this before they arrive."

55

BERNADETTE WATCHED the water encase them as they descended in the small submarine. There was nothing comforting about the thick bubble of Plexiglas that stood between them and the sea.

Getting into the little submarine had taken all of her reserves of courage. The three-seat sub looked like a toy. Percy had given them a quick overview of the craft and shown them how they'd communicate with the surface. A spool of thin wire would release an antenna on the back; this would allow them radio communication in the deepest part of the ocean.

Bernadette looked at the thin-spooled wire and wished it were hooked from the ship to the submarine. She got in, strapped herself in and muttered a silent Hail Mary prayer for their return to the surface.

The first few metres of descent were filled with garbage. Plastic bottles, plastic bags, everything plastic was floating around them in a swirling circle as they blew tanks and began to descend. Bernadette sat beside the Russian sailor who navigated the submarine. Sigurdsson was in the back seat.

The sailor introduced himself as Sergey, he had a brush cut and two gold teeth that flashed when he smiled. He told Bernadette he had been to Canada twice and liked Canadian bacon, but not Canadian hockey players. Russian hockey players were much better according to Sergey. Bernadette smiled at Sergey, trying to hide her absolute horror with the depth they were going to.

The water grew darker. Sergey switched on the lights. Small fish swam into view. They swarmed the submarine to see if it was some predator that might be eating other fish that they could then consume themselves. When they realized this was a sea creature of metal they darted away.

A massive great white shark swam by, then began to circle. Was it checking the submarine to see if it was edible or a threat? After a few more circles it flicked its big tail and shot off into the depths.

They descended deeper. Bernadette could see the depth gage. 500 metres became 750, then 950. Now, they descended slowly. Sergey was feeling his way in the dark, not wanting to bump into the drilling rig.

The stone was affixed firmly in the robotic arm in front of them. It was glowing white. The red glow on board the ship had changed the moment they entered the water.

"There it is," Sigurdsson said, pointing towards a faint object on the sea floor.

They came upon a cage, some twenty metres in diameter with a series of rods inside. Sergey deftly maneuvered the mini-submarine alongside. Sidgurdsson instructed him how to attach the stone to the end of the drill bit.

Bernadette watched as the stone fit perfectly to the drill bit end. How was that possible she thought? It was as if this stone had morphed from a simple stone to a direction finder and now here it was a perfect fit to the end of a drill.

"Push that button on the side of the cage," Sigurdsson said to Sergey.

"How long will it take?" Bernadette asked.

"Not long," Sigurdsson said. "I've been trying to penetrate below the magma for the several days. If this stone works, it will pierce through the magma and into the underwater river. Then we'll see some fireworks—or rather, waterworks."

"I will back off a bit," Sergey said.

"Good idea," Bernadette said trying to mask her terror at being so deep with a potential natural explosion about to take place. The small sub moved off at the speed that resembled a puffer fish to Bernadette. Not a speed that matched the danger they were in.

A stream of bubbles came from the drill. The submarine moved one hundred metres away. The bubbles became a torrent. The submarine was being pushed away by the stream.

"Can we move any faster?" Bernadette asked Sergey. She was trying to mask the tension she felt. Her voice had a noticeable squeak to it.

"This is maximum," Sergey said, his gold teeth flashing a smile. The little sub toddled away with its small propellers at 3 knots.

"It's happening," Sigurdsson said, his voice full of excitement. "We've broken through."

A geyser erupted before them. A column of white water shot up twenty metres wide that became thirty then forty metres wide.

"I think we head to the surface now," Sergey said.

Bernadette had never heard sweeter words. She turned to nod at Sergey. The drilling rig was coming at them when she turned back.

The rig cage tumbled towards the submarine end over end. It was caught in the submarine's lights. Sergey could do nothing at the controls to avoid it. Bernadette hoped it would somehow take one more revolution and pass over them.

It dropped onto the bubble of the submarine in a sickening crunch. They felt the jarring of the heavy metal cage. It shook the submarine then forced it down to the seabed. A cloud of sand rose from the sea floor. Bernadette reached her hand up to the plexi-glass to see if it had cracked. It was cold to the touch, but she felt no moisture. They were safe—for now.

"What do we do now?" Bernadette asked Sergey.

Sergey spoke into his microphone several times. He got no answer. "Our transmission antenna has been ripped off."

"What now?" Sigurdsson asked leaning forward from the back. "Do we have any back up?"

Sergey flashed his ridiculously positive gold teeth. "I am Russian —we always have backup plan." Sergey took out a satellite cellphone; he attached a cable from it to the console and started typing on the keypad.

"That works down here?"

"Russian cell phone with Morse code for deep water," Sergey explained. "I will ask our submarine to come to our aid."

Bernadette looked at Sergey for a moment to try to understand what he had just said. "How is a nuclear-powered submarine going to move this drilling rig off us? They can't even see us down here."

"Not a problem. The submarine will use their hydrophones and I will tell them how close they are getting to us," Sergey said.

"I hope they don't crush us," Bernadette said looking out the bubble at the drilling rig sitting on top of them.

Sergey said nothing. His fingers flew on the cell phone as he gave their coordinates to the submarine. They sat in silence. The sand had cleared. All they could see beyond the lights were the end of the rig.

Sergey broke the silence. "We should be seeing my submarine the Alorsa very soon. I am very proud of this boat. She is 3,000 tons underwater, 74 metres long with a submerged speed of 25 knots." He flashed his gold teeth once more. "I am considered the best driver of the boat. But don't worry. I have told my friend, Dmitri, that in no way is he to crush us."

Bernadette frowned. "I hope he's as good as you say. I'm not much for swimming at this depth."

"Oh, don't worry," Sergey said. "If this bubble cracks, the pressure down here would crush us immediately."

A massive shadow appeared above them. "There it is." Sergey began typing on his phone.

They could feel the rig moving, swaying with the movement from the submarine. The rig scraped right then left on the bubble. It made a loud screeching sound and stopped.

"It's not working," Sigurdsson said.

"I will get them to do an aft propeller wash. This will push the rig off us." Sergey typed in the instructions.

The submarine moved overhead. A single small light from the mini submarine could barely make out its bulk as it moved. Bernadette thought this might be what being dated by a whale would look like.

There was silence again.

A torrent of water washed over them. The submarine was in front of them with propellers fully revved. The rig moved slowly scraping over the bubble and falling off them.

"There. We are free," Sergey said. He pressed the controls for the motors. There was no response. "Ah, the rig must have damaged the electrical system."

Bernadette was amazed at Sergey's composure. It must be the requirement for a submariner. "What do we do now?"

Sergey hit a switch. "We float slowly to the surface. All submarines have a failsafe switch to head for the surface when their propulsion systems fail. We will be on the surface shortly."

The mini-submarine started to float upward. There was a sense of relief. Bernadette sat back in her soft leather chair and began to look above her for the first time with hope that she would be in open sky again.

She felt her feet getting wet. "Sergey. I feel water on my feet, are we breached?"

"Yes, a bit of sea water has seeped in. Don't worry. This often happens when submarines are in stress. We will be fine."

Bernadette switched on the interior cabin lights. The light confirmed what her feet were telling her. The water was rising.

"Sergey. The water is higher," Bernadette said. She hoped her information and the small amount of stress in her voice might get his attention.

"Yes. A seal in the bubble is cracked," Sergey said, his face serene. He watched the depth gauge. It showed they were at 500 metres— half way to the surface.

"Can we raise up any faster?" Sigurdsson asked, placing his hand on Sergey's shoulder as if this might get his point across.

Sergey shook his head. "These submarines are not designed for quick ascents. In my attack submarine, I could be on the surface by now."

Bernadette looked at the depth gauge. They had risen to 200 metres. The water was up to the base of their chairs—it was rising faster. At 100 metres the water was up to their shoulders. They removed their chair harnesses and were floating inside the bubble. Sergey had his cell phone over his head and the ridiculous smile on his face.

Bernadette could no longer see the controls on the console. Light from the surface appeared above them. The water kept rising.

The water lapped at Bernadette's chin as they broke through the surface. They bobbed on the surface in a sea of plastic garbage. Bernadette felt like a goldfish, swimming inside the bubble. Sergey dove to the controls but the hatch wouldn't open.

A zodiac with four Russian sailors and the captain appeared. They climbed onto the mini-sub and opened the bubble. They poured out of it as it rose up.

Bernadette looked at the sky and breathed in deeply. Something about the sky looked odd. There were clouds—lots of clouds.

She stood up in the zodiac to see a column of water gushing into the atmosphere. "Did we create that?"

"Yes, you did," Captain Yelchin said. "The geyser is creating clouds. And it is starting to rain."

Sigurdsson started to dance around in the zodiac. "It's from the River of Thule. You see, I knew I was right. The river is underneath the molten magma. When it was pierced, it created a chute up the magma as the lava cooled. I knew this would work!"

Sergey flashed his gold teeth. "You see, Russian ingenuity has won the day."

"That and a little stone from a beach in Canada's Arctic," Bernadette said. She turned to the Captain Yelchin, "Well, what now? Can we get a lift back to America on your ship?"

"We have repaired your yacht. Your crew is aboard and the Russian Mafia crew is now our guests. We will be taking them back to Russia for trial," Captain Yelchin said.

Bernadette sat back in the zodiac as they motored through the sea of plastic to the yacht. Loud music was coming from the ship. They climbed aboard to find McAllen and the rest of the crew dancing to Reggae music and drinking beer.

They broke into cheers and hugged, handing them ice cold Corona beers. There was backslapping, kisses and kudos to everyone for the opening of The River of Thule.

A fighter jet came low overhead, followed by two more. Everyone hit the deck.

56

"THOSE ARE AMERICAN F35 FIGHTER JETS," Captain Yelchin said, his voice almost drowned out by the roar. "My ship could not detect them. They have stealth capabilities."

Bernadette was lying on the deck. Captain Yelchin was standing, watching the fighter jets swooping low and turning to make another pass. He looked like a kid admiring an air show.

Yelchin looked down at Bernadette. "Are they not beautiful to see?"

Bernadette stood up, shielding her eyes from the sun. "Yes, they are wonderful. You're not concerned they'll attack your ships?"

"Hah," Yelchin scoffed. "If my ships detect a lock on of their missiles we'll throw out counter measures to destroy the missiles and blow them out of the sky. We would show them many surprises. Even the F35s are not superior to our Russian ships."

"This is going to get silly rather quickly," Bernadette said. She turned to Sergey. "I need your satellite cell phone."

Bernadette dialed Anton. He answered on the second ring. "Anton, I need your help—now."

"Bernadette, where are you? I've just noticed some strange

climate changes in the Pacific Ocean. Is that your doing?" Anton asked.

Bernadette blew out a breath. "Well, sure, me and a whole bunch of ancient legends colliding. Look, not a lot of time here. Remember that back up I asked for?"

"Yeah, did the Americans arrive?"

"Sure did, can you get them to back off?"

"Problem?" Anton asked.

"Oh, yeah. We've got some friendly Russians and need the flyboys and whoever else is coming to back off. Can you do that?"

"You're sure you're all safe?" Anton asked.

"Totally. Thanks for caring, Anton." Bernadette ended the call and handed the phone back to Sergey. She turned to Captain Yelchin. "Captain, please have your ships weapons stand down. This is a misunderstanding."

A few minutes later the jet fighter waggled their wings and flew off toward the coast of America. A small American ship did the same. It blew its horn and turned towards home. The Russians ships and submarine blew two farewell blasts.

They were left with the sound of reggae music. Bob Marley was singing, *coming in from the cold.*

Off in the distance, a geyser of water was erupting into the atmosphere. The underwater river was shooting into the sky, creating clouds. The clouds were dropping rain. It was a glorious sight. Bernadette turned her face to the heaven. She felt cool rain. She hadn't felt that in a long time. It felt wonderful.

57

THE RETURN TRIP back to America was like a pleasure cruise for the crew. Grace delved deep into the stores of the ship's galley and found frozen lobster and several cases of filet mignon. Theo found a case of fine French Champagne.

They ate and drank until the wee hours of the morning to celebrate their success. On the day they approached the coast, Bernadette went up to the bridge carrying two coffees to look for McAllen. He was standing at the wheel of the bridge, staring at the coast, his soft blue eyes taking in a homeland that no longer welcomed him. He looked up and smiled at Bernadette when he saw her.

"You here to put me under arrest now that this adventure is over?"

Bernadette handed McAllen a coffee and sipped on her own. "No, I actually have been in touch with both the Canadian and American authorities. They have come up with a deal for you."

"Will I like it?"

Bernadette arched an eyebrow. "They will give all of you amnesty if you agree to never use your science to go after North American Industry. Do you think you could do that?"

McAllen sipped his coffee and looked from Bernadette to the coastline. "That would give all those industrial goons a free ride, wouldn't it? They could keep polluting, making things that hurt the earth, and be sure that if they had enough government hacks in their back pocket they're free to make as much money as they want."

"Okay, hell of a speech, Professor, but the industrial goons as you call them are tax paying citizens who are regulated by environmental controls," Bernadette said.

"Yeah, we can see how well that's worked." He stared straight ahead at the coastline, his eyes fixing on a beach.

"I kind of need an answer," Bernadette said.

"Give me an hour," McAllen replied.

Bernadette went back to her cabin and took a long shower. When she came out of the cabin she felt the ship had stopped. She went up the stairs to the bridge to see Winston standing there with her hands over her head. Sebastian was standing there with a gun pointed at her.

"Sorry, ladies," Sebastian said. "Captain's orders. You two are being put ashore."

"What the hell are you talking about?" Bernadette asked.

McAllen walked up behind her. "You wanted an answer, you got it. There's no way I can live my life with the knowledge I can never act on my own conscience. Tell your authorities, I'll do whatever I want. And if that means you come after me again, well that's the way it is. I'm not going to sit idle and watch bad things happen on this Earth— you got that?"

Bernadette tilted her head to one side and smiled. "You know, I expected you to turn them down. I hope you and your merry band head for somewhere safe. Are you taking Sigurdsson and his family with you?"

"No, Barney wanted to hang out with us, but Samantha put her foot down, I think it's more for Becky's sake," McAllen said. "And Barney's already had offers flowing in to help reduce the Earth's core with other underwater rivers. Seems he's some kind of Icelandic hero now."

"They will sing songs about me back in Reykjavik," Barney said with a smile.

"We'll drop them off down in San Diego," McAllen said.

"And how do you think you'll get around in this stolen super yacht?" Winston asked. She was looking at Sebastian with eyes that said he'd betrayed her and he'd best keep the gun pointed at her.

"We have our ways," Sebastian said. He got the message from Winston; he backed off from her slightly.

Winston and Bernadette stepped off a ladder and into a zodiac, started the motor and headed for the shore. There was a beach some 500 metres away that Bernadette pointed the boat towards.

When they reached the shore, she hopped off the boat and beached it with Winston. They watched the yacht turn and head down south. As it disappeared in the distance, it changed its appearance. Sebastian had turned on the holographic program to hide the boat. It became a tuna boat—a very fast moving one.

58

THE NEXT SEVERAL weeks were a wonder of climate correction for NorthAmerica.

The clouds filled with moisture and it rained. Not a deluge, but a rain that put out the fires and brought the temperatures down. People returned from Latin America and Mexico to the American Midwest where the temperatures were now becoming reasonable. Winter was returning and a cool snow fell.

Bernadette Callahan had made her report. It was long, detailed and listed all the people who had helped along the way. She had Anton De Luca's word that no one would be punished for whatever assistance they had given. She did not mention that Winston and her had been put off McAllen's ship at gunpoint, merely that they had gone their separate ways. She hoped the authorities would give McAllen and his friends a break.

They had after all, saved North America from drought and raging fires. The oceans would take some time to recede. It was already getting much colder in the Arctic and the Antarctic.

The billionaires from Hong Kong, the Philippines and Willa Flowers who was hiding in Panama were tracked down and extradited to the International Court in The Hague in Holland. Willa was finally going home, but not to the reception she'd hoped for.

The Russians were prosecuting the Mafia. Bernadette hoped there were enough non-corrupt judges to convict them. The world's media was being cautiously optimistic.

Bernadette had a phone call from Danny in Iqaluit. He'd wanted to say thank you for returning the stone to its origin. Everyone in the high Arctic knew about the story. He said it would be told for generations to come. She was now part of the legends of the north.

"Do you have your ice back on the ocean?" Bernadette asked.

"Yes, we do. I saw my first Polar Bear stalking some seals yesterday on the ice. It was a beautiful sight," Danny said.

"What about the cruise ships that can no longer sail up there to visit the Arctic. Won't your people miss the added tourist income?" Bernadette asked.

"No, we thought it was getting too busy with them up here. The Arctic is a place of peace and quiet. If the tourists want to come, they can visit in smaller groups and come onto the land. We'll be happy to take them," Danny said.

Danny sent Bernadette a case of tinned walrus meat. She'd opened a tin of it and offered it to her dog, Sprocket. He'd laid his ears back with his tail between his legs and slunk off to the furthest place away from the meat and the smell.

Bernadette shook her head. "There's obviously no wolf blood in you, Sprocket."

She was waiting a phone call from Chris. They'd spoken in the past several weeks. Chris decided to finish his contract on December 31st and Bernadette was going to fly to Paris to meet him.

There was one more trip with his client he needed to take. Chris had sounded anxious about it, but said he wanted to go to make sure the others in his group were safe. Then his calls stopped.

Calls to his cell said his voice mailbox was full. Bernadette tried not to let panic or anxiety set in. There had been many times in their relationship when they couldn't reach each other. Why should this be any different?

On the 30th of December, her cell phone rang. She recognized the number as being from overseas. Her heart beat so hard she could hardly breathe. "Hey baby, is that you?"

"Is this the phone number of Detective Bernadette Callahan?" an official voice asked.

"Yes, it is. Who is this?"

"I'm Vincent Caprinski. I worked with your fiancée. I have to inform you that he's missing."

"What do you mean? How long since he didn't report back from his mission?" Bernadette asked.

"It's been three days," Caprinski said.

"Didn't his people call in every day? Why would you wait three days? Are they injured somewhere. Did their vehicles break down? Where were they travelling too?"

"I'm not at liberty to say."

"What are you at liberty to say?"

"That your fiancée is missing. We have registered this with the Canadian Embassy and the military in Kandahar. That's all we can say for now."

"That's not good enough. I'll need to speak to someone in charge," Bernadette said.

"I'm in charge. And this is all I can tell you."

Bernadette ran her hand through her hair. "Where are you located?"

"I operate out of our company base in Kandahar. Why do you ask?"

"Because I'm coming over there," Bernadette said.

She put down the phone and sent a note to her boss. He'd been telling her she needed some time off. She was taking it now.

DEAR READER

I hope you enjoyed my fantastic tale of Bernadette Callahan saving the world. I know I loved writing it. My inspiration for the story came from my personal climate experience.

One spring we had a torrential downpour of rain that flooded our lakes with a "one hundred year episode," of precipitation—followed by the worst forest fires we'd ever seen.

My home of Kelowna, British Columbia, Canada was filled with smoke. So, I sent Bernadette Callahan off to save the world that fall. I'm a writer, that's how I roll.

The next in the series, is Caught In the Crossfire. Bernadette will head for Afghanistan to find Chris and hopefully, return him home safely. Enjoy!

You can read the next three chapters of the next book in the series on the next page.

CAUGHT IN THE CROSSFIRE

A BERNADETTE CALLAHAN MYSTERY

LYLE NICHOLSON

CAUGHT IN THE CROSSFIRE
CHAPTER ONE, THREE WEEKS AGO

Ghulam Nasim hurried along the darkened streets of Kandahar. Isha, the last call to prayer, had sounded several hours ago. The cleric's short legs moved as fast as they could over the recent snow; his leather shoes had become wet. He cursed leaving without his boots. But this was too important. A boy had appeared at his house telling him Imam Sardar Agha, the leader of Kandahar's largest mosque wanted him at the Shrine of the Cloak of the Prophet.

Something was wrong; Ghulam could feel it in his bones. The ancient cloak, once worn by the Prophet Mohammed, had been kept in the shrine for centuries. Ghulam's sole job was to keep the cloak he'd never seen safe in the shrine. It was kept in an ornate wooden box. The boy said the box had been broken, things in the shrine were scattered. He had to come quickly.

His mind raced over the possibilities, his breaths coming in short bursts. His heart felt like it wanted to explode with fear.

The imam, Sardar, would have his head if the sacred cloak were missing. How would he explain such a thing? Last night after the fourth prayer, when the imam had been meeting with two foreigners, the box had been intact.

Ghulam had opened the shrine and let the imam and the

foreigners in. One was a thin man with blond hair and blue eyes that darted around the room taking in the artifacts as if he was appraising them for sale. The other man was tall and dark with a thick chest and arms; he seemed to be the blond man's bodyguard.

The imam had dismissed Ghulam, telling him to leave the key with him. He could pick it up at the mosque next to the shrine in the morning.

Now, the cleric panted as he reached the stairs of the shrine. He could hardly make it up the stairs from his exertion.

He heaved himself through the front doors. It was, as he feared. The ornate box with the brass hinges that Ghulam had polished so lovingly for many years was in splinters.

He clutched his chest. "What happened? How did this happen?"

"I thought you could tell us, Ghulam Nasim," Imam Sardar said as he walked into the room. The imam was much taller and older than Ghulam. He always carried himself with an air of his religious office, however tonight he wore plain brown robes and only a cap. He looked as if he'd been pulled from bed. His fierce eyes penetrated into Ghulam's, making him feel smaller than his five feet three inches.

"But, but, I left you alone with the two gentlemen tonight. You said you'd leave the key at the mosque for me this morning."

"Enough of your silly explanations, Ghulam. I locked the door myself when I left. I have the key with me. Did you make an extra key and give it to the foreigners?"

"Of course not. I could not, I would do no such thing," Ghulam protested.

"Are you sure? The little one, he seemed quite taken with you last night, asking you many questions. He didn't offer you some extra money to steal our precious cloak?" the imam asked. His eyebrows rose high in two accusing arches.

"No, no, no my Imam. I have been caretaker of the sacred cloak for many years. This shrine is my life, I would never sell it to Infidels —to anyone."

"Yes, we will see what the videos show. All will be revealed...ah, here is the chief of police. We will have an answer to this great tragedy soon, Ghulam. You had better hope that Allah is merciful."

Ghulam felt his heart growing smaller in his chest. How could this be? The sacred cloak, the only thing that mattered in his shrine, was gone. If by some hand of fate he was found at fault, his head would roll, not figuratively, but in the square of Kandahar at the hands of an executioner.

CAUGHT IN THE CROSSFIRE
CHAPTER TWO

Chris Christakos wasn't happy with this morning's mission. He'd been pulled from his room at 0500. His orders were to escort Jannick Lund, their personal protection client out of Kandahar, to a small village so he could do some recon of a water project he wanted to fund.

Jannick Lund was CEO of a Non-Government Agency; they called them NGO's here in the 'Stan, the short name for Afghanistan.

Chris had signed a three-month contract, leaving his fiancé Bernadette Callahan to come here and show his worth. This was the dumbest thing he'd ever done, he thought as he pulled on his bullet-proof vest and strapped his Glock to his leg, then checked his MP5 machine gun.

He was supposed to be heading for the airport the next day on a flight to Paris to meet Bernadette and rekindle their relationship. He couldn't count the number of times he'd apologized for being so brash and accepting this job. Sure, it was one thousand dollars a day, a cool ninety thousand good old US dollars tax-free for three months work. But the work! Damn, it was dangerous.

They'd been shot at and run over IED's, those lovely big 'impro-vised explosive devices' the Taliban liked to dig into the roads and blow up unsuspecting vehicles. Three of their team had gone back home with injuries. This job was getting more dangerous all the time.

And last night, doing the personal protection gig for Lund at the shrine with the crazy imam, that about settled the guy as bat shit crazy. Chris hoped they'd get out, check the village and be back in time for him to call Bernadette one more time before she left for Paris.

They mounted up into the trucks—three dark SUV's with heavy amour, which they hoped would protect them from IED's. Secretly, they all knew the trucks were toast if they were hit.

Stanhope, an ex-British paratrooper was in the lead vehicle with McEwan, a Scot who'd retired from the Black Watch Regiment. He had a wicked sense of humor, while Stanhope had none. With them was Max, his real name was Mahboobolah, which no one could pronounce, their interpreter who spoke Pashtun and Dari. His English was sometimes hard to understand, but they cut through translations with hand signals.

Lund, their asset, was in the second truck with his driver, Douglas, a young kid of 19, who never should have been hired but they were desperate for warm bodies. Douglas was a wash out from the armed forces but could drive anything. He was a big kid from rural Nebraska with a wide smile who didn't get rattled. He actually fit into the team quite well.

Chris was in the last truck, with Cameron who took the wheel. They sped out of their compound, shooting dust into the air. Afghans cursed the convoy as it sped by, scaring their donkeys and chickens. People dove out of the way to avoid being hit by the three large trucks that looked as if they would rather run over someone than stop.

"This is bullshit," Chris said to Cameron.

"Copy that," Cameron said. He was a young former marine from Ohio named Cameron Anderson. He'd done two tours with the Marines in Iraq and how the hell he ended up here took a two-hour story and six beers. His long story short was—insanity.

"Why the hell do we have to drive like we're protecting some five star general? Who does he think he is?"

"Yeah, total dumb ass. But his orders are we drive like hell for his protection. He's paying the bills and Stanhope takes him to the letter. Just like a true Brit," Cameron said. "And we got some kind of rendezvous with a big Afghan in a village."

"Sure, but this just draws attention to us. Kick up a lot of dust when we hit the outskirts of town, you alert every Taliban that you've got something important. Puts a target on us."

Cameron turned to Chris. "Hey, QC, you're finally thinking like a true military guy. Wow, from QC to jarhead in three months. Impressive."

Chris smiled and stared ahead. His nickname had become QC for "Queen's Cowboy" when the guys learned he'd been a constable with the Royal Canadian Mounted Police in Canada. He told them the force was once nicknamed the Queen's Cowboys by Canadians after Queen Elizabeth of England. The name stuck.

The convoy sailed past the markets then onto the main highway. They had several checkpoints to go through before they left the city of Kandahar. The ANP, Afghan National Police, manned the checkpoints, took the bribes and made sure they got their cut of anything that was leaving the city. They did well.

In this case, they'd have to wave the convoy on, for no goods were being transported; Lund always made sure of that or he hid them well. Max showed their credentials and they went through each checkpoint without problem.

They were soon out in the open. Guard towers appeared on the sides of the roads. Machine guns tracked their progress with young Afghan kids barely out of puberty holding the trigger of a 50 MM machine gun. One slip of the finger and their truck would be toast.

The convoy sped on. Chris tensed up as they reached the hills. In his imagination, he saw Taliban behind every hill. The landscape looked like uneven brown pancake batter spread over ominous hills. Each hill could hide a Taliban with an AK47 Russian-made machine gun and a cell phone with a transmitter to an IED.

"We're approaching our first choke point," Cameron said. "Clench your cheeks QC 'cause this is the fun part."

Chris knew what he meant. Choke points were a narrowing of the road. When the road ran right through a hill, leaving a deep valley, they were vulnerable to attack from two sides. The Taliban loved these hills. They could sit there all day and take out anyone they wanted. The only thing that kept them away was U.S. helicopters and drones.

"Skies are clear, we should be okay," Chris said.

"Once again, QC, you're right on, true military thinking," Cameron said with a smile.

When the skies were clear, the drones were flying high on the perimeter of Kandahar. They were loaded with Hellfire missiles that made quick work of any Taliban who decided to linger over a hill staring down at the highway. Clear skies were their friends; cloudy days made them want to cringe.

They relaxed as they came out the other side of the valley and into the clear open spaces of the Afghan countryside. There was one more hill left. As they approached, the lead truck started to slow.

"You think there's a problem?" Chris asked. He racked his machine gun, pulling off the safety and placing his finger on the side of the trigger.

Cameron spoke into his collar mic, "What's the situation?"

"Lund has to take a shit," Stanhope replied from the front vehicle.

Cameron muttered, "Copy that." He turned to Chris. "Well that's the biggest *brown star cluster* I've heard of in sometime."

"Which means?" Chris asked.

"Total bullshit," Cameron said. "You'd think the guy could clear his friggin' bowels before we left town."

"Stay frosty," Stanhope said over the radio. They knew he meant stay sharp.

Chris watched Lund walk towards some low hills. "Is he carrying something?"

"Damn if I know, let me get the binoculars—shit—incoming!"

The whoosh of an RPG round streaked between the trucks and ignited Lund's vehicle. The truck lifted off the ground before dropping back in a ball of flames.

"Get out, get out!" Cameron yelled to Chris.

Chris grabbed his machine gun in one hand, pushing open the door and launching himself out of the truck. He turned on his stomach with his weapon ready. AK47 rounds pinged on the truck. Cameron followed him out the same door, his weapon hitting the ground with a crunching sound.

Cameron yelled, "QC, follow me—head for the BFR!"

Chris crawled behind Cameron. The BFR was military code for big friggin' rock. They got behind it and peered out.

"I make out ten hostiles from the weapons fire," Cameron said.

"Great, that gives us three each. Any chance we can move to that other rock and flank them?" Chris asked. He fired off a quick round of his MP50. It resulted in the other side of their rock being hit with a fusillade of AK47 fire.

"I think you made them mad, QC. I'll call in my friendly American chopper buddies. They'll send a Blackhawk in here to put some missiles up their butts," Cameron said.

"Go for it," Chris said. "This could get old real fast, they got us outnumbered."

Cameron took out his satellite cell and dialed a direct line he had to U.S. Forces, Afghanistan. "Lucky I still got friends there that owe me favors."

Chris fired off another round from his weapon and pulled his head back, "You mean you still haven't paid off your gambling debts to the heli pilots?"

Cameron smiled as he listened for his phone to ring. His smile fell to a frown, "Ah shit, we got no coverage here."

Chris shook his head. "Not possible, your sat phone doesn't work on relay stations, it bounces off satellites. The Taliban must be using cell frequency jammers."

"I hate it when the hostiles go all geeky on us. Do you see any of our crew? Can we communicate by visual?"

Chris looked back to the road. "Looks like they got the lead truck as well. Maybe we can make it to our truck and head back for help."

Cameron was about to respond when an RPG round whooshed

over their heads, striking their truck. A roar of flame threw the truck onto its roof. Cameron shrugged. "There goes our ride."

An Afghan voice yelled out. "Surrender to us and you will not be harmed."

Chris stared at Cameron. "What are our options? I'm out of ammo for my MP50. I got nine rounds in my Glock, which means I need them close in, and you don't have any weapons."

Cameron winced at the obvious. His weapon had jammed when he'd jumped out of the truck. It was useless. The sporadic weapons fire from their team in the other trucks who'd made it out had become silenced. They were all out of ammunition. With no cell coverage, they were done.

"Do you trust these bastards?" Chris asked.

"They don't get any ransom money if we're all dead. Kind of the law of the land," Cameron said in a dry tone.

"What about our interpreter?"

Cameron shook his head. "You know what the Taliban do to interpreters, they shoot them on the spot or torture them to death. There's no debate on that with them. Our interpreter Max knows that."

"Bullshit," Chris said. He moved his face towards the edge of the rock. "Does your promise of protection go to all of us?"

A laughing voice answered, "Of course, Allah is merciful to those who surrender to us, *inshallah*."

Cameron yelled to the others in the crew. "Guys, what's the call? I got no cell, no back up. If we surrender, we do it as a group. No one here does a cowboy and starts firing. You got that?"

A muffled 'copy that' came from a rock a hundred meters away and the other men in the crew put their hands up. Chris and Cameron did the same.

The Afghans came forward with their weapons trained on them. They were herded into a group. Cam looked around; McEwan and Stanhope looked okay.

"Where's Douglas?" Cam asked.

McEwan nodded in the direction of the flaming middle truck. "He didn't make it out."

"What about Lund?"

The question was answered with Lund coming towards them with his hands over his head. He looked pissed. Chris couldn't tell if it was his stupid decision to stop at this obvious choke point or if he thought his security team had failed them. He didn't care; staying alive was his main concern, not the health of this idiot who had gotten them captured.

Chris looked down at their interpreter; Max was sitting on his haunches, his hands cradling his head as if he expected the worst.

Max looked up at him. "You must kill me now, please, I beg of you. The Taliban kill all interpreters, after they torture them. Your bullet would be a mercy to me, please."

"Hey, don't worry, Max. They said they would be merciful to all who surrendered. You'll be fine," Chris said. He couldn't imagine putting a bullet in Max's head.

Max looked up with eyes filled with tears. "You do not understand the true translation of *inshallah*."

"Sure, I do, Max, it means God willing."

"Yes, my friend, and it also means, if God wills it. The Taliban can kill us all and say that God willed it."

CAUGHT IN THE CROSSFIRE
CHAPTER THREE, PRESENT TIME

Bernadette Callahan stared out the airplane window at the cold and barren mountains below. She'd be landing in Kandahar in the next half hour. The captain announced they were arriving on time. The weather was 3C/37 F, snow and wind—a normal January day in Afghanistan.

Nothing about her life was normal. She'd been waiting to hear if Chris had been located for weeks. They were supposed to have met in Paris; she'd even picked out an amazing hotel with a claw foot tub in the Latin Quarter.

All of that changed the moment she got the phone call that Chris was missing on his last security patrol in Afghanistan. She still had no answers. Countless phone calls to the Canadian Embassy and the security company he'd worked for in Kandahar turned up nothing. A series of dead ends led her to this plane flight.

Bernadette Callahan was a detective in the Royal Canadian Police Force in Western Canada. Thirty-five, five-foot eight and medium build with green eyes and red hair and a bronzed skin tone that proclaimed her Irish and Native Cree Indian heritage. The anger that seethed inside of her could come from either of her lineages at this moment.

She shouldn't have let the relationship get to the point that Chris had to prove his worth by taking such a hazardous assignment in Afghanistan, but his leaving was a symptom of the holes that were appearing in the fabric of their relationship.

They'd been together for over a year. He'd proposed to her one evening in December while they were on a trip to Banff National Park. Large snowflakes descended out of the darkness as he'd dropped to one knee and asked her to marry him. She'd said yes even as her heart had cried out in terror at her answer.

She never wanted to leave the police force. Being a detective was her life. For their relationship to work, he had to leave his job as constable for the RCMP on an idyllic island on the west coast of British Columbia. She'd always felt like she'd captured a bear and tried to tame it.

Chris was a Greek-Canadian with a wild nature. He loved the outdoors of Canada. The RCMP had become a way to spend his time at the office—outdoors.

Now, as the plane descended into one of the most dangerous places in the world, she wondered if she should have said yes to that good-looking Greek god with the curly black hair, almond brown eyes and easy smile. If she'd said no, none of this would have happened. He'd still be catching salmon poachers and tracking stolen fishing boats.

Getting to Afghanistan was her greatest challenge. She wanted to be here with every fiber in her body, but you needed a hard to obtain visa to get to Afghanistan. A business visa was the only option, there were no tourist visa's being issued, as the country was deemed too dangerous.

Bernadette had tried every angle with the Afghanistan Consulate. She needed to be working for or consulting for a legitimate agency in Afghanistan. After two weeks of calling in every favor she could think of, she called Agent Carla Winston with the FBI. They'd had some close calls together, and the end result was that neither of them, especially Winston, had suffered any harm, therefore she was willing to help.

Winston was able to procure a special visa for Bernadette as consultant for a company called Apex 5 Security. The company was a front to move FBI, CIA and Homeland Security personnel into Afghanistan without any special attention.

Bernadette was on her own as to her personnel protection and translator. She needed to hire both—the first was costly. A man named Bardulf Brandt, ex German military, would be her bodyguard; his fee was five hundred dollars a day in Kandahar and one thousand if they left the city limits. He had stressed repeatedly in emails that going out of Kandahar was too dangerous.

Her interpreter was a man named Reza. His fee was much less, fifty dollars a day in Kandahar. He gave no fee for leaving Kandahar, which seemed to imply he did not want to leave the city limits.

The plane landed on the tarmac with a thud. Bernadette watched out the window as they taxied past rows and rows of American Air Force planes and Black Hawk helicopters. It looked like a war zone.

She followed the rest of the passengers off the plane. Soldiers were everywhere with AK47 Russian machine guns. They stared hard at the stream of passengers as they walked past. Bernadette pulled on her overcoat and her headscarf as she made her way down the peeling gray walls with the fluorescent lighting. She'd been in prisons with better lighting. The sunglasses she wore made the hallway worse. They were her way of being able to look around her without being noticed. Women in Afghanistan were not to look directly at men. Bernadette was damned if she'd comply with such a custom. The sunglasses would allow her to see men's faces and eyes. Words could hide volumes; eyes could not, as far as she was concerned.

The line of passengers came to a halt at the customs hall. They inched slowly forward as a group of uniformed customs officers, all with beards, scrutinized passports and passengers as if a Taliban infiltrator or drug smuggler was present.

Bernadette's turn came. She marched forward to the officer.

"Sunglasses, off!" the bearded officer commanded.

"Oh, sorry," Bernadette said. She'd been so engrossed in watching all the passengers' interactions she had forgotten.

The officer stared at her Canadian passport and her American consultants' documents. "You are Canadian, yes?"

"Yes, I am Canadian."

"You are working for the Americans?"

"Yes, I am working for the Americans." She decided not to elaborate. She could have told the officer how she was a Canadian detective with the Serious Crimes Division of the Royal Canadian Mounted Police, but all of that was too much.

The officer took her passport and her document and a piece of paper. He wrote as much of her details as he could on the paper. His paper would be sent to the police chief of Kandahar and to the security forces. They would know she was here.

He stamped her passport loudly and handed it back to her, waving her away and summoning the next person.

She felt relieved to have made it through customs. There was a moment when she thought they might refuse her entry, send her back. She pulled on her sunglasses and proceeded to baggage claim. After picking up her bag, she was checked three more times. Every five meters another bearded, officious looking officer stared at her passport, her visa, and ruffled through her bag.

She finally got through and found herself in a sea of Afghans on the other side. An anxious-looking smallish man, with a long black beard, held a sign that read B. Callahan.

He was dressed in the traditional Afghan style, which included a pakol hat, reminiscent of an oversized floppy beret. He wore the traditional perahan tunban, a baggy, loose fitting trouser that came high above his boots and an oversized shirt with short sleeves. Over the shirt with its long tail that came three quarters to the ground, he wore a quilted down vest.

The résumé that Bernadette read online for Reza, one name only, was that he had studied philosophy and linguistics at university. He'd been a teacher but moved into interpreting when the Taliban had overrun his school in rural Afghanistan.

"Hi, you must be Reza," Bernadette said as she strode towards him. She almost reached out her hand, and then quickly put it by her side. Reza saw the movement but made as if he did not notice it. Males and females were forbidden to touch one another in public. Bernadette's gesture would have infuriated the men in the airport.

"Yes, I am Reza. I trust you had a satisfactory flight?"

"Yes, thank you," Bernadette said. She really wanted to say she'd wanted a beer on the plane but knew there was none to be had. Not only was Afghanistan a non-joy for womankind, it was mostly without alcohol. A double buzz kill, as far as she was concerned.

"I will take you to your car and you'll be taken to your guesthouse. All of this has been arranged," Reza said. He took her duffle bag and began leading her out of the airport.

Bernadette caught up to him. "Thanks, but I want to be taken straight to Kandahar Police Headquarters. I need to speak with the chief of police. I want to start the search for my missing fiancé."

Reza stopped. "This is impossible."

"Why, is he not there today?"

"No, he will not meet with you. You are a woman he does not know; he cannot meet with you unless I am there. I cannot be with you today. I'm only here to greet you and see you to your escort."

"I see. Can we set up a meeting for tomorrow then? I want to see the American and Canadian Consulates after that."

"All will be done in the morning. I promise." Reza nodded his head and picked up her bag. "Now, please follow me to your transport."

Bernadette adjusted the headscarf, the hijab she'd been warned she would need, and followed Reza. They walked out to the curbside area of the airport. There was not the usual comings and goings of traffic. Cars were summoned when their passengers arrived and security was tight.

Reza called Bernadette's driver on his cell phone; a black SUV with dark tinted windows pull up almost immediately. Reza opened the back door, Bernadette slid in. The door slammed behind her and the SUV took off.

Reza watched the truck drive away. He hurried away from the airport hoping no Talban had seen him with the foreign lady. He'd told his wife he wouldn't take any more interpreter jobs. His need for money had finally surpassed his fear, for now.

"I am Bardulf Brandt," a Germanic sounding voice said from the driver's seat. "I see you met Reza. That man is a real pussy. I think maybe he's a fag."

"Thanks for your update. I have no problem with gay men, but if you do, you can keep it yourself," Bernadette said.

She looked out the window as they left the airport. Two Afghans were staring at the SUV and dialing into their phones.

"I understand you are here to find your missing fiancé," Bardulf said as he maneuvered the car away from the airport. "You have wasted your time. The Taliban will send word of him in a week or two. You should have stayed in your country arranging his ransom. I hear he is Canadian. That is bad; Canada does not pay ransom, you'll need to do a lot of fundraising."

Bernadette stared into the rearview mirror. She could see only part of Bardulf. He was older, maybe 45, a blond with some streaking of gray in his short-cropped hair. He had blue eyes set in a wide face. He looked well built, someone who spent hours in the gym in his off hours. Thick arms with big hands guided the steering wheel.

"I thought maybe I'd come here, make some inquiries, and then do some recon in the countryside," Bernadette said.

"Ha, you are joking. To do that I need to get four more men and two more trucks. Your cost will be five thousand U.S. per day to venture outside of Kandahar. You have no idea how dangerous it is in the countryside of Afghanistan."

Bernadette could feel her anger growing as her cheeks grew red and her lips set into a tight line. "Really, are all the extra men and trucks for my protection...or yours?"

"Again, you are funny. The Taliban would get special joy in taking a North American woman hostage. I will not tell you all the many things they do to her, but you can guess."

"The joke's on them. I'm Canadian, we don't pay hostage takers like you said...and we have ice cold hearts."

Bardulf laughed. "You'd better have some ice between your legs if you want to fend off the Taliban, lady." He looked into the rearview mirror. His smiling eyes turned to a leer as if he was trying to judge Bernadette's assets beneath all her clothing.

"Giant asshole," were the words she muttered as she turned to look out the window. This conversation with the large Germanic moron was getting boring. She'd dealt with many men just like him in the police force. It was best to stand up to them.

Bernadette turned towards the front and leaned forward. "Listen up, Bardulf, I'm not here in Afghanistan to listen to what you like or don't like about gays or to discuss the temperature of my vagina. In your own language, I believe the term is *Das geht mir am arsch vorbie*."

Bardulf's eyes went wide. He started to laugh so hard he almost went off the road. "Who told you how to say kiss my ass in German?"

"I have German girlfriends back in Canada. Now that we understand each other, maybe you can help me get some intel on how to find my fiancé."

"You have a good sense of humor, maybe you'll keep that if you're caught by the Taliban." Bardulf winked into the rearview mirror.

Bernadette saw his wink—then saw a flash of something alongside the road. She had only seconds to process what it was.

"Take cover!" she screamed.

Bernadette dove down onto the floorboards of the SUV as the rocket hit the right side of the vehicle. She covered her ears and tried to make her body as small as possible. The blast sucked all the air out of the passenger compartment.

She reached up and pushed on the SUV's back door, the blast had destroyed the locks—it was open. She pushed herself out the door as another explosion ripped through the vehicle. Stumbling to a ditch, she fell in. Then, there was darkness as she passed out.

ABOUT THE AUTHOR

Lyle Nicholson is the author of seven novels, two novellas and a short story, as well a contributor of freelance articles to several newspapers and magazines in Canada.

In his former life, he was a bad actor in a Johnny Cash movie, Gospel Road, a disobedient monk in a monastery and a failure in working for others.

He would start his own successful sales agency and retire to write full time in 2011. The many characters and stories that have resided inside his head for years are glad he did.

He lives in Kelowna, British Columbia, Canada with his lovely wife of many years where he indulges in his passion for writing, cooking and fine wines.

ALSO BY LYLE NICHOLSON

Book 1 Polar Bear Dawn

Book 2 Pipeline Killers

Book 3 Climate Killers

Book 4 Caught in the Crossfire

Book 5 Deadly Ancestors

Prequel, Black Wolf Rising

Short Story, Treading Darkness

Stand Alone Fiction

Dolphin Dreams, (Romantic Fantasy)

Misdiagnosis Murder (Cozy Mystery)

Non Fiction

Half Brother Blues (A memoir)

Made in United States
Orlando, FL
16 April 2022

16911229R00180